# ELOISA JAMES

## Say No to the Duke

### THE WILDES OF LINDOW CASTLE

**AVON**BOOKS

*An Imprint of HarperCollinsPublishers*

SAY NO TO THE DUKE. Copyright © 2019 by Eloisa James, Inc. All rights reserved. Printed in the United States of America. No part of this book may be used or reproduced in any manner whatsoever without written permission except in the case of brief quotations embodied in critical articles and reviews. For information, address HarperCollins Publishers, 195 Broadway, New York, NY 10007.

First Avon Books mass market printing: July 2019
First Avon Books hardcover printing: June 2019

Print Edition ISBN: 978-0-06-287782-6
Digital Edition ISBN: 978-0-06-287784-0

*Cover design by Amy Halperin*
*Cover illustrations by Anna Kmet*
*Cover photography by Michael Frost*

Avon, Avon & logo, and Avon Books & logo are registered trademarks of HarperCollins Publishers in the United States of America and other countries.
HarperCollins is a registered trademark of HarperCollins Publishers in the United States of America and other countries.

FIRST EDITION

19 20 21 22 23   QGM   10 9 8 7 6 5 4 3 2 1

*This book is dedicated to my wonderful friend,
the amazing writer Damon Suede.
A good part of* Say No *was written
at 5 am in 25-minute writing bursts,
followed by kvetching on Google Hang-outs—
and starting the clock again.
And again.
Some part of Damon's effortless joy
found its way onto these pages.*

# Acknowledgments

My books are like small children; they take a whole village to get them to a literate state. I want to offer my deep gratitude to my village: my editor, Carrie Feron; my agent, Kim Witherspoon; my Web site designers, Wax Creative; and my personal team: Franzeca Drouin, Leslie Ferdinand, Sharlene Martin Moore, and Zoe Bly. My husband and daughter Anna debated many a plot point with me, and I'm fervently grateful to them. In addition, people in many departments of HarperCollins, from Art to Marketing to PR, have done a wonderful job of getting this book into readers' hands: my heartfelt thanks goes to each of you.

# Chapter One

*Miss Stevenson's Seminary*
*"The Young Ladies' Eton"*
*Queen Square, London*
*September 14, 1776*

*B*y her fourteenth birthday, Lady Boadicea Wilde had wished for a best friend on weeks of first stars. She had created a wishing stone by dunking it in milk under a midnight moon. When that didn't work, she had decided that perhaps fairies preferred adult beverages, so she stole into her father's study and dunked the stone in a decanter of brandy. She had written down her wish and burned the paper in the nursery hearth so it flew up to heaven.

Unfortunately, she'd forgotten to open the flue, so smoke filled the nursery. She had been punished by being confined to bed, where she watched her younger sister Joan and stepsister

Viola cuddle on the nursery sofa and whisper secrets to each other.

It was all her father's fault.

Dukes' daughters, especially those who lived in huge castles, had no chance to meet prospective friends. They were kept in the country like potted violets, waiting for the moment when they would be paraded in front of the world and promptly married off.

From what Betsy could see, her father was her stepmother's best friend. Only a girl with eight brothers could sympathize with the revulsion that swept over Betsy at that thought.

Friends with a *boy*.

Never.

Boys smelled and shouted. They thought nothing of tossing water over one's head, pulling hair, and passing wind deliberately.

How could a boy possibly understand how she felt about life? She longed for a kindred soul, a girl who would sympathize with the unfairness of having to ride sidesaddle, and not being allowed to shoot a bow and arrow from horseback.

A few years ago, when her brothers Alaric and Parth had announced they wanted to visit China, her father's eyes had lit up, and a whole meal flew by talking of three-masted schooners and mountains of tea. True, the duke had forbidden the voyage until the boys were older, but he'd laughed when he discovered they'd sailed off anyway.

If *she* ran away to sea? The idea was unthinkable.

If her wishing stone had worked, she'd be living in a place where girls were allowed to wear breeches and travel wherever they wished.

Lying in bed after her fourteenth birthday party—attended by five brothers, since Viola and Joan were recovering from the chickenpox—Betsy realized that if she wanted a girlfriend, she had to take matters into her own hands. She had wished for a friend before blowing out the candle on her birthday cake, but inside, she no longer had faith.

Magic had proved ineffective, if not irrelevant.

Yet there is more than one way to skin a goat, as the family coachman had it. It took three months of coaxing, pleading, and outright tantrums, but finally Betsy, Joan, and Viola were taken to the very best boarding school in England, an establishment run by Miss Stevenson, who had the distinction of being the daughter of a viscount.

As they walked into the imposing building, Betsy struggled to maintain ladylike comportment. She couldn't stop the giddy smile that curled her lips. When a maid arrived to escort her to the wing for older girls, she hugged her father and stepmother goodbye and danced out the door, leaving them to mop up her stepsister Viola's tears.

Viola was shy, and afraid to live away from home, but as Betsy heard girls' laughter from behind a closed door, her heart swelled with pure joy. She was finally—finally!—where she was meant to be.

"You will share a parlor suite with Lady Octavia Taymor and Miss Clementine Clarke," the maid assigned to escort her said. "Each of you has your own chamber, of course, and your maid will attend you morning and evening. You may become acquainted with Lady Octavia and Miss Clarke over tea."

Betsy's heart was beating so quickly that she felt slightly dizzy. Clementine was such a beautiful name, and hadn't Octavius been a general? Octavia was named after a warrior, just as she was!

The parlor looked like a smaller version of parlors at Lindow Castle, tastefully furnished with a silk rug and rosy velvet curtains. A table before the fireplace was set with a silver tea service.

Betsy's eyes flew to the two girls who rose and came to meet them. Clementine had yellow ringlets and a pursed mouth like a rosebud; Octavia had low, dark eyebrows and a thin face.

"Your name is so pretty," Betsy told Clementine, after the maid left.

"I wish I could say the same for yours," Clementine said, sitting down with a little smile, as if she were merely jesting.

Betsy blinked. "Boadicea is certainly unusual," she said hastily. "I prefer Betsy."

Clementine's nose wrinkled. "We have a second housemaid who used to be called Betsy. My mother changed her name to Perkins."

Betsy couldn't think what to say. "I see," she managed, her voice coming out flat and strange.

"Please, won't you sit down, Lady Betsy?" Octavia asked, gesturing toward a chair.

Betsy sat. "Have you been at the seminary for some time, Lady Octavia?" she asked.

"Clementine and I have been the only parlor boarders since—" Octavia began.

"I have every expectation that my mother will fetch me away within the week," Clementine said, interrupting.

"I see," Betsy repeated, fighting to make her voice cordial. It was ridiculous to feel shaky and a little frightened. This wasn't the way she had imagined her first encounter with possible friends, but Clementine was only one person, and there was a whole school of girls to meet.

"*Do* you?" Clementine demanded.

"Are you good at maths?" Octavia put in, her voice rather desperate.

"No, I am not," Betsy said. "I am sorry to hear that you are departing, Miss Clarke. Is the parlor too small for three of us?"

Clementine snorted.

"The meals are frightfully good here," Octavia said, her voice rising.

"My mother will travel from the country to fetch me as soon as she learns of your arrival," Clementine said, ignoring Octavia. "I sent her a message yesterday."

Betsy had the horrible sense that she'd somehow strayed into a nightmare. She took a deep breath. "Why are you so impolite, Miss Clarke?"

Clementine pursed her lips tighter than nature had made them, and then opened them just wide enough to speak. "No one can blame a child for her mother's lascivious nature, but it would have been more *agreeable* if His Grace had thought how unpleasant it was for young ladies of quality to share a chamber with someone who . . ."

"Who?" Betsy prompted.

"Is bound to have inherited her mother's sinful inclinations," Clementine said, her eyes shining like greased blueberries.

Betsy stared back in horror. Of course Clementine knew that the duke's second duchess—her mother—had run away with a Prussian count when Betsy was a baby. But no one had ever spoken of her mother so demeaningly—nor implied that she, Betsy, would inherit a penchant for debauchery.

"Clementine!" Octavia protested, adding, "You are being frightfully ill-bred!"

Clementine turned toward her. "I'm merely repeating what scientists have proved, Octavia. Strong attributes are always inherited, just as when racehorses are bred for speed. You could call it destiny, but it's really science."

"I don't believe it," Octavia said stoutly.

But Betsy's brother North was fascinated by horse breeding and gave near-nightly disquisitions on which traits were making themselves known in the ducal stables. Betsy knew, better than most ladies, that traits were indeed inherited.

A strange tingle coursed through her body, as if a wall had opened, revealing something frightful behind it, something she'd never imagined. Her Aunt Knowe had never allowed the second duchess's children to become embittered about their mother's absence.

"Your mother didn't belong in a marriage to your father," Aunt Knowe often said. "Thank goodness, she recognized it, because it allowed the duke to find Ophelia."

Family lore had it that the ink on the divorce decree wasn't dry before Aunt Knowe ordered her brother off to London to find a third duchess. Since Betsy adored her dearest papa, her darling stepmother, and even those annoying brothers, she had never given the matter much thought.

Yet it seemed that other people—*all* of polite society, or so Clementine Clarke was shrilly declaiming—had given her mother's circumstances a great deal of thought.

"There is no need to be rude," Octavia said.

"Everyone thinks it," Clementine said, her eyes sliding over Betsy, nose still slightly wrinkled, as if Betsy were a piece of spoiled mutton.

"Are you saying that every girl in this school will think that I am lascivious because my mother was unfaithful?" Betsy asked, just to be very clear.

Octavia turned a hot pink and closed her lips tightly.

"*Will* think?" Clementine retorted. "They *do* think, and so does everyone else important."

Betsy tried not to hear her harsh breath echoing in her ears. Her father was important, but he must not know, because he never would have left her in a den of lionesses.

She almost jerked up from her chair and ran for the door. Perhaps the ducal coach was still at the curb. Or Miss Stevenson could send a groom to the townhouse and they would return and take her and her sisters away.

"Everyone says that the second duchess was never, shall we say, unsullied," Clementine said. "Your mother gave the duke a son—though *my* mother says one has to question his bloodlines—and she was dallying with the Prussian well before you were born."

"My brother Leo is not illegitimate," Betsy said, her voice thick with disbelief and horror. "And neither am I!"

Adulterous mother or no, Betsy stemmed from a long line of dukes, and she was named after a great female warrior. She listened to Clementine until she didn't care to listen any longer.

Then she rose to her feet. "You are quite despicable," she said, controlling her temper as Aunt Knowe had taught her. "Petty and small-minded. I shall not share a parlor with you."

Clementine laughed shrilly. "You should be grateful to sleep in the attic! You're no more than a by-blow, who will be lucky to marry a squire. It would take a miracle for you to attract a spouse from the peerage."

Betsy snatched up a glass of water from the tea tray and dashed it into Clementine's face. "I am a duke's daughter," she stated, enjoying the way Clementine's starched curls wilted onto her shoulders like yellow seaweed. "I have never heard of your family. Clarke?" She curled her lip and said the first consciously nasty thing that she'd said in her life. "I gather you had an ancestor who was a clerk? How amusing to meet you."

Sobbing loudly, Clementine flung herself out of the door.

"Are you going to throw water at me as well?" Octavia asked, her eyes rounded.

"If you say anything unkind about my mother, I shall dump that pitcher of water over your head," Betsy said. "In the middle of the night. I am trained in the art of war."

"I shan't say a word," Octavia said hastily. "I don't like cold water."

Betsy stared at her. Octavia's face wasn't piggish like Clementine's.

"I apologize for Clementine's rudeness," Octavia said. She glanced at her fingers twisting in her lap and then looked back at Betsy. "She's frightfully bad-tempered and considers everyone beneath her. She only allowed me to share the parlor because Miss Stevenson said that she would have to leave the school otherwise. I like your name."

"Boadicea was a warrior queen," Betsy said. She was trembling a little.

Octavia bit her lip. "You'll need that here," she said slowly. "The girls aren't always terribly nice."

Betsy sat down.

"We're supposed to be learning history and the like," Octavia explained. "But in reality, it's all about marriage. Sometimes the only conversation at supper is about how many proposals one should get during one's debut. Clementine's parents have three houses, but that's not enough, of course."

"She's afraid she won't have any suitors."

Octavia nodded.

"If all those girls believe that I won't have any suitors," Betsy said, "I shall prove them wrong." The sick feeling in her stomach was replaced by a red-hot bolt of fury. "I shall have more marriage proposals than anyone."

"I have no doubt," Octavia said, looking rather awed.

BOADICEA HAD COME surprisingly close to winning her rebellion against the Roman invaders, according to the expert on military history the duke had hired to teach all his children, girls included.

By June, three years later, when the time came for Betsy to debut . . .

She *won*.

She came, she saw, she conquered.

*Veni, vidi, vici,* to quote another warrior, Caesar.

By October 1780, Betsy had received—and refused—proposals chaperoned and unchaperoned, in her father's study, in a gazebo, in an alcove at Westminster Cathedral.

She had turned down four peers and fourteen untitled gentlemen, which said something about the paucity of English titles, or the relatively lenient standards of the gentry compared to the aristocracy.

The biggest fish of all—a future duke—had so

far eluded her, but she had the feeling that the deficit would soon be mended.

She was standing in the midst of a costume ball being thrown at Lindow Castle for the wedding of her brother North when her aunt Knowe loomed up at her shoulder.

"Ah, Betsy! I must ask my dear niece to escort Lord Greywick to see the billiard table that just arrived from Paris."

Betsy looked up—and up. The future Duke of Eversley stared down at her.

Did she say that she'd won the battle?

Battles are only won when the biggest fish of all is in one's net.

She smiled.

# Chapter Two

*Lindow Castle*
*A Costume Ball in Honor of the Marriage of*
*Lord Roland Northbridge Wilde to Miss Diana Belgrave*
*October 31, 1780*

*O*nly one gentleman had found his way to the billiard room from the ballroom at Lindow Castle; most revelers were too busy flaunting their charms or their costumes to search out a chamber containing little more than a walnut gaming table and a few armchairs.

Since the castle was larger than most garrisons, no music could be heard in the corner where Lord Jeremy Roden—late of His Majesty's Royal Artillery—sat with his legs sprawled before him, one hand clenched around a glass of whisky.

Which left the other free to irritably prod his halo back in place.

It was composed of stiffened wire supposedly holding up a circlet covered with spangles and brilliants. In his case, the wire wasn't doing its job, and the damned thing listed to the side like a sailor whose pecker wasn't up to shore leave.

Lady Knowe had decreed that all uncostumed guests, which included most of her own nephews, would accept a halo or suffer the consequences. In the resulting plethora of noisy angels thronging the ballroom, no one's curious eyes had noticed that *his* halo was attached to a bandage wound around his head.

If he were the grateful type, he'd be grateful.

Hell, he *was* grateful.

He hadn't been looking forward to explaining that the bandage hid a nearly healed bullet wound—fired by the bride's mother, no less. The poor woman had been dispatched to a sanitarium, and the wound was almost healed.

Unfortunately, the bandage was doing a rotten job of hoisting his halo over his head: Dancing turned from tiresome to mortifying with a limp circlet bobbing next to his ear.

What's more, merely being in a ballroom thronged with angels made a man think hard about war and its damned inconveniences. If he'd died in the American colonies, would an angel have swooped low over the battlefield and caught up his sorry soul?

Not bloody likely.

He took another swig of whisky, telling himself that he wasn't the only man in that ballroom who didn't deserve his sanctified millinery.

The Wilde men had been blessed with beauty, wits, and brilliance—but angelic they were not.

Any more than he was.

Guilt echoed in the void where his soul used to be, and he upended the glass, pushing away the stab of remorse that had become his hourly companion. The whisky scorched down his throat, though (alas) his mind was clear, and his fingers didn't have the slightest tremble.

Liquor stopped doing its job long ago, but it turned out to be an excellent shield against polite society. He plucked up the glass again, relishing the way the last few drops burned his tongue. Perhaps he should try—

The door swung open and he heard a man say, "After you, my lady."

Jeremy shoved his chair farther into the shadowy corner. No one would find his way to this room to play billiards; chances were good he was about to have a front row seat on a visit to Cock Alley, played out on the duke's precious billiard table. Who was he to deny them an audience?

His glass empty, Jeremy was reaching for the bottle when the lady in question replied, "My skirts are caught on the hinge, my lord; would you be so kind as to disentangle me?"

Jeremy slammed back in his chair, eyes narrowing.

Lady Boadicea Wilde.

The wildest of the Wildes, the duke's eldest daughter—who strangely enough demanded that everyone call her Betsy.

A ridiculous name for a woman who could shoot the cork out of a bottle from a galloping horse . . . according to her brothers, at least.

Outside the door, a rustle of silk indicated that her escort was doing his best to free her. She must have forgotten to turn sideways. Betsy's skirts were wider than most doors, and her wigs were always lofty. Tonight her wig was adorned with a halo, which made her taller than most men.

The last was intentional, to Jeremy's mind. She liked being taller than her feckless suitors.

Betsy was the only Wilde whom Jeremy couldn't tolerate. Unfortunately, given that she had an unhealthy obsession with billiards and this room had become his refuge, he had seen all too much of her during his two-month stay at Lindow Castle.

She was damned rash, coming here, a distance from the ballroom, with a man. Just like a Wilde, actually: arrogant to a fault, but in an effortless way that simply expected that lesser mortals would bow to their status.

He'd bet a mountain of ha'pennies that no chaperone had accompanied them.

She didn't understand the way men thought about women. The "gentleman" she was with could be planning to compromise her reputation.

Or worse.

Blood roared through his body, a flood of pure anger chasing away the guilt that was his usual companion. It wasn't the first time Betsy had inspired that reaction. Around her, he tended to be too irritated to think about the fate of his platoon.

He might not actually be a Wilde, but her older brother North was his closest friend in the world.

He would protect her reputation and person in North's stead.

He flexed his fingers, looking down at fabric straining over the unfashionable muscle that bulged in his forearm. North's primitive solution for Jeremy's malaise—to give a fine-sounding title to his sorry existence—was to force him on horseback every day. No matter how much he drank the night before, North shoved him up on an unruly steed. Consequently, he had twice the muscle that he'd had three years ago, when he'd cut an elegant figure as an officer.

"That's it," Betsy exclaimed. "Oh, thank you so much!" She never bothered with such gushing charm around him; they had silently agreed, soon after meeting, that they were oil and water and she would extract no proposal from him, no matter how brilliantly she smiled.

She murmured something else, and it struck him that Betsy might have planned an assignation. Perhaps she had a lover, who had arrived from London in the mass of guests invited to the ball.

His jaw clenched.

Hell, no.

Boadicea Wilde was not going to throw away her virtue on his watch.

"Your skirts are free, Lady Boadicea."

Whoever he was—and his voice sounded vaguely familiar—the man was not her lover. He didn't know his proposed bride well enough to realize how much Betsy loathed her given name.

Wait.

He *did* know that voice. They'd been at school together, a lifetime ago.

Betsy walked into the room. From Jeremy's shadowy corner, she seemed to glow under the light of the lamp hanging directly over the billiard table.

She was outrageously beautiful, like all the Wildes: wide eyes, white teeth, thick hair. Beautiful girls were everywhere, but Betsy's unconscious sensuality? That was matchless. She relished life, and it showed.

The other day some fool described her as prim and proper. Jeremy had had trouble not curling his lip.

Did they not see who she really was?

She turned up the lamp that hung over the table until it illuminated a pool of spotless green wool walled by gleaming wood. Then she turned about, leaning against the table.

Jeremy couldn't see her suitor, who still stood in the doorway.

With an impish smile, Betsy spread her arms. "Here you see my father's billiard table, newly arrived from Paris. A walnut body and bronze motifs in the shape of the Lindow shield, repeated eight times. My stepmother chided my father for extravagant trimming, but His Grace is fond of decoration."

The gentleman chuckled and stepped into the light. "The table is exquisite, but not as beautiful as the woman standing beside it."

Jeremy sighed. His old school friend should be ashamed of that lame compliment.

Likely agreeing with him, Betsy ignored it. "I was very fond of our old billiard table, but this is more fitting for a castle."

"You play billiards yourself?"

He sounded surprised rather than critical, which boded well for his courtship.

"My whole life," Betsy said. "My brothers spent a great deal of their time here. I used to stand on a box to see the play; the table looked like a green ocean."

"I spoke to your father, Lady Boadicea, and he agreed that I might ask you for the honor of your hand in marriage."

This was fantastic. Jeremy had a front row seat on a proposal, and he could mock Betsy about it for weeks.

Her suitor didn't kneel.

Thaddeus would never kneel.

The man currently asking Betsy to marry him was Thaddeus Erskine Shaw, Viscount Greywick.

Duke of some damned place, someday.

Something pinched deep in Jeremy's chest, and he narrowed his eyes. Oh, *hell no.* Whatever that emotion was, he didn't like it.

Wouldn't accept it.

Her Grace, Betsy the Duchess.

Sounded good.

# Chapter Three

$\mathcal{L}$ord Greywick, the honor is mine," Betsy said, allowing her gloved hand to rest in his.

"That sounds very much like a preface to a refusal," the viscount replied, which showed him more observant than most of her suitors, who generally looked stunned, as if they'd never considered the possibility that she might refuse them.

After all, they had weighed her mother's scandalous behavior and her possible illegitimacy against Betsy's beauty, dowry, and exquisite manners. To a man, they judged themselves prescient, even liberal, to ask for her hand at all. They thought her fortunate to receive a proposal.

They couldn't believe it when she rejected them.

She paused for a second, questioning this particular decision. Viscount Greywick was tall and very handsome, with hazel eyes and cheekbones that came straight from some ennobled ancestor.

Her father liked him.

Her brothers liked him.

Aunt Knowe trusted him. She'd waved her hand and sent Betsy off with Lord Greywick without the faintest concern. Actually, since she sent them to the billiard room unchaperoned, she probably wanted Betsy to marry him.

Putting her family's approval to the side, the viscount had no need to marry for her dowry or her status, so presumably he wanted *her*. He wasn't lustful, precisely, but his eyes were warm and appreciative.

Betsy tried to make herself feel excited about that and failed.

"It is indeed a refusal," she said, withdrawing her hand. "I regret to say that we would not suit, my lord. My answer is no."

"Why not?"

That stumped her. No one had anything bad to say about Viscount Greywick. He was, hands down, the most elusive and sought-after bachelor in London. She hadn't even tried to lure him, and yet here he was.

What could she say?

*You're a paragon and I have a weakness for rascals?* Or, worse: *I'm so bored at this moment.*

"We don't know each other," she said, realizing the moment the words crossed her lips that her reasoning was weak. She'd given him an opening to tell her about himself, or worse, suggest that they spend time together.

"Is there someone else?" the viscount asked. "Because if not, and with your permission, I would like to attempt to convince you other-wise."

By now, the wedding guests knew that she had left the ballroom with a future duke. Lord Greywick was the picture of rectitude. He would never spend time with a young lady in private unless he had permission to ask for her hand in marriage.

The *ton* would be surprised to find that she had refused him, but they wouldn't doubt it had happened.

The battle was over.

Won. Done.

A low, rough voice answered him before she could. "You should take him."

Betsy barely stifled a curse that would have shocked her suitor. "For goodness' sake," she cried instead. "I should have guessed that you'd be hiding here." She slid sideways so she could see around Greywick's shoulders.

Sure enough, the bane of her existence was regarding her lazily from the corner of the room.

"I am not hiding," Jeremy Roden protested, managing to sound halfway sober and—even more surprisingly—almost convincing. "To return to the important point, Greywick is a good man and was cleverer than the rest of us at Eton. That includes your brothers, by the way. Not me, but then I put myself in a different category."

The viscount, who had swung about, chuckled at that. "I assure you that we all put you in a different category as well, Lord Jeremy."

"Ne'er-do-wells?" Betsy suggested. "Or perhaps

Lord Jeremy was already cockeyed with drink at that early age."

"Tsk, tsk," Jeremy said, regarding her with an expression that never failed to irritate. "Proper young ladies don't use words like 'cock.' I'm pretty sure angels don't either, and you happen to be wearing a halo at the moment, if you'll forgive my reminder. Angels probably don't even know what a 'cock' is."

The infuriating thing was that everything in her prickled into life the moment Jeremy Roden threw down one of his challenges. He was an intoxicated mess of a man and she still—

The viscount intervened before she could come up with an appropriately blistering response. "I thought I saw you across the ballroom, Lord Jeremy. I was glad to hear that you returned from the army safe and sound."

Perhaps Greywick had no idea what Jeremy had endured in battle, not that she did, precisely. But the viscount was about to say one of those commonplace things that would make darkness roll over Jeremy's face like a storm moving in over the ocean.

"I'm amazed that you missed the spectacle when Lord Jeremy stalked off and left poor Miss Peters on the edge of the dance floor by herself," Betsy said quickly.

Jeremy's dark eyes moved to her face, and to her relief, exasperation smoothed away that other expression, whatever it was.

Well, exasperation or perhaps pure dislike.

She let her smile widen, just to annoy him even more.

She'd decided weeks ago that he was better off irritated than despondent, and fortunately for Jeremy Roden, she had an aptitude for irritating men, thanks to growing up with all those brothers.

Her adopted brother Parth had been the first to put a frog under her covers, probably in league with Alaric. The second time was definitely Alaric, though North had something to do with it.

Aunt Knowe had helped her with slushy tadpole puddles that had mysteriously appeared in their beds.

"My halo failed me," Jeremy said, without a bit of regret in his voice. "Unless I was going to strike Miss Peters in the face with evidence of my piety, I had to get off the floor. She didn't complain. I don't think she liked it when I kept turning the wrong way."

The viscount had a nice chuckle, Betsy had to admit. "All those hours with a dancing master came to nothing?" he asked. He turned back to Betsy. "In our day, Etonian masters believed dancing was a critical skill, whereas we boys were far more interested in swordplay."

Jeremy Roden had broad shoulders that ladies giggled about in the ladies' parlor. They didn't care which direction he turned in the ballroom, as long as he was paying them attention.

"The lessons didn't stick," Jeremy said indifferently.

"He is a disgrace to your tutors," Betsy told the viscount. "He blunders around like a cow on ice."

True to form, Jeremy merely shrugged, making his halo, which was resting on one shoulder, twinkle from the shadows. It was infuriating to find that her pulse sped up at the way shadowy light touched his cheekbones. His black hair had a touch of silver, even though he couldn't be older than North since they had been at Eton together.

Annoyed, she made herself laugh. "Aunt Knowe saw what happened to your headgear, Lord Jeremy, and declared you a fallen angel. 'Fallen' might not be the right word. 'Wilted'? 'Flabby'?" She paused for a moment and then said it anyway, because . . . why not? "Or is the term I want . . . 'flaccid'?" She traded the smile for a mock innocent look.

It felt exhilarating to make a joke in front of one of her suitors. As if she were free to be herself for the first time in a year.

Jeremy pulled off his halo and regarded the way it bent over like a flower in need of water. Then he tossed it to the side. "If you want Greywick to marry you—or *any* gentleman to marry you—you need to do a better job of appearing ladylike."

If the viscount had been put off by her unlady-like pun, it was all to the better. He obviously would want a paragon as his duchess, given how perfect he was.

She was *not* that woman.

Rather to her surprise, Greywick's mouth was

quirked in a smile. "I find Lady Boadicea a perfect lady."

Huh.

The man whom she'd only seen looking as solemn as a judge apparently hadn't taken offense at her play on words.

"I take it back," Jeremy said, his eyes narrowing. "You shouldn't marry that worthless Puritan."

"I'm not a Puritan," the viscount replied. "You're supposed to play the part of one of my oldest school friends, and fight my cause for me. Unless you want the lady in question for yourself?"

The question hung in the air just long enough for Betsy's breath to catch—and then Jeremy Roden snorted.

Yes, snorted.

And upended the bottle of whisky he was holding as if his response wasn't denigrating enough.

# Chapter Four

$\mathcal{J}$eremy thought fast while he allowed the liquor to burn down into his gut. He had to conjure up a reason not to marry Betsy that wasn't too insulting.

Tonight she was dressed all in white, which wasn't unusual for a young lady. Naturally, *her* halo didn't tilt to the side: It sprang from the top of her wig, perfectly positioned to advertise her virtue.

Halo or not, Betsy was far from angelic.

A tempestuous, opinionated, seductive little devil, perhaps.

He didn't want to marry her, or any other woman. He could scarcely manage his own life. In fact, the evidence was pretty clear that he *couldn't* manage his own life since he was living in Lindow Castle rather than his own townhouse.

"I would never marry someone called Betsy," he stated, lowering his bottle. "Everyone knows that a Betsy must be an adorable girl who gathers roses, loves kittens, and scrawls love notes in her diary. Lady Betsy's sweet and modest disposition would be wasted on a reprobate like myself."

"Nothing wrong with kittens," Greywick put in. His tone indicated that not only did he think Betsy charming—the fool—but he would fill his house with felines if she wanted. The man was seduced.

No, that wasn't the right word.

Dazzled.

Sun-struck. It was a bit surprising, given how intelligent Greywick was. But then Betsy had efficiently bewitched all the single gentlemen who had visited the castle since Jeremy arrived at the beginning of September.

Brains or no brains, they couldn't seem to help themselves from falling under the spell of her sugary smiles and blue eyes. To Jeremy's cynical mind, it proved that mankind was endlessly optimistic.

What woman was as simple as she appeared?

Let alone one who appeared to be such a thoroughly proper young lady? Perfection was always a mask.

"To clarify my point," Jeremy said to Greywick, "kittens or no, you have no competition in me. I'm not one to wed, even given the fact that a mere marquess could never take precedence over a duke."

"A title does not determine whom a lady marries," Betsy said tartly. "It may be hard to conceive, but myriad reasons dictate why a lady would choose another man over you."

A less observant man might have been foolish enough to believe the enchanting portrait Betsy offered at this moment: rosy lips and cheeks, a sweetly peaked chin, wide blue eyes that darkened when she was thoughtful.

She appeared angelic.

Sort of. If you ignored the independent look in her eye, and unbelievably, most men seemed to do that.

"So, have you answered Greywick?" he asked, ignoring her comment. Given the women who had tried either to seduce or to compromise Jeremy in the last week alone, he wouldn't have trouble marrying a lady—*if* he had the inclination to do so. "I think you should take him. I've been watching you mow down swaths of suitors in the last two months and he's the best of the lot."

He could read the answer in her eyes.

Poor Greywick.

Being flatly rejected was undoubtedly a new experience.

"You've been staying in Lindow Castle for quite some time?" Greywick asked, looking somewhat displeased. Apparently, he didn't entirely believe that Jeremy was disinclined to court this duke's daughter . . . or any duke's daughter.

Betsy intervened. "Lord Jeremy has been helping my brother North enlarge his stables."

Nice of her not to tell the truth.

Of course, she didn't know the whole truth.

One evening he'd set off to meet Parth in Vauxhall Gardens, only to discover that idiots were setting off fireworks, which sounded remarkably like cannons. Next thing he knew he woke up in Parth's house—having lost the memory of an entire week.

He still couldn't get around that.

Greywick nodded. "You were always excellent with horseflesh. I remember the black mare you brought to university."

"Dolly," Jeremy said, his mouth easing into a shadow of a smile.

"Do you still have her?"

"I—no," he said, pushing away the memory of what happened to Dolly. She had the heart of a lion, but she couldn't save herself on the battlefield, any more than he could save her.

Greywick wasn't interested in Dolly's fate, and why should he be? He had eyes only for Betsy. She certainly looked the part of a docile duchess.

Yet she was as fierce as her brothers—aye, and slightly mad, the way all the Wildes were. God knew, when he and North had been in battle together, North had played the berserker on occasion.

There was that time when North dived off a cliff and swam down the river to the HMS *Vulture* to warn them—but that train of thought led to darkness, and Jeremy forcibly cut it off, returning his attention to the farce about to unfold before him.

Betsy saw bleak desolation cross Jeremy's eyes at the mention of his mare, and decided that chatter with an old friend wasn't helpful. "Now that we've clarified Lord Jeremy's lack of interest in marriage," she said, "perhaps we should return to the ballroom, Lord Greywick."

She gave her suitor a merry smile, emphasizing that she didn't care in the slightest that Jeremy Roden had been so perishingly rude about the possibility of marrying her.

Of course she didn't want a proposal from Jeremy Roden.

But did he have to make it so obvious what he thought of her?

Kittens? Love notes? She didn't even own a diary.

From the age of fourteen, she had never allowed herself to have infatuations, the way other girls did. Half her class in the seminary had swooned at the mere mention of her older brother Alaric. They collected prints of him supposedly engaging in heroic exploits.

They were the only prints Betsy bought as well. Attention to any man other than a family member would be interpreted as erotic interest. Her gowns were a tad more demure than fashion demanded: her hands always gloved, her ankles out of sight, her lips untouched by color. No one could accuse her of flaunting her assets, with her breasts tucked away in a bodice, perhaps with a lace fichu for good measure. Haughty matrons looked in vain for a sign of her mother's weaknesses: Betsy didn't have them.

"It's not that I'm uninterested in marriage, precisely," Jeremy said.

"I stand corrected," she said. "I neglected to

qualify that you are uninterested in a woman with the temerity to call herself Betsy or to keep a kitten."

"An excellent show of affront," Jeremy said appreciatively. "Well-phrased. She will make a perfect duchess, Greywick. Polite to a fault. Untempted by a prime physical specimen like myself."

Betsy narrowed her eyes. Was he subtly referring to her mother? Yvette had famously praised her Prussian's muscled thighs.

No.

Lord Jeremy Roden was objectionable, but he wasn't underhanded. If anything, he was too blunt. His insults were aired for all to hear.

"Luckily, I have consolation in this time of sorrow," Jeremy said, waving his bottle with a madcap grin.

"You can't imagine how devastated I am to find that you're married to a bottle of whisky," Betsy drawled. "I always planned to marry a man with a droopy appendage."

Then she turned to Greywick. "Shall we return to the ballroom, my lord?"

"Not yet, because you're supposed to be getting to know each other," Jeremy said. "I, lucky sod, know you both so I can play the matchmaker. Attest to the fact that you'd make a marvelous pair. Just marvelous."

He stopped and took another swig of whisky. The smell spilled into the room, fierce and hot, as unlike her rose petal perfume as possible. It suited him: Whisky was gritty, bold, and real.

"Lady Boadicea," the viscount said, holding out his arm.

"Oh, for God's sake, call her Betsy," Jeremy said, before Betsy could respond. "She likes it, even though it makes her sound like a milkmaid. Which she's not. Just at the moment, I can't remember her worthy traits, so I'll start with you, Greywick. *Thaddeus*, since we were on a first-name basis as lads."

Jeremy stabbed a finger in their direction and actually straightened in his chair, as if his opinion made an ounce of difference. Betsy barely managed to control her desire to throw a billiard ball at his insufferable head.

Instead she moved closer to Greywick and put a hand on his arm. "Thaddeus? I like that name." She didn't purr, because a Wilde is never obvious. But she did give him a glance from under her lashes that the devil in the corner would never see from her.

"My name is indeed Thaddeus," the viscount replied. "I would be truly honored if you wished to address me as such." He was a bit of a stick, but on the positive side he had marvelously thick eyelashes.

There was nothing more unattractive than skimpy, sandy eyelashes. That was the problem she kept finding with the blond men who had courted her. The hair on their heads might be marvelous, but their eyes had a naked look.

Not Thaddeus. His eyelashes were thick and dark as blackberries.

"Where's *your* halo?" Betsy asked, her face easing into a real smile. "Don't tell me you threw it away, the way this reprobate did. My aunt much enjoyed the irony of turning guests into angels."

One corner of his mouth curled up again. That was a rather fetching trait he had—smiling on one side only.

"I was raised to believe that honors shouldn't be flaunted until earned."

"Nice," came a rumbly voice. "He'll earn it, Betsola, no worries about that. The man's got a corner of heaven all staked out for him. Reserved. Inherited, in fact."

"*Betsola?*" Betsy repeated. "No, don't bother to explain. Thaddeus, shall we return to the ballroom? I think my aunt will be wondering where I am."

"I doubt it," the dark-eyed devil in the corner said. "I expect Lady Knowe is counting the moments, hoping you're behaving indelicately, if not worse. She'll have you married off before Easter. Perhaps before Christmas, if she thinks that Thaddeus here is as forward as her nephews. The next generation of Wildes are all going to be born at six or seven months, if she doesn't look out."

"My aunt is not counting moments or months," Betsy retorted, scowling at him. "You are being quite offensive, Lord Jeremy." Never mind the fact that she agreed with him about the likely arrival of her nieces and nephews.

"Ouch," Jeremy said, grinning. "Now, I think it's worth saying again that Thaddeus was by far the most intelligent of the blighters in our year.

Course, we didn't have Alaric. And I heard that Horatius was—"

"Do *not* mention Horatius," Betsy snapped. Her elder brother had died the day after she turned eleven. To this day, she kept the little ceramic bird he'd given her on her bedside table.

Jeremy was sprawled in his chair again, but he lowered his bottle and gave her a quick nod. "I'm sorry, Bess."

"Bess?" Betsy repeated, desperate to talk of anything else. "I suppose that's better than Betsola."

"Given that your father named all his children after warriors," Jeremy said, "he could have chosen Good Queen Bess instead of Boadicea. Her Majesty Queen Elizabeth dressed up in a suit of armor and rode a white horse to Tilbury. I could see you on a white horse. Your lady is a good rider," he added, waving his bottle at the viscount. "There, you see, I managed to think of a worthy reason to marry her."

She ought to leave. But honestly? This was the most entertaining conversation she'd engaged in all evening. And it was certainly a good idea to hear more details about the viscount.

What's more, her toes hurt. She was wearing a pair of Joan's heeled slippers and they didn't fit. She took her hand from Lord Greywick's arm and moved backward so she could hop up and sit on the side of the billiard table, which made her side panniers flip up in a flurry of silk, so she had to slap them down.

"It's like watching someone wrestle a couple of greased piglets to the ground," Jeremy drawled.

"Thaddeus, I hope you're observant, because your future bride has very nice ankles."

Lord Greywick stiffened, but Betsy tapped him on the arm. "Ignore him. He can't see my ankles; the open door blocks his view."

"I could if I bothered to lean forward," Jeremy argued. "At any rate, I was merely doing a matchmaker's duty. I'm sure Queen Elizabeth had slender ankles."

"I have to point out that Queen Elizabeth didn't wear a suit of armor," the viscount said, moving to lean against the table, hip to hip with Betsy. She didn't mind. He smelled rather good, like some sort of flower.

Not at all like Jeremy, who always smelled of cheroots and whisky.

"Her Majesty wore a silver corselet," Thaddeus continued. "Though some say it was steel. She did have a helmet with white plumes."

"*I know I have the body but of a weak and feeble woman; but I have the heart and stomach of a king, and of a king of England too,*" Betsy put in, quoting Queen Elizabeth.

And shrugged when both men looked at her, surprised. "You surely don't think that my father would name all of us after warriors and leave it there? He had us memorize any number of fiery speeches delivered on battlefields."

Then she flinched, thinking she shouldn't have mentioned a battlefield.

Jeremy's lips compressed. Perhaps it wasn't the battlefield, but the question of what one should say on it. Too late now.

Next to her, Thaddeus moved slightly, his shoulder brushing hers. "Tell Queen Bess how intelligent I was, Jeremy," he said, his voice a command. A gentle one, but a command. "I need help or this queen will look for a consort elsewhere."

For a suspended second, she and Thaddeus watched as Jeremy wrestled with darkness. His chin was square; it seemed even squarer when he ground his teeth.

"Right," he said, just a pulse too late, his voice strained. "I need to hawk the merchandise since the merchandise is failing to do so himself."

"Exactly," Thaddeus said. "The lady says she doesn't know me; who better to explicate my attributes than the most eloquent man in our year?"

"Are you talking about Lord Jeremy?" Betsy asked, startled.

"Eloquent?" Jeremy snorted. "Hardly."

Thaddeus turned to Betsy. "Indeed, he was the best orator at Eton, not just our year, but those above us, even in our first year. Able to coax the stars out of the sky."

"Too bored to stay in their courses once I started babbling," Jeremy said, his voice back to its usual rough indifference. His hair was disheveled, thanks to the bandage that wound over his ears. His neck cloth was half undone, as if he'd tugged it free of his neck.

Betsy glanced up at the viscount, who was a study in contrasts: his wig snowy white, no halo to be seen, and his clothing both exquisitely tailored and beautifully worn. That was one thing she'd realized lately: It wasn't really about how well-made a man's clothing was; it mattered how he wore it.

Thaddeus looked like a king ready to be painted by Holbein.

"You have to imagine all of us blighters sitting around in a schoolroom at Eton, obsessed by women's breasts and playing with ourselves incessantly—those two things not unconnected," Jeremy said, taking another swig from his bottle.

"There is a lady present," Thaddeus said quietly. One knew without hesitation that he would never mention such a topic in the company of women.

He had a nice deep voice. Not as deep as Jeremy's, but that was a matter of whisky and exhaustion, to Betsy's mind. Jeremy never seemed to sleep.

"She's got brothers," Jeremy said indifferently. "And the myth that women don't pleasure themselves, Thaddeus? Just that, a myth. We won't ask Good Queen Bess to confirm, as it might embarrass us."

Thaddeus looked at her. "Do you wish me to escort you to the ballroom, Betsy?" It was the first time he addressed her by her given name, and a nicely judged moment to use it too.

Unfortunately, she hadn't the slightest impulse to blush, and she was still interested to hear what the viscount had been like as a schoolboy.

She smiled at him. "I would like to hear what Lord Jeremy has to say of your prowess in the schoolroom."

"If you're using Greywick's first name, you must do the same for me. Particularly since I've been calling you Betsy for two months," the devil in the corner said. "No longer, though. From now on, Queen Bess will do."

"By addressing you formally, the lady is directing your commentary to a polite level," Thaddeus said. His voice had changed: He was *demanding* that Jeremy stop trying to shock her.

She ought to rethink the question of marrying the viscount. She really, really ought to reconsider it. Marriage wasn't so terrible.

Marriage to a man like Thaddeus would be . . . lovely. Truly.

He would run the country, or whatever it was dukes did if they weren't her father, who only reluctantly went to Parliament.

She had the feeling that Thaddeus would enjoy speaking in the House of Lords.

She would have beautiful daughters with thick eyelashes. That was important. It would break her heart if her babies were born with scrawny eyelashes. She could teach them how to dance and shoot, but no daughter of hers would glue rabbit fur to her eyelids in lieu of eyelashes.

"To return to my theme," Jeremy said, with only the faintest hint of mockery in his voice, "the schoolrooms were bursting with boys thinking of nothing but unmentionable topics. Except for Thaddeus."

Betsy almost said "Excellent," and then saw the trap he'd laid, the one where she would affirm Thaddeus's disinclination to do *that*. Her brother Alaric had explained it to her by means of a flood of synonyms for "gild the lily."

"Churn the butter" confused her at first, but then Alaric handed her an illustrated broadside of an erotic ballad and said that he didn't hold with any of his sisters being surprised by male anatomy.

There were times when she missed the mother she didn't remember. But her siblings, her father, her stepmother, Ophelia, and particularly Aunt Knowe had made up for a mother's loss ten times over.

"You should marry him, Bess. The first Bess made a mistake not marrying, you know."

"I ought to return to the ballroom," Betsy said deciding not to defend Queen Elizabeth's unmarried state. She was uneasily aware that if she stayed away too long, gossipers like Lady Tallow might start a rumor that she'd disgraced herself in order to force the viscount into offering marriage.

"Wait! Was I successful?" Jeremy asked, squinting at her. "Are you overcome with the wonders of the winsome lad beside you?"

Thaddeus crooked an eyebrow. "Lad?"

"North and I are old before our time, and you still have the glow of youth," Jeremy said flatly.

Betsy took it for granted that Thaddeus would be able to translate that as "aging due to time lost in the American colonies in a fruitless war."

Hopefully, he wouldn't be insulted. She'd often heard Jeremy divide mankind into those who had seen a battlefield and those who hadn't.

"Right," she said, sliding down to stand on her aching feet again. "Time to go. I don't want to miss supper."

"May I escort you to the meal?" Thaddeus asked.

She hesitated. If she dined with him, society would assume she had agreed to his proposal.

"Lady Knowe will be disappointed in you, Bess," Jeremy said. "Yet another suitor tossed away."

"I am not yet tossed away," Thaddeus said, smiling down at Betsy. It was a statement . . . and a question.

Betsy was suddenly vividly aware of Jeremy watching them. "Perhaps you are not," she said, pulling in her skirts so she could edge sideways into the corridor. The doors of Lindow Castle were hopelessly narrow, given the current fashion for skirts the width of three women.

Behind her, the viscount bid Jeremy goodbye. Affection deepened his voice and made him far more appealing than did his title or estate. A man who remained friends with a reprobate like Jeremy might not have very good sense, but he had loyalty.

The Wildes valued loyalty above all else. Loyalty to the family, obviously, but also to friends.

"Thank you for showing me the billiard table," Thaddeus said to her, once he had emerged from the room.

"Wouldn't gratitude be in order if I had accepted your proposal?" Betsy said, starting to walk down the corridor. "I am still unconvinced we would suit."

"I never expected you to accept my hand tonight," Thaddeus said, laughter gleaming in his eyes. "A lady of your stature must be won by a lengthy campaign."

Betsy blinked at him, rather surprised. Apparently, Thaddeus had no plans to retreat, the way her other suitors had. Occasionally a man watched her mournfully from the side of the ballroom after she refused a proposal, but generally they accepted her word on the matter and never broached the subject again.

"I'm not very good at accepting no for an answer," the viscount added. His smile was not wide, not overly confident, not arrogant. "Jeremy and I were well-matched in that. He could never bear to lose, and neither could I. We pitted ourselves against each other throughout our boyhoods."

"I am not the prize in some schoolboy contest," she said.

"Certainly not," the viscount said. "I am merely saying that I refined the art of never giving up while arguing with Jeremy." They had walked quite a ways before he said, "Though I think obstinacy is giving my old friend great pain these days. Stubborn people are particularly likely to curse fate rather than accept it."

"I believe his . . . his discomfort stems from unfortunate experiences during the war. I know that my brother North finds himself unable to sleep on occasion."

She was privately convinced that even before today's marriage, North's fiancée, Diana, had learned the trick of exhausting him.

So to speak.

North didn't look nearly as tired in the last few months, whereas Jeremy had black smudges under his eyes.

"As a schoolboy, Lord Jeremy was the most blindly loyal man of us all. Such a man would find it hard to tolerate losses amongst his fellow men, let alone those who served under him."

Betsy nodded.

"I would include his horse in the number," Thaddeus said. "He loved that mare. He boarded her at school, obviously, but most boys left care of their horseflesh to the grooms. Lord Jeremy visited Dolly every day. We were fed horrible slop, but he spent his pocket money on carrots and occasionally a lump of sugar."

"Oh, dear," Betsy said.

"He was rather unkind to you," Thaddeus said. "This may seem absurd, but if you are able, you might take it as a sign of his esteem."

"I don't return that esteem," she said tartly.

It wasn't precisely true. But it was safer to claim not to like Jeremy. More comfortable.

She couldn't imagine a worse fate than having an evil-tongued aristocrat with a dark soul and a penchant for drink jumping to the conclusion that she was infatuated with him.

She'd never hear the end of it.

"I entirely understand. Any young lady would be affronted by his appalling manners. I apologize for not taking you away immediately."

Betsy looked at him, raised an eyebrow. "I did not wish to go."

Thaddeus blinked and visibly absorbed the fact that she was not a woman who needed to be rescued from discomfort that society had decreed she must be experiencing. "I gather from Lord Jeremy's praise that you are a superb horsewoman?" he asked, making a quick recovery.

"I am," Betsy admitted. "We were raised partly in the nursery and partly in the stables. North was always fascinated by horses, and we younger children used to follow the older boys about like ducklings. Do you enjoy riding?"

"I do. The happiest hours of my childhood were spent with our stable master, Barnes. He taught me a great deal about life. Eton was all very well in its way, but the most important lessons are learned at home."

"I and my sisters had governesses, but then we were sent to a seminary for girls," Betsy said. "It was an unusual choice for a duke's progeny, but I loved it there, after a few growing pains. As you say, the lessons I learned were invaluable."

Witness whereof: If she'd stayed at home, she would have debuted in blissful ignorance of the *ton*'s opinion. She would have tried to be *herself* and promptly been relegated to the side of the ballroom, if not thrown out of society altogether.

Her father's rank could do nothing to prevent the judgments of the matrons who ruled polite society.

"Will you send your own daughters to school?"

"It would depend on their wishes," Betsy said. "My sister Viola is extremely shy. She would have been much happier at home. But my smallest sister, Artemisia, will relish a classroom full of other girls."

Thaddeus looked down at her, his eyes glowing. "The more I learn about you, the more perfect you seem."

Betsy cleared her throat. "I assure you that I am far from perfect."

"I necessarily strive for perfection due to my rank and responsibilities," Thaddeus said. "Yet when I fail to achieve my own standards, as any man must, I am reassured by the fact that an excellent reputation can defeat gossip. Your reputation is impeccable."

Betsy nodded her thanks, conscious of a gloomy feeling.

"Small moral faults are allowable under a guise of rectitude," Thaddeus added, digging himself deeper.

It could be that thick eyelashes were not enough to counterbalance such deeply-felt righteousness.

# Chapter Five

$\mathcal{I}$n the first hours after midnight, revelers began to leave. The newly wedded couple had long since vanished. The duke and duchess had bid farewell directly after a light supper was served, retreating to the North Tower, where the family was housed. Guests who lived nearby took to their carriages; those from afar returned to their beds, alone or in pairs.

Still, the ball continued, the music playing on for those who loved to dance or loved to gossip, and wouldn't retire until after Prism served another light meal.

Those guests who had worn masks had removed them at midnight; those with halos had thrown them away long before. The ballroom floor was littered with crushed spangles fallen from angelic headdresses. The expanse of polished floor glittered under the candelabras like a lake shining in the moonlight, the skirts of dancing ladies sweeping spangles into ripples that followed in their wake.

Betsy sighed.

She felt lonely.

She had danced with Thaddeus twice.

Unsurprisingly, the viscount danced with perfect control, maintaining his elbow at just the right level as they wheeled toward and away from each other. One of those dances, late in the evening, had been a new dance called a cotillion. His every move was perfection itself.

As was hers, of course.

People drew back to watch them, a rustle of whispers going through the assembled guests like wind in the trees. Thaddeus's face didn't betray any recognition of the attention they were receiving.

He was used to it.

So was she, but that didn't mean she liked it.

This would be her life if she married him; for a duke and duchess, privacy was a luxury, scrutiny a given. London stationers churned out prints of the Wildes, no matter how spurious the depictions: her brother Alaric wrestling the kraken, North as a Shakespearean villain.

Without a doubt, someone at this ball would report their two dances, not to mention the fact she and Thaddeus had left the ballroom for a time together. By next week, the two of them would be in the front window of every stationer's shop, likely with a wedding ring encircling their heads for good measure.

At this point, the only Wildes remaining in

the ballroom were Betsy and Aunt Knowe. Betsy danced on, ignoring her sore feet, relentlessly cheerful.

People asked her cunning questions about the viscount, which she deftly deflected. *Yes, he is most attractive. Yes, he dances extraordinarily well.*

Just when she decided that she ought to entertain another suitor, if only to quiet the gossips, a candidate presented himself.

He bowed before her, slender and elegant. His wig was ambitious, if not quite the height of hers. She'd met him, of course . . . but who was he?

She fell into a deep curtsy, and managed to make the connection on her way back up. Grégoire Bisset-Caron, who was—oddly enough—Jeremy's first cousin. They certainly didn't appear to have fallen from the same family tree.

"I trust you are having an agreeable evening?" Mr. Bisset-Caron inquired. "I wasn't lucky enough to claim a dance with you, but I thought that we should at least stand together, under the circumstances."

Betsy raised an eyebrow.

Mr. Bisset-Caron indicated his black costume with a sweep of his hand. He was wearing a black coat with a flaring velvet collar stitched in red. "Mephistopheles, at your service. Your heavenly beauty might, if you forgive my presumption, be enough to transform the darkest of devils."

"Didn't Mephistopheles sell his soul to the devil, rather than being one himself?" Betsy asked.

"I'm not much of a reader," Mr. Bisset-Caron said. "Black velvet suits me."

Perhaps he referred to the way he had powdered his face to an unnaturally pale color; certainly all that gleaming velvet enhanced his pallor.

"Lady Boadicea, might I recite a p'hoem that I wrote in your honor this morning?"

Betsy jumped, startled. The Honorable Adrian Parswallow had crept up beside them. Or P'harswallow, her siblings called him, with reference to his lisp. His family's country house was only a few miles away and they'd played together as children—which meant the Wildes had taken notice when the lisp appeared around his eighteenth birthday.

Adrian had a very high forehead, accented by a wig that had been powdered an unfortunate shade of orange. Perhaps he was a good poet; he definitely showed originality by appearing at a wedding ball in a coat and breeches of bright orange.

Masquerading as a carrot, perhaps.

"Good evening," she said, curtsying. "What an unusual costume."

Adrian bowed to a depth that threatened to split his extremely tight orange pantaloons. "I aim to be unexp'hected in all respects. Dressing in black is for old men."

"How frightfully rude of you," Mr. Bisset-Caron said with frosty emphasis.

"Mr. Bisset-Caron," Adrian cried, catching sight of Mephistopheles. "I would never include you in my rep'hroof." He had an extraordinary way of speaking; his intonation was so superior that it sounded as if he was yawning between words, adding random H's here and there.

Betsy managed to summon a smile.

"I shall recite my p'hoem," Adrian prompted.

Poetry was like sketching, embroidering, flower arranging, and counting linens.

Boring.

When she debuted eight months ago, Betsy had professed high delight in the first poem written about her. Consequently, more and more verses had been composed in her honor.

If only she'd been honest when the first p'hoem was thrown at her feet.

"We devils have no interest in literature," Mr. Bisset-Caron said. "I prefer the art of the pencil." And then, in response to Betsy's confusion, "I have a gift for sketching from life. I would be happy to show you my book, Lady Boadicea." He gave her a naughty smirk. "I brought it with me into the chapel this morning and I fancy I created a lovely profile of you."

Betsy managed a smile. Like poems, she found portraits of herself remarkably uninteresting.

Mr. Bisset-Caron's smile widened. "My sketches are not like the rest," he said silkily. "They rival any of those you might have seen in stationers' windows."

"A sketch could never render its subject as well as a p'hoem," Parswallow said.

"I beg to differ," Mr. Bisset-Caron said. "My images of the royal family are recognizable by anyone in London, whereas the poem I heard you recite earlier today, on your mother's voice, could apply to virtually any woman who has chosen to be fruitful and multiply. "

Adrian greeted this insult with the furious gaze with which he might have greeted Mephistopheles himself. "My p'hoem, Lady Boadicea," he prompted, turning his shoulder to Bisset-Caron.

The artist smirked. "We devils have no time for versification." He slid away.

"I'm afraid that I cannot accompany you to a quiet corner," Betsy told Adrian.

"While silence and p'hrivacy are p'hoetry's greatest companions," Adrian pronounced, "I am happy to recite the verse to you in p'hublic view and earshot. I wouldn't wish anyone to cast asp'hersions on your honor."

No one would wish to be dishonored by a carrot with a lisp.

"An Ode to the Name Betsy," Adrian began. *"The soft and comp'hassionate tone in her voice could heal a grieving heart . . . Ahhh, Betsy!"* He paused.

"An interesting first line," she observed.

"There is more," said the poet, unsurprisingly.

Luckily, before he got more than eight or nine lines in, Aunt Knowe appeared. Betsy clutched at her hand. "Darling Aunt, do listen to this marvelous poem."

"I thought the poem you recited this morning, the ode to a mother's soft and compassionate voice, was very interesting," Aunt Knowe said to Parswallow, "though not being a parent myself, I couldn't entirely sympathize."

"But we have all been mothered," the poet said.

Then he stopped in confusion, turning beet red. "Forgive me, Lady Boadicea, if I—"

Betsy shot him her signature blithe smile and nestled closer to her aunt. "I consider myself deeply lucky to have been mothered by Aunt Knowe in the absence of my own mother." She threw her aunt a mischievous glance. "Though I can't recall hearing your soft and compassionate voice very often." She turned back to Adrian. "There were so many Wildes in the nursery, you know. She had to bellow at us daily."

Aunt Knowe burst into laughter, snapped her fan shut, and rapped Betsy on the shoulder. "Wicked girl, I always present the image of a soft and tender lady." Nodding briskly to Adrian, she drew Betsy away. "Do you realize that you are the only angel to have endured the entire ball with a perfectly erect halo? I can always count on you to outdo your rivals."

"Millinery is not a blood sport, Aunt Knowe," Betsy observed. "It's absurd to congratulate me for such a foolish reason."

"Oh, fudge," her aunt said. "I gather you are not in a good mood. I recognize that look from your childhood. Create all the scandals you wish, once you have a husband to protect you from the world's opinion."

"I don't need a husband," Betsy protested. "I have Father, and a million brothers, and you. That's enough."

Aunt Knowe ignored her comment. "Your father thinks Greywick would be a good husband for you. I agree, as you could tell, since I sent the two of you off together. Needless to say, the ballroom was transfixed by your absence. Did you play a round of billiards? Perhaps more to the point, did you win?"

"We did not play billiards," Betsy said, rather surprised. "I thought you sent me off to receive his proposal."

"Naturally, I knew Greywick would blurt that out, but the more important question was whether he could beat you at billiards, no? I rather thought you might be there all night if he had to try more than once. I was merely hoping that the boy had a way with a cue. And," she added, "that was *not* meant to be a double entendre."

"I did not play billiards with the viscount," Betsy said. "When did that become a good standard for choosing a spouse, Aunt Knowe? If that was customary, I'd have married Parth, even though Lavinia would have murdered me. He's the only man outside the family to have soundly beaten me."

"The standard would pertain only to your marriage," her aunt said. "Billiards is so important to you, my dear, though Parth would have been a terrible husband for you. First of all, he's your brother by family ties, if not blood. And second, he's too cheerful."

Prism, the castle butler, was ushering the musicians from the ballroom. It truly was time to leave; for a young lady to remain to the end of a party implied desperation.

"I like cheerful people," Betsy said flatly, turning toward the ballroom door. "I don't want to face a morose man over the dinner table every night for the rest of my life."

She didn't voice it, but an image of grumpy eyes went through her head, followed directly by Jeremy's taut stomach. One day she'd walked up to the stable yard just as he caught a fresh shirt tossed by a groom.

Not that it was relevant in any way, but his stomach had chiseled muscles all down his front, his chest roughened by a light sprinkling of hair.

Aunt Knowe patted her on the shoulder. "Of course you do, darling. All the same, one could make an argument that you bounce enough for one household."

Betsy narrowed her eyes at her beloved aunt. "I do not *bounce*."

"Wrong word," her aunt said. "Fell off my tongue, when I meant to say that you bubble with joy."

Betsy shook her head. There was nothing wrong with being cheerful. It was a perfect defense against the world's indignities.

Aunt Knowe didn't say anything, but just enfolded Betsy in her arms. After Yvette, Betsy's mother, left the country, Aunt Knowe had happily mothered Her Grace's children.

She was as sturdy as an ancient oak tree. She smelled of chamomile and sweet ginger and felt like home.

"I don't want to marry any of them," Betsy whispered.

"You needn't, dearest," her aunt said, rocking

her back and forth. "You can stay with me. I'll teach you how to dry herbs, and we need never leave Cheshire."

Then she roared with laughter as Betsy pulled back, horrified by the idea of growing old at Lindow Castle.

"I always thought you were more like Alaric than the other children," Aunt Knowe observed. "Longing for adventure, I gather?"

"Yes." It was true. Betsy had mastered the rules of polite society because she had to. But she wanted . . . more.

More than billiard games late at night, usually played by herself.

More of the things that men were able to do, and women weren't.

She liked being a woman. But it didn't seem too much to ask to be able to ride astride, to be able to bid at an auction or to buy a horse. To go to clubs and play billiards.

To go to places where men congregated and talked and did business. To do something risky, the way men did: They bet fortunes on the flip of a dime. They swept around corners, leaving a hairsbreadth between the carriage wheel and the curb.

She was so tired of sitting in throngs of women and listening to them gossip about who would marry whom, and who would die soon, and who was being unfaithful. When it came to the last, she couldn't even offer an opinion—young ladies weren't supposed to conceive of adultery, even when the act was discussed in their presence.

She seemed to be the only person who realized how damaging those conversations could be. It took everything she had not to bite out a reprimand. Casual gossip about a woman's infidelity could ruin her children's future. Could destroy lives.

And yet who could blame ladies for chatter? Every woman she knew would categorically deny that she'd ever brewed up a scandal. Yet they spent their days doing little else, because there wasn't anything else *to* do.

Betsy's mother's flight to Prussia had burned away any interest she might have had in other people's intimacies. In her perfect world, a man and woman would stay together as long as they cared to, and then part, if they must. No one would pay notice to their private lives.

Aunt Knowe groaned. "I know that expression."

"What expression?"

"You're the precise image of your brother Alaric at this moment, and that look on his face signaled flat rebellion. You know, your father forbade him to go to China as a young man, and he not only went, but he took Parth with him."

"Yes," Betsy answered. "Though as I remember it, Father welcomed the idea."

"My point is that if I had suggested Alaric stay home and learn how to sort herbs, he would have looked just as tragic as you."

"Alaric is so lucky," Betsy said, wistfully. "I would love to turn my back on society and sail away."

"Marry, then travel," her aunt advised.

She didn't want to be a wife. She wanted to be herself, but without a notorious mother and a famous father. Just a person among strangers. Not a *wife*.

Aunt Knowe clucked her tongue and wrapped her arm around Betsy's shoulder. "It seems my twin brother spawned not one but two adventurers. You behave with such perfection that I didn't realize, Betsy. I feel a terrible aunt not to have known what was in your heart."

"You are the best of all aunts," Betsy said, leaning her head against Lady Knowe's shoulder. "I am merely tired of being perfect."

"You have been the belle of this ball and every other this Season as well," her aunt said, giving her a squeeze. "The news has spread that you turned down the viscount, and all the young ladies are green with jealousy."

"They guessed?"

"He readily told his mother, the duchess, that you had refused him. Are you certain that you don't want Thaddeus, my dear? I've known him since he was a child, and what a darling boy he was. I don't believe he'll give up easily. If anything, I would say that he is twice as interested now that you turned him down."

"He told me as much," Betsy said, trying to find some part of her that cared.

No, she didn't care.

"It would be pleasant to be a duchess," her aunt said, beginning to stroll toward the door and drawing Betsy with her. "Let's go, my dear. It's time to retire."

"I've watched my stepmother play the role," Betsy pointed out. "I would like to live a more private life. What's more, my brand-new sister-in-law strongly believes that being a duchess would be more dreary than working as a governess. Or a barmaid."

"Hopefully, you won't have a chance to test that theory as regards the pub," Aunt Knowe said tartly. "I am still appalled by the fact that my eldest surviving nephew married a woman who had frequented the servants' hall."

Betsy kissed her on the cheek. "It's too late to pretend that you don't adore Diana, my darling aunt."

"I do adore her. But I trust that you would never contemplate entering domestic service, Betsy. You are not suited to taking orders."

"I could take orders!" Betsy said indignantly.

Aunt Knowe shook her head. "You are practically a duchess already, which is one of the reasons why every bachelor peer in London wants to marry you. They know their households will be perfectly ordered."

Betsy scowled at her. "I don't know what you're talking about."

"In the nicest possible way, you expect the world to dance to your tune—and it does."

"You don't understand," Betsy said, nodding politely to Lady Tallow, who was lurking by the door. "It hasn't been easy to cultivate a perfect Lady Betsy that they all see and believe in."

Her aunt smiled at her. "I do see your armor and admire it—and you. But, my dear, people respond to other people instinctively, like animals in a pack. You take after your father: You are a leader in the pack, whether you wish it or no."

Betsy burst into laughter. "You are mad, Aunt Knowe. In the best of all fashions, of course."

The castle butler, Prism, was waiting in the entry with a bevy of footmen at his shoulder, ready to escort people to their bedchambers. The family had learned from sad experience that the castle was so large that gentlemen often lost their way and managed to blunder into ladies' chambers at the wrong moment.

"I suppose you will retreat to the billiard room before bed, since you didn't offer Thaddeus a game," Aunt Knowe said.

Betsy opened her mouth to say that she would be going to bed. "I would like to play one game," she found herself saying instead.

"You might see Jeremy down there," her aunt replied. "He disappeared some time ago."

"He couldn't dance with a halo bobbing on his shoulder," Betsy said, surprising herself by defending Jeremy.

"That wasn't the reason," Aunt Knowe said, pausing. "He was gamely circling the floor and doing a decent job—for North's sake—of acting as if he didn't mind being in society. But Erskine Gedding, that despicable creature, came over and commiserated about the loss of Jeremy's entire platoon."

"Every single soldier was lost?" Betsy asked. She swallowed hard. "I didn't know . . . I wondered what had happened."

"Not my story to tell," her aunt muttered. "But let me just say that it was a despicable thing to say, especially from one who clearly knew the details. Gedding shan't be invited to Lindow again, not if he marries a royal princess. *Never.*"

"Aunt Knowe," Betsy said, grinning at her. "You suddenly resemble the big bad wolf in a fairy tale."

"I'd bite off Gedding's head with pleasure," Aunt Knowe said. "Jeremy is healing. He's much better than he was two months ago. But it's rank cruelty to go after a man on the mend and try to provoke him."

"Is he mending?" Betsy asked dubiously. "He was in the billiard room nursing a bottle of whisky when I arrived with Greywick."

Aunt Knowe gave a bark of laughter. "So he played the Greek chorus in your proposal?"

"He urged me to accept the viscount," Betsy said, feeling a sting of irritation again. "Apparently, Greywick was the smartest lad at Eton, for what that's worth."

"Quite a lot," her aunt said. "I am not in the least surprised."

"My point is that Lord Jeremy was swigging whisky straight out of a bottle. An empty glass sat on the floor beside his chair, but he must have decided that upending the bottle was a faster way to imbibe. To become drunk, in other words."

Lady Knowe had one hand on the polished knob at the bottom of the grand staircase leading to the castle bedchambers, but she turned back.

"You surprise me, Betsy. I think of you as quite observant. You think that Jeremy gets drunk?"

"Of course I do. Were you in the room the night when he slid under the billiard table and had to be dragged upright by Parth?"

Her aunt smiled. "He must have been very bored."

"Nonsense," Betsy said tartly. "The man consistently looks as if he's lost his rudder. Three sheets to the wind."

"Not a bad description," Aunt Knowe said. "But you've got the wrong end of the stick. Have you ever heard him slur his words?"

"I'm sure I have."

"I'm fairly sure you haven't."

"He passed out on the floor, Aunt Knowe. On. The. Floor."

"Boredom is a powerful enervator," her aunt said. "Darling, do take one of the footmen as an escort to the billiard room, won't you? He can wait outside while you play a game or two and then escort you to bed."

Betsy opened her mouth to protest, but her aunt cut her off. "There are too many strangers in the castle. That dreadful man Gedding, for example. I wouldn't put anything past him."

Betsy rolled her eyes. "He's sixty if he's a day, Aunt."

"Cruelty is not bounded by age. By the way, I want to see you at breakfast tomorrow morning, no matter how long you fool around in the billiard room."

"I'll be there," Betsy said, sighing. "Lady Betsy"

was always among the first at breakfast, face shining, ribbons in her hair, a cheerful smile on her lips.

She rarely saw Jeremy at that hour.

Not that the fact was relevant. Whatever Aunt Knowe thought about it, he probably spent his mornings sleeping off a heavy head after drinking all that whisky.

Likely she would find him in the billiard room, passed out under the table again.

She dropped into a curtsy and bid her aunt good night. If Jeremy was lying on the floor she would prod him with her toe and *prove* that he was inert with drink.

At a nod from Betsy, the family butler hastened to her side. "Could you spare a footman to accompany me to the billiard room, Prism?" Betsy asked. "My aunt feels I should be escorted, given the number of guests in the castle."

"She is quite right," he replied. "Carper." A tall footman appeared at his shoulder. "Wait for Her Ladyship to finish a game of billiards and accompany her to the door of her bedchamber."

He turned back to Betsy. "I shall inform your lady's maid that you will not return for an hour or so."

"Please give her my apologies," Betsy said, uncomfortably aware that Winnie wouldn't go to her own chamber until she returned.

"Very kind of you, Lady Betsy," Prism said. "Winnie will be happy to rest on the truckle bed until you return."

Betsy nodded and took off down the corridor,

trailed by a silent young man with a thatch of yellow hair. As a girl, she thought she liked blond men better than dark-haired ones. But there was something wrong about men with yellow hair. It took away from their . . .

Their manhood.

She pushed the thought away.

# Chapter Six

On the way, Betsy decided that if Jeremy Roden was still in the billiard room, she would retire to her chamber.

Of course, she could order him to leave instead. She was a daughter of the house and if she wanted to play a game of billiards alone—as she often did, late at night—she had a right to the room.

The sad fact was that wicked men were interesting and good ones were boring. Thaddeus, with his kindly eyes and generous mouth, with his title and excellent estate, was so *boring*.

And Jeremy . . . wasn't.

God knew why he was often found in the billiard room, since he refused to play her or anyone else. She suspected it was because the room was so quiet. Her older brother North used to haunt the room, but now he was in love, and that drew him to other games.

Ha.

Betsy walked into the room, leaving Carper in the passageway outside. The lamp was burning brightly over the table, just as she'd left it. She glanced immediately at the corner where Jeremy had been lurking.

The chair was unoccupied, the bottle on the floor beside his empty glass.

She was glad, of course. He was outrageously rude and what's more, he refused to play her at billiards.

Sometimes she felt as if billiards was the only thing that gave her any interest in life. Unlike the balls that made up the Season, each new game offered a challenge. She walked over to the rack and picked up her favorite cue.

She would play one game and then retire to bed. A smile involuntarily formed on her lips as she took up the cue. It was made of rosewood, inlaid with mother-of-pearl butterflies. More importantly, it had a perfect weight and slid like silk through her fingers. And best of all, her brother Alaric had brought it home from China for her, even though she had been a very young girl at that point, and girls were not supposed to play.

Yet Alaric and North had never excluded her from the room. For a moment, loneliness flashed through her, but she pushed it away. It was absurd to feel alone when the castle was filled to the brim with guests, not to mention her own relatives. If flesh and blood didn't suit, North and Parth had both managed to snare funny, charming women who would be happy to chat.

Except, given as it was well past midnight, those women were likely cuddled up with her brothers. North and Diana were now married, but Parth and Lavinia merely betrothed.

All the same, Betsy had no illusions about the levels of morality in the castle; copulating couples abounded.

That was rather clever, not that she had anyone to share it with.

The door opened, and Jeremy slipped in.

Absurdly, her heart thumped, and she instantly felt happier. Before she thought better of it, she blurted out, "Why aren't you in bed? Where were you?"

"Is that a question to ask a red-blooded man?" he countered, going to his corner and throwing himself into his chair. "I could have been tupping Lady Tallow, because I don't mind telling you that she made me a *very* indiscreet proposal in earshot of any number of people, luckily not including her husband."

Betsy stopped herself from narrowing her eyes, but it was a close thing. She didn't care about his *tupping* or lack thereof. She was irritated only because Jeremy had become something of a friend.

She cleared her throat and set the red ball down with precision. "Were you tempted?"

"Would you want to rip off Lady Tallow's nightdress with your teeth?" Jeremy countered. He reached for his bottle of whisky.

Something eased in the general area of Betsy's chest. "No." She couldn't think what else to say and Jeremy was paying her no attention, pouring whisky into his glass as if it were melted gold. "It might be adventuresome," she added, on second thought.

"No, it wouldn't," Jeremy said, plunking the bottle back down onto the floor. "I'll bet you anything that she wears sturdy flannel at night. It would ruin a man's jaw to rip that fabric."

"There are other ways to remove a nightdress," Betsy said, bending down to take her first shot. She decided to start with an easy angle. "Lord Tallow has apparently mastered the art of disrobing a woman in flannel."

"They do have a full nursery," Jeremy conceded. "At any rate, being as I'm an old-fashioned type and prefer not to sleep with women with spouses, I was taking a piss, if you must know. I had to go a damned long way down the passageway to find a room with a chamber pot."

"Rude," Betsy remarked. "Profane, and indecent. It's a wonder you aren't drummed out of society."

"Nonsense. See how well-mannered I'm being? Using a glass, just for you." He took a deep draught of whisky, throwing it back as easily as if it were tea. "And by the way, you'd find me unbearably tedious if I reformed."

That was so close to what Betsy had just been thinking that she was silenced and took the shot without proper preparation. The ball ricocheted off the side rail in the wrong place and missed its target.

"Anything interesting happen after you returned to the ballroom?" Jeremy asked, slouching down in his chair.

"No."

"Surely you rejected at least two more proposals before midnight?"

Betsy had to counter Lady Tallow with *something*. But no one ever offered an illicit proposition to the perfect Lady Betsy. To be fair, any man so inclined likely guessed that her father would rip him limb from limb.

In fact, it was a good thing that His Grace rarely entered the billiard room these days. This rude, not to mention profane, exchange she was having with Jeremy?

Her father would not approve.

Suddenly she realized that she had received something of an illicit proposition. "Did you know that your cousin, Mr. Bisset-Caron, is an artist?"

"That does not surprise me," Jeremy said. "He was an intolerable boy."

"Apparently he surreptitiously brought a sketchbook with him into the chapel during the wedding—which Aunt Knowe would undoubtedly consider a grievous breach of manners—and he offered to show me his sketches, which, you must admit, is a mere step from offering to show me his etchings."

Jeremy snorted.

"Are you implying that I shouldn't accompany your cousin to his chamber to view his sketchbook?" Betsy asked, putting on an innocent air.

He just rolled his eyes.

"In lieu of private art," Betsy said, "I listened to a public recitation of a poem a neighbor had written about me."

"Do share," Jeremy drawled.

"It was about my name. Not my real name, but Betsy." She looked up and their eyes met, a smile flashing between them. Yes, they squabbled, but they had similar senses of humor.

"Of course it was," Jeremy agreed. "Did he manage to rhyme it? *Let's see, Bet-sy.* That's not bad."

She wrinkled her nose at him. "Surely you jest. My name is a liquid melody that suits a gentle life like mine. Plus there was something about the tears of my tender girlhood. Then Aunt Knowe came along, and that was the end of the artistic part of my evening."

They laughed at the same moment.

"My cousin is lucky that Lady Knowe didn't hear of his sketches," Jeremy said.

Betsy picked up the red billiard ball and replaced it in the center of the table. "I have a question. Do you actually get drunk, or are you just fooling?"

"Who could drink the better part of a bottle of whisky without becoming bosky at the least, and completely foxed at the worst?"

"So are you foxed? Because I don't think you are. Your speech is very clear."

"I was sent to Eton and Cambridge," he told her. "The accent disguises any amount of folly."

"Untrue," Betsy said. "On his fifteenth birthday, Alaric drank two bowls of punch all by himself. He could barely speak. We lured him up to the nursery so Aunt Knowe couldn't sober him up, and then fell about in fits of laughter."

"From what I know of your brother Alaric," Jeremy said, "I'd wager a guinea that he was bent on amusing the youngsters and enjoyed playing the part of a drunkard as much as you enjoyed seeing it."

Betsy took another shot and botched the angle again. "I can't remember well enough." She met his eyes. "I don't remember whether *he* slid under the table and went to sleep, for example, but I definitely remember *you* being fished off the floor like a sleepy toddler."

Jeremy raised an eyebrow. "Likely the nursery was a lively place and your squeals kept him awake."

"Aunt Knowe was right!" she cried, straightening and planting her cue on the floor. "You didn't pass out. You were merely bored!"

"Which time?" he asked genially. "Do you suppose if I ring the bell, Prism will send a footman? I could use another bottle of whisky."

"Carper is outside the door, waiting to escort me to my chamber," Betsy said. "You can send him if you like. Why do you bother drinking whisky if it does nothing for you? It leads to dropsy and tremors, and will turn your nose red."

Jeremy's eyebrow flew up. "That seems oddly specific."

"Aunt Knowe made all of us read *An Inquiry into the Effects of Ardent Spirits on the Human Mind and Body.* Or perhaps it was *Human Body and Mind.* Are you hoping that liquor will send you to sleep if you drink enough of it?"

"I wouldn't be so lucky."

She sighed. There was nothing worse than a person who nagged about a friend's bad habits. For example, her stepsister Viola kept urging Betsy to "be herself," now that Betsy had proved so popular on the marriage market.

Won the war of the debutantes.

Whatever you wanted to call it.

"You should stop drinking," she said, because Jeremy Roden was so ferocious that people likely felt they couldn't tell him the truth. "If not for the sake of your liver, then because Shakespeare said it takes away the 'performance.' You don't want to find yourself in proximity to a nightdress, flannel or otherwise, and be unable to play your part."

He raised an eyebrow. "You think I'm losing my teeth at this young age? I assure you I can rip silk with one incisor."

"You did tell Thaddeus that you had aged." She rearranged the table, banking a right-angle shot off the left side.

"You are uncannily like your aunt," Jeremy observed.

"I can't imagine a better compliment," Betsy replied. "Tell me again why you won't give me a game?"

Silence.

Then a low voice drawled, "I'd be bored."

"You're a brute," Betsy tossed over her shoulder.

Jeremy didn't see any reason to answer that because, of course, she was right. "Why do you like billiards so much?" he asked instead.

That made Betsy actually turn around, her precious cue—he'd noticed how much she adored it—cradled in her arms. "It takes a great deal of concentration to stand on the back of a moving horse," she announced.

"North boasted about your ability to do that. Just think: If all the gentlemen at your feet disappoint, you could join the circus."

"It takes even more concentration to play billiards."

"The tricky shots," Jeremy said, nodding. "I have a friend who likes to send the ball backward." He'd taught Jeremy the trick, though Jeremy didn't add that.

Betsy made a scornful sound. "Billiards isn't about flamboyance; those players lose to anyone who can make six or seven simple shots without making a mistake. *I* could beat your friend."

He had no doubt of that, so in lieu of reply, he stood up and stuck his head out the door. A footman leaned against the wall, eyes half closed. "A pot of tea, if you please," he said. "You might as well get yourself a cup before you return, as Lady Boadicea will be an hour or two at least. You're no use to her if you're asleep on your feet."

"Of course, my lord," the footman said, trotting away.

It was astonishing to realize that everyone in the

castle—from Lady Knowe to a lowly footman—appeared to have concluded that he posed no danger to Betsy. That footman left without a second thought.

Jeremy could ravish her. Didn't they think of that? They were putting a lot of weight on loyalty to the Wilde family, if that was their reasoning.

Maybe the household considered him akin to a Wilde, but that was absurd.

He'd only met Betsy two months ago. He wasn't Parth, for God's sake, who wasn't related to the Wildes by blood, but a member of the family in every way that mattered.

He was just a friend of North's and no more.

Jeremy returned to his chair. If he tried something untoward, she would ram the billiard cue into his stomach.

Maybe that was it. Maybe they knew Betsy would defend her honor to the death and they trusted her to fight him off.

She was bent over the table, lining up the cue and ball, her upper teeth clamped on her lower lip the way she did when she concentrated. She was a hell of a billiard player.

If they ever played and he actually wanted to win—because the two times she'd bullied him into it, he hadn't given a damn—he could give her a true match. His father and he rarely saw eye-to-eye, but they had been most civil to each other over a billiard table.

Now he thought of it, that's probably why he wouldn't play her. Too much of an echo of his childhood.

Of course, the Wildes were right, whatever their reasoning: He would never ravish a woman. But that didn't mean he couldn't enjoy the view from the corner. Every time Betsy bent over the table, he had a delicious view of either her breasts or her arse.

The fact her skirts extended to the sides emphasized the round swell of her bottom. Her breasts peeked out the top of her corseted bodice, gorgeous handfuls that blushed pink when she was angry.

A man lucky enough to bed her would probably think up ways to annoy her, just to see that delightful haze of color flood from her bosom to her cheeks.

Perhaps when she was aroused . . .

Proving that she had no idea that his thoughts had wandered in a lascivious direction, Betsy bent down, eased her cue forward, and lined up a shot that apparently was meant to go from the left rail to the right, and from thence to the pocket.

Her eyes betrayed the angle she wanted, but her arm was at the wrong height. It wouldn't work. And it didn't.

One thing you could say for Betsy Wilde: She didn't give up. She didn't even sigh, just plucked up the ball and returned it to its place.

"You're holding your right elbow too high," Jeremy growled.

She immediately adjusted her elbow, one of the rare instances in which she'd listened to him. Then she replaced the ball and tried the shot again. It worked.

"Now try from this side, but bend lower over the table," he ordered.

She obediently moved around the table so her back was to him and bent over to put the ball into place—and froze. She put her cue across the table with a click and turned about, crossing her arms over her chest. "Why?"

"So I have a better look at your arse, of course," he said.

"I should whack you over the head and put you out of your misery," Betsy muttered, moving back around the table to the other side.

"This angle isn't bad either," he said a few minutes later, after she'd managed to finesse the angle twice. He was beginning to feel slightly repentant about ogling her bosom, though not enough to force him to his feet and out of the room.

A glimmer of the gentleman he used to be was making itself known, pointing out that he oughtn't to gawk at a lady's curves without permission.

Betsy would never give permission, obviously. She wasn't Lady Tallow, who shook her bosom in front of him like a bowl full of jelly, reminded him of the castle's two peacocks.

Lacking a peahen, they spent their time rattling their feathers open in colorful but fruitless displays.

When Lady Tallow did the same, he couldn't even manage a twitch of his cock, a failure she had read in his eyes, given that she'd flounced away before he could refuse her offer.

Yet his cock twitched every time Betsy neared

him. And now, when she was leaning over as if she were offering her breasts for his pleasure, he was far past a twitch.

It felt damned good to have a hard cock again after months of inertia.

That had nothing to do with *her*. It just meant that his body was getting ahold of itself again. He was healing, the way Lady Knowe kept promising when she poured noxious cups of soothing draughts down his throat.

Betsy glanced up at him, and apparently realized her breasts were on full view. "You must be desperate," she said, straightening and hauling up her bodice.

"Oh, I am," he agreed, upending his glass. "These old stone walls are crowded with Wildes, each more luscious than the last. I meant the Wildes, obviously, not the walls."

"You're desperate *and* blind," Betsy snapped, setting up the table again. Whatever else you could say about her, she was not a quitter. He'd never seen anyone work so hard to master the angles that ruled billiards.

Blind?

Surely, she knew how beautiful she was. One of the things he liked about Boadicea Wilde was that she wasn't nervous about her looks. She wasn't one of those women who were forever peering into their glasses and poking at their hair or coloring their lips.

She sailed into every room, the confidence of a beautiful woman hovering around her like an ermine wrap. She was fit for a king, in other words.

Or a duke.

"I don't have proper breasts," she said, surprising him. "Not like Lady Tallow's, for example."

He blinked but managed to keep his face expressionless. "I can assure you that from a man's point of view, every pair of breasts is 'proper.'"

"I could put on boy's clothing and no one would know the difference."

She was probably right about that. Other women overflowed with fleshy parts, lush breasts so plump that they rose from their chests like overgrown gourds.

Betsy was perfectly proportioned. Nothing overly ripe.

Jesus.

"Not true." He managed to give the words a touch of contempt, even though the contempt was really about his unruly desire for her. He set his glass down on the floor. Maybe whisky was finally affecting him. "You don't walk like a boy."

What's more, he couldn't be anywhere near her breasts without noticing them. Even flattened by the wretched bodices women wore, you could see—

He wrenched himself back from the edge of saying something stupid and resorted to brutal honesty instead.

"If a man hadn't already noticed your breasts, you might get away with it on top. But you wiggle when you walk. Makes a man want to watch your arse."

Likely that would shock her. He was tired of

prevarication. Talking of men who "passed to a better reward," for example.

They died.

They were buried. Gone.

After a moment, he wrestled his mind back into the room. Betsy's mouth had eased. She wasn't shocked; she was complimented.

"You hurt my feelings," Betsy told him, the plaintive note in her voice obviously false. She pursed her lips in a mock pout that made his cock throb against his silk breeches.

He eased backward in the chair to hide his condition, just in case she happened to glance in that direction.

"I didn't hurt your feelings," he said, taking another swig. "I can tell."

"You must play me a game of billiards, or I'll tell my father that you praised my arse, and guess who'll be asked to leave the castle?" Her voice was triumphant.

He'd walked straight into her trap.

He didn't want to leave. This shadowy room was a perfect place to wrestle with his demons. And now he had his cock back . . .

Fine.

He stood up. "I don't play without a wager."

Betsy shrugged. "What will you wager?" Her voice was confident. Of course, she expected to win. He had sat around the billiard room for weeks, not to play but to brood. Or heal, as Lady Knowe had it.

That and to argue with Betsy. And watch her play.

Her bosom and her arse were simple pleasures. Private ones. She had no idea that he could have drawn the outline of her body with charcoal if he wanted. Hell, he could do it in the dark, his fingers tracing her curves.

Not that he ever did anything about it, even in the privacy of his room. Forget his boasts to Thaddeus about self-pleasuring. He couldn't remember the last time he touched himself.

For months he had felt as if his body was merely a container for emotions that he didn't want and couldn't get rid of. The fierce pleasure he used to experience from righteous exercise of his favorite body part?

Gone.

Instead of raging desire, the kind that reminded a man that he *was* a man, Jeremy went through the day with a muted, passive lack of interest in anything connected to the female body.

Perhaps every soldier felt that way.

But a memory countered that thought. A few weeks ago, he'd walked around a corner silently and come on North in the act, his fiancée hitched high against a wall, her skirts spilling over his braced arms, her legs curled around his waist.

North had laughed unsteadily as Diana threw her head back and cried out as if—

Jeremy wasn't a pig. He had retreated as silently as he'd come, eyes squeezed shut. But that one image was burned in his memory.

He hadn't felt even a twitch in his loins, though.

Until now.

"What do you want if you win?" he asked. Obviously, Betsy assumed he was a rotten billiard player.

"An adventure," she said instantly, propping her hip against the table and staring at him.

That was surprising. Perhaps that was Betsy Wilde's appeal: She was surprising, and nothing else in life was.

"Adventure," he repeated, trying to imagine what a young lady considered to be an adventure. Going to the theater? Betsy had spent a good part of her life in London; hell, her father had brought in an entire troupe to act the outrageously successful drama *Wilde in Love*, written about Alaric.

"Three syllables shouldn't be too hard for a drunkard like yourself to understand."

Jeremy dismissed that taunt. She had caught on to the fact that he couldn't get drunk. Perhaps Lady Knowe had told her. The duke's sister was one of the most observant people he'd ever met. She would have made a hell of a general.

"What sort of adventure?" he asked.

Betsy gave him a fierce look, nothing like the gentle, sweet gaze with which she mowed down her suitors. "The sort men can have," she stated. "I want to put on breeches and be a boy for a day."

Jeremy's mouth fell open. "*What?*"

His mind immediately presented him with an image of Betsy wearing a snug pair of breeches. What had been desire became a forest fire. He took a deep breath.

It was very uncomfortable to discover that he

wanted her more than he'd ever wanted a woman before.

She was *not* the right woman.

*Not* the right moment.

"I want you to take me to London and show me things that only men can see," Betsy added.

He scowled at her.

"Not a brothel," she said, obviously disgusted. "A gentlemen's club like White's or Brook's, where I can play billiards."

"Just billiards?" he clarified.

She nodded.

Actually, that made sense. She was obsessed by billiards.

"That's it? That's your adventure? Going to London and playing billiards? You'll likely beat almost anyone," Jeremy pointed out.

"You're not as drunk as I thought, if you realize that," Betsy said.

"Much to my dismay, I never am."

"I'd like to go to an auction at Christie's too, and bid on something. I *loathe* the fact that women aren't allowed to place bids."

"Why so much passion?"

She stared at him. "As a woman, I'm not allowed to have my own money. I am required to buy fripperies, but nothing of any import, reflected in the fact that I am not allowed to place a bid at auction. And you ask me why it matters?"

Jeremy winced. "I apologize for my sex."

She gave him a lopsided grin. "So, are you ready to take me on an adventure?"

"Impossible." He brought out the one weapon

he knew would horrify her. "You might be compromised. Forced to marry me."

"Nonsense. A woman can't be compromised unless a man wants to sleep with her."

Jeremy narrowed his eyes. It was almost as if she knew that he hadn't had a cockstand in months, not until this evening. She was treating him like a toothless old dog.

He rose to his feet and stepped toward her. The fact she brought a footman with her to protect her from male attention went through his brain, along with the fact that she hadn't blinked an eye when he sent her chaperone away. In fact, she suggested the man leave.

Damn it, she thought he was neutered.

"What is it?" she demanded. "My father wouldn't let the two of us spend so much time together if you were a man who felt—" She broke off.

Jeremy stared at her, incredulous. *"Desire?"* The duke himself had declared him castrated?

Betsy frowned at him. "Are you going to be missish with me? Yes, *desire.*"

"I feel desire." The words growled from deep in his chest.

"Oh, for goodness' sake," Betsy cried. "For *me*, you philistine! I don't mean you leering at my bottom. I mean proper desire, the sort that makes people behave like fools."

"I could be that sort of fool."

He was still hard, and exhilaration filled him. He felt alive again, as if his body and mind had clicked back together like a huge puzzle piece.

Betsy narrowed her eyes, her instincts finally driving her to see him as a man. She shifted her weight from foot to foot, thinking.

"Of course," she said, her voice careful. Not tentative, but careful.

"If I win, I want a night with you," Jeremy said, staring down at her. "One night and no ring to follow."

Betsy's mouth fell open. "What in the bloody hell—"

Joy rose within him. He wouldn't take it, but damn, it felt wonderful to *desire* it.

"You don't want me, and even if you did, you're a gentleman," she said.

He raised an eyebrow.

Betsy gave a theatrical sigh, but he could see that she wasn't entirely certain of her statement. From now on, she'd never see him as a toothless old dog again. She'd keep her damned footman within earshot in the future. "If you won, you could never claim your wager," she pointed out.

"War burns the gentleman out of a man." It was true.

Betsy scowled. "I don't believe that."

*Oh, sweetheart.*

That was why men went to fight on battlefields far from home, if they possibly could. No one wanted a woman to see what happened there. What it cost a man to survive, let alone what happened to those who didn't.

He would never take a woman's virtue, but that didn't mean he wasn't enjoying himself. "Believe it," he said, dropping his voice to a growl.

Desire burned in his gut and down his legs. He hadn't wanted anything since he left the service. But now?

He wanted her.

He wanted this complicated, mad girl who had managed to fool most of polite society into thinking she was docile and demure.

Betsy didn't show the faintest sign of being unnerved; indeed, her mouth curled into a genuine smile. "You've had most of a bottle of whisky this evening, and you've never beaten me, even once."

He had never tried to beat her. He didn't say a word, just looked down at her and waited, letting his eyes do the speaking.

"Ladies play first," Betsy pointed out.

She was planning to shut him out of the game entirely. This wager came down to whether he had a chance to play at all.

She'd been missing shots in the last hour, probably tired from the long day, so he had a chance.

He nodded.

Betsy cracked a smile, a naughty smile even for a Wilde. "Would you truly bring me to the city? You'd have to show me how to walk like a man."

Jesus.

Would he?

He'd have to speak to her father. Or her brothers. But look at her: She was like a bomb on the verge of exploding. If he refused, she might do something mad that would truly ruin her reputation. Or get her married to the wrong man.

No lady he knew would dream of traveling to London in boy's clothing. But he got it. Betsy's older brothers went out into the world, and she stayed at home and arranged flowers. Listened to poetry. Ladies weren't allowed to have adventures. Or own property. It wasn't fair.

He nodded.

"All right," Betsy said, turning away.

Jeremy reached out, and his fingers slid down the silky skin of her arm. "Is the wager on?"

"You're going to lose," she told him. The faint melancholy that had cloaked her all night was gone. She looked cheerful.

"You cannot travel alone with me," he pointed out, just to be fair. She opened her mouth, but he shook his head. "Put it down to fear of *my* lost reputation, if not yours. Your aunt must come along. Or one of your brothers."

"I suppose," she agreed reluctantly.

He moved to the other side of the table and stood there, arms crossed, watching like a hawk. A few moves later, he flinched, and she hastily lowered her elbow. "Better?"

"Yes."

"You're hardly helping your own cause by correcting my stance," she said, glancing up.

Mostly Jeremy watched her breasts rather than her stance.

He felt surprisingly alive. What's more, the realization didn't throw him into a cauldron of grief, the way it usually did. Tonight, in this shadowy, quiet room, it seemed a good thing to be alive.

To be making a foolish wager, and lusting after

a woman's breasts, and generally behaving like a member of the human race.

She caught him looking at her bosom again.

He cocked an eyebrow.

"Last shot," Betsy said, scowling at him. If she made this, the game was over.

She kept her elbow down. He watched her eyes and realized that she was planning a simple shot: left wall to the right pocket.

The cue struck the ball, the ball struck the wall . . .

Jeremy's mouth curled into a smile.

Slowly, Betsy straightened and met his eyes.

# Chapter Seven

*T*hat's the game," Betsy said, feeling a wave of relief that put her slightly off-balance.

She'd won an adventure.

She would go to London in a pair of breeches. She would play billiards with the best players to be found in England. She sucked in a deep breath.

Jeremy had come around the table and was standing before her. "You did indeed win, Bess."

For the moment, she ignored his adulteration of her name. "I get to wear a pair of breeches," she said, smiling. "I used to borrow a pair of Leonidas's breeches and put them on under my dress when I was a girl. I adored wearing them."

"That would explain why you have such a damned good seat on a horse."

"Yes." Betsy's heart lit with the pure joy of sharing a secret. "I'd take my sidesaddle off in the meadow and practice riding bareback."

"How improper," he observed, but his eyes were laughing.

"I also practiced archery," she confessed. "I had a target. And standing on top of my horse's back, as I told you before. She was an old mare with a broad back. It was so much fun."

"Why did you stop?"

"I could only do it because an accommodating stableboy, Peter, never told anyone. He helped me with the saddle and the rest. I was only ten years old when I first showed him my breeches."

"He must have been horrified!"

She shrugged. "He was twelve. We rode out together whenever I could arrange it, but a couple of years later he decided to apprentice to a blacksmith."

"I'm amazed your brothers didn't stop you."

"Alaric and North are quite a bit older than I am," she pointed out. "Leonidas was always away at school. I'm very close to Joan and Viola, but they are both far more ladylike than I am, and Viola is afraid of horses."

Jeremy bellowed with laughter.

"What's so funny?"

"You are widely seen as the most ladylike maiden on the marriage market."

"And so I am . . . in public." Happiness swelled up inside Betsy. "Could we leave on Monday, do you think?"

"Not without a chaperone." He stepped backward. "I'm sorry, Bess. You did win, and I agreed—but I highly doubt that anyone will agree to chaperone us. I am friends with North and Parth, and neither of them will approve."

"*Why* do we need a chaperone? I'll be dressed

as a boy! No one will know who I am, and I trust you implicitly."

"How do you intend to explain your absence from the castle? With me? The family would be within rights to believe that I had kidnapped you and was planning to marry you at Gretna Green or something equally absurd."

"They would *never* believe that," Betsy said, wrinkling her nose.

"Why not?"

She gave him a little push. "Your lack of interest in me is obvious and everyone's seen it."

Either that, or they'd decided he was as feeble as an octogenarian. "Your reputation would be damaged," he said, stating the obvious. "Your downfall would be all the greater because so many fools have put you on a pedestal. We'd be forced to marry."

"Who would possibly find out?" Betsy grinned at him, mischief glowing deep in her eyes. "You don't understand, Jeremy. I look *good* in a pair of breeches. No one will guess I'm not a boy."

How in the hell had she been able to conceal that she was the wildest of the Wildes?

"I won't do it unless you tell a member of your family and that person accompanies us," Jeremy said, putting his cards on the table. "If I marry someone, I'd prefer to choose the woman myself than face the end of His Grace's dueling pistol."

"I am so tired of being treated like a piece of china that will break at the slightest jarring," Betsy growled. "I am a grown woman."

Jeremy stepped forward again, eyes intent on

hers. Suddenly she was acutely aware of his size. Her mind neatly supplied her with an image of the sharply defined muscles on his chest.

If she pushed him again, she might feel those muscles under her fingertips.

Slowly she raised her eyes from his powerful neck that a half-open neck cloth did nothing to conceal. To his square chin and blunt cheekbones.

Jeremy looked like a warrior. He could have been in the legions of angels commanded to guard heaven's door. Until he fell.

A dark angel, then.

She lifted her eyes all the way to his, because the room had gone peculiarly silent. She could hear his breathing, and her own.

For most of the evening, he'd sat in the shadows. But now they both stood within the pool of light thrown by the lamp hanging over the billiard table. The light was bold and bright, since a shadow might throw off a player's calculations.

Jeremy's eyes were not black, as she'd always thought, but flecked with gray. Dark gray with a lighter ring around the outside.

She stilled when she saw the expression in them.

In the last two months since he had arrived at the castle, she had seen him scornful, bitter, grieving, desolate. Buried in guilt. Pained as if he'd been stabbed in the chest. Issuing withering sarcasm, mostly directed at her but occasionally flaring in all directions, even at Aunt Knowe.

Outrageously arrogant.

But this she had never seen.

*Need.*

What was in his eyes was pure physical *need.* For her?

Her lips parted, surprised, and her hand began to rise to his chest before she snatched it back.

"That's right, Bess," he said, his voice cordial but still low, a growl hidden in its depths. "I am not a safe companion. Especially not if you put on breeches and I could see every outline of your luscious bottom."

"Jeremy!" she breathed. "Don't."

"Don't what? Don't lust after you? They all lust after you, princess, don't you understand? All those men who proposed to you."

"No, they don't!" she said stoutly.

"Surely you don't believe they've fallen in love with you, poetry or no poetry."

"Love doesn't enter into the calculation. I've presented a lady whom they want to marry: obedient, demure, quiet." Her voice had an edge. "Well-bred on one side, if not the other."

He made a noise, somewhere between a laugh and a snort. "You're wrong, Bess. They aren't in love with you, but damn, they are in lust. You walk across the ballroom, looking like the perfect embodiment of a future duchess—and at the same time, the most sensual woman in England."

Betsy gasped, and ice went down her spine. She lost all inclination to pat his chest and glared at him, stepping back until she bumped the table. "No, I do not! You are absolutely incorrect."

He frowned. "It was a compliment of a sort,

Bess. I can assure you that gentlemen watch you with your duchess airs, your touch-me-not innocence, and the main thing that comes to mind is a violent wish to *have* you. To be the one to break that ice and set free the fire inside you."

Betsy gasped, horror welling up in her chest. If he was right, all those proposals she'd received were *because* of her mother, rather than despite her.

What if those men thought they saw the shadow of her mother's debauched behavior? The kind of lust that drove a woman to throw away the best match in the land? To leave her children?

Acid burned up her throat from her stomach, and for a moment she thought she'd vomit.

Jeremy's eyes sharpened with puzzlement, and he wrapped his large hands around her upper arms. "I meant it as a compliment."

He had no idea that he was making her heart burn with disgust, and she certainly wasn't going to explain.

Her mother, Yvette, was *her* burden, and the last thing she'd do was reveal that weakness to one of the few men in the world who had always told her the truth. A shudder ran through her body, and Jeremy's hands tightened on her arms.

"What's the matter, Bess? It doesn't make sense that you'd fall for the idea that men view ladies like delicate angels. You don't turn up your nose at a bawdy joke. Hell, you were the one who called me 'flaccid'!"

"Excuse me," Betsy said, marshaling all her strength to remain calm. "But any man who thinks about me that way is quite mistaken. I am *not* a loose woman, puns or no, and there is *nothing* about me that might suggest I would readily fall into bed with a man."

That included her future husband, but she kept that to herself.

She'd decided years ago that she had to get through the bedding part of marriage without giving her husband even the faintest suspicion that she enjoyed the act—if indeed she did. Enjoyment would be fatal.

If she expressed pleasure, he would watch her like a hawk. And rightly so. Just look at her mother, giving birth to four children in five years, before fleeing with the count. The evidence of her *enjoyment* of men's favors had been written on Yvette's body in language that anyone could understand.

"That is exactly why you and I cannot make a five-day journey in which you are dressed as a boy," Jeremy said, his voice patient, as if he were instructing a slow student.

Betsy opened her mouth and stopped, floundering. He was right, of course. She rarely accompanied a man out of a ballroom without a chaperone. She zealously guarded her reputation.

And yet—

"It wouldn't be *me*," she said, looking back up at his eyes. "You could call me by a boy's name. Fred or Pete. Don't you see, Jeremy? It wouldn't be me, so how could I lose my reputation?"

"Are you planning to bed down in the stables with the grooms and other male servants?" His eyes were sympathetic, but his voice was unrelenting. "It would still be you, albeit in breeches, and if you were discovered—which is likely—the consequences would be terrible."

"How would I be discovered?"

"London is five days' journey from here. Anything could betray you. Did you know that men whip out their cocks and piss against the wall?"

She blinked.

"You want to masquerade as a man," he said. "What are you going to do if someone wagers that they can pee farther than you?"

"Is that likely?"

"It's not unlikely. Men like to measure their prowess in ways that are related to the performance of their private parts, ridiculous though it seems."

"I needn't be disguised as a stableboy," she pointed out. "I could pose as a young relative of yours."

"If I travel from Lindow Castle to London with a well-dressed young lad, almost all will wonder if you are one of the Wildes. Everyone knows the duke has thirteen or fourteen children. They would stare at you."

"Oh."

"On the other hand, if I am merely part of a group that includes Lady Knowe, or North, or even one of your younger brothers, you simply become a young Wilde, traveling with an older relative. Nothing interesting to see . . . *move along, if you please.*"

"What?"

"Constables say that during street riots," Jeremy explained. "My point is that if I travel to London with you, you would be a subject of interest. But if we brought along one of the older Wildes, that person would absorb the attention. People are fascinated by your family, in case you haven't noticed."

She harrumphed. "I've lived with their attention my entire life, so yes, I have noticed."

"They would focus on Lady Knowe, or North, or Leonidas, not on a mere boy."

"I think your argument is a weak one, Lord Jeremy."

"We agreed on first names."

"We didn't really."

"You have already addressed me as Jeremy. And I'm calling you Bess, or *in extremis*, Boadicea. Frankly, this breeches play you're suggesting is not far from the warrior queen who took on the Romans. I don't suppose she was wearing skirts, let alone panniers, when she led the charge."

"I still don't think a chaperone is necessary."

"I suggest Lady Knowe."

"This is ridiculous!" The words burst past her lips. "Yes, I see the danger if I pretend to be a stableboy, if I'm alone with a group of men. But I could be a stray young cousin of yours whom you were escorting to London."

He shook his head. "You have the Wilde profile and eyebrows, Bess. There's no mistaking the look. Every Wilde has it, except—"

"Except for my sister Joan," Betsy said resignedly. "You needn't elaborate. We all know that

Joan's hair is the precise shade of the infamous Prussian's."

"More to the point, the Wildes are well-known for eyebrows, high cheekbones, blue eyes with a tilt at the edges . . . Anyone in the south of England and most people in the north are able to identify a Wilde even from the worst-drawn prints."

Betsy groaned.

She hated to admit that he was right. She did look like her father and her aunt. Joan stood out in the midst of them like a rose in a bunch of lilacs. Even the three younger children, Ophelia's brood, had the Wilde eyebrows. And the Wilde cheekbones as well.

"Right," she said. Her mouth drooped. "I suppose it was a stupid idea."

"Yes, it was," Jeremy stated, not softening the blow.

She straightened and forced a blithe smile on her lips. "It was a happy dream while it lasted, so thank you for indulging me."

He flinched. "That smile is terrifying."

"What do you mean?" she asked, scowling at him instead.

"Has anyone recognized how much desperation lies behind that particular smile, the false cheerful one?" Jeremy asked.

He had her hedged against the billiard table. In an effort to gain a little space, she pushed up so she was seated on the table and wiggled backward, making sure to pin her panniers at her sides.

"I am never desperate," she told him. "Despair is an emotion unbecoming to a Wilde."

"Believe me, my father expressed similar feelings about my condition on returning from war. And yet . . . when desperation becomes one's companion, no calls to better behavior seem to ward it off."

Betsy shook her head. "I'm not desperate. I'm simply fatigued, after a long Season." She had an idea. "Could we go to Wilmslow for an afternoon instead? I am so . . ."

"Bored," Jeremy supplied, his voice solid and steady. "You are tired of pretending to be a woman whom you are not. You are tired of laughing at unfunny jokes and listening to terrible poetry. You are tired of receiving and rejecting proposals of marriage from strangers."

"Yes."

"I'll take you to Wilmslow if we are accompanied by a chaperone." His voice was indomitable.

"You just tried to win a night in my bed!" she cried, frustrated. "Where were all your principles a half hour ago?"

"You believed me?" A glinting smile spread across his face. "I rather thought you had put me in the category of a wilted vegetable, Bess."

"What?" She eyed him. "You know exactly what you look like, Jeremy. Don't be absurd."

"You're the one who is here with me, late at night, without a footman within call, though he should be coming with tea any moment, now I think on it."

"Because you are . . . *you*," she said, exasper-

ated. "Could we go to Wilmslow just for one afternoon?" True desperation was leaking into her
voice but she couldn't stop it. "We needn't have
a chaperone if we merely walked around the
town."

"Aunt Knowe," Jeremy said firmly.

Betsy groaned.

"If she accompanies us, I'll agree. As an older
woman, she can visit any place we might fre-
quent. The attention will focus on her, rather
than on you."

"I will ask her," Betsy said reluctantly.

"Then it's as good as done."

"I still don't see why we can't go alone," Betsy
grumbled.

"There's this as a reason," Jeremy said. There
was something in his voice that made her head
jerk up. He braced his arms on the billiard table
on either side of her.

His face was so close to hers that she could see
his eyes even more clearly than before. The gray,
flecked with a lighter color, made them look like
granite. This close, his expression was still enig-
matic.

But not his eyes. Jeremy's eyes burned with
lust. Her own widened in surprise, but he didn't
move. He just watched her, his breath touching
her face.

# Chapter Eight

$\mathcal{B}$etsy had never been kissed.

She had made it clear to her suitors in hundreds of ways that she would not welcome any physical protestations of affection. If gentlemen cared to go on their knees, they could remain at a reasonable distance and make their case from below.

But this was different.

Jeremy wasn't kissing her. He was just waiting, and all of a sudden, the world narrowed to the two of them. A flare of adventure swept through her. She had never wanted to kiss her suitors, but Jeremy?

She leaned forward and put her lips tentatively on his.

To her surprise, his tongue swept her lips and dipped inside.

Jeremy tasted so good that he stole away her common sense. His tongue curled around hers and sensation streaked down the backs of her knees.

This kiss was unsanitary, but Jeremy tasted so good. Like cherries in summer, when you can't stop eating them until your lips and fingers are stained purple. Hot and luscious and carnal.

Her tongue twisted around his. She hadn't realized that eating cherries was carnal, not until this moment, when she tried to make sense of the way he tasted, better than summer fruit. Her heart was pounding with the frantic pace of a woodpecker. And she was . . .

Loose.

Her knees felt loose and her arms felt boneless and her mouth was open against his and she felt . . .

This was lust, presumably.

That thing she'd told herself that she would never, ever succumb to.

She jerked backward.

Thank goodness she did, because through the open door she heard approaching footsteps. "Carper . . . the tea!" she whispered.

Jeremy moved to the side just as Carper appeared. The footman was toting a heavy silver tray laden with a steaming pot of tea.

"Apologies from myself and Cook, Lady Boadicea," he said, looking around for a place to set down the tea tray. "A number of guests decided they'd like a tea tray before bed, and the boiling water had run out."

"Our game is finished," Jeremy said. "Lady

Boadicea, would you like the tea tray brought to your chamber?"

"No, thank you," Betsy said, giving Carper an apologetic smile.

"I shall be glad of a cup before bed," Jeremy said. "Tell my man I'll be there directly." Carper trotted away, the sound of his footsteps fading into the castle's silence.

Jeremy moved back between her legs and bent his head, his lips brushing hers with leisurely pleasure.

Words and thoughts jostled in Betsy's head, but her body claimed the lion's share of her attention. Somehow her arms wound around his neck. A tendon flexed under her fingertips and she was glad that billiards required she remove her gloves.

It wouldn't be proper to run her hands down his back.

His hands didn't move, clamped onto the table.

His lips drifted over hers, his tongue dragging over her bottom lip. It felt fuller and her tongue hovered in front of her teeth, waiting for his.

Every time his lips caressed hers, she felt a kind of greed rising up inside her for more, more of his touch, more of his taste.

*More.*

The thought made her recoil so hard that she actually reeled backward and would have fallen onto the table except his hands flashed forward and caught her.

"No more," Betsy said shakily as he brought her back upright.

"No more kisses?" Jeremy cocked an eyebrow at her. She'd never realized how winglike his eyebrows were. They went up like curved blades, suiting the sharp planes of his face.

"I don't kiss like that," she said, her voice rasping in an embarrassing fashion. "In fact, I don't kiss at all."

Because he'd had to catch her, he was leaning over her, which was somehow even more sensual than when they were mouth to mouth.

"That was certainly an awkward first kiss," Jeremy said, straightening and backing away. "I'm sure that your hordes of suitors have offered you far more graceful busses."

She didn't reply to that.

A wicked little smile was playing on his lips. "I didn't even know that I wanted a kiss," he said, all friendly as if what happened was nothing. "But I do believe you've healed me, Bess."

"Healed you?" She felt as if her brain were drowning in a river of sweet honey. She could see why lust was addictive. An anxious voice had popped up in the back of her mind, reminding her that lust *had* to be addictive.

Otherwise, her mother never would have abandoned her babies, would she? It wasn't as if Betsy's father was abusive, or even intrusive. The way Aunt Knowe told her, the duke had remained in the castle at the same time her mother was in London, conducting an *affaire*.

Her younger sister Joan was conceived that year: born at the castle, but conceived in London.

"Cured you of what?" she clarified.

"Disinterest," he said. His smile widened. "War knocked it out of me, but by God, one kiss from you . . . no wonder all those suitors are lined up to ask for your hand in marriage!"

"I don't suppose you'll be joining them," she said, a shrewish note leaking into her voice because . . . honestly? She felt shaken to the bone by that kiss. It did something to her. She had loved it.

Jeremy was ranging about the room, grinning with the sort of cheer that she pulled over herself like a coverlet when she was in society.

On him, it was real.

She put a hand to her lips and they pulsed at her touch. She wanted to slide from the table and leap into his arms. Paste her lips to his and welcome whatever kiss he'd give her. The only thing stopping her was the certain knowledge that lust was irrational. Wicked.

"I must go to bed," she said, sliding off the edge of the table and coming to her feet. Her knees felt weak.

Thankfully, Jeremy was gentleman enough not to make a joke or even leer at her. Kisses were nothing; she knew that from other girls. But she didn't know anyone who'd kissed a man in the middle of the night, in a deserted room.

She dropped into a curtsy. "Lord Jeremy."

"Here," he said, visibly alarmed. "Are you angry? Did you not wish to kiss me?"

She met his eyes and grimaced, something like a smile. "Of course I did."

"Then why are you giving me such an odd

look?" he asked. "That's one of those smiles that you don't mean, where your mouth curls up, but your eyes stay flat. Look, if you didn't want me to kiss you, I am truly sorry. I misinterpreted."

"I kissed you first, remember? It was a surprising experience, that's all." She shook out her skirts so she didn't have to meet his eyes. "I've been kissed before, as you surmised. This was one of many."

"I knew that. No man proposes marriage these days without at least claiming a woman's lips first. What if you found out that she had false teeth?"

"Shocking," Betsy said, walking to the door. "Are you retiring as well?"

"You know, I believe I shall," he said, looking absurdly jolly. "I haven't been sleeping more than a few hours a night, but at the moment I feel as if I could lie down and sleep."

"That's what you meant by being 'cured'? By a kiss, like a frog who used to be a prince?"

"No. But I've learned to be thankful for small gifts. You have given me something, but I can't elaborate because you're a young lady."

She stopped.

The castle echoed with silence around them. The sound of their feet on stone pavement had been swallowed up by the long corridors that ran before and behind them.

"I want to know. It was *my* kiss, after all."

"You've given me a cockstand," he said, tilting his head and watching her as if she were a chess problem. "The first in months."

"A—oh."

Well, that made sense. Fallen women, loose women, inspired that sort of thing in men. Her mother surely had. It made sense that Betsy inherited the ability.

"We shall not ever do that again," she said, meeting his eyes to make certain that he completely understood.

"Of course not. I expect you have a quota."

"A what?"

"One kiss per man? One to confound his senses, and then he is supposed to flop down on his knees and blurt out a proposal? You already know that I'm not going to do that, so I'll take my allotted kiss and head back to London before I lose my head and propose."

"You may do as you wish," Betsy said, feeling nauseated. She put a hand on her stomach to steady herself and walked faster.

A large hand clamped on her shoulder. "Bess."

She pulled away. "I have to be up early in the morning."

"What's the matter?"

She kept silent until they reached the end of the corridor.

"It wasn't a deep metaphysical question," Jeremy observed.

"Why would anything be the matter with me?" She looked up at him, certain that her face was composed.

"Damned if I know."

They walked up a half flight of steps. They were heading toward the family wing, in the North

Tower, by a shortcut that hopefully avoided servants.

Jeremy felt a sudden conviction that whatever Bess was feeling, he should not allow her to retire to her room without discussion. Everything wouldn't be better in the morning, as when they had had a squabble, and then met again the next day with a silent agreement to let bygones be bygones.

This was something else. Their kiss might have ruined the only connection he had that amused him.

"You tell me," he said, "and I'll tell you."

"What are you talking about?" Her voice was steady. But he heard a thread of tension there. Something *was* wrong.

Damn it, he shouldn't have kissed her. But hadn't she done the kissing? He couldn't remember clearly, because of the burst of pure desire that went down his spine when their lips met.

"I'll answer your question," he said, "the one you posed to me back in the billiard room, and then you answer mine."

He was appealing to her curiosity. Over the last two months he'd noticed that mysteries were anathema to this particular Wilde. She wanted to know where people were and what they were thinking.

"There's nothing for me to tell. I'm merely tired. And I don't remember what it was I asked you."

That was untrue, or he'd eat his hat. He'd seen her save up a question and ask one of her brothers weeks later for the answer.

"I haven't had a cockstand in months," he told her, conversationally. "No interest. Not in Lady Tallow or anyone else. But you, with the way you glare at me, and then bite your lower lip, you brought me back to life, or at least the part of me below my waist. You do have a delicious lower lip, Bess."

She shuddered visibly. He saw it.

"All right, I told you what I meant by that comment about being healed. I did something wrong in our kiss," he said. "You have to tell me, Bess."

"Nothing was wrong," she said stonily.

He felt a prickle of anger, so he stepped in front of her. "There were two of us in the room. We kissed, and now you've got a desperate look about you, as if I took you by force, or lured you into something indecent, and we both know that didn't happen. So what in the hell is going on?"

His stomach clenched as he saw a tear running down one of her cheeks.

"It was just a kiss," he said, about to reach for her and stopping himself.

She moved to put her back against the corridor wall. He backed up so he was against the opposite wall. He tried to make his voice as gentle as possible, which didn't come easily to him. "Did something happen to you that Ophelia or Lady Knowe should know about? Or your father?"

Betsy frowned at him.

What on earth was he talking about?

Then she recoiled, her shoulders striking the stone wall behind her. "No. Thank goodness."

His jaw eased.

"That was my first kiss," she blurted out.

"Really? It wasn't *that* bad." Jeremy's brow furrowed. "I could do better if you give me another chance but honestly, Bess, as kisses go, it wasn't terrible. Not too much spit, our teeth didn't clang together, and you have very good breath. Like roses, as a matter of fact. Delightful."

"Yours too," Betsy said mechanically, having been trained to return compliments. "You don't understand."

"I should have given you a slug of that whisky," he said. "Who knew my kisses were so powerful? Would you like to sit down? You're looking white as a sheet. I think I'd better fetch Lady Knowe."

"No!" Betsy squeaked.

"In that case, I suggest we have another go at it." Jeremy gazed at her, eyes somber. He meant it. "I can't leave you with a terrible experience of kissing. Lord knows what it would do for your future marital life."

Betsy pushed herself away from the wall and began walking again. "You've got the wrong end of the stick," she said, over her shoulder. "I'm merely overtired. It's been a long day, given the wedding and the ball."

"And our kiss," he said, catching up. "So you would rather I believe that you were overcome by the pure bliss of kissing me than acknowledge that I did a terrible job, and put you off men for life?"

"It was pure bliss," Betsy said, wishing that he wasn't so close to the truth. "Absolutely. No need for a repeat."

The problem was just that: It had been blissful. For a moment she had been flooded with a kind of giddy pleasure that was poison to a woman like herself. Like a future drunkard after his first glass of stout.

"This is my bedchamber," she said. Jeremy had terribly searching eyes. How did she ever imagine he was drunk?

No inebriate could see straight through the smiles that had charmed polite society, knitting his brow and looking as if he planned to have a word with Aunt Knowe. Or even worse, her stepmother, Ophelia.

She hesitated, hand on the door. "So when are we going to Wilmslow?"

"Are we still going?" He sounded startled.

"Of course we are." She pushed open the door, then turned around and put into her voice every bit of command she'd learned in a lifetime of being the duke's eldest daughter. "Surely you don't think that one second-rate kiss would put me off a wager honestly won?"

"Second-rate is it now? I thought it was blissful."

A gleam in his eye showed that he was thinking of trying again, but Betsy would never allow him to kiss her again. Or any other man.

"I'll leave you," Jeremy said, apparently reading her eyes as easily as she could read his.

"Yes, you do that," she said. "We can discuss our plans tomorrow."

"Those would be the plans involving you donning a pair of breeches?" He grinned. "I'm looking forward to it."

"Hush!"

"It's not as if you will be able to keep your maid in the dark. You must trust her. I kissed you for one reason, Bess: to convince you of the need for a chaperone. I fancy you get the point? Because if we were alone together, and you in a pair of breeches, I'm quite likely going to think that I could persuade you to enjoy kissing."

Betsy ground her teeth. "I see your point," she said woodenly. "I will ask Aunt Knowe to accompany us."

"Excellent. I might sleep tonight," he said, looking surprised.

"I knew it," Betsy said, before she could stop herself.

"What?"

"I guessed how Diana had cured North's sleeplessness."

He chuckled. "With kisses?"

Betsy's cheeks were burning. "We shared only one kiss. Imagine what she could accomplish with four or five."

He leaned close. "I *shall* imagine that, shall I?"

"You are appalling." She went into her bedchamber and almost closed the door, but stuck her head back out.

He was still there, waiting for her, as if he knew that she would return. "I want to go to Wilmslow soon. Perhaps we should visit in our normal garb and find out if there is an auction we might attend."

"Good idea. I need to brace myself."

She frowned.

"You . . . in breeches. No kissing. I might have to find a woman between now and then." A slow smile spread over his face. "You won't mind knowing about it, Bess, because you've no interest in me or my kisses."

She pulled her head back and closed the door.

Winnie was fast asleep on the truckle bed in the corner and didn't even stir. Betsy leaned back against the door, eyes searching the ceiling. She would have to wake her maid in order to undress, but she could wait.

Why was she so upset? She had always known that she might have inherited her mother's pleasure in bed sport. That didn't mean she had to give in to weakness.

What a way to discover it, though: with a man who showed her no respect. If one kiss from *him* melted her resolution and made her weak at the knees, just imagine how she would feel when kissing a man for whom she actually cared.

Her mother's bequest, so to speak, was this volcano of erotic desire swirling around in her, waiting to take over and force her to abandon her husband and babies. Lust felt like a windstorm that could sweep away her prudence. Her common sense.

She slid down the door until she was sitting against it. She could deal with this. She'd known it was a possibility. In fact, she'd sensed inside that it was a certainty. Look at how readily she'd gaped at Jeremy's bare chest.

If Thaddeus kissed her, would she leap on him like an untamed cur? She had the feeling that she would not. But if she married Thaddeus, and then some years later met a Prussian with golden hair?

She could actually imagine lust driving her to extremes.

After twenty minutes of hard crying, she finally stopped and blew her nose.

Fate had offered her a chance to ameliorate her mother's shame. Her mother had left a duke and her own children behind. She, Betsy, would be a good duchess. A *perfect* duchess. And a good mother too.

She would be everything her mother hadn't been. She would never flirt with another man after marriage, or even consider such an abomination. She would be loyal and true and a perfect wife.

No one would ever whisper about her daughter's corrupted blood.

She would marry Thaddeus.

# Chapter Nine

*I*t was ridiculous to hope that one kiss would make him sleep. Instead Jeremy stared into the dark, as he had night after night.

But somehow, tonight, the dark was a little less murky. For one thing, he kept puzzling over what went wrong with that kiss.

Betsy—*Bess*—had curved her arms around his neck and leaned into him as if she felt the same jolt of staggering pleasure as he had. For a moment, he'd been blinded by the ferocity of it.

The passion had to be due to his two-year drought: Desire returned in a rush that brought him near to groaning at the taste of her, every sense in his body flaming to unruly life.

He could have sworn she felt the same.

Her tongue had curled around his shyly, but he felt the breath catch in the back of her throat. He kept his hands to himself, but he felt her tremble with desire.

Then it all changed, which was a puzzle. He

hadn't done anything extraordinary. He hadn't nipped her lip even though it was plump and delicious.

The memory seared down his body and his cock jerked up and fell back against his belly. It was still hard, an hour later. Straining to be—

Near her.

Heat sizzled across his skin and he almost moved to grip himself, but that didn't feel right. Betsy hadn't liked his kiss; it wouldn't be right to relieve himself with thoughts of her.

Another thought occurred to him and he crossed his arms behind his head, trapping his hands to make certain that they didn't wrap around his cock and pull, hard.

What if it was he? What if she liked the kiss—it was her first, after all—but then she realized she was kissing *him*?

Maybe she knew about his lost week after those bloody fireworks. The details that Parth had promised to keep to himself.

No.

He trusted Parth the way he trusted North and Betsy—all the Wildes. He and Betsy could trade insults all day long, but she'd never stab a man in the back.

He had faith in the Wildes, a gut-deep faith, the way some men believe in God, and others in king and country.

Betsy probably formed her own opinion about why he spent his evenings in a corner, brooding over lost men and lost opportunities.

A worse thought occurred, and he stiffened.

Perhaps she knew what had happened in Massachusetts. No Wilde would have lost his entire platoon. Her brother North had brought his men through multiple engagements safe and sound, but for an unlucky few.

Not he.

Every single man was lost; only he had walked off the battlefield without an injury.

His tool fell against his belly, and there was no need to trap his hands.

Someone could have told her. The War Office had investigated and declared him a hero—but who cared for that? They hadn't been there, in the smoke and the sweat and the blood.

So much blood.

He had taken his men into the belly of the beast as he had been ordered to, rallied them again and again, went back and forth across that bloody battlefield—the one he still walked in his dreams—and every musket ball flew by his ear or his shoulder, never touching him, always striking one of his men instead.

At the time, he didn't realize what was happening, too desperate to keep his men together, to get the wounded to safety. Waiting, waiting for the sign to retreat because the bloody engagement was lost from the beginning.

The order never came, and he found out later that his colonel had fled rather than bring in his battalion as ordered.

His men, his brave men, fought on because he rallied them. And perished, because he didn't save them.

His cock lay on his thigh now, as dead to the world as the rest of him.

With an effort, Jeremy forced the memories away, even though they were so vivid that he could have sworn he smelled an acrid whiff of gunpowder.

Dawn would come.

He would get through this week, and carry out his promise to Betsy. Then he would leave. What had he been doing, sitting among good people as if he had a right to be here?

Kissing a woman who deserved so much better than he that she actually looked ill when she realized who she'd kissed?

He'd take Betsy to Wilmslow, let her bid on some fool thing, then leave. Go somewhere. Perhaps to his townhouse in London.

After a while he got up and moved to a chair by the open window. He lit a cheroot and sat in the dark, waiting for the sky to lighten, the only light in the room the glowing end of his cheroot. Hours later, the bullfinches woke, and began twittering.

They must have made nests in the gaps in the stones, because as soon as the sky turned a chilly pink they shot out from the castle, straight into the sky like arrows from a bow.

His throat burned from tobacco; he'd smoked three of the four cheroots he still had, imported from Madras. And he had told himself that he would buy no more.

As the finches dipped their wings against the sunrise, he realized with slow surprise that he wouldn't even smoke the last of them.

He'd had his last glass of whisky as well.

A burning throat—caused by whisky or tobacco—was a reminder that he was alive. But it was no more than that; just a reminder that the body that breathed and coughed and peed was still on the earth.

# Chapter Ten

*B*etsy woke the next morning and shook off the remnants of her sorry mood. Her fear was realized: She had inherited her mother's lusty nature. It was no excuse for feeling sorry for herself.

Instead she would go on just as she had, but with special attention to anything that could destroy her reason and common sense. Send her into a haze of desire.

In short: Jeremy.

It was actually a fortunate event that she now had experience with a disreputable man, who'd kissed her only after making it clear that he had no wish for marriage. She had to avoid situations in which she might lose her head and end up married to the wrong man, for the wrong reasons.

Today the remaining wedding guests would return home. Parth and Lavinia were returning to London. Diana and North were leaving as well, planning to take Diana's nephew Godfrey to Scotland to visit the clan that the little boy would someday lead. Last night, her stepmother, Ophelia, had decided that she and the duke would accompany them, since Artie, Betsy's little sister, didn't like to be separated from Godfrey.

Among the family, only Aunt Knowe would remain to chaperone Betsy, Viola, and Joan. And that meant that only her aunt would be available to forbid Betsy's plan to masquerade as a boy. Kiss or no, Betsy couldn't ignore the yearning inside her to do something that wasn't ladylike.

By the time she climbed from the bath, her good humor was restored. With her father and stepmother on the way to Scotland, it would be easy for her to escape the castle for a day. She merely had to talk Aunt Knowe into accompanying her to Wilmslow.

She was fairly confident that her aunt would agree. Every naughty idea she had as a young girl had been seconded by Aunt Knowe, who had even helped her collect tadpoles, so she could turn the boys' beds into wet and squishy ponds.

"Everyone is chattering about you and Lord Greywick," Winnie, her lady's maid, reported as she helped Betsy towel her long hair.

"His proposal?"

Winnie nodded. "Are you quite certain that you don't wish to accept him? He'll be a duke someday. He's handsomer than any footman I've met, I can tell you that. And his voice, the way it rumbles: I can feel it to the tips of my toes."

Betsy straightened, pushing her wet hair over her shoulder, and grinned at Winnie. "Rumbles?"

"Deep and dark," Winnie said, shaking out a chemise. "I'd marry him even if he didn't have a ha'penny to his name, and that's the truth."

"I might marry him," Betsy said cautiously.

"His mother's lady's maid says that Her Grace is very precise in her ways. She approves of you."

Betsy had met Her Grace, the Duchess of Eversley, several times. She was a plump lady with her son's beautiful bone structure, but her eyes were quite different. His were solemn. Hers were bright. Confident. She was . . . Betsy searched for the right word.

Capricious.

That was it: The Duchess of Eversley was her opposite. Betsy watched every gesture and facial expression to make certain that no one could judge her by her mother's mistakes. Whereas the Duchess of Eversley expressed herself freely, and the self she expressed was unique.

To put it mildly.

"Oh!" Winnie squealed. She dropped the gown she was holding onto the bed, darted back over to the wardrobe, and pulled open a door. "I have an idea what you should wear this morning. This dress!"

It was a pale rose silk with a violet petticoat, a gown that Parth's fiancée, Lavinia, had ordered for Betsy in London.

"I was saving that for a special day," Betsy reminded her.

"Today *is* a special day," Winnie said, her fingers

flying over the gown's fastenings. "Last night you refused Lord Greywick's hand in marriage. Today his mother will seek you out and demand to know why you rejected her son."

"Surely not," Betsy said, somewhat horrified. "No other mother has done such a thing."

"Her son will be a duke," Winnie said, as if that explained everything. "Do you know that Her Grace always wears pink?" She deftly turned Betsy and began lacing her corset. "Everything, including her shoes, must be pink. Except her undergarments, of course. Carper asked Her Grace's maid about her intimates and got a sharp reprimand from Mr. Prism. But not before she answered. They are white."

Betsy couldn't remember the color she herself wore to dinner a week ago, and she certainly hadn't noted Her Grace's penchant for pink.

"Why?" she asked, keeping it simple.

"The duchess believes in the healing power of the color," Winnie said.

"Oh."

"Lord Greywick is ever such a good son. He has a pink coat and pantaloons that he ordered solely so that he can wear them when his mother is worried about his health."

"An excellent point in favor of marrying him," Betsy said, though she privately felt unenthusiastic about a man in pink pantaloons.

"I would put the title first," Winnie said, and then, with a giggle, "followed by his thighs. His legs are very fine for a man of his stature."

"I hadn't noticed," Betsy said. She truly hadn't

noticed. That suggested that Thaddeus would make a good spouse. She hadn't the faintest interest in sleeping with him.

She probably ought to marry him.

"There you are," Winnie said sometime later. In Her Grace's honor, Betsy wore the pink dress, with pink ribbons rather than powder in her hair.

"This doesn't mean that I agree to marry Thaddeus," Betsy said, staring at herself in the glass.

"*Thaddeus?*" Winnie's eyebrows flew up. "You have never referred to any other suitor by his first name, Lady Betsy."

Betsy's bodice was a trifle lower than she liked. "Please hand me a fichu," she said to Winnie.

"That bodice is absurdly high! It's practically at your collarbone, and by rights it should skim your nipples."

Betsy shook her head. "A fichu, Winnie."

Her maid sighed and handed over a square of silver lace. Betsy folded it into a triangle, put it around her neck, and tucked the ends into her bodice.

She opened the door and almost collided into one of her sisters running down the corridor. "Viola!" she cried. "Where are you going?"

Viola turned around and ran back in her direction. "Joan needs a dentist," she gasped. "We rang for Prism, but no one came, so I think the footmen must be busy putting people into their carriages. The courtyard is crowded with vehicles."

"She has a sore tooth?"

"Aunt Knowe says it must be pulled. It's in the very back, and it's making the other teeth ache as well. All night Joan kept groaning and clutching her jaw. Hot flannel isn't working, and neither is a cut onion."

"How unpleasant for her." Betsy turned to go to the nursery, but Viola caught her arm.

"Mother said to tell everyone to stay away. You know how Joan is; she hates crying when anyone can see her. She even asked *me* to leave."

"Oh, but—"

"No," Viola said firmly, pulling her in the other direction. "We shall tell Prism about the dentist, and then you must go in to breakfast. I expect Lord Greywick is waiting for you."

Betsy looked down at her stepsister's earnest face and felt a wash of love. The Wildes were tall, imposing creatures, but her stepsister was petite and delicate, with chestnut ringlets and a heart-shaped face. "You're a dear," she said, gathering her into a hug. "Joan is so lucky to have you as a best friend and sister."

As soon as they arrived in the great marble entry, a groom was sent to fetch the dentist.

"Please join me for breakfast?" Betsy asked her stepsister.

Viola instantly shook her head and backed up a step. "I couldn't."

"You promised your mother that you would try to join us in the mornings."

"Not when the castle is full of guests!" Viola whispered. "I can't, Betsy. Please don't ask me." She took two more steps backward.

If Viola had her way, she would remain in the safety of her chamber or the library all day long and never encounter strangers. Especially unmarried male strangers.

After an initial shock, Miss Stevenson's Seminary had been a happy experience for Viola; she had grown from a shy child, unwilling to meet any strangers, to one who was comfortable in female company.

But not with males, unless they were family.

"Please?" Betsy asked, reaching for Viola's hand. "I don't wish to encounter Lord Greywick's mother by myself. Winnie thinks that Her Grace will demand to know why I refused her son's proposal."

Viola looked appalled. "We should avoid breakfast altogether."

"Girls!"

They looked up as Aunt Knowe galloped down the stairs. "I heard that foolishness," their aunt said cheerfully, when she reached the bottom and put her arm through Viola's. "My dear, I've told you that the only way to exorcise your shyness is to force yourself into rooms full of strangers."

Viola gulped.

"I will sit with you," Betsy promised.

"I came downstairs to fetch my dandelion syrup to dose poor Joan or I would join you as well," Aunt Knowe said. "Not a single person in that room will bite you."

"If a man engages me in conversation, you must rescue me," Viola said to Betsy.

"Of course. Last night I saw you talking easily to the vicar."

"Oh, well, Father Duddleston," Viola said. "He's different."

Viola was capable of chatting with an eighty-year-old man like their vicar, but give her a flirtatious young man, and she had been known to throw up in a potted plant.

"Did Father Duddleston mention that he is retiring?" Aunt Knowe asked. "The position will soon be vacant. In normal circumstances, a younger son of the family would take the living."

"It goes without saying my brothers are not suited for the position," Betsy said.

"The Wildes are manifestly unfit for holy orders," Aunt Knowe agreed. "I must fetch that dandelion syrup from the stillroom. Viola, if you must be sick, avoid the lemon tree. It hasn't recovered from the last time."

"I don't want to do this," Viola moaned. But she obediently began walking down the corridor to the breakfast room.

"It's like acting in a pantomime," Betsy advised. "Not real."

"Not real *to you*," Viola said, her voice rising a bit. "Everything comes easily to you, Betsy. You want to present London with an ideal debutante, so you do. You just *do* it, even though everyone in this family knows that the only person in the family naughtier than you was Parth. But all these people think you're sweet. *Sweet!*"

"I'm—aren't I sweet?" Betsy asked, disconcerted.

"In a way," Viola said, hunching her shoulders. "But in most ways, you're not. My point is that you don't ever throw up on meeting a stranger, do you?"

"No. But I'm worried about meeting the duchess," she reminded Viola. "Life is full of discomforting events."

Viola gave her a bleak look. "I know."

They'd reached the breakfast room, where Prism guarded the door, the better to guide guests to precisely the right table.

"Good morning, Miss Astley, Lady Boadicea," he said. "Miss Astley, may I say how pleased I am that you will breakfast with our guests this morning?"

"There's nothing to be pleased about," Viola said morosely. Then she added: "I lurked in the ladies' retiring room at the ball last night, Prism, and I heard nothing but praise for the household."

Prism's smile widened to cover his entire face.

"*You* are the true lady of the two of us," Betsy told her sister as a footman pushed the door to the breakfast room. "Perhaps *you* should marry Lord Greywick."

Viola looked at her in horror. "Don't make jests like that."

The breakfast room was one of Betsy's favorite chambers in all of Lindow Castle. Her grandfather had seen the room in a decaying palazzo in Venice and had the whole thing shipped home to England. The wood paneling was painted delphinium blue with elaborate swirls picked out in white.

The matching cabinets were filled with exquisite spun-glass vases. They were never used, as the late duke had bought the contents along with the cabinets and considered them akin to wallpaper. "Can't replace 'em, might as well leave 'em be," or so legend had it.

This morning Prism had rearranged the breakfast room due to the press of guests visiting the castle. Rather than a single board, small tables were dotted around the room, set with white cloths embroidered with forget-me-nots.

Viola's hand tightened around Betsy's arm like an outgrown bracelet.

"Mind your skirts," Prism said, with the familiarity of a butler who had watched both of them grow from toddlers to ladies. "The tables are set close together."

Betsy pasted a blithe smile on her face as she walked across the room. Some fifty persons of worth and consequence looked up and nodded their greetings. Thankfully, there was no sign of a pink-clad duchess. Beside her, she heard an almost soundless moan.

Prism came to a halt. Betsy heard a rustle spread through the room, as the guests realized that the Wilde sisters had been placed at a table holding a future duke and a future marquess, not to mention Adrian Parswallow.

Prism pulled out a chair. "Lady Betsy."

"Viola, you first," Betsy said, keeping her voice carefree as she pushed her trembling sister into a seat. That was a breach of etiquette, since she was the elder sister, but she had the distinct impression that Viola was thinking about dashing from the room.

"I'll sit beside my sister," Betsy said to Prism, before he could try to place a gentleman between them.

Only once she was seated did Betsy realize that Prism had attempted to put her in a chair beside Thaddeus, but instead Viola now sat there. Which meant Betsy had Jeremy on her left. Both men were on their feet, naturally.

Betsy shot a quick look at Jeremy under her lashes. He looked frightful, with smudges under both eyes. So much for the idea that their kiss would send him to sleep. Then she remembered the other rude things he'd said.

Perhaps he was up all night tupping Lady Tallow.

She shot him a frown.

He swayed a little. "Sorry, I haven't had any sleep," he murmured, sitting down as a footman placed buttered eggs on Betsy's plate. "Did you just frown at me? In public? You never do that. In public you generally resemble a china doll with a painted smile."

"That is frightfully rude," Betsy said, although she had to admit that he had a point. Her smile was a powerful weapon and she didn't hesitate to employ it.

She turned to the table at large and beamed. "How are you all today? Mr. Parswallow, I hope to hear the rest of your poem before you leave."

"I can stay in the castle a day or two longer," the gentleman said eagerly. "Last night I wrote an ode to p'heacocks." He struck a pose, not easy while seated. *"An obscene grandeur and a decadent feather with green-groping eyes . . ."*

He paused. There was a deafening silence.

"An evocative line," Betsy said hastily, picking up her sister's cold hand and giving it a squeeze. No one knew how much courage it took for Viola to do something as simple as attend breakfast.

"What are the family peacocks' names, Miss Astley?" Thaddeus asked Viola.

Betsy took a bite of egg and gave him an approving nod. Most people didn't notice that Viola's shyness was crippling, and if they did, they didn't guess that she could be distracted by talk of animals.

"Fitzy and Floyd," Viola replied, brightening slightly.

"P'heacocks are glorious pl'humed beasts," Parswallow put in. "They belong on castle grounds."

"They seem to be fantastically quarrelsome," Jeremy remarked, waving his fork. "I witnessed a battle royal during which bucketfuls of dirt were scratched from the ground and flung about. The air was blue with cursing."

"Peacocks are territorial," Thaddeus said in his placid way. "Has His Grace ever considered acquiring a peahen or two, Miss Astley?"

"We're afraid it would give them more reason to fight," Viola answered.

From the table behind them, Betsy heard a penetrating whisper. "Miss Astley isn't often seen in public."

Hopefully Viola hadn't heard that; Thaddeus

was inquiring about the battles between aging Fitzy and the young upstart, Floyd.

The woman behind them seemed to believe she was inaudible, even though she was seated so close to Betsy that their skirts were almost overlapping. "No, no! She's not a *real* Wilde. Her mother is the third duchess, but she's a child of Her Grace's first marriage. She's quite peculiar, from what I hear."

The reply to this extraordinarily rude comment came in a murmur, while Betsy chomped on her eggs, anger churning in her stomach. How dare anyone label Viola as "peculiar," simply because she was shy?

"Yes, chatting to Greywick," the first woman said clearly. "Of course, she can't have him. Everyone knows he was on his knees last night."

"Eavesdropping, Bess?" a husky voice said.

She scowled at Jeremy.

He glanced behind her. "Ah, the less-than-beloved Lady Tallow," he murmured. "I warned you about her last night, did I not?"

"You said nothing about her loud voice."

"Some people are like peacocks," he said. "They offer their opinions and their bosoms at inopportune times."

Betsy bit back a smile.

Lady Tallow continued, remorseless, "Of course, she'll have an excellent dowry, but one has to wonder what the going rate is for such a cow-hearted girl."

Just as Betsy was about to swing around and say something—*anything!*—Lady Tallow apparently noticed that one of her neighbors was engaged in a different conversation. "Poppycock!" she said loudly. "That Norwegian prince is a dapper fellow."

"There is no—" Betsy began, and stopped. She never aired negative opinions in public. Young ladies weren't allowed anything as controversial as an opinion.

"No what?" Jeremy said. "Eat your eggs. You're too thin."

She narrowed her eyes at him. "This level of consideration isn't characteristic. You must want something."

Jeremy felt a germ of thoroughly uncharacteristic laughter stealing up his chest. "Now what could that be?" he asked, pitching his tone to mock innocence.

Betsy blinked and then caught on. A look of horror crossed her face. "I didn't mean it that way."

"That's why it was so funny," he agreed.

The funny thing was that he actually *did* feel desire, even if it was for an annoying girl who thought he was an irredeemable ass.

Common sense told him that there was nothing special about his feelings. A good quarter of the castle was in love—or lust—with the duke's eldest daughter. She hadn't powdered her hair this morning, and her skin looked particularly creamy against her dark locks.

Locks?

He truly was losing his mind, finally.

*Locks.* He felt his mouth twist into a sneer.

"That expression looks more like you," Betsy said cordially. "Thank goodness. I was growing worried that you might have transformed into the sort of man who offers compliments and poetry over the breakfast table, when the only thing one wants is some buttered toast and silence."

"Not poetry?" Jeremy asked. "Dear me, Mr. Parswallow, it seems you broke one of Lady Betsy's cardinal rules."

The poet bridled, but Betsy flashed her smile and he melted into an embarrassing puddle of adoration.

"I discovered my calling at Eton," Parswallow announced, "and as a p'hoet, I can assure you that p'hoetry belongs at every meal."

When no one showed much enthusiasm for this idea, he lapsed into sulky silence.

"I don't remember being taught to write poetry at Eton," Jeremy said. "You?" he asked Thaddeus.

"I was more engaged by the sciences," Thaddeus replied.

"He was brilliant," Jeremy informed the table at large. "I've never forgotten when Master Swinkler got irritated and said that if Thaddeus wanted to teach at Eton, he had to wait until he graduated from Cambridge."

"Did you go to Cambridge?" Betsy asked Thaddeus.

"Of course he did," Jeremy answered. "Bucked tradition, too, because generally dukes' progeny are off to Oxford, in witness whereof: your brothers. But the brilliant lads all went to Cambridge."

"Lord Jeremy and I were there together," Thaddeus said. "Almost lived together one year."

"I got in trouble and was sent down," Jeremy said, unrepentantly. "Putting my disreputable career at Cambridge to the side, let's return to Eton. Thaddeus had got hold of a book by a fellow named Kant, arguing that stars aren't stars, but that each twinkle is a collection of them. He used to drive Swinkler mad by quoting from it."

Thaddeus intervened. "Master Swinkler was teaching us theology, and he had an unreasonable attachment to the idea that God created our planet and put us at the center of it, the stars existing as a mere embellishment for the pleasure of our nightly strolls."

"That is not the case?" Betsy asked, curiously. No one had ever indicated otherwise to her. She nudged her sister. "Did you know that, Viola?"

Viola was staring down at her plate, and just shook her head.

"Astronomers—Mr. Kant among them—surmise that what we see is a galaxy, or rather universes of them, at such a far distance from us that they can scarcely be seen," Jeremy said.

Betsy looked at him, astonished. "Each star is one of these galaxies? Universes?"

"Single stars are close to us and those that seem far away are actually groups," Thaddeus put in. "It's an interesting idea, and astronomers since Kant first posed the theory have confirmed it, as far as they were able."

Jeremy gave a bark of laughter. "Thaddeus was a galaxy above the rest of us."

Then he watched as Betsy buttered toast and gave a piece to her little mouse of a stepsister, who looked as if she'd like to slide under the table. Jeremy narrowed his eyes. The poor girl was convulsively swallowing, a sensation he'd come to know all too well.

A cluster of smells could drive him to lose a meal—the obvious ones like blood and gunpowder, but also rotting autumn leaves, wet hay, wood smoke . . .

He wrenched his mind away from the battlefields of America because, damn it, Betsy's younger sister was about to make a scene that people wouldn't readily forget. Vomiting Viola wouldn't do well on the marriage market.

Behind Betsy, Lady Tallow had returned to her original topic. "The girl's peculiar, if you ask me," she hissed. "Of course, she doesn't have bad blood, unlike . . ." She finally lowered her voice to a discreet level, apparently realizing that insulting the children of her host might not be a good idea.

Betsy was turned in her chair to face Viola. "Oh, no," Jeremy heard. "Viola, please *don't*."

Jeremy would have snorted, but there wasn't time. "Please" would never stop his stomach from emptying if the right smell came along. His body had learned the trick of expelling emotion along with his breakfast, and he had the feeling Viola was a kindred spirit.

He pushed back in his chair and launched into his favorite, well-practiced performance: drunken lout. He stumbled, clutched the back of

Betsy's chair, and let out a loud belch, followed by a curse and a belated "'Scuse me, ladies."

Back when he was in school, he had specialized in belches on demand. Who would have thought they'd be so useful, years on?

Everyone in the vicinity turned to him, surprised. No—strike that. Thaddeus glanced up and then went back to eating smoked haddock. Of course, he had been party to many a self-induced belch when they were schoolboys.

Viola was staring straight down at her plate, her lips tightly pressed together. That wouldn't do.

He reached back and grabbed his cup of cold tea and held it high. "Let's drink to the duke's health! Nothing better than a little tipple in the morning!"

He realized suddenly that most of the room was male—since married ladies were allowed to take breakfast on a tray in their beds—and they agreed with him. A number of narrow glances toward the footmen suggested that they were taking affront at not being offered a stronger libation than tea.

"What a fraud," Betsy muttered, under her breath, but he heard her.

Briefly he considered dumping the tea on her instead of her sister—but no. Viola needed a shock, no matter how much he'd like to see Betsy's bosom drenched. Other women flaunted their assets but Betsy hid hers from view.

Not realizing, obviously, that it only made her more enticing.

"We should have a toast," he said, lurching again, and then falling back against Betsy's chair in hopes of exasperating her.

He hoisted the teacup in the air and bellowed, "To Lady Tallow and her talent for . . ." He let silence hang in the air just long enough so that all the men who had succumbed to her obvious charms would wonder. ". . . gossip!"

As he brought the cup to his lips, he pretended to slip sideways, flinging the tea in a graceful arc so that it coursed directly down Viola's neck and then completed its arc by splashing over Lady Tallow.

Viola reacted to cold tea on her neck with a squeal, jumping to her feet, which knocked Jeremy to the side . . . allowing him to slump into Betsy's lap.

"Oh, hello," he said, bracing his elbow on the table so he didn't crush her. His legs sprawled across the floor. "Do I know you?"

Lady Tallow was shrieking; behind them chatter filled the room as if a chicken coop had admitted a fox.

"You don't even smell like brandy," Betsy said, not sounding angry. "Why are you bothering?"

Jeremy shrugged.

"That was very clumsy, Lord Jeremy," Viola said, her cheeks pink with indignation. She turned and marched out of the room, and he was gratified to notice that she didn't run, even when hailed by a number of guests on the way out of the room.

Apparently, cold water to the back of the neck was as effective for her as it was for him when it came to preventing vomiting.

"Do I have to get up?" he asked Betsy. "Your lap is remarkably soft."

"I'm about to dump my tea on you, and it's hot rather than cold."

Her expression was rather odd; if he had to guess, he'd say that she didn't mind the fact he was sprawled on top of her.

Most of the Wildes had blue eyes. It was part of their charm: They were a pack of beautiful people, tall and athletic, with aristocratic cheekbones and the rest of it. Betsy's eyes were darker blue than her brothers'.

"Very well," Jeremy said, hoisting himself back onto his feet. "I should make my apologies to Lady Tallow."

"You needn't bother," the lady said acidly. She was patting her bosom with a linen napkin while a footman hovered with an additional stack. "You, sir, are a reprobate who has no place in polite society! To this point, we have excused your disgraceful behavior due to your birth and your grievous circumstances, but no gentleman acts the drunken lout at breakfast."

"Only in the evening?" Jeremy asked curiously.

"What?"

"Are we gentlemen allowed to be drunken louts in the evening?" he clarified to Lady Tallow. "I gather you make exceptions for me at one time of day but not another."

"In the normal course of events, no. Only those

who have sacrificed their entire platoon are allowed such leniency." The lady's voice rose. "We make exceptions for—for *those* men, though thankfully, there are not many. *Most* English gentlemen put their soldiers' safety above their own."

The words struck him like a blow, and for a second the world rocked around him. Suddenly, in the corner of his eye, the great silver escutcheon on the sideboard began sparking light as if it were on fire.

He clenched his teeth and focused on Lady Tallow, willing himself to ignore the glinting lights invading his vision. He refused to show any reaction to her words. *Refused.*

Sickeningly, he was no more in control of his body and brain than Viola had been. *She* had been about to vomit; *he* was on the verge of collapse.

Lady Tallow's bosom was heaving under the napkin as if a live animal were concealed there. "Hiding behind a tree, as I heard, with no survivors to say different!" she spat.

The *London Times* had reported on the loss of his entire platoon, hailing him as a hero. He thought about his men every day—every hour—yet he'd fooled himself into believing that perhaps society didn't think of him in the same cruel terms he thought of himself.

"In fact, I heard on the best of authority that Thomas Cromie let it be known on his deathbed that you were nowhere to be seen. Thomas deserved better than that; he was a baron's son!"

"Actually, Thomas didn't die on a bed," Jeremy said, feeling his face twist into some horrible semblance of a smile. "He died in my arms. And do you know what he *did* say? His last words?"

Lady Tallow's mouth fell open slightly and she began blinking rapidly, but he was caught in the horror of that memory.

"He apologized to me. He said he was sorry that he couldn't keep going. 'Sorry to fail you.'" Jeremy cleared his throat. "That's what he said. 'Sorry to fail you.'"

Beside him, Betsy stepped into his vision. He was used to seeing her look like a ceramic doll, but just at the moment she looked like a warrior.

Her face resembled the sky when a thunderstorm is on the horizon. She was about to destroy her reputation for placid, ladylike behavior.

For nothing. For him, who deserved every unkind word.

Before he could croak something to cut Betsy off, a deep, calm voice intervened. Every head in the room turned to Thaddeus. He was now standing shoulder-to-shoulder with Betsy.

They looked like a golden couple, paired by the shimmering beauty that comes with noble family trees and layers of silk.

"Lady Tallow, you are beside yourself," Thaddeus stated. "A true Englishwoman never maligns those who have served our country. Those aristocrats among us who stayed at home, mere moths of peace, owe *everything* to the men who risked all to defend our shores. I count myself among them."

Betsy opened her lips, and Thaddeus put a hand on her arm.

Jeremy realized with a thump of his heart that every person in the room would assume they had an understanding. Perhaps they *did* have an understanding. Perhaps Thaddeus had found Betsy before breakfast and returned to his knees.

Without realizing it, Jeremy took a deep breath of air.

"I am ashamed that I did not see service in the Americas," Thaddeus continued. "Tommy Cromie was failed not by Lord Jeremy, but by me. Every able-bodied man in this room who stayed home shares my feelings."

Jeremy very much doubted that, but no matter.

"Anyone who tarnishes the name of one of the king's men, whether he died in the service of our country, or survived with the burden of grieving for those lost . . . that person will never be an acquaintance of mine. Ever."

A moment of silence hung over the room.

Betsy cleared her throat. "I speak for my family." Her voice was as calm as Thaddeus's but more forceful. "Lady Tallow, you are no longer an acquaintance of mine, or of any Wilde."

A man stood at the next table. "Or mine."

"Mine, mine, mine, mine . . ." The sound came staccato, falling on Jeremy's ears like . . .

Like a benediction.

Which was ridiculous. He twisted his lips into a sneer. Lady Tallow was looking about her, tight red spots high in her cheeks, a touch of uncertainty in her long upper lip. Presumably she could read the mood of a room.

Or the mood of the calls that came now from every corner.

Thaddeus stood calmly, his eyes moving from person to person as they spoke, with the air of a man who would expect no less of his fellow mortals. Jeremy could have told him how often his fellow aristocrats had tried to comfort him by discounting the lost men as mere cannon fodder.

Yet Thaddeus was a leader, and just at this moment, every damned man in the room was following him. If Lady Tallow had cared to count, she would have seen her welcome in polite society shrinking, voice by voice, house by house.

Thaddeus still had a hand on Betsy's left arm. But behind her back, hidden in her voluminous skirts, her right hand grabbed Jeremy's.

Warm, strong fingers curled around his.

As "mine" continued to ring out around the room, he leaned against the table in pure exhaustion, letting her hand anchor him to this moment, to this country.

To this life.

# Chapter Eleven

*J*eremy, Thaddeus, and Betsy left the breakfast room together, but in the corridor, Prism bowed and said, "Her Grace, the Duchess of Eversley, requests that you join her in the library, Lady Betsy."

Jeremy rumbled with laughter and wished her luck. Then he demanded that Thaddeus play him at billiards.

Betsy tried to not mind that Jeremy was eager to challenge Thaddeus, although he generally refused to bestir himself for her. She walked to the library feeling a prickle of curiosity overtaking her dread. If she married Thaddeus, she would necessarily spend time with his mother.

The Lindow library was a large room with a number of comfortable chairs and shabby sofas scattered about amid glass-fronted bookshelves containing moldering books, and open-shelved ones crowded with volumes one might actually wish to read.

Since Aunt Knowe was the biggest reader in the

family, almost every table held a stack of books to do with medicine, biology, or herbology. A bust of Shakespeare, lent a jaunty air by the tricorne hat tipped over one eye, held the place of honor on the mantel.

At first, Betsy thought the room was empty. Then, as she was wandering toward the fireplace, a short woman jumped from a high-backed chair.

"There you are!" the duchess cried, coming over to Betsy and taking both her hands. "I know we've met but I didn't take note of you. You are monstrously tall, and very pretty. And you look so very healthy! That's important, isn't it?"

Her Grace had an infectious smile set in a plump face with a dimple in each cheek. She had the air of a lady who has grown old without noticing and doesn't see the point of bothering about it now. Her eyes twinkled, and she shook Betsy's hands, both of them, with great energy.

"Good morning, Your Grace," Betsy said. Rather awkwardly, she couldn't curtsy, as the duchess kept hold of her hands.

"Thaddeus tells me that you have refused him," Her Grace said, drawing Betsy over to a sofa.

Rather than challenging her, as her maid had expected, the duchess sounded thoroughly pleased about Betsy's rejection.

"I am not convinced we will suit," Betsy said, sitting down.

"I suspect you won't," Thaddeus's mother said promptly. "But the question is: Does it matter? It is far more important that you and I are able to hobble along together. You are the first woman who has caught Thaddeus's eye—at least, in an official capacity."

"I see," Betsy said.

"Men are generally not in the house, and my husband certainly is not, but we would be there together," the duchess clarified. "Thus, when Thaddeus informed me that he intended to ask for your hand, I made up my mind to join him at Lindow. Please don't think me selfish, dear, but if I find myself *in extremis*, it won't be my husband who comes to my aid."

"Do you often find yourself *in extremis*?" Betsy inquired.

"Very often, over tea," the duchess said promptly. "I find tea parties unbearably tedious, and yet they occur with appalling regularity. I could not bear it if Thaddeus marries a woman who adores tea more than ale."

She looked expectantly at Betsy.

"Ale," Betsy said, choosing to tell the truth.

"October or March?" the duchess asked.

"October by far," Betsy replied. "March is weakened by last year's hops and malt."

"Excellent. Have you ever suffered from a spasm, or have you ambitions toward such lady-like behavior?"

"No," Betsy said.

"My last question," the duchess said, "and the most important: My husband's name is Marmaduke and he fancies the name should be given to his first grandson." She paused.

"No child of mine will be named Marmaduke," Betsy assured her.

The duchess's face broke into a beaming smile.

"Your Grace, I have no intention of marrying your son," Betsy said, feeling particularly apologetic now that she seemed to have passed an examination.

"Perhaps he will grow on you," the duchess said. "I like Thaddeus quite well, of course, but I realize that I am biased. I will try to think up some good tales to convince you of his eligibility."

She came to her feet and Betsy jumped up as well.

"I mustn't keep you, Lady Boadicea. From what my dear friend Lady Knowe tells me, any number of gentlemen are elbowing each other aside in their eagerness to win your hand."

Betsy sank into a curtsy.

"Lady Knowe tells me that you are an excellent billiard player," the duchess said. Then she smiled. "So is my son. You should challenge him to a game."

Naturally, Betsy headed directly to the billiard room. "I can't believe it!" she cried, stopping in the doorway. "You are a misogynist maggot, Jeremy. How dare you play Lord Greywick when you so often refuse to play me?"

"*Thaddeus*," the viscount said, raising his head and nodding at her. "Not Lord Greywick, at least in private. I, for one, would never refuse you a game."

Oh, dear. His eyes were definitely warm. Betsy had been very careful never to allow her suitors to go beyond affection; she didn't want to break any hearts. One of the startling lessons of her debut had been how many men asked for her hand in marriage although they were no more than slight acquaintances.

"I think I prefer to be Lord Jeremy," Jeremy drawled, "if the alternative is to be a maggot."

"You know what I mean," she said, waving her hand at him. "I'll play the winner."

They were both startlingly handsome, Thaddeus particularly. He had a noble look about him, with a straight nose and a strong jaw. Any woman would want to marry him. He even smelled good.

Not Jeremy.

"Why do you always smell like a horse in the morning?" she demanded.

Jeremy raised an eyebrow. "Don't you like horses?"

She would rather die than admit that she loved the way he smelled, like saddle leather and pomade, with an edge of the wind that blew over the bog. It was arousing.

No.

She pulled herself back together. "Of course I like horses. They have their time and place."

"That time and place is five in the morning, at break of dawn," Jeremy said. "Don't you agree, Thaddeus?"

"Ladies generally ride in the afternoon," Thaddeus said. "I am not as enamored with the stables as you are."

"You don't need to be," Jeremy said.

"Is your equestrian enthusiasm the result of sleeplessness?" Betsy asked.

Jeremy shrugged.

Thaddeus leaned down, sighted down the cue, banked a ball off two walls, and slammed it into the red ball, which pocketed.

Betsy swallowed. He could play. He could *really* play.

That was a sign she ought to marry him. Aunt Knowe had sent her to the billiard room last night for a reason. Was she a coward that panic flooded her entire body?

"He's showing off," Jeremy said, an edge to his voice. "It's amazing what men will do when a beautiful woman is watching."

Betsy felt her cheeks redden but she kept her eyes on the table. Jeremy thought she was beautiful? He'd never shown an iota of—

Not true. He had kissed her.

But kissing was a pastime.

Apparently, Jeremy had no wish to show off, because he missed the ball entirely on his turn.

"Oh, look at that," he said flatly. "You'll have to play Thaddeus." He turned around and dropped into his usual chair.

Thaddeus caught her eye, and a glimmer of the worry she felt was reflected in his. "If you'll forgive me, Lady Betsy—"

"Betsy," she corrected him.

"Bess," Jeremy put in. "You mustn't confuse your wife with a nursemaid."

They both swung about to stare at him.

"What?" he demanded. "I saw your first proposal, but presumably you can do better than that, Thaddeus."

"My next attempt will be without an audience," Thaddeus said.

Betsy felt herself growing even redder.

"A maidenly blush," Jeremy said approvingly. "One might imagine you'd run out of those after all the proposals you've received. Englishwomen are endlessly inventive, one finds."

"Endlessly patient, more like," Betsy muttered under her breath, but he heard her.

"It's not my fault that your suitors are bores," he pointed out.

"I'd like to go for a drive," Thaddeus said. "I need fresh air. Betsy, would you be so kind as to accompany me?"

Jeremy abruptly hoisted himself out of his chair. "Nice try, Thaddeus, but you'll have to schedule your next proposal for some other time. Betsy and I have plans to visit Wilmslow."

"We do?" Betsy asked. She felt as if her head were spinning. Jeremy wasn't wrong. After spending a Season being proposed to, she knew the hidden language behind an invitation to go for a drive.

"We need to spy out the town," Jeremy said.

It was Thaddeus's turn to ask "Why?" His manner was polite but confused. And just a trifle, the smallest trifle, displeased.

Betsy turned to Thaddeus. "We have a prank in mind, a silly thing."

"Perhaps we could make up a party," Thaddeus suggested.

Betsy replied before Jeremy could make things worse. "Aunt Knowe just told me that you and your mother will stay with us for a few more days," she said to Thaddeus. "Do you think that Her Grace would like to visit Wilmslow?"

Thaddeus's mouth eased into a smile. "I believe it quite likely."

"Excellent," Betsy said, her heart thudding in her chest. By issuing an invitation to the duchess, she had as much as accepted Thaddeus's hand in marriage. For the first time in her memory, she felt a degree of panic akin to Viola's.

Jeremy walked out the door and said, without looking back, "Right, I'll convey your invitation to Her Grace, Betsy. And I'll see you both in the entry in an hour, mama in tow, Thaddeus."

He strode away before Betsy had a chance to respond.

"He's not himself," Thaddeus said, touching her elbow to indicate that she should leave the room before him.

"Are you trying to bamboozle me into believing that Jeremy Roden was a courteous youngster?" Betsy asked, forcing herself to smile at Thaddeus.

The viscount drew the door closed and held out his arm, so he could escort her down the corridor. She slipped her hand around his elbow.

"Jeremy was always foul-mouthed and brilliant, an odd combination that made him the head of any classroom."

"I didn't imagine that students swore in front of professors," Betsy remarked.

"Most learning in college is done outside of the classroom," Thaddeus said. "In the debating societies, for instance. I think there is a reasonable argument to be made for the future of Britain being staked out in debates at Eton and nuanced in debates at Oxford and Cambridge."

"I see," Betsy said, wondering what the House of Commons did in that case, not to mention the king himself.

"Jeremy's brittleness is new," Thaddeus added.

"What you said at breakfast was marvelous," Betsy said, looking up at him with a genuine smile. "I was about to scream at Lady Tallow and that would have done nothing to the purpose."

"I spoke before you collected your thoughts, but I'm certain you would have been more eloquent than I." His eyes were distinctly warm.

Damn it.

She had to make up her mind before he became more attached. But perhaps she'd already made up her mind? If so, she had to be honest with him. "Thaddeus, last night you asked for my hand in marriage."

He drew her to a halt. "Dare I hope that you have changed your mind?"

"No," she said hastily. "That is, not yet. Or—*no*."

He smiled. "I understand."

He did? Good for him, because she didn't.

"I wanted to tell you that I present a duchess-worthy face to the world," Betsy said, forcing herself to focus. "I am not truly as sweet as I appear. I may have the semblance of a duchess, but in truth, I am far more . . ."

She stopped, unable to explain.

"Wild without an E?" Thaddeus supplied. "I

would expect no less. I think you to be honest, loyal, honorable, and intelligent. Those qualities are far more important to me than the fact you are both exquisite and have exquisite manners."

Betsy cleared her throat. "Also I should add that there are those who believe that my mother was unfaithful to my father before I was born."

He laughed. "You don't believe that any more than I do, nor does any other person with common sense. You have your father's eyebrows." He touched her right eyebrow lightly. "You are beautiful, Betsy, but I admired your eyebrows first."

"Goodness, why?" she asked, dumbfounded, barely stopping herself from touching her eyebrow herself. It arched, like any eyebrow.

"Yours is a mischievous eyebrow," Thaddeus said. "That of a woman who will never settle for domestic peace but will be a true partner."

Betsy swallowed. It was too late. *She* was too late. Somehow, he'd given his heart away before she noticed.

"You make me sound like a paragon," she said weakly. "I assure you that I am all too human."

"That's just what I'm saying," Thaddeus said, raising her hand to his lips and kissing it.

"Eyebrows are not indicative of parentage," Betsy told him.

"*You* are a Wilde, through and through."

"Would you court me if I didn't have my father's eyebrows?" Betsy asked, thinking of her sister Joan's straight, golden eyebrows.

"I would have to think carefully," Thaddeus said. "I hold the honor of my family line in my hand. My younger brother passed away, and I have no first cousins. So whomever I marry will be the mother of the sons that will carry dukedom into the future."

"I don't believe that ancestry matters," Betsy said, not entirely truthfully. "Were I actually the daughter of that Prussian who lured my mother away, I would still be myself."

Thaddeus looked embarrassed. "I was raised to believe that my land and my title are sacred. As sacred as England itself."

"You will only marry a woman whose parentage you revere?" Betsy asked. She was starting to dislike him, just a little.

"What I am trying to say is that I don't care if the likes of Lady Tallow says unkind things about your mother. *I* am absolutely certain that you are your father's daughter."

Betsy walked along, trying to pick the best words. The kindest words. "What you are saying is that you are brave enough to confront society as regards your wife's illegitimacy only if you were convinced of her legitimacy. You wouldn't do it if you suspected she was illegitimate."

"You make me sound like a coward," Thaddeus said after a moment. "My lineage is important to me, Betsy. Not as important as it was to my father—who fell in love with a local tradesman's daughter but gave her up for the sake of the family. I was raised to think that my Norman blood is all-important."

Betsy would have argued . . . but how different was his view from her own? She knew that she had inherited undesirable traits from her mother. She should just be grateful that Thaddeus was willing to overlook them, and not wish that he didn't care about her ancestors.

"I was raised to think that *people* are all-important," she said. "Kind hearts are more than coronets, etcetera."

He raised an eyebrow.

"Kind hearts are more than coronets, and simple faith than Norman blood," she said, changing the phrase to suit her purpose.

"Family may be more important than coronets," Thaddeus said. "The Wildes are all-important to each other; anyone can see that."

Betsy was silenced.

"It's part of the family charm," he added, after waiting a few seconds. "You take such pleasure in each other."

"Did you mean that to sound distasteful?" Betsy asked.

He looked down at her, obviously surprised. "Not in the least. Envious, if anything. My father did his duty in marrying my mother, but the union is not a happy one. We were not a happy family."

"Do you suppose that your father regrets not marrying the tradesman's daughter?"

Thaddeus shook his head. "He—" But he cut off his words.

They were nearing the stairs leading up to the next floor. Betsy came to a halt. "Yes?"

"It's not a story for a young lady," Thaddeus said, apology in his voice.

"I can guess," Betsy said. "Your father had fallen in love. I expect that he turned his beloved into his mistress, and he has a great many children with her, and only two with the unwanted but nobly-born wife. The second family grew up like a happy pile of puppies, which must have made you feel lonely. Did I get it right?"

"Not entirely accurate but disturbingly close."

Betsy began to respond, but she was cut off by a bellow from above stairs. "Louisa, you are a rat!"

"My mother," Thaddeus said.

"She just called Aunt Knowe a rat," Betsy said, astounded.

Thaddeus smiled, his eyes glinting in a very attractive way.

"If I am a rodent, you are a dormouse." Aunt Knowe's voice drifted down the stairs. "The older you get, the more your nose quivers, Emily."

"A cruel rat," the duchess declared.

"I must change into a walking costume," Betsy said.

She nearly dropped a curtsy, thinking it would be good to create distance between her noble suitor and herself, but she caught Thaddeus's eye and changed her mind.

"A pink dormouse," Aunt Knowe said, laughing.

"May I escort you upstairs?" Thaddeus asked.

"No," Betsy said. She cleared her throat.

"May I escort you to town?"

"You may escort your mother," Betsy said.

His eyes darkened. "So Jeremy will escort you?"

"Oh, for goodness' sake," Betsy said, and took her leave without further conversation. She ran up one of the many back staircases that laced Lindow Castle together like a pair of stays.

By all rights, she should like Thaddeus madly. Love him, even.

"One of the mysteries of life," she said aloud, starting down the corridor to her bedchamber just as Aunt Knowe rounded the corridor.

"Oh, dearest, there you are! Her Grace is frightfully pleased that you invited her to Wilmslow." She lowered her voice. "As mothers-in-law go, the Duchess of Eversley will be a good one."

"It's too late to refer to her so politely," Betsy said, walking briskly toward her bedchamber. "I heard you call her Emily, and a dormouse, and so did her son."

"She *is* a dormouse; her nose is the most delicious pink. I've called her a dormouse on and off since we were children. Not that we were schooled together, of course, but our mothers enjoyed each other's company."

"I believe I shall wear my striped walking dress," Betsy said, dismissing talk of duchesses.

"Excellent," Aunt Knowe said amiably. They paused outside Betsy's door.

Then Aunt Knowe swooped down as she often did—she was precisely the same height as her twin, which made her remarkably tall for a woman—and enclosed Betsy in a warm embrace. "You don't have to marry him, dearest."

"Is that a new scent?" Betsy was nothing if not cunning when it came to changing the subject of conversation.

"From Paris!" her aunt exclaimed, instantly distracted. "Après Something or Other."

Betsy came up on her toes and kissed her aunt's cheek. "I must change."

Aunt Knowe widened her eyes. "I've just had a frightful thought, Betsy. Your daughters might look like dormice. Characteristics from noses to teeth are hereditary."

As if Betsy could forget that salient fact.

Her mother's sinful blood was racketing about her body, because she had no sooner caught sight of Jeremy's shoulders in the billiard room than her heart started racing, and she felt bewilderingly weak at the knees.

Whereas the dormouse's son had a noble nose that didn't quiver like his mother's, and thick hair that appeared to be always in order, and a deep voice that by rights should make a maiden's heart go tippity-tap.

He was The One, obviously. She would never horrify him in the bedchamber. Their headmistress had been very straightforward about wedding nights, over a special tea Miss Stevenson had held with girls about to debut.

"Welcome in the bedchamber is expected," Miss Stevenson had said. "Enthusiasm would be a grave mistake; vulgarities, even in secret, destroy a man's love for his wife."

Betsy had felt her face burning with shame, but she hadn't said a word. And no one had spoken to her.

But she hadn't forgotten.

Inside her room, Betsy leaned against the door and tried to shore up her resolve. Her weakness for Jeremy posed a challenge, by which she could prove to herself that a golden-haired Prussian would never cause her to desert her husband and children.

She had the bloodlines that Thaddeus required.

But if she wanted a happy marriage, she could never, ever let him know that she had inherited her mother's passionate nature.

# Chapter Twelve

*A*n hour later, Jeremy strolled down to the entry feeling extremely irritated with himself. Betsy was a perfect mate for Thaddeus. He should be celebrating the fact, but instead he was combating an ever-growing feeling of possession, as if somehow the snappish billiard-playing girl who wanted to wear breeches was *his*.

Ridiculous thought.

He hardly knew her.

The feeling he had was as awkward and conflicted as the shame and guilt he felt for surviving the war. He was thinking about how useful it would be if one could simply excise uncomfortable emotions out of one's mind, when he realized that Betsy's future mother-in-law had reached the entry before him.

She was shaped like a small barrel, the kind that holds beer. Barrels weren't painted pink, nor embellished with a great many feathers, but the duchess was patently uninterested in such dictates. She had likely been told she was charming in pink as a girl, and had seized on the color as a rule, never interested enough to try green or blue.

Jeremy liked her. He'd found that eccentrics didn't bother to make unkind or pitying remarks; as a whole, they weren't interested in him.

"I saw you leaving the ballroom last night," Her Grace said, without preamble. "Your halo was a mess, but now I see you're bandaged about the head. Wounded in an affair of honor, were you?"

"No," Jeremy said. "Shot by a madwoman, if you must know."

"It's a bleak world when a person can simply shoot whomever they wish," the duchess proclaimed.

"Yes," Jeremy agreed, shoving images of pistols and cannon smoke into the corner of his mind.

"I don't agree with war," the duchess stated.

"Neither do I," Lady Knowe said. They both jerked about to discover she had emerged from the study, drawing on a pair of long lilac-colored gloves. "Where is Prism, for goodness' sake? Or a footman? What is this, a castle or a dairy?"

"Why a dairy?" the duchess asked.

"Because the two of you look somber enough to milk a cow. It's a very serious business, milking. I tried it as a girl."

"*There* she is," the duchess said with satisfaction, looking past Jeremy.

Betsy was descending the stairs wearing blue stripes, which was an agreeable color with all her dark hair. Jeremy wasn't good at that sort

of thing, but her costume had a little collar that
stood up around the back of her neck and flirted
with her hair.

She'd be a frightfully expensive wife.

He pushed away the small voice in the back
of his head that reminded him just how much
money he had. Never mind his future inheritance as a marquess; his mother had left him a
fortune. He could afford striped gowns and anything else a wife might wish for.

Not that he wanted one, of course.

Thaddeus arrived next, very properly attired,
looking every inch the future duke. Lady Knowe
sidled up to him, and his mother took his other
arm, which left Jeremy with Betsy. He held out
his elbow without speaking.

She slipped a hand around his arm and they
walked together through the great door of the castle into chilly, bright sunshine. Jeremy squinted
at the sun.

"The light is green today," Betsy said suddenly.

"What are you talking about?" He glanced
down at her and then thought he'd better not do
that too often, because her face was unnervingly
dear.

"Squint again," she prompted.

Obedience led to the realization that there was
indeed a faintly green shade to the sunshine.

"By evening, the light will be purple," Betsy
said.

"Come along, you two," Lady Knowe bellowed
from the door of the carriage. "Spit spot! There's
an excellent teahouse in Wilmslow."

"Coming!" Betsy called.

In the carriage, Jeremy seated himself beside Betsy, who had Thaddeus on her other side. Across from them, the older ladies took up the entire seat with their voluminous skirts.

"There's a vehicle coming down the lane," Lady Knowe said, as he pulled the door shut. She gave the roof a hard knock. "I ought to remain and greet whomever it is, but I am tired of guests."

Jeremy looked out the window and bit back a curse.

"You should be very proud of the wedding," the duchess said, patting Lady Knowe on the knee. "It went off without a hitch."

Jeremy felt Betsy's eyes on his face.

The carriage started.

"As for the person who just arrived, I am a firm believer that guests should send a card the day previous, or not be received at all," the duchess said with the air of someone accustomed to being begged for an audience.

Jeremy took a deep breath.

"Who was in that carriage?" Betsy asked in a low voice, when they were well on the way to Wilmslow. Lady Knowe was busy interrogating Thaddeus about the proper height of hedgerows, while the duchess put in a word now and then. "You recognized it, didn't you?"

"My father's," he said.

"You are estranged?"

"That is a strong word." But inside he knew it wasn't strong enough. "We rarely speak."

"You won't be able to avoid him now," Betsy pointed out.

"Unless I leave for London," Jeremy said, which was true enough. But he wasn't a man who fled like a coward. If so, he would have run away from the increasingly irritating emotions that tugged at him when he was around Betsy.

Even more so when he was seated beside her, as he was now. She smelled like a beautiful woman, which was a foolish observation but true. She smelled delectable and English, like all the good, clean things in the world that he'd turned his back on when he went to war.

"You cannot leave the castle yet," Betsy said, with a distinct tone of satisfaction in her voice. The two seated on the other side of the carriage paused, and she said, "Aunt Knowe, you'll be so pleased to know that Lord Jeremy recognized the carriage as his father's."

The duchess clapped her hands. "The marquess is one of my husband's close friends."

"I've met him once," Lady Knowe said, knitting her brow. "Years ago."

Jeremy held his tongue. He and his father hadn't spoken since he came back from war a shuddering mess of a man, knowing he wasn't worthy to become a marquess. Luckily, his cousin Grégoire would relish the title. He had told his father as much, left for London, and not seen the marquess since.

"Would you like to return to the castle?" Lady Knowe inquired.

"My father and I are estranged," he said, using Betsy's word.

His father's response to his weakness had sent him into a trembling fury. He had slammed out of the house.

"I suspect the marquess has not come to see the Wildes, but you, my dear," Lady Knowe said to Jeremy.

When had he become her "dear"? Sometime over the last months of dandelion tea and sleeping draughts made from comfrey and peppermint?

"I made a gentleman's wager with Lady Boadicea regarding Wilmslow, so there's no going back now," he said. "My father will undoubtedly need to rest from his journey, and he will enjoy spending time with my cousin, Mr. Bisset-Caron."

That wasn't true, as his father disliked Grégoire, the offspring of his younger brother's lamentable marriage to a Frenchwoman. He also loathed the way his brother had adapted his wife's family name as the requirement for inheriting a considerable estate.

"It's true that you gave me your word of honor," Betsy said.

The duchess wrinkled her nose. "I do not care for wagering."

"Oh, for goodness' sake, Emily," Lady Knowe said, "don't be a prude. I still have that bunch of dried violets from when you dared me to approach the pastor and ask for his thoughts on dance."

"We were children," the duchess said dismissively, waving a pink-clad hand.

"So are these three," Lady Knowe said. "A cheerful wager is a pleasure. Now, what did you wager, Betsy?"

"Lord Jeremy has promised to accompany me on a tour of Wilmslow. I shall be in disguise," Betsy said, adding, "I had the idea in the middle of the fancy dress ball. He agreed to do so only if you accompany us, Aunt Knowe."

"Why on earth—" the duchess began.

Thaddeus spoke at the same moment. "What disguise?"

Jeremy realized, not for the first time, he must be a very shallow person, because he was enjoying the shock in Thaddeus's face.

"The disguise was chosen by the lady," he said, giving Betsy time to change her mind about the breeches. "As for the 'why,' Your Grace, Lady Boadicea expressed the wish to visit an auction."

"An auction?" the duchess asked wonderingly. "Do you mean the sort of thing where disgraceful men sell their wives?"

"Sell their wives? You surprise me, Mama," Thaddeus said.

Jeremy thought about whether he would call his mother Mama if she were still alive. That was a firm no. Never. Not even if she had been a duchess rather than a marchioness.

"The auction in Wilmslow is an important affair," Lady Knowe put in. "Works of art and the like. I sent the estate manager to secure that lovely Rembrandt that hangs in the back parlor."

Jeremy thought that Betsy had better speak up soon if she wanted to preserve her illustrious future as a duchess. She was running the risk of setting Thaddeus's mother against her.

"Lady Boadicea collects miniatures," he said, making that up on the spot. "She would like to bid on a piece herself."

Lady Knowe blinked at Betsy. "My dear, I thought *I* was the only person in the family interested in miniatures. If there is one for sale you fancy, Prism will send a factotum to bid for you."

"I wish to bid in the auction myself," Betsy stated. She straightened in the seat. Surely, she wouldn't inform Thaddeus, let alone his mother—

Yes, she would.

"I plan to go to the auction disguised as a boy and bid on a work of art," Betsy said, looking directly at the duchess. "I would have liked to play billiards, in an establishment where ladies were not allowed to pick up a cue, but Lord Jeremy does not think that advisable."

There was dead silence in the carriage.

"Billiards while dressed in boy's clothing," Betsy clarified.

Because why put in just one coffin nail when two will do better?

More silence.

Just as Jeremy was trying to decide whether he wished to exacerbate the situation by inquiring whether Betsy planned to wear breeches or pantaloons, the duchess began laughing. Thaddeus's brow had knit, likely thinking deeply about propriety, but he lifted his chin and stared at his mother.

"One of my friends told me to go to Lindow because Lady Boadicea would be a perfect duchess," Her Grace said, fairly gasping with laughter. "Here you are. A perfect duchess indeed."

She leaned forward and patted Betsy's knee. "We don't follow fashion or standards, my dear. We make them. If you decide to dress as a boy, you'll be doing nothing that my relatives—my female relatives—haven't done before."

"I am surprised to hear that," Thaddeus said.

To Jeremy's mind, if Thaddeus wanted the "perfect duchess" he'd chosen, he'd better start defending Betsy's ideas, no matter how unusual.

"My great-aunt was a plucky gal," the duchess said. "Rumor has it that her father tried to marry her to an older man, and she didn't agree. So she put on breeches and snuck out of the house, meaning to make her way to Italy or some such."

"How romantic," Lady Knowe said. "I gather she didn't make it to a boat, or did she?"

"Caught at the pier," Her Grace said. "Hauled back and married off the next morning. Rumor has it she was tied to a bedpost all night to make certain that she didn't escape, but my mother said that was apocryphal. She never liked my great-great-uncle, though, and we children considered him an ogre who might well have imprisoned his daughter, albeit temporarily."

"I don't expect that their marriage was very happy," Betsy said, which showed that she hadn't been around *le monde* very long.

"Oh, no, it was very happy," the duchess said, sounding as surprised as Betsy was sorry. "Now if my great-aunt had scampered off to Italy with some black-haired *conte*, she likely would have been miserable. Not a good draught of ale in the whole country."

Betsy grinned at that, and Jeremy could practically see the duchess's happiness blossom as she smiled back.

They liked each other; Thaddeus and Betsy was a marriage made in heaven.

"Beer is what saves a marriage," the duchess said, spilling all her secrets before her son even had a ring on Betsy's finger. "A good ale has often saved this country from rack and ruin at the hands of the idiots in Lords. The husbands go home at night, and their wives explain what they should do after they're mellowed by a tankard of excellent beer."

"I could drink some ale," Jeremy said, mostly to cover up the fact that Thaddeus still hadn't said a word.

Just then the coach began bouncing as the duke's springs encountered the knobbly stones lining Wilmslow's main street.

"I wish I had more to contribute to a discussion of successful marriage," Lady Knowe said, "but given my ignorance, and our impending arrival at the teahouse, I think we'll have to postpone the conversation."

"We shall all go," the duchess announced.

"To tea? I should hope so," Lady Knowe responded. She had clearly noticed Thaddeus's silence. In fact, Jeremy had the sense that not much ever got past Lady Knowe. "I like ale, but it has its time and place."

"No, to the auction," Her Grace said.

She was smiling at Betsy as if she'd found a long-lost daughter. Perhaps she felt that way. Jeremy had the sudden realization that the duchess's pink-clad barrel shape disguised a heart that would have loved to rampage about in breeches.

"We will all go to the auction," she continued. "Lady Boadicea can pose as one of my nephews a few times removed. I have hundreds of them."

"Unfortunately, not even duchesses are allowed to appear at the auction house in Wilmslow," Lady Knowe said. "They have a rule keeping out ladies, which is frightfully old-fashioned."

"I could wear pantaloons," the duchess remarked.

"No, you couldn't," Lady Knowe retorted. "Your figure is unsuited to the task."

The duchess looked down thoughtfully at her plump hips. "I know an excellent tailor in London."

"Few men are shaped like a beehive," Lady Knowe said, not unkindly. "My figure would not be flattered by breeches either. We're like the girls in that Shakespeare play: One of them was a beanpole and the other was an acorn."

"*A Midsummer Night's Dream*," Betsy supplied.

Thaddeus still hadn't said a word.

The carriage door swung open. Her Grace rose to leave the carriage, taking the hand of a waiting groom, followed by Lady Knowe, and finally Betsy.

Jeremy scowled at Thaddeus, who looked back at him with that imperturbable calm he'd affected ever since Eton. Yet Jeremy could see a tic near his eye.

Thaddeus didn't want a wife who fancied wearing breeches.

How foolish.

Jeremy didn't want a wife, but for the sake of seeing Betsy in breeches, he'd marry the baker's daughter.

"Don't make an ass of yourself," he said. Though why he was helping Thaddeus in his courtship, he didn't know.

"I shall not," Thaddeus stated.

Others might have believed him, but Jeremy had his doubts. Thaddeus had always been obsessed by lineage. His father had drummed it into his head, the better to excuse himself for not marrying the woman of his heart.

Old fool.

By the time Jeremy left the carriage, Lady Knowe was already escorting the duchess into the teahouse. For her part, Betsy beamed up at Thaddeus with that sweetly biddable—and utterly dishonest, now Jeremy thought of it— expression with which she'd won over polite society.

"Betsy," Thaddeus said haltingly.

Jeremy probably should leave the two of them to have this uncomfortable conversation in private, but instead he stayed where he was. His life had been sorely short of amusement lately.

"Yes?" Betsy asked.

"Perhaps you were joking about wearing breeches in public?"

"No, I was not," Betsy replied. Her charming smile widened.

Thaddeus looked disconcerted. "Not a merry jest?"

"I often wore breeches as a young girl. It is easier to ride horses astride," Betsy informed him, making it worse.

"I talked her into going to Wilmslow. She wanted to visit London and play billiards in White's," Jeremy said, feeling that he might as well chime in.

Betsy was testing her future husband, and he was failing the test. Not fair, because Thaddeus was a decent fellow.

"Come on, Betsy," he said. "Tell him the truth: This is merely a taradiddle. You don't plan to walk around your own house every day wearing breeches."

Betsy had her eyes fastened on Thaddeus's face. "I might," she stated. "In the privacy of my own house."

She was a minx who deserved to lose a dukedom.

"Come along!" Lady Knowe cried from the door of the teahouse. She was prone to acting as if people were a flock of sheep, likely because she had been in charge of her brother's nursery. There were eight Wilde offspring. Or was it twelve?

The duchess appeared at her shoulder, like a plump duckling nestled beside its mother. "We have plans to make!" Her Grace called, with a surprisingly girlish laugh.

Thaddeus moved toward his mother, so Jeremy held out his elbow to Betsy. This time he decided that her hair smelled like morning sunshine with a touch of river water.

"The breeches were a stroke of genius, don't you think?" Betsy whispered.

Jeremy looked down into her laughing, naughty eyes and felt the world shaking around him and settling into a different shape. As happens in the midst of battle, when all of a sudden you realize the skirmish is lost.

This battle had probably been lost from the beginning. He was beginning to suspect that mankind merely believed they governed their own affairs. Some embodiment of Fate, a deity with a sardonic humor, controlled them.

Betsy poked him in the side. "Don't you see what's happened?"

"What has happened?" Jeremy inquired.

"The duchess would marry me now, except that we're the wrong ages for each other and not the right gender and the rest of it."

"There are some serious barriers to that union," he agreed.

"Come along," Betsy said, drawing him toward the teahouse. Whoever married her was clearly going to be herded about, since Betsy had learned her skills at Lady Knowe's knee.

Not the worst of all fates.

In fact, when Betsy gave him a genuine smile and whispered, "I don't believe that Thaddeus agrees with his mother," Jeremy decided that perhaps the fates . . .

Well.

The teahouse was small, with a few tables angled in front of windows composed of leaded glass triangles. Lamps glowed on every table, and a large fire burned on the hearth. The air smelled like gingerbread and strong tea. Their hostess was a cheerful woman wearing a mob-cap embellished with four layers of ruffles.

"I am so honored!" she cried, excitement making all her ruffles tremble.

Likely, she collected prints of the Wilde family—as did most of England—since she was staring at Betsy with awe.

"I'm so glad to be here," Betsy said, with a warm smile. "Your gingerbread smells heavenly."

Jeremy frowned, struck by a thought. He could wander into any inn in the country and no one would have the faintest idea who he was. Perhaps there was more to Betsy's wish to wear boy's clothing than he had imagined.

"Lady Boadicea, you must sit beside me," the duchess called to Betsy. She had saved a seat between herself and her son.

Jeremy sat beside Lady Knowe.

"How charming these pink napkins are," Her Grace said, shaking hers out.

"Don't you dare turn your linens as pink as

your gowns," Lady Knowe exclaimed. "My dear, when *are* you planning to drop all that pink? There is a moment when an affectation becomes a burden."

"It simplifies my life," the duchess said, utterly unperturbed. "If I wore breeches, they would have to be pink."

"We already agreed that breeches are not for you," Lady Knowe proclaimed.

Her Grace snorted. "So you said, but I disagree. My coachman is a tremendously clever fellow; he can find me a pair and my maid will fit them to my shape."

Thaddeus's mouth tightened, but his mother jumped to another topic.

She began telling the table about their house in Bordeaux, from which she nimbly skipped to a discussion of the hall at Falconleigh, the seat of the duchy. The marble floors had been recently ground down. "His Grace insists on bringing a pack of bloodhounds with him into the study and they scratch the floors," the duchess said, a distinct chill entering her voice.

"I don't suppose you have a dog," Jeremy asked Thaddeus, doing his small part to impress the pleasures of ducal life upon Betsy.

"I plan to have a pack someday," Thaddeus said, showing the first spark of rebellion Jeremy had ever seen in the man.

"He had a spaniel as a boy," the duchess said. "It found its way into the butler's pantry and chewed up all the polishing rags. Of course, when there are children in the house, we shall reconsider the situation. A boy ought to have a dog."

Betsy bore it all with a charming smile, and Jeremy had the distinct impression that Her Grace wasn't the first mother to decide that Lady Boadicea would be a perfect mother for her unborn grandchildren.

After a half hour, Thaddeus still had a guarded look in his eyes, but the duchess seemed to consider her job finished. She summoned a waiter and ascertained that there was an auction the very next afternoon.

"Has anyone looked outside?" she asked. "It's snowing. I suggest we spend the night in the inn and attend the auction tomorrow."

"I agree with you about spending the night," Lady Knowe said. "I shall send the groom back to Lindow for our necessaries. Maids and the like."

"Those of us who wish to don male clothing tomorrow can attempt it," the duchess said, ignoring the question of necessaries. She was patently uninterested in practicalities. "I may decide to go as myself."

"Women are not allowed in this particular auction house," Betsy reminded her.

"Nonsense. I have been to Christie's several times. Quite likely they would have preferred the duke, but they certainly didn't bar the door," Her Grace said with a drop of scorn. "Don't ever believe the word 'no' unless you say it yourself, dear. It makes life much more agreeable."

"While ladies may visit auction houses in London, it is different out here in the provinces," Lady Knowe put in. "I'm afraid that Mr. Phillips has a strict policy against females. I was most annoyed when I learned of it."

That settled it; Her Grace was determined to visit Mr. Phillips's auction house wearing breeches. "If they think I'm a woman, I *dare* them to say a word about it!" she declared.

From there the conversation turned to a discussion of men's clothing.

Jeremy put a word into the conversation now and then, and kept an eye on Thaddeus, who courteously answered any question put to him directly, but spent most of his time brooding. This was familiar behavior from Eton; even at a young age, Thaddeus had to feel his way through an ethical problem before he reached a decision.

At some point Thaddeus must have decided to marry a perfect lady, and Betsy was now proving to have uncomfortable edges to her. He apparently didn't mind overlooking her adulterous mother, but breeches seemed to be a bridge too far.

Jeremy felt a flash of disdain. His friend was hoping for bucolic bliss with an uninteresting wife and a passel of children and dogs.

The duchess, meanwhile, seemed blissfully convinced that the only matter at hand was how to facilitate Betsy's trip to the auction. "A wig will cover her hair, of course. You'd better instruct your butler to send a variety of them," she advised Lady Knowe. "Footmen have such oddly shaped heads."

"That won't work," Jeremy objected.

"Why not?" Betsy demanded.

"You have too much hair for a small wig." It was a simple fact. This morning it was caught up all over in loops and puffs. It stood out around her head in such profusion that a man could imagine it falling to her waist if she pulled out all the pins.

He shifted, discreetly rearranging his breeches to make room for his reaction to that image.

"We'll braid her hair tightly," Lady Knowe told him. "There are ways of keeping a wig on one's scalp."

"When we're in the Scottish house," the duchess told Betsy, "I braid my hair and make the housemaids do theirs as well. Scotland is overrun by head lice."

Thankfully, teacakes, cream biscuits, and cucumber sandwiches arrived before that subject received more attention.

Jeremy ate a surprising amount, given his customary lack of appetite, while trying very hard not to notice the pale skin of Betsy's wrists. Why should a wrist be erotic, after all?

And yet it was.

If he had his way, he'd run his tongue around that creamy skin and cover it with little bites, lick his way to her palm, wrap his lips around one finger . . .

He came back to himself with a jolt, realizing that the party was looking at him expectantly. "Yes?"

"Thaddeus is going to escort Lady Knowe and

myself to the auction house so we can spy around the premises," the duchess told him. "We don't think that Lady Boadicea should be seen in the vicinity, so the two of you must wait for us to return. If she is seen in our company, they might suspect who she is tomorrow when we return."

If he were Thaddeus, he wouldn't leave his fiancée in the care of another man.

But he wasn't Thaddeus, and Thaddeus seemed perfectly agreeable about the prospect of losing the company of his supposed beloved.

"He doesn't want to marry me anymore," Betsy said a few minutes later, after the party left. She didn't sound disappointed.

"You could have been a duchess," Jeremy said. "Actually, you probably will still be a duchess, because Thaddeus's mother wants you, even if Thaddeus doesn't. You're going to be permitted, if not goaded into, all the pranks that she wasn't allowed as a child."

"No one will goad me into anything," Betsy said, finishing her last bite of crumpet. "Where shall we go, by the way? Not that I don't enjoy your company, but I hate sitting in front of crumbly plates. It's so depressing."

"I would suggest a visit to St. Bartholomew's," the hostess suggested, appearing with Betsy's pelisse over her arm. "Your Ladyship will find it pleasing. It has a turreted bell tower and an ancient crypt, and dates to the 1600s."

Jeremy kept his utter disinterest in turreted bell towers to himself, took the pelisse from the woman, and helped Betsy put it on. "Do you suppose your future mother-in-law thought about the fact that she'd left you unchaperoned?" he asked.

"Should she have?" Betsy asked, looking up at him.

"Certainly not," Jeremy said. "I'm as safe as a toothless dog and they know it."

A smile glimmered in the depths of Betsy's eyes. He wasn't . . . and she knew it. For a moment the air between them sang with a promise of purely earthly delights. The kind that keep a man and woman in their room for hours, contemplating an effort to rise and then collapsing back into bed.

There were reasons why young women weren't allowed to spend time alone with men unless betrothed or married.

"I like her for it," Betsy said, unexpectedly. "There are many who expect me to be as immoral as my mother. That prospect didn't even cross her mind, did it?"

"No," Jeremy said. "The duchess has come to an orderly conclusion about you and her son, and she can't conceive that you might prefer another man."

There was a funny little silence after that.

"Shall we tour St. Bartholomew's?" he asked.

"Yes," Betsy replied, taking his arm. On the doorstep she paused and pulled up the hood of her pelisse.

The snowfall was thicker than it seemed from

the teahouse windows. Through a veil of white, the town looked bleak and dark. Wilmslow was an old town, with narrow streets that wove back and forth, cobbles curving around a massive oak tree.

"You are certain that you don't wish to return to the teahouse?" he asked Betsy. "We could ask to have the plates cleared. We could start over with fresh crumpets and tea."

"I'm sorry to drag you through the snow," she said, "but I couldn't take another moment. Did you notice the hostess staring at me from the side of the room?"

"It did occur to me that she might have collected a print or two of the Wildes," Jeremy admitted cautiously.

"If I marry Thaddeus, she will begin collecting prints of duchesses," Betsy said, wrinkling her nose.

"Perhaps I am being obtuse, but how are you injured if she wastes her money on prints of you posing in a ballroom?"

"You haven't made a study of Wilde prints, obviously."

"True."

"The stationers pry and investigate in order to create different prints that will tempt their customers. They often make up the subjects from whole cloth. I've been shown in dalliance with Lord Merland, for example—and he's married! More to the point, I scarcely know the man."

"Unpleasant," Jeremy acknowledged.

"They are often disagreeable," Betsy said. "My

mother, you see. You know about the Prussian, don't you?"

Jeremy blinked at her.

"My mother's lover," Betsy said, scowling at him. "Golden hair, good teeth, looked just like—" She bit the sentence off.

"Looked like?"

She looked up at him. "I shan't finish that sentence, and I hope you will forget I ever said anything."

"Looked like your sister Joan," Jeremy said, realizing. "You mentioned that yesterday but I forgot. I don't listen to that sort of gossip, so I had no idea of the color of the man's hair, or his origins, or any of it."

"You are singular in that respect," Betsy said. "Reporters dog my footsteps, hoping to see me mimic my mother. If we were in London, I would never be so imprudent as to walk in the open with you, even with a maid trailing behind."

They walked without speaking for a few minutes, their steps muted by snow. Around them, the windowsills and doorsteps were turning white. A few locks of Betsy's hair curled around her forehead, and snow was falling softly on them as well.

Jeremy had the disconcerting realization that he didn't care if the church they were walking toward was holy ground or consecrated from the crypt to the bell tower: He meant to kiss Betsy again. With thoroughly profane intentions.

Simple lust.

Albeit with a touch of giddiness.

A stiff wind cut around the corners of the narrow street and shot past Jeremy's ears with a whistle, carrying a whiff of coal smoke.

"It's growing frightfully cold," Betsy said, her words nipped away and flung over her shoulder.

"The wind sounds like a musket ball going past one's ears," Jeremy said, his thoughts spilling out. "Except," he added, "wind isn't dangerous, of course."

Betsy gave his arm a squeeze, which was the perfect response.

"Would you like to return to the teahouse?" Jeremy asked again.

She shook her head. "I like fighting the wind."

They were walking along when a rumbling coach pulled up.

Jeremy glanced to the side and his heart sank. The window was open, and a lean face topped with a great deal of fluffy salt-and-pepper hair peered out. He had a majestic nose, the kind that was meant to be attached to a man standing in the prow of a ship or the House of Lords.

"Oh, bloody hell," Jeremy said, and came to an abrupt halt. He hadn't seen his father since well before the Vauxhall fireworks and subsequent visit to Lindow.

Betsy stumbled. They had been walking quickly, their bodies shoved along the pavement by the wind.

"My father," Jeremy said, with a wave of his hand. "He can't have stayed more than an hour at the castle before following us here."

"I think my eyelashes have frozen," Betsy said, rubbing an eye. "Did you say your father?" She peered around his shoulder. "In that carriage?"

"Unfortunately." Jeremy quickly unwound the bandage from his head, thrust it in his pocket, and slapped his hat back on. His father wouldn't be pleased to learn his son escaped war only to be nearly felled by a madwoman.

The Marquess of Thurrock was clambering out of the vehicle. He had seemed impossibly tall and lean when Jeremy was a child, his eyes bright, a near-visible sense of *competence* hanging about his shoulders. He was still tall, obviously. And competent, presumably.

"Good afternoon, Lord Thurrock," Jeremy said, bowing.

The marquess was fussing with his greatcoat and busily acting like a British aristocrat avoiding an awkward reunion.

Not that Jeremy didn't feel the same way.

Finally, the marquess took a step forward, as if he meant to sweep Jeremy into the sort of hugs with which he had always greeted him when Jeremy came home from Eton. But he caught himself.

"Son," he said. "Who's this?" His voice was full and hearty, like a fishmonger, and his eyes—damn it!—were hopeful.

"Lady Boadicea, may I introduce my father, the Marquess of Thurrock?" Jeremy said.

Betsy cocked her head slightly to the side and smiled.

Jeremy waited for her beatific smile to dazzle, as it had dazzled most of polite society, but his father merely blinked and said, "I recognize the eyebrows, of course. Haven't seen your father for a few years."

Betsy's curtsy was particularly graceful, given the fact the wind was trying to drive them along the walk. "Lord Thurrock, it is a pleasure to meet you."

The carriage door opened again, and Grégoire Bisset-Caron stepped to the sidewalk. Jeremy's cousin was wearing a fur cape and hat instead of a tricorne. "Here I am," he called. "Forgive me for keeping you waiting!"

"Lady Boadicea, may I present my nephew, Mr. Bisset-Caron?" Jeremy's father asked, sounding distinctly unenthusiastic.

Betsy curtsied again. "It's a pleasure to see you, sir. I thought you had returned to London."

"I intended to do so, but my uncle surprised me," Grégoire said, with a languid nod to Jeremy. "I decided to accompany him to this town . . . what is it called?"

"Wilmslow," Jeremy said, wondering whether Grégoire had plans to court Betsy. Surely his cousin didn't think that he could compete with a future duke. Grégoire could be considered the heir to a marquess—but only if Jeremy died without a son.

At times that seemed eminently possible. Grégoire might even be counting on it.

"A pleasure and a surprise," the marquess said to Betsy. "I didn't know that my son was keeping company with a young lady, to call a spade a spade."

Grégoire snorted. "Your spade is misplaced, Uncle. Lady Boadicea is all but promised to the future Duke of Eversley."

"I am not keeping company with Lord Jeremy," Betsy confirmed.

"Ah well," his father said. "It'd take a thief catcher to tie the boy down."

"I'm no longer a boy," Jeremy said.

His father was grinning at Betsy. Her charm was warm and cheery, albeit fake. His father's was laid on a foundation of ancient silver, an ancient title, and rows and rows of tenant farmers.

The marquess actually paid his farmers, which was more than his great-grandfather had done. Jeremy had never forgotten being told by a wizened old relative that the new way of doing things—which included paying a wage—was bollocks.

The marquess moved to Betsy's other side, leaning slightly on a silver-topped cane. As he crossed before them, the wind blew a whiff of cigars and starched linen into Jeremy's face that reminded him of childhood.

"Where are we going?" the marquess asked.

"St. Bartholomew's," Betsy replied.

"An unusual destination for a member of our family," Jeremy's father observed. "I remembered on the way here that my old friend Samuel Finney hails from Wilmslow. He paints miniatures. Has a terrible squint. Last I heard, he'd become a justice of the peace. He exhibited a miniature of Queen Charlotte, and the money allowed him to pay off all his family debts. How far is this church?"

"At the end of the street," Betsy said.

"It is too cold to walk even that far," Grégoire stated. "It's positively barbaric the way the wind cuts through my cloak." He waved his stick at the coachman. "I will wait for you."

"Just how interested are you in seeing the church, Lady Boadicea?" the marquess asked.

A groom jumped down and opened the carriage door. "Grégoire is right; it's too cold for walking," Jeremy said, drawing Betsy toward the vehicle.

Once they were all seated, in the sudden silence that follows an escape from a storm, the marquess asked, "Lady Boadicea, might we change your mind as regards the church? I'm afraid the building will be bitterly cold."

"I will admit to feeling chilled," Betsy said, her teeth chattering. "Perhaps we should join the Duchess of Eversley, Lord Greywick, and my aunt, Lady Knowe, at the auction house instead of continuing to the church."

Jeremy wrapped an arm around her shoulder and then, as his father looked surprised: "We are merely friends. As Grégoire said, Lady Boadicea is almost betrothed to Greywick. In fact, the duchess treats her as a daughter-in-law."

"*Almost*," his father repeated. He smiled, and a flame lit somewhere in the region of Jeremy's frozen heart. He used to love that smile: It appeared rarely, and as a boy, Jeremy would do anything for it. Learn three Latin declensions before bedtime, bring home top marks in history, argue his instructors to a standstill . . . knowing his father was doing the same in Lords.

"I don't mean this unkindly, but I doubt very much that the Duke of Lindow would embrace my cousin as a son-in-law," Grégoire said in his most waspish manner.

The marquess leveled a tremendous scowl. "What did you mean by that?"

"Since Lady Boadicea has, as we established, very nearly reached an understanding with Lord Greywick, I can say freely, amongst the family as it were, that Jeremy's nerves are not at their best."

"What in the hell are you talking about?" the marquess thundered.

"I had an unfortunate episode after some fireworks exploded in Vauxhall Gardens," Jeremy said. It wasn't how he would have chosen to inform his father, let alone Betsy. "I lost sensibility for some time."

Betsy said nothing, but shifted closer to him, her side pressing against his.

"The details are unpleasant," Grégoire agreed with a sniff. "I wouldn't wish you to have misplaced hopes, Uncle. Nothing has leaked to the stationers about Jeremy's illness, but one can't count on that."

The marquess regarded Grégoire with withering scorn and pointedly gave him his shoulder. "I suggest that you visit St. Bartholomew's on a summer day, Lady Boadicea. My coachman knows something about these parts. Earlier, he suggested we retire to the Honeypot for hot drinks. Best inn for miles around."

At Betsy's nod, his father opened the window and shouted to his coachman, and the vehicle lurched into movement.

*"Dieu soit loué!"* Grégoire said, under his breath.

"Lady Boadicea, are churches a particular interest of yours?" the marquess asked.

Jeremy stared out the window at the gathering swirls of snowflakes while his father and Betsy talked about churches they had visited. He had decided never to see his father again. That seemed childish in retrospect and yet—

His ownership of a blackened soul was not childish. Next to him, Betsy's warm hip—or at least all the skirts that bunched up next to her hip—pressed against his greatcoat.

That slight touch inspired a flash of desire so intense that he felt it in the back of his teeth, along with an inexplicable dose of comfort.

The carriage wheels were muffled by snow as they trundled along the cobblestones. At some point, spring would come. Robins and wood pigeons would sing again. Hawthorn would blossom.

"If this snow keeps up, we'll have to spend the night in Wilmslow," his father said, twitching aside the curtains. "Hopefully the Honeypot has enough rooms. Apparently, there's another inn as well. Not the Fox & Hound, a more interesting name than that."

"My aunt is fond of the Gherkin & Cheese," Betsy said.

"That's the one," his father said. He turned to Grégoire. "We'll let you out at the Honeypot; if the duchess and her party are there, send to us at the Gherkin. If not, take a carriage and join us."

"Dropping off a groom would be sufficient," Grégoire said sulkily. "Or you could simply wait for me while I inquire about Her Grace."

The marquess looked at his nephew down the length of his nose. "One does not keep a lady waiting in a chilly carriage."

Betsy burst into a flurry of small talk, as marked as if butterflies suddenly fluttered all around her head. She peppered the marquess with charm, but Jeremy had known him a lifetime. He saw a puzzled light at the back of his eyes. Betsy was hiding herself so well that his father was confused.

They pulled up to the Honeypot. Grégoire got out of the carriage and disappeared into the blowing snow.

"That boy soured while you were at war," the marquess said, tapping a hand on his knee. "Mayhap he talked himself into a belief the title was his."

"Did you notice that his mention of a Vauxhall print was close to a threat, Jeremy?" Betsy said, as the carriage set off for the Gherkin & Cheese.

She used his first name before his father—and the marquess took note. With an effort, Jeremy wrenched his mind back to Betsy, who was explaining the times when the Wildes had discovered acquaintances were selling sketches, or even just ideas for them, to stationers in London.

"The prints travel all about the country on tinkers' carts," she was saying. "They have plagued my brothers."

"Was Grégoire with you at Vauxhall when you fell ill?" his father asked.

"No," Jeremy replied. "You and I haven't spoken in many months," he added. "Have you been well?" The marquess looked older, his nose beakier, his eyes paler blue than a year ago.

"Yes. Other than the fact I have worried about you." He turned to Betsy. "I hope I didn't make you uncomfortable by answering so truthfully. I can see you are my son's dear friend."

"I am honored," Betsy said.

The carriage was quiet for a moment. Jeremy and his father hadn't spoken since shortly after he staggered off the boat from America, shuddering at the faintest sound, waves of shame and grief cutting him to the bone on a daily basis. They had quarreled within days of his landing in England, and after that, Jeremy couldn't face him.

"You are so bloody effective," Jeremy said, forcing the words out of his mouth. "If you'd been there, in the colonies, the whole thing would have been done right. You'd have brought your men home."

The marquess shook his head, his eyes unreadable in the dim light in the carriage. "There is no right in war. There's only what happened."

"I followed orders," Jeremy said, a swell of bitterness riding his tongue. "You wouldn't have followed orders. It wasn't fair of me to blame you for it."

The marquess frowned.

"Oh, for God's sake," Jeremy said. "You would have marched your men out of there and discovered that the colonel in charge had fled. Your men would be home with their wives now. I just kept running across that field, from side to side."

"Had I taken an oath to serve in His Majesty's forces, I would have followed orders," his father stated. "The fact that the War Office decided not to court-martial that blasted colonel is an outrage, an affront to every man who fell on the field."

Jeremy quirked up the side of his mouth in a failed attempt at a smile. "Be that as it may, I shouldn't have blamed you for my failures."

"You thought I would have succeeded where you failed—but you *didn't* fail," the marquess said.

"He did," Betsy said suddenly.

The coach went silent again, but for the slush of the wheels on snow.

The marquess's eyes narrowed and if he'd looked confused before, now he looked at Betsy with daggerlike contempt. "I assure you, Lady Boadicea, that I have read the reports of my son's service myself. He kept his men together in battle, in the face of insurmountable odds. Had the coward's battalion joined them, as planned, Jeremy's actions likely would have turned the fate of that particular battle."

"I know that," Betsy said.

"My son received an honorable mention in the dispatches," the marquess barked.

The carriage was drawing to a halt, but Betsy leaned forward like a gladiator about to whip up her steeds. "A true leader feels he has failed every man he loses," she said, contained anger equal to the marquess's in her voice. "My brother North is such a leader. And your son is such a leader."

Jeremy's mouth twitched, an involuntary movement.

"If you ask him, Jeremy will deny it," Betsy said.

Jeremy opened his mouth. "Because—"

Betsy cut him off. "He will say that North is a better man. The guilt is intolerable. You couldn't understand it. If you say his experience was not a failure, you ignore his feelings."

"Balderdash!" his father barked. He turned to Jeremy, his eyebrows nearly meeting. "Do you think that I know nothing of guilt?"

The wind had picked up and was rocking the carriage.

"An entire platoon was lost," Betsy said. "With all due respect, Lord Thurrock, no guilt you feel could equal that which your son experienced."

Jeremy's mouth curled in a genuine smile. "I can fight this particular battle," he said to Betsy. "If not the other."

"You did fight," Betsy said. "You just didn't win. You tried. To my mind, every battle is a failure."

"You have a point." The knowledge settled into his bones with surprising warmth.

"I know guilt," his father said stubbornly.

Without any of the three of them noticing, the carriage had halted. Now the door opened, letting in a swirl of freezing air. Outside the door a groom in red livery stood stiffly next to a mounting box rapidly turning white with snow.

Betsy bent forward and left the carriage without a word to Jeremy or the marquess, holding out her gloved hand for the groom's aid.

His father made no move to leave. "I don't know why you thought I blamed you, Jeremy, but I didn't. God knows I never would."

"I didn't truly think that," Jeremy said, touched despite himself. "I was an idiot, that's all. I've always thought of you as one of the most competent men I've ever met."

His father's mouth wobbled.

"I couldn't help making the comparison. I didn't look outside the battlefield, you see. On one level I followed orders. But on another, I should have realized that something had gone wrong. I should have sent someone to investigate. Instead, I just kept running across that bloody field."

"And what were you running toward?"

"My men kept falling, one after another," Jeremy said, swallowing.

"If you had left the field, your men would have fallen without notice," his father said. "A general watches the battle as a whole, but you were told to watch over your men. You did that, Jeremy. You did that. The fact your colonel shamefully deserted his post is not your responsibility."

Jeremy clenched his jaw because the English language didn't seem to have the words for what he felt. Or what he should say.

"We can't leave your warrior queen out in the snow." The marquess's hand closed tightly around Jeremy's knee for a second before he bent forward and stepped out the door.

Jeremy sat still, capturing the whiff of linen and tobacco in his memory. He finally jolted himself out of the carriage and gave the shivering footman a shilling.

By the time he entered the inn, the marquess and Betsy were seated on opposite sides of a private parlor, which wasn't as awkward as it might have been because Lady Knowe, Thaddeus, and the duchess were crowded around the fireplace with them.

Apparently, they had appropriated the entire inn.

"Isn't this marvelous?" Lady Knowe called, flying to meet him. "We are warming up, and then we shall retire upstairs for baths. We can feel as comfortable as if we were in Lindow Castle. There was only one guest for the night, and he was perfectly happy to go off to the Honeypot. I'm paying for his stay, of course."

She burbled on, but Jeremy looked to Betsy. She looked back at him, wide mouth solemn and one eyebrow arched, so delicious that Jeremy moved directly toward her.

A hand on his arm stopped him. "Lord Jeremy," the duchess said, "I wish to apologize."

"There is no need," Jeremy said mechanically, bowing. He had no idea what she was talking about.

"I left you and Lady Boadicea at a teahouse unchaperoned. Naturally you both felt uncomfortable, which forced you out into a winter storm. What a marvelous piece of luck that you found your father's carriage when needed!"

Jeremy forced himself to nod. "Lady Knowe

sent the duke's carriage back for our servants," the duchess went on. "They should be here within the hour. I could not sit down to dine in this gown."

"No, indeed," Jeremy murmured.

Thaddeus was sitting beside Betsy. She would be a marvelous duchess. Just look at the squabble she had with his father in the carriage. Only a future duchess could lecture a marquess and then walk straight past him without a word of farewell.

Her Grace was blathering on about her lady's maid—why would she think he was interested?— and Betsy was giving Thaddeus that smile, the one that would likely turn his head and make him forget that she was a breeches-wearing scandal in the making.

Damn it.

"If you'll excuse me, Your Grace," he said to the duchess, and made his way across the room.

Betsy and Thaddeus looked like a ceramic lord and lady, a flirtatious pair fashioned in France by a man who'd never seen a queen but pictured aristocrats with sweet faces and strong chins.

"Hello," Jeremy said, pulling over a seat to Betsy's other side. "How was the auction house?"

"Lady Knowe decided that the weather precluded the trip," Thaddeus said, all amiable and gentlemanlike. "We came here, and she sent the carriage back to the castle."

There was something in his eyes. Thaddeus had made up his mind.

Perhaps because the auction itself would be put off due to the weather. Yet if he thought that

Betsy would forget the idea of breeches, he was due for a surprise.

"Lady Knowe has ascertained that the auction will be held tomorrow," Thaddeus continued. "All the ladies plan to attend, dressed as men."

"I thought you felt it disreputable for a lady to appear in breeches," Jeremy observed.

"My mother has impressed upon me that she should be my guide in such matters," Thaddeus said. "I have apologized to Betsy for any discomfort I caused with my naïve and inept response."

"There's nothing that makes an aristocrat look like a grocer as much as a robust love of respectability," Jeremy observed. "My father is the first in my family to bother with reputation at all."

"Aunt Knowe claims that the aristocracy is like a pond full of swans," Betsy said, her eyes sparkling. "From above, we look elegant, if not regal. But under the surface, we're all swimming madly, with not much difference between us and the ducks."

"An acute observation," Thaddeus said.

"The snow tonight looks rather swanlike," Jeremy said idly. "Like the feathers of an unimaginable bird."

The duchess called to her son, so Thaddeus rose and escorted her from the room.

"You can't marry him," Jeremy said. "You'll spend your adult life watching a man ferry his mother about."

Betsy threw him an inscrutable look and rose

to her feet. "I would escort my mother, had she cared for my company."

"Our maids have arrived, thank the Lord," Aunt Knowe announced from the door. "Come along, you two. No dilly-dallying. Jeremy, your cousin is in a frightful state; Mr. Bisset-Caron fears he's caught a cold. He shall have supper in bed." She disappeared.

"Unchaperoned once again," Jeremy said, strolling across the room. "One would almost think that Lady Knowe wasn't championing Thaddeus as your future spouse."

It was madness to discuss marriage with Jeremy, but Betsy found it irresistible as well. "If I became a duchess, the world would be at my feet."

"You don't want the world at your feet," Jeremy said, shrugging. "You certainly don't want the whole world to have your likeness on the wall. What do you want, Bess?"

*You*, she thought involuntarily.

But that way was madness. There was no question but that Jeremy brought out her worst, the carnal impulses she'd inherited from her mother.

"I want to be a duchess," she said, echoing her fourteen-year-old self, the girl who fiercely longed to win at the game of marriage. "Thaddeus is a true gentleman."

Jeremy leaned forward and brushed his knuckle across her cheek. "But are you a lady?"

She flinched.

"What's the matter?" he asked, his eyebrows

drawing together. "I didn't mean it as an insult, Bess."

"Why did you agree to walk me to the church?"

His eyes searched hers, and she saw the moment when he decided to be honest. "I hoped to kiss you again."

She had always been so careful, so sure that she could avoid her mother's mistakes. Yet she had walked out of the tearoom without thought of a chaperone, beside a man who lusted after her.

"Betsy," Jeremy said softly. His eyes looked almost tender. "Don't. Don't think whatever it is you're thinking."

"I think nothing," she said, walking out and leaving him behind.

He was confusing, bitter, dark-tempered. For all she yearned to soothe the anguish he sometimes let slip, she couldn't.

She caught up with Aunt Knowe in silence. Once they had climbed a flight of stairs, her aunt paused.

"You're going to have to choose between them."

"There's no choice," Betsy said immediately. "The duchess is marvelous. She's funny and kind."

"I didn't mean between the duchess and her son. You are not marrying Emily," Aunt Knowe said dryly. "The choice is between Jeremy and Thaddeus."

"A man's mother is the mirror of her son," Betsy said airily. "How could I be luckier? Everyone loves Thaddeus."

Aunt Knowe pushed open a bedchamber door, and Betsy saw Winnie changing the bed into linens brought from Lindow Castle. Aunt Knowe was a firm believer that to sleep in strange linen, even once, was to court vermin, if not illness.

"Take a warm bath," her aunt suggested, her eyes softening. "Remember, you have more choices than these two. The men flinging themselves at your feet are legion."

Betsy came up on her toes and kissed her aunt's cheek. "You're wonderful."

"I'm lucky," her aunt said. "You children are endlessly amusing."

As Winnie dosed her bath with vervain, Betsy sat next to the fire and tried to collect her thoughts.

If she was honest with herself, she loved flirting with Jeremy. She wanted to kiss him in a dark corner. She wanted *him*, with his dark soul and furious eyes, his brandy-drinking, sober-sided sarcasm.

His broad chest, battered hands, and beautiful lips. What man had lips like his? She was fascinated by his lower lip, by the little crease in the center of it. The way his tongue had slipped past her lips.

The way he spoke idly, a flow of words, and all the time his eyes ranged over her lips . . . her bosom, her neck.

He seemed to like her wrists. Was that possible? She caught him looking, his eyes drowsy.

She could swear . . .

But what did she know of lust?

Only that it danced in her limbs and made her mind flood with scandalous ideas. What if she teased Jeremy with kisses, with a lap of her tongue, even with a nip from her teeth? What if she kissed him so passionately that he—

That he what?

She knew nothing.

Oh, she knew the mechanics. But that was nothing.

# Chapter Thirteen

They gathered for dinner in the inn dining room, and even Grégoire Bisset-Caron joined them, complaining of a cold but never sniffling.

The duchess carried the conversation through the first course, as she had apparently decided to woo Betsy by describing Thaddeus's innate aptitude for being a duke, on display from the age of two months.

Betsy listened carefully to the story of Thaddeus's generosity toward an orphaned hedgehog, but she allowed her mind to wander when his mother described his courage after being stricken with ringworm.

"His beautiful curls fell off in patches all over his scalp," the duchess lamented.

"Oh, for God's sake," Thaddeus groaned under his breath.

Betsy liked him for that, because he was irritated but didn't cut his mother off.

The ringworm finally vanquished, the marquess entered the lists, and the table was treated to the harrowing tale of Jeremy's childhood bout of mumps.

"You've missed the point," Jeremy observed, when the story of bulbous glands wound down. "You forgot to say how wildly courageous I was in the face of near death."

"Death?" His father snorted. "You were a frightfully naughty child, but your disobedience wasn't fatal or near to it."

"I notice you are not mentioning my cousin's service in the colonies," Grégoire said.

Jeremy smiled faintly. "Mumps is easier to excuse."

"Nonsense," the marquess said, frowning mightily at his son. "Your military service earned you a rare mention in the dispatches, even if you chose to ignore it."

The duchess nimbly jumped in at this point and launched into a tale about Thaddeus's remarkable talent at the billiard table.

"As has my son," the marquess said mulishly.

Each story the duchess told was capped with a parallel. Thaddeus was brave; so was Jeremy.

Both men greeted these stories with silence, but Betsy noticed that Grégoire was becoming more peevish with every passing minute.

"I find tales of childish heroics frightfully tedious," he said after a third glass of wine.

"Do you indeed?" the duchess asked, dangerous quiet in her voice.

But Grégoire had apparently reached the point of inebriation at which one no longer pays attention to disapproval, even when wielded by those at the very top of polite society. "Who cares if a boy was brave when he fell into a horse pond?" he demanded, waving his wineglass. "The real test of a man is how he behaves as a man."

"I take it you are accusing me of lack of courage," Jeremy said with complete indifference. "I will readily admit to being terrified on the battlefield."

"That says a great deal about you, doesn't it?" Grégoire replied with a smirk. "In school, I was forced to memorize a speech given by your namesake, Lady Boadicea. Jeremy could have used it to rally his men rather than leaving them to die." He leapt to his feet and struck a pose. "*Have no fear whatever of the Romans; for they are superior to us neither in numbers nor in bravery.*"

Aunt Knowe turned to the marquess. "Have you ever suspected that there may be madness in your family?"

"We're all mad as March hares," Grégoire said, seating himself. "Only a fool would marry into our family, more's the pity."

"I beg to differ," the marquess said frigidly.

Grégoire shrugged. "I wish it wasn't the case, but I'm afraid that Jeremy doesn't make a good case for our bloodline."

"It's all true," Jeremy said, sighing. His eyes, gleaming with amusement, met Betsy's. "If only I could have sparkled on the battlefield. Perhaps

I should woo a wife in a vaudeville troupe in order to give my children the ability to scintillate at the dinner table."

"My family does not approve of dramatics," the duchess said. She had obviously written off Grégoire, who just as obviously didn't care.

Betsy was struck by curiosity. What possible goal could Grégoire have for discouraging her from marrying his cousin—not that Jeremy showed any sign of proposing to her?

Could he truly believe that Jeremy would die without leaving a son, allowing him to inherit?

That was absurd.

But Grégoire launched into a supposedly amusing reference to a print sold in London that showed Jeremy hiding behind a tree. Aunt Knowe was regarding him with narrowed eyes and the marquess was apoplectic.

"You are an ill-bred young man," Her Grace decreed, before launching into an account of the time when Thaddeus almost brought down a Scottish stag with an arrow.

Betsy watched as Thaddeus winced at the depiction of the stag leaping over his eight-year-old body and disappearing into the Highlands, an arrow waving from its haunch.

It wasn't until the dessert course that Betsy's mind presented her with a dilemma. What if she married Thaddeus, and then Jeremy accepted an invitation to their country house?

Had her mother felt the insistent desire that crawled through Betsy's veins and urged her to glance at Jeremy under her lashes? Think about licking his bottom lip? Think about what his arms felt like around her? Think about what his hands would feel—

One of the more irritating aspects of attending a girls' school was that Clementine's voice was vividly memorable. If Clementine knew of the seething lust Betsy felt for a sarcastic, annoying man, who was adamantly not an appropriate suitor, she would scoff.

Betsy sighed. Miss Clementine Clarke had married a wealthy man who might, someday, be the Lord Mayor of London. They were unlikely to meet again. So why, why couldn't she simply forget Clementine's insults? She saw Octavia frequently during the Season, so why couldn't she remember Octavia's laughter rather than Clementine's slights?

Jeremy's white neck cloth brought out the shadows under his eyes and made him look like a devil, but not the sort who began as an angel and fell. He was the Demon King from a Ben Jonson play, frolicking about while plotting how to condemn the entire cast to the fiery depths.

"Drinks by the fire in the parlor," Aunt Knowe announced. "I recommend stiff brandies all around as the bedchambers promise to be chilly tonight."

"I have requested another eiderdown," Grégoire said. "The one I have is entirely insufficient. I demanded that the innkeeper change the sheets as well. I suggest everyone do the same; it can be fatal to sleep in damp sheets."

It seemed that Aunt Knowe had not instructed

the Lindow maids to change Grégoire's bedding. Betsy was certain that the marquess's and Jeremy's bed linens had been switched for those embroidered with the Lindow crest.

After the meal, Grégoire headed to bed to nurse his cold, and the rest of them set out for the room Aunt Knowe had designated as the parlor. Betsy found herself walking beside Jeremy, who prowled down the corridor, brows knitted, not bothering to speak after giving her a burning glance.

Once they were all in the parlor, the duchess demanded a game of piquet, and cast a betrayed frown in Betsy's direction when she confessed to disliking the game. The marquess banded with Thaddeus, and Lady Knowe claimed the duchess.

Which left Betsy sitting with the Demon King. Jeremy glared into the fireplace as if each flame was an enemy combatant. She had accepted brandy; he was nursing a cup of tea. In fact, he seemed to have left his ever-present whisky bottle back at Lindow.

No member of the Duke of Lindow's family was allowed to be missish about liquor, so Betsy savored every drop and tried not to feel as if she were seated next to a steaming volcano.

"What is it?" she asked finally, not lowering her voice because Aunt Knowe was in a pitched battle with her childhood friend over a betting fiasco.

"What?" he growled.

*Growled.*

She didn't like men who growled. She liked men who kept their temper to themselves.

"Your sulk," she said, not bothering to curb the irritation in her voice. "Presumably from the aggravation caused by your father's arrival, but one never knows with two-year-olds; it's so difficult to coax them into coherence."

Jeremy stared at her in slack-jawed astonishment.

"Yes?" she asked, when he didn't reply.

Only to feel disconcerted when he broke into laughter.

She saw from the corner of her eye that all four players glanced up from their cards. Since Thaddeus was watching, Betsy smiled at Jeremy.

Who recoiled.

"Jesus," he muttered. "What was *that* in aid of? One moment you're scolding me like a nanny after a sleepless night, and the next you're serving up a society grimace?"

Thaddeus turned back to his cards.

"Well, what are you brooding about?" she asked.

"I wasn't sitting about in a melancholy. My face merely falls into detestable lines. Likely a matter of inheritance."

"Your father appears perfectly cheerful," she said, taking another sip of brandy. "Particularly when he told the story of your adoration for that shaggy little pony. He glowed with cheerful pride."

*"What a blow was there given,"* Jeremy recited.

"Are you being clever?" she asked. "Thanks to your father, I know about your brilliance at Latin declension. While my education was excellent for a young lady, it didn't extend to memorizing the classics."

"A quote from *The Tempest*," Jeremy said. "I was being a conceited, if well-educated, fool." The firelight caught his hair and made it shine like burnished dark bronze.

"Your cousin was pettish at dinner as well," she said thoughtfully. "It could be that your temper is inherited."

"My mother had an optimistic frame of mind," he offered.

"But you're prone to allowing your temper to get the better of you?"

"I find myself in the grip of strong emotion." Their eyes met. "I'm considering taking a wife."

Betsy's throat closed, and she spluttered, coughing as brandy went down the wrong way.

"If I appear to be glaring into the fire, it's the effect of deep thought," he added.

It seemed impossible. He had tolerated her. He regularly made fun of her.

Although they *had* kissed.

"There's no need to propose simply because of a kiss," she hissed, taking advantage of another burst of irritation among the players.

He raised an eyebrow. "I wasn't planning on it."

Betsy felt color crawling up her neck. "Good," she said, taking another sip of brandy. She wanted to touch him. Put a hand on his arm and see if she could make him shiver. Trail a finger over the back of his hand and see if it made *her* shiver, deep in her core.

It would. She knew it would.

"I was actually considering the attributes one should look for in a wife," Jeremy said. "One can hardly avoid the thought, given the deluge of information emanating from Her Grace about the attributes that commend Thaddeus as a prospective husband."

"Your father rose to the challenge as well," Betsy pointed out.

"A failed endeavor," Jeremy said. "I was such a boring child. Mumps are nothing compared to the hairless horrors of ringworm."

Betsy giggled. Brandy was spreading through her stomach in a pleasant way, making her feel as if the world was a kindly, glowing place.

"Don't get drunk," Jeremy said, giving her a sharp glance.

"Why not?" Betsy asked. She lowered her voice. "It's frightfully *déclassé* to go bald at an early age."

"The opposite," Jeremy said, pouring himself more tea. "Only a duchess boasts of something as distasteful as ringworm. It displays utter disregard for the cautious mores of the socially anxious. I shouldn't say this to you, though."

"Why not?"

"Because you're so anxious yourself," he said, glancing at her. "Charming, snobbish, anxious."

Betsy's first instinct was to fling the dregs of her brandy at him, but she drank them instead. He was right. Why should she take umbrage?

She lived in the grip of a profound fear instilled in her by Clementine and her fellow scholars.

"No answer?" Jeremy asked.

"You are correct," she said, holding out her glass. "More brandy, please."

He rose, strolled over to the decanters arranged on a sideboard, and poured her a healthy slug of liquor.

"You told me that you wouldn't drink after the midday meal," Aunt Knowe said, her voice displeased. "You'll never sleep at this rate, Jeremy."

"It's for Betsy," he replied.

"Oh, all right then." She returned to her cards.

Betsy looked over to find Thaddeus looking at her, so she raised the glass that Jeremy had just handed her. "Luckily, I have no trouble sleeping," she informed him.

"I've taught all my girls to hold their liquor," Aunt Knowe said. "You needn't worry about your future wife becoming tiddly and flirting with the vicar." Then she put down some cards with a shout of triumph. "I fancy that's cooked your goose!"

"You're anxious because of your mother, aren't you?" Jeremy asked in a low voice.

Betsy looked at him. Despite Aunt Knowe's pride, she was definitely feeling on the tiddly side of sober. "Wouldn't you be, were you I?"

He pondered that, staring narrow-eyed into the fire.

"Well?"

"I'm trying to imagine my mother running away with a footman rather than dying while I was in the colonies. I'd prefer she was alive and in the world, even if she lived in a different country with the footman. Is that unkind to tell you as much?"

Betsy took a healthy swallow. "It is, rather. Your mother's death did not shape you as an adult, and others feel nothing but sympathy for you. You've made me feel shallow, although my mother's adultery has had a significant effect on me."

"Only because you allow it," he said, without hesitation.

"You know nothing," Betsy stated. "Nothing at all. Of all the contemptuous things you've said to me, that is probably the worst."

She could tell from his expression that he was surprised and, rather sweetly, taken aback.

"I didn't mean it contemptuously."

"That excuse only works once or twice."

Yet when she met his dark eyes, desire flared up between them. She bit her lip, fighting back against instincts that suggested—madness!—that she transfer herself from her chair to his lap. That she tilt back her head and invite a kiss. That he would kiss her, and her hands would clutch his shoulders.

She jerked her gaze away and put a hand to her burning cheek.

"You just watched two peers parade their respective sons' virtues before you, and still you think that you have a damaged reputation?" Jeremy asked. "You're a duke's daughter. Your mother's blood is as noble as mine, albeit her morals were a trifle elastic. Morals are not inherited."

"All characteristics are inherited," Betsy said. "Have you ignored North's diatribes on the subject of a horse's stride?"

"You may have inherited your mother's legs, but morals are taught," Jeremy retorted. "You learned your morals from Lady Knowe. I would be extremely surprised if any child in a nursery she oversaw would behave in a less than resolutely English fashion—and by that I mean the behavior befitting an English nobleman."

"Horatius raced his horse over the bog while inebriated," Betsy said. Her older brother had perished in that bog.

"Did he ever cheat at cards?"

"Of course not!" she flashed.

"Being reckless with one's life is practically a British pastime," Jeremy said. He reached over and picked up her glass of brandy, which she had placed on the floor beside her chair.

"Not good for your sleep," Aunt Knowe barked from the table.

Jeremy sighed and put the glass back down. "Your mother has had no real effect on your morals, Bess. Lady Knowe shaped you, through and through."

"I can't think of anyone better," Betsy said stoutly, aware that her aunt was apparently listening.

Just then the duchess launched into a diatribe that implied Aunt Knowe had cards up her sleeve. Which made the other three players break into laughter and led to the dissolution of the games.

"If I had the ability to hide cards up my sleeve, we wouldn't be playing for walnuts," Aunt Knowe declared. "I would wager you for your diamond set, Emily, see if I wouldn't."

Thaddeus eased his long body into the empty chair beside Betsy and then nodded at her half-full glass. "May I?" he asked.

Thaddeus's clear eyes made no demands. Marriage to him would be peaceful.

Betsy gave him a genuine smile, and handed him the glass. "You would do me a kindness; I am not used to copious amounts of brandy."

"I like a woman who can hold her liquor," Jeremy's father said, dropping into a seat beside his son. Betsy felt as if a gray heron had suddenly folded its knees in ways unknown in the avian kingdom and perched on the edge of a seat.

"Drink can lead to indiscretions," Her Grace put in. "Remember the French ambassador's wife? I put that scandal down to her passion for brandy. She told me herself that she brought over three cases, disguised as household goods."

Thaddeus's coat pulled across broad shoulders as he drank. Jeremy's beauty was of a brutal kind that slapped you in the face with a wave of desire. Thaddeus's was quieter, accompanied by a nobleman's confidence that he was welcome in any company. Betsy let her eyes wander over his chest, wondering if he too had a muscled stomach. Likely he did. His legs stretched black silk pantaloons—

This was terrible.

She was losing hold of convictions she'd held for most of her life. The good thing was that she didn't feel a raging wish to crawl into Thaddeus's lap, which boded well for their future married life, should it come about.

He smiled, eyes warm, and fleetingly touched her cheek. "If there was a billiard table in the inn, I would love to have a match with you."

On her other side, Jeremy growled something, too low for Thaddeus to have heard, thank goodness.

The evening was growing all too confusing. "Your Grace, Aunt Knowe, I believe I shall retire to bed, if you will excuse me."

After bidding everyone good night, Betsy headed toward the door.

"I plan to have a debate with the marquess about his mistaken approach to grain policy," her aunt declared behind her, which roused a groan from Jeremy's father. "Thaddeus will surely support my point of view. I'm certain that you're more liberal than your hidebound father."

As Betsy neared the door, Jeremy reached over her to open it.

"You mustn't accompany me. This isn't proper," she whispered.

"I don't care to have you walking about the inn at night by yourself," Jeremy said. "Thaddeus's eyes are drilling into my back; what a dog in the manger."

"Just what do you mean by that?" Betsy glared

at him. "He doesn't want me, but he doesn't want you to have me either? In your conception, I am no more than a feeding trough?"

"Exactly," he said, holding the door for her.

"If I were a manger," she said haughtily, "I believe that Thaddeus would—" Too late she realized the error in going anywhere near "lie."

Jeremy chuckled.

She swept past him and started toward the stairs.

"A manger by any other name," he said behind her. "A refuge from the storm, a calm center in a whirling world, a funny, passionate woman who is lethal in a billiard game."

Despite herself, she walked slower.

"Beloved and loving, of course."

She turned around. The paneled hallway had very high ceilings, and lamps had been affixed to the walls just above her head. The shadows thrown by light falling down made Jeremy's face look like a judge's.

"That's why Thaddeus wants to marry you," he finished.

"You have been making a list of pros and cons," she said. "As part of your thoughts regarding marriage?"

He nodded.

"Might I know the cons?"

"Eccentric. Often likely to triumph at billiards, which might lead to ulcers."

His eyes were glinting at her with that special look he seemed to reserve for her: mischief, wickedness, a hint of desire . . . No, a lot of desire. Mixed with self-reproach, as if he found it beneath him to desire her.

"Prone to falsehood," he added.

"I am not!"

"You are. You create a face and a smile and put it on like a suit of armor. Who wants to marry a suit of armor? Your entire life is like a *bal masqué*."

"It isn't," Betsy protested.

He just kept going, relentless. "Will you teach your children to plaster fake smiles on their faces and pipe inanities in a twittering voice? Will they be driven to collect proposals as if gentlemen were daisies in an invisible, wilting chain of flowers?"

Betsy stood in that corridor feeling sick. What could she possibly say to that? "You are unkind," she managed.

"I like the real you: witty, charming, and intelligent. Sensual and deeply lovable. You are a delight, Bess. A true delight. If I were the marrying kind, I'd be lining up in the queue, bumping Thaddeus out of the way in a rush to win your hand."

"Charming," Betsy said. Her mind was rushing this way and that. Fury burned up her spine, and angry words trembled on her lips about his behavior.

"Have you anything further to add?" she asked. "I don't want to cut you short." She managed her voice perfectly: It was as calm as if he were remarking on the weather.

His eyes searched hers. "Bess—"

She could accept his opinion of her. She refused to argue with it, because he was right, though he didn't understand her motives. She made a sudden jerky motion. "Don't."

"You could have laughed at me, the way you always do."

"I laugh when you squabble with me or make fun of my halo. You aren't making fun." Hurt, angry words were bubbling up in her chest. What good would it do to say, *I thought we were friends.*

Or particularly, *I thought you were courting me.*

Because she had. In some small part of her heart she had begun to nurture affection for a foul-tempered wreck of a man.

"Good night," she said, turning on her heel and walking away. What a fool she was. There could be nothing worse than being tied to a cruel man. She didn't deserve his rebuke. She hadn't been unkind. She had merely tried to befriend him.

She walked faster, knowing he was following. The corridor widened into a flight of stairs that curved to the right and around an indoor balcony. She went up those steps as quickly as she could without running.

She made it halfway around the balcony, the door to her bedchamber in view, when Jeremy caught her arm.

"No," she spat, her voice nearly cracking despite herself.

"Talk to me. Please."

Betsy took a deep breath and faced him. "I gather that you are troubled by my response to your summary of my character. You needn't be.

My behavior in polite society has been crafted since the age of fourteen; I am as aware as you are that I create a 'face' when I'm in public."

"My room is just here. Please talk to me for a moment."

"In your *room*?" That question destroyed any claim she had to control. "I think not. In fact, I think that you have lost your mind. Everything you said to me was true. You are a guest in my father's house, and yet you ask me to visit your bedchamber? I do you the courtesy of believing that you are not trying to destroy my reputation or compromise me. After all, you are not a marrying man."

"I hurt you. I'm sorry."

As far as Betsy was concerned, no explanations were necessary. An apology would do little, and in any case, his voice was not particularly apologetic. There was a note of command there, as if the Jeremy who had ruled the battlefield was making an appearance.

"I accept your apology." With a tug she freed her arm and walked to her chamber, opened the door, and escaped without looking back.

# Chapter Fourteen

*J*eremy stood in the corridor feeling gutted. He had grown accustomed to trading barbed comments with Betsy. With Bess. They had squabbled and disagreed, and her fire kept him tied to the room and not back on a smoke-filled battleground.

Then he had turned sparring into an unkind assault, from pure jealousy.

She had been his friend and he'd watched her turn white. Unkind? He was more than unkind.

He had been cruel.

For one reason. For one damned reason. Because she gave Thaddeus a smile, and because Thaddeus touched her on the cheek.

For that, Jeremy excoriated her behavior, even though he was beginning to understand her pretend smile and the way she collected proposals the way strangers collected Wilde prints.

He entered his room but couldn't settle. It was one thing to be a failure on the battlefield. Betsy was right: Any man who went to war was a failure, if he lost even one man, one companion. It made him feel better, somehow, to acknowledge it.

She'd made him feel better, and to repay her, he'd made her feel horrible. He was an unforgivable lout.

The raging hypocrisy of his chiding anyone— for *anything*—wasn't lost on him either. Betsy hurt no one with her masquerade. Thaddeus looked at her with genuine affection and admiration. Damn it. And he was a good man. The best.

Better by far than Jeremy with his blackened soul.

He walked restlessly from one end of the room to the other. Snow was still coming down outside, so he stood at the window watching the way drifts bunched up in the corners of the courtyard, looking deceptively soft and warm.

His eyes fell on a bundle he'd found earlier. Lady Knowe must have ordered it brought from Lindow. Seeing it held male clothing, a groom had delivered it to his room, but in fact the clothes inside were too small: boy's clothing for a girl with too much exuberance to be confined to skirts, no matter how wide. He could go along the corridor and knock on Betsy's door. It was only two down from his; he'd noted her chamber, of course.

No.

Likely Betsy's maid was in her room, helping her disrobe.

He wrenched his mind away from that vision because it wasn't his to think about.

His room faced the front of the inn, as did Betsy's. Perhaps she was staring out the window as well. His hands curled into fists at the idea she might be crying.

Her pointed comment about his being a guest at the castle was a signal. He could leave in the morning in grand style, in his father's carriage. No one would guess that he was fleeing the scene of a crime.

He discovered that he was grinding his teeth when his jaw started aching.

Snow was drifting higher against the stone walls in the courtyard. The iron-wrought railings outside his window were decorated with ornate metal spears, each of which held its own snowy nightcap, like a line of thin, old men.

Iron-wrought railings.

A balcony . . .

He brought back an image of the inn. A narrow balcony ran along the front of the house and curved around both sides.

Looking out the window, the balcony seemed wide enough. A man could walk to the left, pass one window, stop at the next.

He waited until he hadn't heard any footsteps for a good half hour. Then he opened his French window and stepped into snow that mounded over his ankle. It was coming down in an irresolute fashion, appearing from the blackness to float through the circle of light cast at his back.

He walked past the room next to his. It was lit from within, the curtains well-drawn against the cold. With a start, he realized that his father was inside, belting out "Amazing Grace," which meant he was in the bathtub. The marquess always sang in the bath.

The sound brought him back to the family pew at Thurrock, standing beside his father as a little boy, listening to his deep voice growl out lyrics.

*"I once was lost but now am found,"* his father sang now. *"Was blind but now I see."*

Jeremy kept walking, cold biting at the back of his neck. The next window was Betsy's. Only a muted glow came from the split in the curtains. With luck she was tucked in bed, her maid . . .

What would he say if her maid came to the window? He could hand her the bundle and walk silently back to his room. Presumably her lady's maid wouldn't destroy her mistress's reputation by telling others that a man had visited the room.

Before he changed his mind, he put his palm on the left-hand glass and pushed. Sure enough, the glass swung open gently, stopped by thick velvet.

He heard a muffled exclamation, so he stayed where he was on the balcony, snow building up on his shoulders and freezing his fingers.

The drape pulled back with a rattle of ironmongery and—

There she was.

God, she was beautiful. The fire burning in the hearth bathed her in golden light. Her hair was down, tumbling over one shoulder. Her dark eyebrows stood out in her face; her eyes were shadowed but, thank God, showed no signs of being swollen with tears.

He cleared his throat. "It's me."

"I can't imagine that you somehow feel that your disquisition on my character gave you entry to my bedchamber."

There was just a hint of a rasp in her throat. Jeremy's gut clenched involuntarily. If he'd reduced her to tears, he would leave in the morning and never see her again.

"May I come in?" He held up the snowy bundle. "To deliver breeches."

Her eyes flicked down and then back to his face. "I don't think so." She stepped backward.

"I was wrong," he said. "I was jealous because Thaddeus caressed your cheek."

She frowned. She apparently hadn't noticed.

"Downstairs," he clarified.

"He touched my face in passing, and you took it as an invitation to piss all over me and my life?"

One side of his mouth rose involuntarily because she was simply so *delightful* when she forgot to be a lady.

"No," she said sharply. "You don't get to feel better. Friends don't speak that way to each other, and I was stupid enough to think we were friends. I won't make that mistake again."

"You *are* my friend," he said.

"I may have been your friend, but you were not mine."

He was silenced.

She reached out and took the bundle.

"I'm learning," he said, hearing his hoarseness. "I won't do it again. Ever. I don't have other friends like you and I—I reacted badly. I didn't mean to hurt you."

"You do have friends. My brother North among them. Parth, who brought you to the castle, if you remember. Thaddeus. My aunt. Moreover, your father, who would love to be your friend and is worth your regard."

"I was trying to talk myself into marrying you."

"Better and better," she said, biting off the words. "If you'll forgive me, Lord Jeremy, it's very cold standing before an open window."

"I want to marry you."

Betsy froze.

The light from the fire behind her cast rosy light on Jeremy's face. If he had acted like a judge below, in the corridor, now he seemed a boy with true regret in his eyes.

"You want to marry me," she said slowly. "Why?"

Snow had fallen on his shoulders. "Love, I suppose. I'm not certain how to recognize it. But I can't marry you, Bess. I can't."

"Do you have a mad wife hidden in the attic?" Her heart pounded erratically.

"No," he said, a minute too late.

"A sane wife, then?"

"No."

Despite herself, a sigh eased from her mouth.

"I'm the madman. I should probably be in an attic. I'll end up there." He hunched his shoulders.

She took a step back, and another.

"You'd better come in."

# Chapter Fifteen

$\mathcal{H}$er bedchamber suddenly shrank to the size of a mousehole, all because of a large man, dripping melting snow, holding his hands out to the fire.

"Why didn't you put on a coat and gloves? Or a hat?"

"I couldn't call down for my coat or they'd wonder where I was going. As it was, I had to wait for people to stop climbing those bloody stairs. Every fifteen minutes, some other fool would set the steps creaking again."

His broad shoulders were rigid and not because he was shivering. Apparently he was too manly to shiver, even though she felt like an icicle after a brief conversation at the window.

Taking up a blanket from the end of her bed, she marched over and pushed it at him. Then she pulled the eiderdown off, wrapped it around herself, and sat down by the fire, putting out one bare foot to make her chair rock before she tucked her legs under the coverlet.

And waited.

Meanwhile he looked at the fire, grim as could be, jaw set, and a vein ticking in his forehead.

"Madness," she reminded him. "Yours, as opposed to the madmen in my family, or even the madwoman who fell in love with Alaric, or Diana's mother, who shot you and will likely spend her life in the sanitarium."

He raised his head and the edge of his mouth eased. "You're trying to tell me that I'm only one amongst a crowd of madmen in Cheshire?"

"It could be the bog," Betsy said. "Evil contagion caused by peat moss."

"I caught mine in the American colonies."

"On the battlefield, I expect," Betsy said, curling her toes. She considered informing him that she'd decided not to marry either of them but rethought it. Jeremy ought to make this uncomfortable apology. Why should she let him off the hook?

"All jesting aside, Parth actually found me in Bedlam after that Vauxhall incident." His voice echoed queerly in the room.

Betsy gasped before she could stop herself. "What were you doing there?"

"Lying about in a straitjacket, as I understand it. Drugged with laudanum. Supposedly incoherent and violent, though I have no memory of it."

Betsy's breath caught in her throat. Even through her shock, she realized that the worst thing she could do would be to dole out lashings of sympathy. He was glaring at the fire as if the flames were responsible for his failure of nerve. Or however he would describe that terrible experience.

"Did you murder anyone?" She put a fair amount of interest in her voice.

"Not so far as I know."

That wasn't the right tack. She tried again. "What brought on the attack?"

"Fireworks. They sounded like cannons, which is all I remember."

"That makes sense," Betsy said. "No Guy Fawkes Day for you. You'll have to limit yourself to a peaceful bonfire in your garden."

That brought his head about, if only so he could scowl at her, rather than the blameless logs. "I lost consciousness, Bess. Fell over like a log. More than a day passed before Parth's household could rouse me."

She nodded. Inside she was horrified and afraid for him, but she was used to playing a role. "How did they wake you up?"

His mouth twitched.

"Come on, then," she said. "Now you have the dramatic announcement out of the way, let's have it."

"Sausages," he said with a wry smile.

He smiled so infrequently that the gesture struck Betsy like a blow. She had to stop herself from throwing herself at him like a maiden encountering the prince in a bad play.

"Sausages," she echoed.

"Fried them up and stuck them under my nose and I awoke," he confirmed.

Betsy couldn't help giggling at the look on his face. "It could have been worse."

"It could have been better," Jeremy countered, rocking back on his toes and shoving his hands into his pockets.

"True. Whisky has a manly air. On the other hand, *sal volatile* is given to fainting maidens. Legend has it that my great-aunt Genevieve was so horrified by her wedding night that she fell into a faint and was only roused by having a chamber pot poured over her head by her indignant groom."

When she saw the laughter in his eyes, she added: "My great-uncle always insisted that it was an accident."

"Do you mind if I take off my coat? It's cold and wet. I promise that it's not a first step to an undressing in your chamber."

"You may."

His white shirt was sodden as well and clung to the dips and valleys of his chest. If they married, she would have the right to sit here nightly and watch him undress.

Except she wouldn't, because if they were married, she would pull that shirt off his head and rub him down in the warmth of the fire and then pepper his chest with kisses—

"It would help if you didn't look at me with that expression," he said.

Betsy felt red flood her cheeks. "What expression?" It would be awful if everyone could tell when she was overcome by desire. She had to learn how to disguise it.

He picked up his blanket, wrapped it back around his shoulders, and sat down in the chair beside her. Apparently, he refused to answer idiotic questions, because he stretched out his legs and contemplated his sopping breeches.

Betsy watched just long enough to register his muscled thighs and then looked away.

"I saw that," Jeremy said.

"You should return to your chamber," Betsy said. "Now that you've told me your dark secret. Unless there's more to it?"

"Isn't that enough?"

"Madness, et al? I am a Wilde. A good swath of the country considers us mad, and we've had many a madman in and about the house. You are a bad-tempered version but at least you aren't writing a play."

"How do you know?"

Betsy rolled her eyes. "In that case, good luck with it. Alaric's madwoman made pots of money with *Wilde in Love*."

"I have no need for money," Jeremy said.

"Do you feel the need to elaborate on your madness? Do you sleepwalk like Lady Macbeth?"

"No."

"Eat in your sleep? We had a footman who ate most of a cake that had been reserved for the queen's visit."

"No."

Betsy's heart was aching for him, but she was determined to show him no pity. She felt instinctively that he would hate her for it. He was the sort of man who spent his life solving problems.

She'd bet that from the age of five he was toddling around after his father, being as competent as a five-year-old could be.

Until he found himself on that beastly battlefield.

"I can't say much more than that," he said. "I didn't catch lice in Bedlam, which Parth thought was very good luck. Apparently, the sleeping quarters were not salubrious, though I can't remember the hospital at all."

"Your lack of memory suggests they gave you opium," Betsy said. "If you fall into a stupor again, no one should bother with a hospital. Your man can tether you to a tree in the shade and ply you with sausages."

She'd managed to shock him into a better mood. "It's a good thing I decided not to marry you, isn't it?" he said musingly. "Tether me to a tree like an unruly puppy?"

"I'll just remind you," she said loftily, "that marriage to me would only follow my decision to accept your hand."

"I was saving you the trouble of making a decision by telling you about Bedlam."

"Oh, that." She waved her hand. Was she overdoing it? No, she didn't think she was. When Jeremy first came to Lindow, a few months ago, he was drawn and white. Now his eyes were shadowed but his skin was healthy, thanks to spending most of the day in the stables.

"Yes, that."

"You shouldn't think of a stint in Bedlam as

putting you out of the sweepstakes for marriage. I say that in the spirit of friendship, mind you, not as one who would want to string your proposal onto my daisy chain."

Silence.

Then: "I'm sorry I was so brutal."

"So you said."

"I was a shite to say any of it."

"You weren't incorrect," Betsy said, throwing him a bone.

"I like you as you are, as you truly are. You're not very sweet, thank God. No, don't glare at me. That's a good thing. Sweet people skim along the surface of life. For example, you tell them you've been in Bedlam, and they cluck like hens."

"Whom have you told?" Betsy asked.

"You."

"Not your father?"

"No."

"You can't tell me that Parth clucked, when he found you in the asylum. Parth would *never* cluck."

"After I woke up, he threw me in a carriage and blackmailed me into coming to Lindow so he could chase that woman of his."

"You see? He didn't leave you alone, but he didn't fuss over you."

"Your aunt pried it out of me."

"Aunt Knowe is not a clucker either."

"She fusses, though." He reached out his hand.

Betsy looked at it thoughtfully. A man like Jeremy never asked for help. People had to intrude on his life, pouring tea down his throat and tossing him into carriages. Blackmailing him from pure love.

Yet here he was, holding out his hand.

She took her hand out of the cozy warmth of her eiderdown and reached toward him. His palm and fingers were callused from working with horses.

All she was doing was comforting him, the way any kind person would do. And she *was* kind, no matter what he said, and "kind" was almost the same as "sweet."

After staring into the fire and parsing the two words, she felt a prickling awareness and discovered that he was staring at her.

"Is there a smut on my nose?" she asked.

"I give you fair warning: I'm about to be brutally honest."

"I've had enough of your type of honesty for one day," she said, pulling away her hand. "Why don't you go back out in the snow instead?"

"I've never desired a woman the way I desire you. It's like being in the teeth of a damned inferno."

Betsy found herself smiling. "That's frightfully improper, and a mixed metaphor as well."

"You sound very pleased."

"Oh, I am. I like to win, and if you remember, Lady Tallow made a play for your attentions, if not affections."

"Are you tempted to marry me and take me off the market?"

Betsy snorted. "You just announced that you

refuse to propose. And frankly, you're not such a prize that I'd go out of my way. Lying about in the billiard room, pretending to be drunk and sliding under tables from pure boredom, saying fantastically unkind truths due to a whiff of jealousy. Throwing tea around the breakfast room. Now *there's* a man I want to spend my life with!"

He laughed. "You're not including Bedlam in the list?"

"Bedlam? No. It's the daily encounters that make marriage intolerable, from what I've seen. You're unlikely to go insensible again, but if you did, I'd stow you in that nice sanitarium where Diana's murderous mother lives."

"So she could shoot me again, thereby making you a merry widow?"

She grinned at him. "Exactly. There are women who are cut out to be widows, you know. I wouldn't have to worry about—" She stopped.

"About what?"

"My reputation," she answered. "Widows are expected to be lascivious and make their way through bevies of men. No one excludes them from society for it. They create scandal after scandal with anyone from a cannibal king to a pirate, and people throw dinner invitations at their feet."

"Would that make you happy? The pirate king? I'll leave the cannibal king out of it because one has to think that a dinner invitation from him might not be entirely desirable."

She giggled at that, and then realized that he had pushed over his chair so that it was just next to hers, which allowed him to reach out, scoop her up, and plop her onto his lap.

"What the bloody hell!" she cried, exploding to her feet, wheeling about, hands on her hips. "I allowed you into my chamber with the understanding that you wouldn't infringe on my person!"

Jeremy stood, eyes locked on hers. "I'm sorry, Bess."

"Don't call me Bess!" Betsy snapped. "No one says cruel things to someone they—they treasure."

"Where in God's name did you get this idea of marital bliss?" he asked. "Married people say all sorts of things to each other. It's the nature of the beast. Your spouse is the one person who *can* be honest with you and still be loved."

"You have a strange idea of marriage," Betsy said, trying to make her voice chilly, and not quite succeeding. His eyes made it hard to be lofty. They were deep, dark, and whatever that expression was, she couldn't stop drinking it in.

She hadn't known him before he went to war, but presumably he had been more courtly. Now he was rough around the edges, untamed. He looked like a man who would enter a woman's bedchamber and end up with her on his lap.

"More to the point," Betsy said, reeling her imagination back to its proper confines, "we are not married, and we never will be. Out," she said, keeping it short. "Now."

"One kiss. Please."

"No." And then, "Why would I kiss you again? It wasn't something worth repeating."

"To me, it was."

Ugh. Her whole body responded to his expression. And his truthfulness. But she didn't like his brand of honesty. Did she?

She could jerk her head toward the window and he would leave. She knew that in every part of her being. Even if she lost her head and followed her most reckless impulses . . . she could trust him to stop whenever she wished.

The thought that exploded into her head next was life-changing. If a yellow-haired Prussian came to a country house party hosted by Jeremy . . . she would never leave him. Never.

Perhaps she would have fled marriage with Thaddeus, but never Jeremy.

So she stayed where she was and he took that final step and put his arms around her. By rights he should feel cold and damp, but instead his chest was hot. She eased forward until her breasts flattened against him.

He said something under his breath and his arms tightened. Heat spread through her body, spiraling from every place they touched: his arms on her back, her cheek on his shoulder, her right foot against his boot. His cheek against her hair.

Fire kindled in improper places. She would like him to slide one of his callused hands down to her rump and pull her even closer.

"May I kiss you?" His voice sounded irritable, the tone with which he snarled comments from the corner of the room.

Those eyes that seemed mercilessly unkind were hot and desirous.

For her.

She leaned forward and put her lips on his, because if she was going to throw in her lot with her mother, she might as well go all the way. Their lips brushed softly for a moment and his tongue caressed her bottom lip.

All that lazy fire spilled into open flame. Her body prickled until even the backs of her knees felt hot and weak. She wound her arms around his neck and melted against him until her nipples flattened against his chest. Finally, *finally*, one of the hands on her back slid down and cupped her bottom.

She shivered and nipped his lower lip, which made him growl. She wanted more.

Yet Jeremy didn't seem to follow her inclination to move toward the bed and she didn't have the courage to step in that direction herself. In fact, he pulled away and she swayed toward him before she caught herself.

His eyes were raw with an emotion that went far past her experience of lust. Need, perhaps. Need for *her*.

"Not a good idea?" she asked with a little gasp.

"Not at this moment." His eyes skated down her front and then jerked back to her face.

Betsy looked down too, and found her nipples making little bumps in the soft fabric of her nightdress. She squared her shoulders and gazed back at him.

"There's my Bess," he said, voice rasping.

She had floated through the Season as if it were

a prolonged masquerade, a game in which the prize was a wedding ring. Here, in the middle of the night, facing a man with stubble on his jaw and no coat, with no more apparent similarity to a gentleman than she had to a queen . . .

This was real.

*He* was real.

"Please sit," she said, pointing to the chair by the fire.

One eyebrow arched, but he sat.

"I will sit in your lap," she told him. "We had better not kiss again, though. It seems to go to my head."

"Nothing so depraved," he promised, seating himself. Betsy sank onto his lap, his arms came around her, and her head settled against his chest. It felt like the end of a book, the part of a marriage that authors leave to the reader's imagination: daily affection and sweetness, a layer of desire never alluded to on the page.

"So you're my friend again, even though I was an ass?" he asked.

"If you find yourself in the grip of another temper, you must keep it to yourself."

Jeremy rested his chin on her head. "He touched you." There wasn't an ounce of apology in his voice.

"What will you do if I marry him?" she inquired.

"Move to Italy, I suspect. Or Russia, as that's even further away."

He didn't sound as if he was jesting, and his

arms tightened possessively. Betsy felt a stab of such pure joy that she didn't bother searching for a response, just snuggled closer.

"The Season is a game," she said later, drowsily. "My father says I allow men to hang about me like horseflies at the trough."

"I shouldn't have been harsh."

"Before I debuted, everyone viewed me as a version of my mother, and now they don't. They think women can be *bred* for chastity and obedience."

"You are a Wilde, and a magnificent example of the breed."

Betsy puzzled over that and decided it was a compliment. Her eyes kept closing because the thump of his heart against her ear was mesmerizing. She almost missed what he said next.

"You're the best of the Wildes," he murmured. "The most loyal and true, a brilliant player at billiards and life."

Did he really say that?

Betsy woke up when her maid pulled the curtains open the next morning. She was tucked in bed, alone.

"We won't be returning to Lindow today," Winnie said. "There's more snow on the way." She opened the door and ushered in a procession of Lindow grooms carrying buckets of hot water. Lady Knowe would never allow strange servants into an inn bedchamber when one of the family was in bed. It was too easy for strangers to be bribed.

Betsy lay watching and trying to think through a fog of happiness. Just at the moment, she didn't care about wearing breeches to the auction, or playing billiards in a men's club. She was contemplating a far more scandalous move, from the view of polite society: rejecting a future duke in favor of a war-damaged man with a lesser title.

She was out of the bath and dressed by the time Winnie discovered Jeremy's bundle tucked behind a chair. "What on earth is this?" her maid asked.

"Oh, that'll be my breeches," Betsy said airily. "There's an auction in Wilmslow this afternoon, and I plan to wear boy's clothing."

"Lady Boadicea!" Winnie cried—using Betsy's full name as a measure of her distress—"after all the work we've done to make you into a proper duchess! With the future duke and his mother in the inn. You mustn't, you really mustn't!"

"The duchess plans to wear men's clothing as well, if they can be made to fit in time. Her great-aunt tried to escape a marriage by fleeing in breeches. Think of it like a fancy dress party."

"How very peculiar," Winnie observed. "I have no wish to wear men's clothing." She took a pair of green velvet breeches from the bundle. "I suppose if Her Grace . . . I can't imagine her in men's clothing!"

"My Aunt Knowe will wear breeches as well."

"I wouldn't want to put on nasty old breeches." Winnie shook out the matching coat. "I think it will fit you, but this costume is wretchedly out-of-date."

"There's a portrait of my brother Alaric wearing it in one of the east wing bedchambers. I think he was around twelve. He threatened to slice the painting to ribbons and feed it to the goats, so it had to be stowed in a guest room."

"He's a wild one," Winnie sighed. Like the rest of the nation, she had succumbed to Alaric's books depicting his adventures. No one had cried harder when *Wilde in Love* was performed at the castle and Alaric's supposed fiancée was eaten by cannibals.

"I suppose if I steam these carefully, I can make them look respectable." And with that she tucked them under her arm and set off for the nether depths of the inn.

Aunt Knowe poked her head in the door shortly afterward. "Breakfast, Betsy."

"Mayn't I stay here and read?" Betsy was seated with her toes close to a burning log, reading a rather bawdy play she found on the mantelpiece.

"You, my dear, are wearing a pink morning gown, the better to dazzle Emily. Why waste it?"

Betsy looked down, disconcerted. She hadn't registered that Winnie had dressed her to suit the duchess's taste. "I don't feel dazzling." She inched her feet a little closer to the fire. "I feel like staying here until it's time to leave for the auction."

"Emily has gone to church, but she will be back soon. Given that she's a lackadaisical church-goer at best, I think she means to pray that the three of us be forgiven for our breeches-begotten sins. You must come to breakfast and thank her. She's so pleased that you are both perfectly behaved and wild, not with an E."

Betsy sighed.

"You've made her happier than she's been in years. From Emily's point of view, the curtain is rising on a new duchess who promises to perform the role with verve. She can't wait to play a supporting role."

"She understands my so-called perfection is a performance?"

Aunt Knowe waggled her eyebrows. "Everyone does. Most of polite society is agog, waiting to see you throw off the shackles of propriety and arise from the ashes like a phoenix. That would be the female half, as the men are too foolish to discern that you are no demure maiden."

"You mean those ladies are waiting for a Prussian to cross my path," Betsy pointed out. The prediction of her disgrace still stung, but it had lost the power it wielded when she was fourteen.

"You're a Wilde, my dear. Your mother was not a Wilde. Those are the only two facts that matter: My friends are intrigued by the fact that one of the Wildes appears to be a model of propriety."

"You're wrong," Betsy said with conviction. "They're waiting to see me make a fool of myself over a yellow-haired man."

A tremendous frown gathered Aunt Knowe's forehead into pleats. "Are you jesting, Boadicea?"

"No," Betsy said. "I assure you, Aunt Knowe, I learned that lesson on the very first day I went to school."

Aunt Knowe closed the door and sat down in the chair where Jeremy had seated himself the night before. Not that the fact was relevant.

"My dear," she said, "you're moonstruck. Batty. Mad as a March hare. Put your book aside."

Betsy obeyed, because she was used to obeying her aunt.

"I have wondered why you constructed such a medieval portrait of a lady to perform before polite society," Aunt Knowe said. "I see now that I have been a very bad aunt because I thought you deserved privacy. I considered your perfection a result of nervousness. It seemed unlikely, but one never knows. That wasn't it, was it?"

Betsy shook her head.

"I'm a fool," her aunt muttered.

"The story of my mother and the Prussian was a dragon that had to be slain before I could join society without whispers behind my back."

"You are a *Wilde*, Betsy! You have no need to genuflect before foolish matrons who gossip at the side of ballrooms."

"Because my eyebrows mark me a Wilde?"

"Among other things," Aunt Knowe said. "No one could possibly think that you were illegitimate."

"My legitimacy doesn't alter the fact that my mother ran away with a man and left her children."

"Yvette's flight doesn't mean that her daughter must collect proposals the way a boy collects butterflies. Just sticking in a pin and turning the page."

"School was difficult—"

"You think I don't know that?" Aunt Knowe's cheeks had become as red as her hair. "I heard about the unpleasant gossip; the headmistress warned us. But I never thought you'd pay attention to that rubbish! You are a duke's daughter."

"Yes, but—" Betsy began.

"Just look at Joan," Aunt Knowe said, talking right over her. "She can't wait to debut—and she has the Prussian's hair! Why on earth would you think that jealous gossip can define a Wilde? Rubbish!"

"It's not rubbish," Betsy said, fumbling to defend herself. "Horses inherit characteristics, so why not people?"

"Characteristics!" Aunt Knowe waved her hands in the air. "Rubbish! Double rubbish! Your mother fell in love. Have you ever asked your father about their marriage?"

"It's not my business."

"It is if you behave like a brainless widgeon on account of it," her aunt retorted. "Your father believed that Yvette would be a good mother to his orphaned sons, but he was wrong."

Betsy nodded. "The matrons believe I'll be overcome by lust and invite a man to my bed, as Yvette did."

"Yvette did nothing remarkable. Just think of your brother Alaric having to flee Russia in order to escape a command visit to the royal bedchamber. Behave like an empress, not like a mouse, Betsy. Although," she added, "if you intend to invite someone to your chamber, you must be prepared to marry him."

"I haven't invited anyone to my room," Betsy said truthfully.

"Because you don't *have* a fiancé," her aunt continued, "and until you have chosen one, no invitations. Marriage is not like a stable, where you might try riding two or three stallions before buying one, so don't you dream of comparing those two men on alternate nights."

"The Empress Catherine does not have to navigate a London ballroom," Betsy said.

Her aunt grinned. "I'll echo Viola: Just be yourself, Betsy. You have nothing to worry about." She rose to her feet. "Come along now; I'm starving."

Betsy came to her feet, thinking hard.

"I can't wait until you are in charge of your own nursery," her aunt said with relish. "I shall visit frequently, once fate gives you the children you deserve."

"Judging by the Duchess of Eversley's stories of Thaddeus, her ducal progeny are far better behaved than those whom you raised," Betsy noted, as they descended the creaking wooden stair.

"Thaddeus's calm might balance out the Wilde blood," her aunt acknowledged. "Or you could choose Jeremy, and end up with mop-headed devils with no manners. Climbing on the furniture. *Peeing* on it."

"That seems unnecessarily judgmental," Betsy said.

"Based on harsh experience," Aunt Knowe said. "Speak of the devil . . ."

Jeremy appeared in the door of the dining room. He bowed and bid them good morning. "The innkeeper has a question about salmon delivered from Lindow, Lady Knowe."

She rolled her eyes. "I should have brought our chef, but Frederic has such a loathing for strange kitchens." With that, she marched off toward the back of the inn.

Jeremy's hand closed around Betsy's wrist and then she was enveloped in clean starched linen and a rough, open-mouthed kiss.

It was like being hit by a gale-force wind: She melted against him, one hand gripping his lapel to hold him close.

A shuffling step from the passageway leading to the kitchens broke them apart like the sides of a clam shell. Betsy's heart was pounding in her chest. Down the corridor to their right, Carper bore a tea tray through a swinging door to the kitchen.

"Bloody hell," Jeremy breathed.

Betsy raised a trembling finger to her lips and took a deep breath. "Was that your morning greeting?"

"I don't offer it to all and sundry," Jeremy said.

Clatter from the kitchen suggested that the footman would emerge again at any moment.

"I was waiting for herring or at least a strong cup of tea, and then you appeared. You're very kissable."

"More appealing than herring?"

"Infinitely. Enthralling, actually, as fish never seems to be."

She drew in a deep breath and met his eyes.

"I don't use the word lightly," he added.

Carper reappeared and came down the corridor, a tray held high on one shoulder. Betsy remained on her side of the corridor and Jeremy on his. With a muttered apology, Carper walked between them into the dining room, his eyes resolutely fixed on the air.

"I smell sausages," Jeremy muttered.

"And Pekoe tea," Betsy countered. "Aunt Knowe must have had it brought from the castle." Neither of them moved until Carper reemerged and walked back down the corridor.

The kitchen door hadn't swung shut before Betsy tumbled into Jeremy's arms. Their mouths met as if they'd kissed every morning for twenty years.

She feverishly absorbed each sensation. He smelled like fresh apples, rather than horse and leather. His shoulders flexed under her fingers and *need* rose in her like a windstorm. She lost her train of thought, but then roused to the caress of a hand on her back that transformed her skin from mere covering to something sensitive and longing.

Another sound down the corridor, and Jeremy put her from him, tweaked the small ruffle on her bodice, adjusted the lace around her left wrist, smiled.

"You'll do," he said. "Gorgeous as you are."

She raised an eyebrow.

"Even more gorgeous with a Wildean eyebrow in the air," he muttered. "Time for sausages. I don't fancy your aunt catching us dallying in the corridor."

His eyes had that burning look she'd never seen

him direct to anyone else. Usually he viewed the world with a sardonic air.

Betsy walked into the dining room feeling dizzily happy. Jeremy put herring on her plate. She hated fish in the morning, but she ate a bite of one. He poured tea and she nodded when he asked about milk, although she never had milk, especially with Pekoe tea.

They talked and didn't kiss, although his eyes kept catching on her lips and she kept shifting in her chair, small frustrated movements, because her body felt as wound up as a top.

After a while, Aunt Knowe marched in the door and checked her step when she saw the two of them sitting there alone, then launched into the innkeeper's appalling ignorance of baked salmon.

Betsy felt keenly aware of her heartbeat galloping along. She looked down at her plate, thinking about all the moments and hours when one's heart beats without notice, and then after a few kisses, it felt like an unbroken horse that couldn't be ignored.

Aunt Knowe wound down her discourse on the proper care and cooking of salmon—wasted on two people who didn't say a word in response. "The innkeeper tells me that the auction will happen today, snow or no snow."

"What time will it take place?" Jeremy asked.

"It begins in a couple of hours," Aunt Knowe replied. "Betsy, was your costume delivered to you?"

"Yes, it was," Betsy said, not daring to look at Jeremy.

"I sent for a costume of my brother's," her aunt said. "I expect it will fit very well. Thankfully, neither of us has fattened with age."

"Three ladies in breeches will attend this auction?" Jeremy asked.

"That's the size of it," Aunt Knowe said, finishing off a piece of buttered toast. "I have no fear for myself. I look uncannily like my brother and I could impersonate the duke in a pinch. I might even introduce myself as him. I haven't been sufficiently groveled to in my life. This is the chance to make up for lost time."

"I feel the same!" Betsy exclaimed. "I plan to make up for lost time wearing a corset."

Jeremy choked back a laugh.

Aunt Knowe patted his hand. "No jesting, my dear. Until you've experienced whalebones, you must bite your tongue. That's true of you as well, Betsy, when we enter the auction house. Your voice is too high, even for a boy. You can bid with a wave of your catalogue."

"Certainly," Betsy said, excitement bubbling in her stomach.

"Emily's voice is even higher than yours," Aunt Knowe continued. "What's more, you've spent an entire Season practicing maidenly tranquility, but she was married out of the schoolroom, so silence will be a trial for her."

"Maidenly tranquility," Jeremy said, his eyes glinting with laughter. "I gather I should have spent more time in the ballroom this last Season.

You didn't bother with that trait in the billiard room."

"You were silent enough for both of us," Betsy retorted. "Sitting in the corner, brooding over your whisky, pretending to be inebriated."

"Better than pretending to be maidenly?" He raised a devilish eyebrow. "Hmmm."

"Hush, both of you," Aunt Knowe ordered. "Back to my point, Betsy. You must keep your mouth shut or risk discovery."

"Will there be dire consequences if we are caught?" she asked.

Her aunt was busily buttering her third piece of toast. "Emily and I will be with you. If we're all in fancy dress, the event turns from a scandal to a lark."

"In that case, *you* should wear a gown!" Betsy told Jeremy. "Perhaps one of yours would fit him, Aunt Knowe." Two appalled looks greeted this idea.

"Absolutely not," Aunt Knowe cried. "His chest is twice the breadth of mine, Betsy. He'd ruin my bodice!"

Jeremy appeared to be struck dumb with horror.

"I think Jeremy would make a delectable lady," Betsy said, giggling. "Yes, his chest is somewhat hairy—"

"I do *not* want to know how you are aware of that fact!" Aunt Knowe barked.

"He changed shirts in the stables," Betsy said, ignoring Jeremy's intrigued response to her comment.

"I believe it is likely that our escapade will

result in more prints," her aunt said. "If you will forgive my presumption, Jeremy, I have a strong feeling that Mr. Bisset-Caron will dine out on the story for weeks."

Jeremy's eyes darkened. "He'll do nothing of the sort."

The duchess marched into the room, her cheeks bright red from cold.

"We've been to St. Bartholomew's," Her Grace announced. "The butcher and baker are open no matter the snow, and the auction opens in two hours!"

Thaddeus followed her into the room, his brows knit. "There's no sign of a footman," he said testily. "Unless I burdened my mother's maid, I had no one to take my coat." He took off his snowy caped greatcoat and slung it over the chair, put his hat and gloves on a side table, and leaned his cane against the wall.

Apparently he didn't care to eat in the vicinity of his outerwear, and he was visibly cross as the dickens. Though to be fair, he must have risen at six to escort his mother to church.

With that in mind, Betsy gave him a warm smile and handed him a platter of coddled eggs.

After eggs, toast, herring, and sausage had been consumed, the duchess let out a crow of excitement. "My goodness, I clean forgot! We picked up the auction catalogue." She turned to Thaddeus. "Where has it gone to?"

He rose and took a rolled sheaf of paper from his greatcoat pocket.

The duchess flattened it on the table, putting a teacup on one corner and a sugar bowl on the other.

*"Presenting a very extensive and valuable assemblage of drawings of all schools, and several specimens of the most valuable and rare works of the master of the miniature, Samuel Finney.* I shall bid upon a miniature," she announced.

"We were all painted by Finney a few years ago," Aunt Knowe said idly. "Dear me, I wonder what happened to them. Small things are so hard to keep track of, don't you think? In fact, I have been painted by him several times. I do like miniatures."

"If your likeness is being auctioned, we shan't let you go to a stranger's home," Betsy promised.

"I thought miniatures were primarily exchanged between lovers," Her Grace observed, twinkling at her old friend.

Aunt Knowe waved her fork at the duchess. "Fiddlesticks! I am a pattern card of decorum, as you well know."

Just when the tea had gone quite cold, the innkeeper appeared with a fresh pot and a message. The marquess never ate before noon, and Mr. Bisset-Caron would spend the day in bed.

"That will make the escapade easier, though I'm certain Bisset-Caron'll hear of it from his manservant," Aunt Knowe declared.

Thaddeus and Jeremy exchanged a glance that suggested Grégoire would risk his head if he gossiped.

To Betsy, Jeremy looked like a man ready to support her in wearing breeches, a man with a burden on his soul, with too many lines at the corners of his eyes.

He looked as if he were hers.

# Chapter Sixteen

$\mathcal{B}$etsy's breeches were tight over her bottom, and the stockings itched. The shirt was so long that it hung to her knees and made it hard to stuff into her breeches.

"Hopefully no one will pay much attention," her maid said, looking her up and down.

Betsy turned to the mirror. Her hair was braided, ready for a small wig that sat waiting. The wool stockings made her legs thicker, as if they might be a boy's. She peered over her shoulder at her bottom. "I never knew my arse was so round. And I think of my bosom as small." The shirt was tucked in but the buttons on her waistcoat gaped at the top.

"Your bosom is not small," Winnie stated. "I wound the muslin as tightly as I could."

"Your profile is not manly," Winnie observed, after Betsy put on the velvet coat.

Betsy turned to the side. Her chest curved and her bottom curved. "I have a much better figure than I thought," she said wonderingly, running her hands down her front.

"The problem is that no boy has that figure," Winnie said.

"I will be wearing a greatcoat," Betsy said. "That would cover up the rear, at least."

"I'll have to fetch it myself," Winnie said. "You're not going into the corridor dressed like that. Not with Lord Greywick and Lord Jeremy looking at you the way they do."

"And how is that?"

"As if you're a bone they're scrapping over."

Betsy wrinkled her nose and moved over to the window. Snow was still mounded on top of the stone wall, but the inn yard was mostly clear and she could see carriages tooling slowly up and down the road. A robin was hopping along the top of the stone wall, its feet leaving marks that looked like the scratchings of an ancient civilization.

Three grooms were clearing snow from the courtyard. The one on the right, with his back to her, had dark hair tied in a queue. It gleamed in the chilly sunlight. His shoulders rose and fell, scooping huge amounts of snow onto a shovel and throwing them on a pile to the side.

"Which one of the two do you think I should marry?" she asked Winnie.

"The viscount," Winnie said from behind her back. "He'll be a duke someday. What's more,

Lord Jeremy can be cross as the dickens. Mind you," she added, "his valet talks about him as if he walked on water."

Betsy put a great deal of store by what servants thought of their masters. Two of the grooms trotted away, as if the third had dispatched them.

He straightened and ran the back of his hand over his forehead. His breath puffed white as he wrenched off his greatcoat and tossed it over a hitching post. Then he began shoveling again. She knew those shoulders, even from the rear.

"The household loves Lord Jeremy," Winnie said. "Mind you, the same goes for the viscount. I haven't heard a bad word about him, whereas Lord Jeremy drinks himself into a stupor and slides on the floor. No, there's no question at all about which to marry."

"He is never truly inebriated," Betsy said. The robin was tugging on a twig sticking out from the snow. It tilted its head and tugged, its claws tramping a flat space in the snow.

The shoveler was working so hard that Betsy was amazed his linen shirt didn't split between the shoulders. As he threw snow on the mound she caught sight of his profile.

Nose. Chin. Shoulders.

Jeremy.

Winnie made an exasperated sound. "So says Lady Knowe, but evidence doesn't agree, does it? Lord Jeremy drinks a whole bottle and then falls to the floor. It's not as if he didn't drink the bottle. Plus there was unpleasantness over in the colonies."

Betsy kept watching.

"What are you looking at?" Winnie joined her at the window. "That's a very nice back. I can see why you're ogling the fellow."

"He's not a 'fellow,'" Betsy said.

Was she "ogling"? Yes, she was. She would never have allowed herself to do something so improper a month ago.

Winnie leaned closer to the window. "Lord Jeremy!"

They stood in silent appreciation of the smooth motion with which Jeremy threw huge amounts of snow onto a shoulder-high mound.

"He doesn't suffer from ill effects of inebriation," Winnie admitted.

He was attacking the last patch of snow as if . . .

Well, as if every snowflake were an enemy.

"Something happened over there in the colonies," Winnie said. "Something terrible. There are rumors . . ."

"You mustn't listen to them," Betsy said sharply.

"My point is that a man with darkness in his soul isn't an easy one to tame. Husbands need taming, everyone knows that. You can tell that the viscount would never flaunt a mistress in front of you."

"Neither would Jeremy!"

Winnie snorted. "I've heard stories as you wouldn't believe—"

"About him?"

Down below them, Jeremy had straightened, wiping his forehead with his arm. Betsy's skin prickled.

What would those girls from school say if they knew what she was thinking? Did they ever watch a man doing honest labor and wonder if his sweat tasted salty or sweet?

They would think she was lascivious, and they would be right.

He pulled the strip of leather from his hair and shook it free.

"Lord, but he's a pretty man," Winnie said with a sigh. "His shoulders are much bigger than they seem in a jacket, aren't they? Or perhaps his hips are narrower."

Betsy bit back a remark. He wasn't hers. Any woman could admire him. The snow was casting bright light, making Jeremy's sculpted features stand out clearly. In the dark of the billiard room, they looked as if they were chiseled in harsh lines, but in clear morning sunlight, his profile appeared to be drawn by an old master.

"Stop gawping over that man," Winnie said, turning away. "Did you hear what I said?"

Betsy remained glued to the window, irritatingly aware that her breath was quick and shallow, and her toes were curling. Jeremy's shirt was damp with sweat, clinging to his arms and chest. Of course he wouldn't strip it off, the way he had done at the stables. It was freezing outside.

"Yes," she said absentmindedly.

He gave his hair a last shake and stretched. His

shirt pulled free of his breeches, and she caught sight of his ridged stomach, an arrow of hair disappearing into his waistband.

Her breath caught in her throat.

Unheeding, unknowing, he strode toward the inn, out of her sight in a moment.

# Chapter Seventeen

*J*eremy had discovered to his surprise that vigorous exercise in the morning had become a necessity. He had managed a few hours of sleep before he woke at dawn. After fruitlessly staring at the ceiling, he flung himself out of doors and tackled the snow.

It pulled his mind from the battlefield to the present. He wasn't in the colonies. He was in a small inn crowded with eccentric, loud people of whom he was growing inordinately fond. Especially one of them.

The corridor leading from the courtyard seemed dark and musty after squinting at piles of shining snow. There was no mistaking the tall figure of Lady Knowe, waiting for him.

"Betsy has tamped herself down in the last years," she said without introduction. Her eyes searched his face. "Believe it or not, she was the wildest of my children."

"I believe you," Jeremy said.

"Do you?" she demanded.

How was he supposed to answer that? "I gather that you approve of Bess's"—he caught himself—"Betsy's wish to dress herself in men's clothing. Since you are doing the same."

"Are you being judgmental?" Lady Knowe said. "It never suits a man to be judgmental. Life is far too easy for you, so you must reel in your tendency to censure others."

Life was too easy? Jeremy could feel his jaw tightening, but he nodded.

Lady Knowe's eyes softened. "Not in all ways, my dear," she said, more gently. "But believe me, when it comes to relations between men and women, men hold all the cards. Betsy is finally letting herself out of a box she created."

"I see." And he did.

"Emily as well. She has been an excellent duchess and mother, and she's finally doing something that *she* wants to do."

Jeremy nodded.

"You and your father must watch out for Betsy, and Thaddeus will do the same for his mother."

Her Grace emerged from the door behind Lady Knowe, her mouth tight. "Thaddeus and I have come to a mutual decision that he should remain in the inn and not accompany us to the auction."

Lady Knowe muttered something under her breath.

"I am going," the duchess said, her voice rising loud enough so that it could easily be heard in the room behind her. "I shall attend the auc-

tion, with or without him, and frankly, I'd rather
it was without. I can't believe that a son of mine is
such a priggish, self-righteous, prudish—"

"We understand," Lady Knowe said.

"—puff of air!" the duchess finished triumphantly.

Thaddeus appeared in the doorway, his expression imperturbable. "As you will have ascertained, Her Grace and I do not agree."

Lady Knowe shook her head. "Not the time to
play the haughty duke, Thaddeus."

"I merely expressed concern," he said.

"I'd be honored to accompany you, Your Grace,"
Jeremy said.

"No, you will be accompanying Betsy," Lady
Knowe said. "In case the worst happens, I want
someone with her who has a talent for fisticuffs,
which I do not have, obviously. Your father can
accompany the duchess."

Thaddeus's eyes narrowed. "Your concern in-
creases my own, Lady Knowe."

"No reason for you to worry," Lady Knowe
said dismissively. "In the unlikely event that an
auction-goer has the temerity to question Betsy's
costume, I want him thrown out of the establishment." Lady Knowe stared at Jeremy. "Do you
understand?"

"Completely." The very idea of someone ogling
Betsy's arse—other than himself—made his
blood boil.

Thaddeus and his mother had begun to argue
again.

"Go have a bath," Lady Knowe said to Jeremy.

"You're sweaty as a pig and Betsy will be downstairs, in breeches, soon."

Jeremy bounded to the top of the stairs. As he walked by Betsy's door, it sprang open and a slender hand emerged, curled around his wrist, and tugged.

"I need you," Betsy whispered. She tugged again.

He went, because although she didn't know it, he would always come when she needed him. Whenever she needed him.

Inside the chamber, his eyes went straight to Betsy's face. She looked as exquisite as ever: A man's wig suited her. She generally wore towering creations or arranged her own hair into powdered mounds on her head.

A small white wig focused attention on her face, especially her dark, arched eyebrows. She looked unmistakably like a Wilde. She was damned beautiful.

But then, Wilde men were beautiful. It was one of the irritating things about them, to Jeremy's mind. North and Parth didn't even have spots, back in school when every normal boy was a pimply mess.

"Did you get spots as a girl?" he asked.

"What? Jeremy, pay attention!"

He *was* paying attention. Every part of his body longed to look below her chin but he was a gentleman.

"Spots!" she cried. "Who cares? I need help!"

"May I look?" he asked, gesturing toward her lower area.

"Of course, you may look!" Betsy replied, her

voice rising. "No one is going to believe I'm a boy."

His eyes drifted to a decently tied cravat and down to her chest. "How on earth did you flatten yourself to that extent?" he asked, rather stupefied.

"I bound my breasts," she said impatiently. "Besides, a corset—oh, never mind. That's an improper subject of conversation."

"Most of our subjects of conversation are improper," Jeremy pointed out. "Do you normally stuff your corset? Not that I mind in the least."

"You needn't share your opinion of my breasts!" she shot back.

"Your breasts—" But he broke off. A better man than he wouldn't have ogled her from the corner of the billiard room until he could trace her breasts in his mind's eye and almost feel them plump into his hands.

"I like your breasts," he said flatly.

She was wearing a velvet coat buttoned to her cravat. Savoring the moment, he looked lower.

"Well?" she asked, when he remained silent.

"Women should wear breeches all the time," he said, registering the hoarse sound in his voice without embarrassment.

"You oughtn't look at me that way," Betsy said, sounding somewhat delighted.

"What way?" He couldn't pull his eyes from her rounded thighs, though every gentlemanly instinct in his body—luckily, there weren't many—demanded that he gaze somewhere else, say, to the corner of the room.

"Heated," Betsy said.

Jeremy forced his gaze back to her face.

"I am too curvy, especially in profile. If every man looks at me the way you do, I can't go to the auction."

Jeremy took a deep breath and rubbed his hands over his face. "Give me a moment. I'll try to look at you as if you were a stranger."

Betsy turned and started fussing with her wig, pulling it lower on her brow.

From behind . . .

Her coat was quite short—designed for a young boy—with double vents in the back that were not lying flat. Betsy had an arse designed by the gods. Her coat displayed that curve in all its magnificence. Now he knew what she meant.

"That coat won't do," he said, steel in his voice.

"I know!" Betsy cried, whirling about. "I look like a fool, don't I? It's far too short and not fashionable."

"Among other problems."

She turned to the mirror again. "I can't go to the auction."

To his horror, her lower lip trembled before she bit down with even, white teeth. "It was a stupid, stupid idea. Looking like this, I'd be found out. I'd have to live in the country like a hermit because I wouldn't be received anywhere." She took in a shaky breath.

Some part of Jeremy's brain, an ancient, wary part, was instructing him to leave the room. But the part of him that had watched Boadicea Wilde practice with a billiard cue day after day before she sailed into the ballroom to play a role as a demure maiden opened his arms and pulled her against his chest.

Sweaty or no.

"You can do it," he murmured. "We'll do it together."

She snuggled against him, cheek against his chest. "You smell good." Her voice trembled. "I knew inside that it would never work."

Jeremy tightened his arms and rested his chin on her bristly wig. "It *will* work. I am taking you to the auction. I will not fail you."

"What if we are caught? We'd have to marry and then you'd have to become a hermit as well."

"I am already a hermit," Jeremy said, dodging the question of marriage. If and when he proposed to Betsy, it would be at a time of his choosing.

If?

*When* he proposed to Betsy. She had somehow carved a place in his chest and it wasn't going to go away.

"All right," he said, reluctantly stepping back. "I shall pretend that I don't know you."

He raked his eyes up and down, pushing away the scorching wave of desire that followed.

"We should make you plump. It would be better if we could find you a different coat, but if you didn't have such a slim waist, your rear wouldn't be so obvious."

Betsy frowned at him. "My rear?" She peered over her shoulder. "What about my legs?"

Jeremy obediently looked down. Lovely thighs. Plump above, slender below.

"Your ankles are rather small," he said.

"I have boots!" Betsy pulled forward a pair of battered boots and stamped into them. "I used to wear them riding when I was a girl, so I asked Aunt Knowe to have them taken from the attic."

"You wore riding boots as a girl?"

She nodded. "It looks better, doesn't it?" she said, before the mirror again. "My legs don't look as skinny."

No wonder lust was one of the seven deadly sins. It was as strong as the instinct to live.

"No, they don't." His voice could be classified as a groan, if one were so inclined.

A grin crossed Betsy's face. "Jeremy! Regard me as if I were a stranger, remember?"

"Do you have any more of the material you bound your breasts with?"

"Muslin? Yes. My maid brought rolls of bandages."

"Wind them around your waist until you look like a stocky young lad."

Nodding, her hands went to the buttons on her jacket.

"Not until I leave. Where's your sense of self-protection, Bess?"

"I don't need that around you." But she dropped her hands.

It was the work of a moment to wrap his hands around her shoulders, bend his head, and catch her lips in a hard kiss. He was no tamed and toothless alley cat.

She giggled and kissed him back, her tongue lapping his until his mind blurred. And when her teeth closed on his bottom lip? He growled and his hands slid down her back, rounding that luscious bottom.

"You're sweaty," she said, sometime later.

That was when Jeremy realized that Betsy had her hands under his shirt in the back, tracing his muscles. He jerked. "Bloody hell."

Her hands slid from his back. "I watched you pitching snow in the courtyard. I couldn't stop wondering . . ." To his shock, she raised a slender finger and licked it. His tool throbbed, demanding attention. Demanding her.

"Mmmm," she said with throaty pleasure. "Salt."

Jeremy's brain had seized up, and he came up with only one response. "You must say *No* to the duke," he said. "Conclusively."

She licked another finger. "Duke? What duke?"

"Greywick."

"Thaddeus is not a duke, but a viscount."

"*Bess*. He's courting you."

"Oh, all right. I must say no to being a duchess, is that your command?"

"Precisely."

Her hands went back to her coat. "Unless you want to help me transform into a plump school-boy, you'd better leave."

For a moment, time froze. Jeremy's eyes caught on the laughing curve of her red lips, the heat of her gaze as it met his.

"I do want that," he said, his voice a ragged groan.

"Next time?"

Next time. His mind obediently served up an image of Betsy in her breeches, laughing from horseback.

It wasn't until he was sluicing himself in water that he realized he'd imagined her in the courtyard of the house where he grew up.

The house he had sworn never to return to after he'd disgraced his name.

When he first returned from the colonies, he and his father had fought bitterly; he couldn't remember the precise words now. But he had left believing that he was thrown out.

It seemed he had been entirely wrong. Unsurprising. In those first months, anger had raged inside him to the point where he hadn't been able to sleep or think. The only sounds in his ears were the ricochet of bullets, and the moans of dying men.

The anger was still there, the grief and guilt too. But it felt as if a snowstorm had covered those emotions. They were muted by soft mounds of snow. The voices of dying men quieted.

Not silenced . . . but muted.

The voices of his men would always be with him. His experience on the battlefield had changed him forever.

But he could live in this wintry landscape better than the hellfire he had walked through for the last months.

He shook his hair, drops of water flying across the chamber. He felt clean.

# Chapter Eighteen

$\mathcal{W}$hile Betsy waited for Winnie to return with a greatcoat, she stripped off her coat, waist-coat, and the long white shirt underneath. Her breasts were tightly bound. Below them her waist curved in and her hips curved out.

The breeches strained over her hips, and when she turned to peer in the glass over her shoulder, she could actually see the stitches that held the fabric together over the roundest part of her bottom. She'd be lucky not to split them down the middle.

A giggle escaped her at the memory of Jeremy's expression. She put a hand on her rear and slowly ran it over the curve. There *was* something erotic about breeches on a woman.

Her hand slipped off her rear as a frisson of anxiety hit her. This excursion was mad. It was as if she'd pent up her love of mischief and her reckless impulses, and now they were exploding.

It had been an interesting year. She had fulfilled her fourteen-year-old self's ambitions. She had collected enough proposals to prove that her mother's disgrace didn't define her.

Every time she refused a proposal, she wielded a small amount of power over her own future. But the world wasn't ready for the unnerving prospect of women who made their own decisions, society be damned. In fact . . .

She sank into a chair, feeling stunned.

The only woman she knew who had made her own decisions in the face of social disgrace was her mother.

The infamous second duchess. She still didn't agree with Yvette's choice.

But now she understood it.

The one decision Betsy had made in defiance of social rules—going to an auction in breeches—was almost as likely to cause a scandal as Yvette's flight with the Prussian. The scandal wouldn't be on the same scale, but still . . .

It could be that she *did* have an inheritance from her mother. She had looked at Yvette through the lens of Clementine's disgust.

But what if Betsy inherited courage and decisiveness from her mother? What if she inherited a wish to create her own future? A dislike of being penned in by society?

What if she inherited the ability and the wish to astonish people?

What if *that* drove Yvette?

Until that moment Betsy hadn't realized how

taxing it was to dislike one's mother, even an unknown one.

The door swung open and Winnie flew in. "Here I am! Oh, you undressed again."

"We have to make me fatter," Betsy said, standing up and trying to ignore her giddy feeling. Freedom? Was this what freedom felt like?

"Fatter?" Winnie didn't like that. "Why?"

Betsy turned around and pointed to her rear. "It's too obvious."

"I suppose I see your bottom every day, but I don't think about it," Winnie said, taking the bundle of muslin strips Betsy handed her.

"If I'm rounder all over, it won't be so obvious."

"Hopefully that's true." Winnie began to wrap Betsy like a mummy from the British Museum. "Straining over the belly means that straining over the bottom won't matter."

"I'm filling in back and front," Betsy said, a moment later. "That's good enough." When she buttoned up the last button, she turned to face the glass and they both broke out laughing.

"You look like a stuffed goose, ready for Christmas!"

"More like a goose egg," Betsy said, giggling. "I'm so round in the middle!"

"No one will think of you as a woman," Winnie said.

"More like a pillow out for an excursion," Betsy said, pulling down the hem of her coat.

"Time to go!" Aunt Knowe bellowed from the bottom of the stairs.

"It's a good thing there aren't other guests in the inn," Betsy said.

"You'll do," Winnie said, adding a final hairpin to Betsy's wig. "Just don't bend over because the egg might crack."

Betsy nodded, savoring the feeling of adventure that flooded her. She took pleasure thumping down the stairs in her riding boots because her demi-boots always tapped in a ladylike way and her slippers swished.

The corridor was full of people. With a rapid glance, she saw that the duchess resembled a round-faced mayor. Jeremy's father had an expression of suppressed glee, and Lady Knowe looked exactly like her twin brother, the duke. Jeremy . . .

He was waiting for her. Looking for her. As if she were the only person who mattered.

Somehow her feet kept thumping down the stairs, her hand holding the rail. Aunt Knowe cried, "Here's the gentleman we've been waiting for! I wondered if you would be attractive as a boy. Now I have my answer!"

Betsy walked toward her. "No?"

"You look like a turnip," her aunt remarked. "All right, everyone. The carriages are waiting."

Betsy's heart was beating quickly, but not because she was about to take her first step out of doors in breeches. No, it was the way that Jeremy stepped toward her as if he would always walk at her side.

"Jeremy, Betsy, and the marquess in one carriage," Aunt Knowe ordered.

"We'll take my carriage," the duchess cried, grabbing Aunt Knowe's elbow.

Betsy glanced up at Jeremy from under her lashes and her heart beat even faster. "Are you ready to take a turnip on an outing, Lord Jeremy?"

"It's been one of my long-held ambitions," he said gravely. "Lady Knowe, I think we should congregate in the sitting room first."

"Why?" Lady Knowe demanded. "I don't want to miss anything!"

"A lesson in manhood is in order," he said, nodding to the duchess. "For one thing, Her Grace is now *His* Grace and probably shouldn't be holding your elbow."

"Oh, my!" the duchess squealed.

"Fine," Lady Knowe said grumpily. "You can give us a few brief lessons. How hard can it be to be a man?"

"To be a gentleman?" Jeremy corrected, his eyes glinting with an edge of wicked laughter. "Hard. Very hard."

Lady Knowe took off her cocked hat and swatted him, and he laughed like a boy, ducking through the door into the sitting room.

Betsy found herself watching Jeremy's father, whose eyes were clear and shining.

She followed the group into the sitting room, feeling a complicated knot of emotions: uncertainty warring with excitement warring with desire, happiness, recklessness . . .

"I like wearing these breeches," she told the room.

"You enjoy looking like a stuffed sausage?" Jeremy asked.

"You have obviously never worn a corset if you think there's anything new to the sensation."

Whatever was going on between them felt risky and exhilarating, not like the practiced chatter with which she had enticed her suitors.

"I might wear a corset someday," Jeremy said conversationally.

Her mouth fell open. "Why?"

"My grandfather used to creak when he bent over; I was twelve by the time I realized that the sound was protesting whalebones."

"'Protesting whalebones,'" she repeated, and then laughed. "Are you planning to grow into your grandfather's girth?" She flicked a glance at his body. "You'll need to eat more regularly than you do now."

"I'll take that under advisement," he said.

They'd reached the duchess. Walking like a man wasn't an easy task if you had large hips, as did the duchess.

"That's better!" Lady Knowe cried, clapping her hands. "Lengthen your stride!"

"This is as long as physically possible," Her Grace said, with an edge.

"You try it, Betsy," Lady Knowe said. "Walk from the fireplace to the chair."

Betsy was waddling, but Jeremy's imagination nimbly removed the padding from her waist and freed her poor, confined breasts.

Her aunt narrowed her eyes at him.

He moved his gaze to Betsy's neck. The curls

of her white wig hid the back of her neck, but framed the proud lift of her chin. Her throat was satin smooth. He'd like to pull off her cravat, lick her throat, and then bite her ear. She would gasp. He let himself think about what Betsy's gasp would sound like, until it occurred to him that his breeches were now as ill-fitting as hers.

Lady Knowe had her hands on her hips. "Betsy is passable, but Emily, if you don't stop swinging your hips, we shall have to leave you in the inn. Do you need me or the marquess to demonstrate again?"

Lady Knowe had perfected a long-legged, raw stride without a trace of femininity.

"Good enough," the duchess barked, ignoring her comment. "The horses will take a chill if we don't make haste. Has anyone seen my son?"

"No," Lady Knowe said.

"He was cross as a child too," Her Grace said. "Didn't get his way and he'd be as pickled as a pear."

Jeremy saw Betsy's eyes light up. Her pink lips shaped the phrase "pickled as a pear."

He allowed the duchess to leave the room, followed by Lady Knowe and his father, and then he said, "It wouldn't be comfortable to be matched with a pickled pear, Betsy."

"I didn't know that pears could be pickled," Betsy said, her eyes shining.

He'd been driven half mad, hungering after the curve of her neck, so he drew her into his arms and waited just long enough so that her eyelashes swept shut before he brought their lips together.

She sighed, a sound so erotic that wildfire leapt over his body.

Their tongues were shameless, but Jeremy didn't allow his hands to slide down to her arse and grip it the way he'd love to do. He didn't pull Betsy against him so that her legs in those scandalous breeches could wind around his hips, and the better parts of each of them would rub against each other in fierce pleasure.

She tasted joyful and sweet and lustful. "I want to ravish you," he said, his voice rasping like that of a boy of fifteen. "For God's sake—"

"Say *No* to the duke?"

"Exactly."

"Then you'll ravish me?" She had a bewitching twinkle in her eyes.

"No, no, I won't," he said hastily.

He saw a flash of hurt go through her beautiful eyes.

"Not until we're married."

He had spoken the word aloud.

"An ultimatum." She looked over her shoulder as she walked from the room, giving him an impish—sweetly feminine—smile. Which he didn't entirely understand until he realized that she was swaying her hips.

Her bottom in breeches was enough to drive a man to madness. Or to marriage.

"You are the most erotic turnip I've ever seen," he called.

She just laughed.

# Chapter Nineteen

The auction house was a large building fronted with shallow steps and a sign decorated in gold that announced the ownership of Mr. Phillips, renowned auctioneer of London, Stratford-upon-Avon, and Wilmslow.

A butler opened the door as they approached, bowed, and asked for their names.

"The Marquess of Thurrock and party," Jeremy's father said, pulling off his tricorne.

A well-proportioned man wearing an excellent suit and a superior, though not extravagant, wig made his appearance. "Your Lordship," Mr. Phillips said to the marquess, "it is my honor to welcome you to the smallest of my auction houses."

"I knew Finney as a boy," the marquess told him. "I've a mind to acquire one of his little pieces, as long as the price is right. Brought some friends with me."

The auctioneer's shrewd eyes paused for a moment on Betsy, who gave him the smallest of chin nods. For a moment, he looked puzzled, then, to Betsy's satisfaction, he looked past her to Jeremy, Aunt Knowe, and the duchess. He blinked, visibly registering their clothing and deciding that the Marquess of Thurrock's party was not as tasteful a group as he would expect of a nobleman's friends.

"You are most welcome to enter the salon," he said, waving in a stately manner toward large open doors. "We will begin with drawings that I acquired at great effort on the continent and follow with exquisite examples of Samuel Finney's miniatures."

The salon proved to be a tall-ceilinged room, every inch of which was painted with a relentless number of cupids, interspersed with a cloud here or there.

"Look up," Jeremy murmured in Betsy's ear, nudging her as they sat down.

Obediently, she tilted her head back, and her mouth fell open. The ceiling was a riot of cherubs, lying on clouds, playing harps, quaffing wine, and—

Aunt Knowe's familiar bellow of laughter rang out as the rest of the party seated themselves. It sounded reasonably manly.

"Don't speak loudly," Jeremy reminded Betsy, just in time.

"The cupids," Betsy whispered.

"Engaging in intimacies." His eyes had a devilish, laughing glint. "I'm reassured to discover that heaven won't be as tedious as one is led to believe. I've never been able to sing, let alone strum a harp."

"Indeed," Betsy murmured. She couldn't keep her eyes off the joyous, erotic cupids. Some acts she readily recognized. But others were more mysterious. In fact, the more she looked, the more curious she grew.

Their chairs were positioned close together, Jeremy's leg and arm pressed against hers. Under normal circumstances, she never felt a gentleman's leg if it was close to hers; her skirts precluded any such intimacy.

But now . . .

Two pairs of breeches was an entirely different situation. Her heart had quickened, thanks to the riotous cupids, but that was nothing compared to how she felt when she saw their legs pressed together.

"Are your sensibilities offended by the ceiling?" Jeremy asked, a deep ribbon of amusement running through his voice.

"I'm not missish," Betsy informed him. "I would—" She coughed and deepened her voice. "I would like a closer look at the pair in the left corner to the front."

Jeremy took a swift glance in that direction and laughed. "You delight me."

The marquess, Aunt Knowe, and the duchess were seated on his other side. Slowly the seats behind them began to fill. Some men looked to be merchants, and some of them were obviously factotums, ready to bid for their masters. In the row just behind them, one gentleman sat by himself.

She sat quietly as the first few drawings were knocked down, enjoying herself more keenly than she had in months. In the rows behind her, men were shouting, bidding and outbidding, cursing freely.

All the things they never did in a ballroom.

She was half turned so as to see the ranks of men behind her when Jeremy leaned close and whispered, "I have been paying close attention to the ceiling."

"Oh?"

"The couple you identified is particularly adventuresome. You have good taste."

Betsy was having the best afternoon of her entire life. Jeremy's arm was touching hers, and her leg was tingling as if she were immersed in a hot bath.

"I have never doubted my taste," she told him. "Aunt Knowe assured us many times that she had shaped our tastes after her own, and therefore we need never doubt that our instincts were beyond criticism."

Jeremy laughed under his breath. "I grow more fond of Lady Knowe by the moment. Shall I inquire what she thinks of that particular set of cupids?"

Betsy narrowed her eyes. "Don't you dare."

"Gentlemen discuss these matters amongst themselves," he assured her. He made a case of looking up. "I particularly like that cupid on his knees, happily engaged in his work. One wouldn't want to see reluctance on his face during that particular act."

"No," Betsy said faintly.

The auctioneer had already knocked down any number of drawings, but now he cleared his throat with particular emphasis. "Five drawings, by Rubens and Rembrandt, to be sold as a lot."

Before he began the bidding, Aunt Knowe brandished her catalogue in the air.

"In the front row, at twenty shillings."

After that the bidding was fast and furious, but Aunt Knowe was not to be beaten, waving her catalogue as if she were a butler summoning a hackney.

"Do you wish to bid?" Jeremy asked.

"Against my aunt?"

"Or for the next lot," he suggested. "That's what we came here for, after all."

"Sold!" the auctioneer bellowed, his smile widening. "Sold to the Marquess of Thurrock's party for five pounds two shillings."

"Your turn to bid," Jeremy said.

"If I see something I love, I shall," she replied. "I thought I wanted to bid for the sake of it, simply to play a man."

He raised an eyebrow. "No?"

"Being a man is not the act of buying things. It's the freedom to sit here under shameless cupids and spread my legs in a most improper fashion. I am *slouching* in my chair!" She couldn't stop the grin on her face.

Jeremy frowned. "You never slump?"

"I wear a corset and, often, a high wig," she

told him. "Slumping is inadvisable. Sometimes my back is in agony by the end of a long evening."

Hopefully, no one saw one gentleman's large hand slipping under his neighbor's coat, the better to caress his spine.

"You'll make me blush!" Betsy whispered.

Jeremy withdrew his hand with a low laugh. "Fair warning: I may make it my life's ambition to bring that color to your cheeks."

The auctioneer had burst into another flurry of activity, as drawings by "the youthful prodigy, William Beechey" were being knocked down.

*"After Rembrandt,"* Aunt Knowe said to the marquess in a penetrating whisper. "Poppycock! I hardly consider that the action of a prodigy!"

"What I most like about these cherubs," Jeremy murmured, "is the fact that they do not worry about the color of their faces, or even their expressions."

"I would care," Betsy said, leaning back in her chair so that it wasn't as obvious that she was craning her neck. "I will always care."

"No, you won't."

"You have no idea what it's like to be a woman," she whispered, glancing behind them to make certain that the gentleman wasn't paying attention. Luckily, he seemed entirely engrossed in the auction. "No woman could abandon herself to . . . to that degree! Such intemperance isn't proper."

"My experience of women suggests otherwise," Jeremy said, stretching his long legs so he could cross his ankles. "A woman can find herself so engaged in the moment that she entirely forgets about her appearance. Of course, ladies may be more circumspect."

Betsy was thinking so hard about lust and ladies that she didn't answer until he nudged her with his elbow.

"Didn't offend you, did I?"

Betsy started. "No. I'm simply thinking about what it's like to be a lady."

"We men don't know much," Jeremy said, obviously enjoying himself, "but it seems the very devil to me."

"Why so?"

"We agree that these cupids are shameless," Jeremy said.

"Indeed." Betsy nodded.

"British ladies are taught so much about shame that they are rarely shameless. They're married off to near-strangers, which doesn't help, of course."

"Shame is not merely a lady's affliction," Betsy pointed out.

"But ladies wield it against each other like a club."

"I think one ought to be ashamed to break certain rules." She was thinking of the prints that people made of the Wildes, and her growing suspicion that Grégoire was supplementing his income by shaming Jeremy in print. Or in *prints*, to be more exact.

"At certain times one ought to be lost to shame," Jeremy said.

"Only if other people aren't hurt." Betsy was trying to think her way into an understanding that would encompass shameless pleasure and babies and a husband.

"I can agree with that," Jeremy said. "Loyalty outranks shameless pleasure."

"Are all rooms frequented by men decorated in this fashion?" Betsy whispered to Jeremy. She had discovered a pair she'd overlooked. She'd like to ask what they were doing; perhaps she could mention it later, in private.

"Only the good ones," he responded. "This ceiling is particularly creative."

"I have very little with which to compare," Betsy said.

"Nicely put," Jeremy said. "'With which to compare,' indeed. I like a man who maintains grammar in the face of erotic art."

She frowned at him.

"Men can become incoherent when presented with a plethora of erotic activities."

Suddenly, a head poked between their shoulders. "A plethora implies too much, an extravagance, a superfluity, or a surfeit. Are you discouraging your young friend from engaging in such heavenly activities?"

Betsy jumped and let out a squeak. Then she quickly cleared her throat. "A good question," she said, pitching her voice as low as she could.

The man who had been seated behind them and apparently eavesdropping had coarse gray hair that frizzed from under a carelessly positioned wig. He wore a striped coat and a lace-trimmed cravat. His eyes were very bright, and his eyebrows very bushy.

"Good afternoon," Jeremy said.

"I apologize for intruding," the gentleman said. "I am extraordinarily precise by nature. It's practically agony to hear a word misused."

"I did not misuse it," Jeremy replied. He waved his hand at the ceiling. "This activity is entertaining, but it reminds me of morning prayers in a chilly chapel: too much of a good thing."

"Very clever to contrast one heavenly activity with another that claims to lead to clouds, cupids, and the rest," the gentleman said approvingly.

Whatever he might have said next on the subject was lost when the auctioneer announced, "And now for the miniatures of the renowned Samuel Finney, portrait painter to our beloved Queen Charlotte, member of the Royal Academy of Arts."

The room went silent. Lady Knowe snapped to attention as the auctioneer's assistant began unwrapping the first miniature from a silk cloth.

"Aha!" the gentleman said, and flung himself back in his chair so that it creaked in protest.

"Do you intend to acquire a miniature, sir?" Jeremy asked, turning.

The man snorted. "Absolutely not! I've come along to see what they sell for."

"Do you own some of Mr. Finney's artworks?" Betsy inquired.

He looked at her, and one of his bushy eyebrows sprang up. "You could say that."

She turned about quickly and faced the front, feeling certain that he knew she was a woman.

"I painted them," said the man, in a more disinterested than boastful fashion.

Betsy couldn't stop herself from turning about again. "How do you do, Mr. Finney? I've admired your work."

Then, as his eyes crinkled in amusement, she realized that she'd forgotten to pitch her voice to a lower register.

Mr. Finney leaned forward and tapped her on the shoulder. "I don't paint any longer. I'm justice of the peace for the parts around here, and it keeps me busy. But damned if I wouldn't like to paint *you*, my dear."

Jeremy's face suddenly grew dark. "Mr. Peters is not 'your dear,'" he said, managing to sound pleasant yet threatening.

"Mr. Peters, is it?" Mr. Finney beamed. "I've got the best of references. Why, I painted several people in this room, though they haven't yet recognized me. Growing old is an excellent disguise, better than breeches."

Betsy managed to choke back a laugh.

"I only occasionally dabble these days, but I'd take you on, Mr. Peters."

The auctioneer held up a small oval painting in a gold frame. "*Portrait of a Lady in a White Dress and Matching Under-Dress*," he announced. "Starting at twenty shillings."

The painter snorted, but settled into silence.

Betsy had hoped to buy a miniature, but she quickly realized that Mr. Finney's miniatures cost far more than she could afford. Jeremy glanced at her a few times, but she shook her head. Aunt Knowe, on the other hand, bid with gusto and won two miniatures, one of a young boy and another labeled *The Virgin Mary*, which led to robust snorting from the row behind.

"The baker's wife," he said. "Eight children, if she had one!"

"*A Young Man*," announced the auctioneer. "Verso reads, 'To P, with all my love.'"

Betsy looked down at her catalogue. It was her favorite among them; not only did the boy have a longing expression, but his eyebrows suggested a Wilde.

Her aunt must have thought so too, because she leapt into bidding with a frenzy, and when she realized that the duchess had bid against her, she pointed at Her Grace and bellowed, "Cease at once, sir!"

"Your aunt plays an *excellent* man," Jeremy murmured in her ear. "Surely you wish to bid against both of them?"

Betsy saw that the duchess was backing down with a great waggling of her eyebrows. "We should have arranged among ourselves which paintings we wished to buy. Thank you, but no. These are far too expensive."

"I agree," said a grumpy voice behind her. "That's an early effort, and it isn't even enameled."

"Money is not a concern," Jeremy told Betsy.

His father leaned from his other side. "Neither of us has anyone to spend money on." He began to lift his catalogue.

"Make him stop!" Betsy whispered, laughing. "Just imagine how angry my aunt will be if your father outbids her."

"I shall paint Mr. Peters with enamels," Mr. Finney said conversationally, hitching his chair forward. "That's the great thing now. I might as well turn out a few more of them between quelling riots and jailing malcontents and the like. Enamels catch the tender gloss of a beautiful woman's cheeks as mere paints can never do."

Betsy smiled at him. "Stop," she whispered.

But the old man was irrepressible. "I'll paint you in breeches," he whispered back, "but perhaps with an overskirt? In a rose garden."

"Sir," Jeremy said, turning to him with a ferocious scowl.

"You *are* lucky to have such a protective companion." Mr. Finney reached over to tap on Aunt Knowe's shoulder.

She startled on seeing him and smiled. The moment she won the miniature of the boy, she rose and beckoned to Mr. Finney. They left the room together.

"You're going to be painted by a famous miniaturist," Jeremy said. "What do you think of that?"

"He wants to paint me in breeches," Betsy breathed into his ear.

"So do I," Jeremy said. "I don't know how to paint so you'd have to pose for hours. Days."

Another miniature was knocked off, but without Mr. Finney's exclamations and Aunt Knowe's excitable bidding, the auction was less interesting. The duchess managed to win a portrait, *A Lady in Brown*.

Aunt Knowe was waiting for them in the carriage. "Yoo-hoo," she called, opening the door. "The most marvelous thing, darlings! We're going to Fulshaw Hall for supper. It's Samuel Finney's manor house, just south of here."

Snowflakes were whirling around Jeremy's shoulders, tiny ones catching the light from the open door of the auction house.

"I have one addendum to our discussion of shame," he said to Betsy.

"Yes?"

"Shame cannot be *my* daily companion, if I'd like *you* to be my daily companion."

The duchess was being hoisted into her carriage; apparently she found breeches somewhat confining.

"The same is true for you," Jeremy said, his eyes searching hers: tender, ferocious, longing. All kinds of emotions that she'd never seen from any man who'd proposed to her. There was nothing *respectful* about Jeremy. He would challenge her every day. Her whole life.

Her aunt was biding her time in the carriage, but any moment she would bellow for them.

"Or you can say *Yes* to the duke, instead of *No*," Jeremy continued. "When you are certain about your choice, let me know. If you decide to become a duchess, tomorrow my father and I will return to his—to *our*—house."

# Chapter Twenty

$\mathcal{T}$he temperature had fallen by the time the carriages reached the inn, allowing their passengers to dress for dinner, including Thaddeus but not Grégoire, who was still bed-bound, before taking them on to Fulshaw Hall. The air had turned to a thick blanket, hanging close to the ground. Snowflakes were everywhere, quickly blinked from eyelashes and settling again a moment later.

The manor was barely visible through the swirling snow, although light spilled from windows and the open front door. Jeremy squinted at it. Seven bays, plum-colored, patterned brick . . . the painter had done nicely for himself.

Or perhaps Finney had inherited it.

Inside, he looked for miniatures, but didn't find any: In fact, it was a perfectly ordinary house. Mr. Finney lived with a widowed cousin named Mrs. Grabell-Pitt, who looked somewhat faint when she realized that her house had been graced not merely with a duchess, but with two Wildes. After that, she did nothing but smile, displaying long rows of saffron-colored teeth.

Jeremy went through the meal without looking at Betsy more than three or four times. She was seated beside Samuel Finney, the canny old man who had known instantly that she was a woman and a Wilde.

He was at the other end of the table, seated beside his hostess. She talked about snow and quince jelly and her fear that songbirds would freeze on their boughs.

"Not a song will be heard in the spring," she predicted, her eyes owlish with alarm.

He and his father stayed mostly silent, watching Thaddeus, Betsy, and Lady Knowe draw out Mr. Finney regarding his career, the experience of painting a queen, the reasons he left the painting world behind.

After the meal, Lady Knowe talked Mr. Finney into displaying his miniatures, but neither Jeremy nor his father moved to join the group hovering around a glass-topped cabinet.

"Were we always this silent together?" Jeremy asked.

"I do not easily put things into words," the marquess replied, regret and love in his eyes.

"I thought you condemned me for cowardice," Jeremy admitted. "I heard your words wrong, or I remembered them wrong. You didn't follow me to London; I decided that I had been thrown out of the family. I felt I didn't deserve to be in the family any longer."

His father scrubbed his hands over his face, and

Jeremy realized with a shock that his favorite gesture was borrowed.

"I failed you." The marquess's eyes were anguished. "I was trying to explain that I understood guilt, and you thought I was blaming you. You were gone before I could mend it. I thought . . . I gave you time."

"Exactly one year," Jeremy realized.

"To the day," his father said. "As for guilt . . . your mother died in childbirth while you were at war. We didn't let it be generally known."

Jeremy froze.

"We were so startled to find she was with child," his father continued. "She was too old. Sometimes I think that perhaps if I had begged her . . . I should have begged her to take a draught." His eyes met Jeremy's. "Yet I wanted the child too. So I lost them both."

His jaw clenched. Jeremy knew that gesture, the way it felt when the press of guilt clamps one's jaws tight to stop agony from escaping.

He was seated on a sofa beside his father; he turned toward him and awkwardly put one arm and then the other around his father's shoulders. Their embrace was brief and embarrassing.

"The child was my brother or sister," he told his father, after they drew apart. "My mother would never have taken a draught. You did the best with the hand that fate dealt you."

"As did you."

"Right," Jeremy said. "I know. Now I know."

And finally, perhaps, he was beginning to believe it.

# *Chapter Twenty-one*

*B*etsy waited until Aunt Knowe was poring over Mr. Finney's miniatures before she drew Thaddeus to the side under the pretense of looking out at the snow.

Which meant that they stood shoulder-to-shoulder before a window that showed nothing back but their reflection.

"We look like a couple, but we are not, are we?" Thaddeus asked very quietly.

Betsy was staring at their reflection, thinking the same thing. They looked like etchings of aristocrats. After her day in breeches, Betsy had felt gloriously feminine. She was wearing a coquettish gown of raspberry pink, as Winnie had brought from Lindow only gowns in shades of pink. Much to her maid's approval, she hadn't added a fichu, so her breasts were on display.

"We are not a couple," Betsy confirmed, meeting Thaddeus's eyes in the mirrored glass.

A rueful smile cocked one corner of his lips. "I couldn't lose to a better man. I mean that."

"You and I would never suit," Betsy said, putting a hand on his arm and smiling up at him. "You truly disapproved of our wearing breeches today, didn't you?"

"Not simply from a puritanical impulse, but because gossip can be damaging. I loathe scandal." He hesitated. "My mother has often been hurt over the years on hearing gossip concerning my father's second family."

Betsy nodded.

"That filth affected my mother, never my father. It is dangerous for women to stray outside the bounds of proper society."

"I don't think that 'filth' would describe the gossip following a revelation that a duchess mischievously dressed in breeches to attend an auction," Betsy said. "My guess is that it would begin a craze, and ladies would begin crowding into the doors of White's and other gentlemen's clubs."

The appalled look in his eyes made her laugh.

"I am grateful that you asked me to marry you, given the scandal attached to my mother's name."

He frowned at that. "No one should besmirch you based on your mother's decisions."

"Nor you or your mother, based on your father's," she pointed out gently.

"*Touché*," he replied. "Are you absolutely certain that you don't wish to be my duchess? I think we would be happy. I would very much like to marry you, Betsy."

He meant it; she could see that in his eyes.

"No," she said, shaking her head. "I'll choose a less decorous path."

"I have a feeling it will be a happier one," Thaddeus said. He raised her hand to his lips and kissed it, before bowing and walking away.

After everyone bid farewell to Mr. Finney and his cousin and returned to the inn, Betsy retired to her bedchamber very conscious of one thing: She did not care to be ignored by Jeremy as she had been during the meal.

She was used to meeting his eyes when someone said something foolish. She'd overheard a prediction that all the songbirds in England had died in the storm, but Jeremy just nodded, his head courteously bent toward Mrs. Grabell-Pitt. She was used to being the one he turned to, and virtually the only person he spoke to.

That realization made her twitch because she wanted Jeremy to have friends, to carry on conversations with others.

She just didn't want him to overlook *her*.

Sometime later she sat by the fire, drying her hair as Winnie fluttered about the room, then finally took her leave. Slowly the old inn quieted, with just a shudder now and then as a gust of snow struck the windows with particular force. What had been pretty swirls of snow had transformed into a gale that hurled itself against the building with the force of gravel tossed at a lover's window.

Clementine's hateful voice kept echoing in Betsy's ears. But she had made up her mind to do this thing that society forbade.

As *her* choice.

She chose Jeremy, here and now, and not merely when a ring would mark her as his possession. In fact, he hadn't even asked her to marry him; simply discussed their marital future. It was that memory that brought her to her feet and into the dark, chilly corridor.

She paused, hand flat against his door, just to make certain that her inside landscape entirely agreed with this decision.

It did.

Jeremy was hers.

His door swung open soundlessly and she walked forward just enough to ease the door shut behind her. His fire was still burning high, so it cast rosy light around the room: over the great four-poster and its high canopy, over the looming chest of drawers—

Over the man who had risen to his feet from a chair by the fireplace. Light flickered over him as if with love, shaping the planes of his face like one of Mr. Finney's artworks.

"Hello," Betsy said, reminding herself that she didn't believe in being nervous. She had allowed herself that emotion only when she met the queen.

"Hello," Jeremy replied. His smile said a great deal more.

They moved toward each other as if they were following the steps of a very slow, very grand country dance. One that was danced by kings and queens and countryfolk alike.

When they were beside each other, she squared

her shoulders and met his eyes. "I decided to come to you. I hope that is all right."

"I do believe that you are the bravest woman I've ever met," he replied.

He couldn't have said anything better; Betsy felt herself begin to glow. "I haven't been brave to this point, but I have made up my mind to change. I outlawed being nervous, but now I need to outlaw being afraid." She hesitated. "I have chosen courage, and now I choose happiness."

"I love you as you are," he whispered, and then his mouth came down on hers.

Her breath caught in her throat because their tongues met as if they kissed every day, every night. He tasted *right*, which sent a shiver through her whole body, and pushed her against him gently, the way a pebble might roll up a beach when the tide comes in.

One doesn't fight the tide.

All the time they kissed, Betsy's tongue danced to the pulse she felt in her throat. Her arms were around his neck, but it wasn't enough, so she let one slip down his side and then around to his back, caressing him through the thin fabric of his shirt.

She was delighting in the pure strength under her fingers when he eased away.

"No," she said, her voice an aching whisper.

"I have to know that you want me, not just this," Jeremy said. His lips ghosted down her throat, and the tip of his tongue traced patterns over the tender patch under her ear.

"I want you," Betsy said. And then, not in answer to what he said, but because it was the truth of her heart: "I love you."

He stiffened and lifted his head, then drew her over to the fireplace. "I need to see your face," he muttered.

Betsy could feel her lips were swollen by his kisses. Her hair tumbled down her back. Her nipples were tenting the fabric of her nightdress.

She smiled at him, letting her hands hang loosely by her sides. From the time she was fourteen, she'd concealed her body in underskirts and corsets, fichus and side panniers. Not tonight.

His eyes came back to her face, and the desire in them felt like a lick of fire over her body.

"You had a question?" Betsy prompted, smiling at him. Fear was gone.

"You love me?"

She nodded, not a shred of reluctance in her, and then spread her arms, letting them drop to her sides again. "Not a future duchess to be seen in this room."

"Will you become my future marchioness, instead, Bess? I cannot—I cannot allow you to be here without marriage."

"Because you are a gentleman," she said, nodding.

"No."

She raised an eyebrow.

"Because you'll break my heart. It's already cracked," he said, his voice steady. "All those men knelt at your feet, Bess. Do you wish me to kneel?"

The image of cavorting cherubs came straight into her mind.

He caught it, of course. Likely he'd always catch her errant thoughts.

"Next time," he promised, a glint in his eye. "I need to know that you didn't just say *No* to the duke: You said *Yes* to the marquess."

Betsy took his hands in hers. "I don't want you to kneel at my feet. I want you to be my partner and stand at my side."

"I fell in love with you one of those days that I spent lurking in the corner of the billiard room," Jeremy said, drawing her hands toward him and holding them over his heart. "With *you*, Betsy, not with the lovely woman you present in the ballroom."

Betsy's heart bounded and she swallowed hard. "You did?"

She was holding her breath, memorizing every intonation, the strength of his large hands curled around hers, the way his eyes were searching hers. Joy crashed through her as if that gentle surge of the tide had turned to a wave larger than her body.

"I would run away to Prussia with you, Jeremy," she said, truth ringing in every word. "I wouldn't leave my children, but I would leave everything and everyone else."

"In the face of society's outrage?" His voice was almost casual, curious. And yet they both knew that the question carried a huge weight.

Betsy smiled at him. And then she drew her hands free and threw herself at him, arms around his neck. "Yes, I would," she said fiercely, against his mouth. "It's you, and only you, even when you were rude to me, when you slid under the table, when you laughed at me. When you were the only person who really listened, and knew what I loved most. When you actually *saw* me."

He grunted as her weight hit him and then he kissed her. Or they kissed each other, because her hands were in his hair, pulling his head down to hers. Then she walked backward, one, two, three steps until she reached the side of the bed.

He scooped her up and put her on the bed, his eyes full of feeling. Then he stood back and pulled his shirt from his breeches.

"I was looking forward to seeing you in a nightshirt," she breathed.

"I don't wear one." He wrenched his breeches over his thighs and they fell to the floor.

Betsy rolled on one side and propped her head on her elbow. Their bodies couldn't be more different. His was chiseled, from broad shoulders to a narrow waist, and below it . . .

"The cupids weren't that size," she said faintly.

"I noticed the poor fellows didn't seem to be properly endowed," Jeremy said, cheerfully. "As small as their wings." He ran a hand under his balls and then slowly up his length. "This is designed for a woman, not a naughty cherub."

Betsy sat up, fascinated. She had known what a man looked like. She even knew what they were about to do—and no thanks to those frolicking cupids, either. But she had imagined something smaller and less *virile*.

Courage, she reminded herself.

"Come here," she said, reaching out her arms. "Come here."

"Always." Jeremy had a knee on the bed and she toppled back again, her hands flat against the thick muscles of his chest.

Her hands slid lower and his body went rigid.

"Yes?" he whispered, his voice a rasp.

"Yes," she said. Then, her hand finally curling around the hard, silky length he had caressed a moment ago, she said, "Don't ask me again, Jeremy. You and I are here, and this is the way it's going to be. I'll follow you wherever you go."

Seeing a flicker in his eyes, she added, "Yes, to Bedlam, but you won't go there. I'll wave sausages under your nose until you wake up."

"You could just take me into the bedroom and undress before me, slowly," he suggested. "I'll come back to my senses."

"What if I undressed *you* instead?" She gave him an impish smile and tightened her hand.

A rough sound erupted from his throat. "You could do that," he managed.

"What about this?"

His answer was a hoarse curse. And then: "Enough, unless you want to unman me."

"It's more the opposite," Betsy said, giggling. But she brought her hands back to his chest. He had a scattering of black hair that arrowed down his stomach. "This feels wonderful against my breasts," she whispered, arching to press her taut nipples against him.

Their groans entwined, the breathless, rapturous echo of bodily pleasure.

"I have to see your breasts," he said, moving to the side and slowly easing her nightgown up her legs and then over her head.

"You don't know how many times I've traced their curves in my head, imagined *these*." His fingers shaped her. "You're so much softer than I could have imagined," he whispered. His fingers reached her nipples, and her breath quickened.

"There's a wonderful bit in *Romeo and Juliet*," he murmured. *"Let lips do what hands do,* or something like that."

Betsy closed her eyes. His warm mouth was tracing a pattern on her right breast, coming closer to her nipple and then falling away until she was shivering with anticipation. Even so, his rough lick startled her into a throaty sound that turned to a moan.

One large hand held her breast, and as if his fingers were hers, she felt the heavy weight of its curve, the silky feel of her skin. Heat forked through her as if the veins of her body had dissolved and her body had become a conduit for sparks and fire.

She found herself arching instinctively, pushing her breast more firmly into his caress, silently begging for a rougher touch. He responded instantly, his mouth tightening into a delicious pull that made her cry out, her hips writhing, one knee coming up as she turned toward him. Eyes still shut, her hands blindly closed on his shoulders, taut muscles flexing under her touch.

Betsy was gasping for air by the time Jeremy raised his head, his eyes hungry but with a gleam of satisfaction. Betsy could feel sweat on her forehead and behind her knees, which was disconcerting and slightly embarrassing.

Jeremy smiled, a slow, *happy* smile. "Hello, you," he said, his voice a rasp.

Betsy managed to catch her breath, but she was still reverberating inside from his smile. "We should marry and stay in bed all day," she whispered, tracing his lips with her fingers. His tongue swept over her fingertips and she shivered again.

"Mmm," he groaned, and rolled on top of her again, his thumb rubbing over her nipple and his tool throbbing against her legs. With a throaty moan she arched, rubbing herself against him.

He said something, husky and too low for hearing, and took her mouth in a kiss that had her shaking and pressing against him desperately.

In the back of her mind her hunger led to a flare of alarm. Was she being too—too forward? It seemed a ridiculous thought to be having at this precise moment, but it wasn't easy to cast off years of determination to make certain her husband never thought she found bed play pleasurable.

Embarrassment flooded her and she pulled away from his kiss. She felt suddenly messy and sweaty.

"I would spend my life in bed with you, if you asked me to," Jeremy said, his eyes on hers. He braced himself on his elbows, nipped her ear, and whispered, "I'm enthralled, in case you haven't noticed, Bess. I'm at your feet, or I would be if you wanted it. Perhaps you do want it?"

She bit her lip, trying to think what a lady would say. He didn't wait, just moved down the bed and began kissing her toes, and then suckled one, which made her squeal—and lose the embarrassment that was making her shoulders tight.

"Exquisite," Jeremy said, his teeth nipping her right toes. "Were I a shoemaker, I would weep with joy to make shoes for this foot."

Betsy began giggling, joy mixed with burning desire, which came back as if it hadn't been quenched by mortification.

One rough hand circled her ankle. "Remember when Thaddeus proposed and your panniers flew up in the billiard room?"

"Uh," she gasped, because his other hand was tracing a slow caress up the inside of her thigh.

"I *could* see your ankles from my chair in the corner," Jeremy said, punctuating his words with kisses on her legs. "I nearly lunged out of my chair to smash Thaddeus in the jaw for being within eyesight of these ankles."

"You did?" She raised her head and stared at him.

His mouth twisted ruefully. "Never underestimate a man's primitive nature. If Thaddeus hadn't instantly turned his head away, like the excellent gentleman he is, he would have had a black eye the next day."

"I had no idea," Betsy gasped.

"I tried to convince myself that my outrage was

on behalf of your brothers. That I was merely a proxy for North."

"North wouldn't have paid any attention to my ankles," Betsy pointed out.

"I couldn't look away. The idea that any other man might share the pleasure swamped me with rage."

His eyes holding hers, he slid both hands up her legs. "Remember when I told you that going to war burned the gentleman out of a man?"

She half gasped, half laughed. "Not true?"

"Very true. In proof whereof, you are here with me, in this bed, at night, about to be ravished, our marriage about to be consummated, though we are not yet betrothed."

He dropped his head and kissed her thigh. Her inner thigh.

Betsy closed her eyes, embarrassment striking a blow again. With his face so close to her leg, he could see her most private parts. They should be making love under the sheets in the dark. She should hold herself still instead of quivering at every touch of his lips. Her legs went rigid.

"Bess," he said, his voice encouraging.

"Just give me a moment," she said, her mind rabbiting in fearful circles. "I just need to . . ."

"That's not important," he said. "Not between us, Bess." But he ran his hands down to her ankles in silent, tacit acceptance of whatever she decided.

Betsy closed her eyes, listening to the sound of his breath.

If he was no gentleman, then she was no lady. At least when they were together.

She would never leave him; she knew that with every instinct she had. He was her Prussian, not her duke. Shared pleasure wouldn't change her character and turn her to a faithless woman. Still, she had to conquer this insidious fear or she would diminish *his* pleasure.

"How did you know what I was feeling?" She propped herself up on her elbows, curiosity trumping mortification.

"I know you," he said, pressing a kiss on her left knee. His hair slid over her bare skin, making her shake. His hands traced higher, caressing the sensitive skin of her inner thighs.

Betsy sank into mindless need, raw desire. She *wanted* him to move his hands higher. She wanted his lips to touch her thighs, and higher. She even wanted him to look at her.

To lick her.

Men and women did that service for each other, and according to the ceiling of the auction house, cherubs were intoxicated by the act.

"Are you planning to kiss me, ah, intimately?" she whispered.

"I was." He met her eyes, the hunger in his making her dizzy. "We can wait until you are more accustomed to bedding."

"I would like to kiss you that way," she said, the words stumbling out of her mouth.

He froze, his fingers tightening on the full curve of her upper thighs. It gave her courage, because his eyes didn't look scandalized. Quite the opposite.

"We don't have any pillowy clouds," she said.

"I'd like to act out any number of angelic postures." She began to sit up. "In fact—"

"No." His hands slid forward, pinning her legs to the bed.

She cocked an eyebrow. "Dictatorial, are we?"

"Always, in the bedchamber." He said it without apology, although he added, "If I do something you don't care for, tell me."

"Those two statements are in opposition," she teased.

He growled and then rose on his hands and knees and moved to kiss her. Breathless moments later, Betsy returned to sanity to find she was shaking with impatience and muttering pleas under her breath.

A half hour later, after Jeremy had reacquainted himself with her breasts, and began leaving kisses on the curve of her stomach, her pleas were breathless.

"Couldn't we do that later?" she begged, looking down without a shred of embarrassment at the man who had positioned himself between her legs, and was doing things with his thumbs that made her breath catch and turn to cries.

Proving her own courage, to herself and to him, she put it in words: "I'd be happy now to find myself deflowered."

He glanced up, eyes full of wicked laughter. "You're rushing your fences, Bess." Holding her gaze, he leaned forward just enough to lick her. A long, slow, lap.

Betsy tried to keep her mouth closed, but a needy whimper escaped her.

"You taste wonderful," Jeremy said, his voice guttural.

She fell back, shaking, and put an arm over her eyes. He was holding her legs apart so he could lick her. She'd never felt anything so acutely in her life. Shudders wracked her body, and when one of his fingers slid inside, she called his name, clenching tightly around his finger, her legs restlessly moving against the sheets.

"What did you say?" Jeremy asked.

She dropped her arm and gasped, "More."

"Like this?"

He eased a second finger inside her and she arched her back, breath shuddering in her chest, pushing against his hand because it wasn't enough.

Jeremy said something in a low growl and his fingers slipped from her. She cried out, reaching down for him, but suddenly he was there, above her, and in a single, smooth stroke, he slid home.

For one moment, Betsy went still around him, her eyes widening with surprise. He was so much larger than his fingers.

"It doesn't hurt," she said, shocked. And again: "It *doesn't hurt.*"

She daringly bumped her hips upward because he was still, his eyes searching hers.

"No?"

That joyful smile again, the one that she saw so rarely.

"Time to try for more than not hurting," he muttered.

In answer, she nudged him again, her body burning to feel more. He drew back and claimed her again with a devastating thrust that brought fire in its wake.

A groan tore from his lips. "You feel . . . Bess, love, I've never felt anything like you."

She tried to answer but words didn't seem to have a part in a world narrowed to sweaty limbs and sobbing breaths.

He withdrew and thrust again. Betsy arched up, clinging to his shoulders, sucking in air, writhing in an attempt to get closer. She felt graceless and desperate, uncertain how to play her part.

He grabbed one of her knees and pulled it against his side, showing her. She was completely open to his every stroke now, and each made fire lick through her.

How could she ever have imagined she could lie still while making love? Every thrust made her nerves dance, and as he fell into a smooth rhythm, pushing deep inside her and then withdrawing, she kept shifting her hips upward, hanging on to him.

Behind her closed eyes, relentless pleasure was building like water trapped behind a dam, so ferocious that she was almost frightened.

"I've never felt like this," Jeremy rasped, his lips brushing hers. "You were made for me. We were made for this."

Betsy kissed him back, her hips rising to meet his thrusts, ragged cries escaping her lips. His movements were smooth and relentless while her hands flew over all the parts of his body she could reach, caressing him, loving him.

Still the pleasure built and built, until the moment came when the dam cracked and broke. He bent his head just in time and his lips covered hers, his hips moving faster and harder. Her fingers dug into his shoulders as waves of pleasure shook through her body.

She came back to herself, finding that sweat had slicked the backs of her legs and her body was shaking.

Jeremy was braced above her, his shoulders gleaming with sweat. He smiled at her, eyes slumberous, heavy lidded. "That looked like fun."

His voice sounded as if he was barely holding himself in check. Betsy had a sudden realization that Jeremy never let himself go. Perhaps that's why he gave way when fireworks exploded around him.

No, that was too simple.

"Rapture," she whispered. She turned her head and rubbed her cheek against his sweaty shoulder because tears were misting in her eyes. "I love you," she whispered. She wrapped her arms around him and then, daringly, her legs, and let her head fall back so their eyes could meet. "You feel so hard, and so right that I ache."

His eyes flickered.

"In the *best* way," she amended throatily.

He dipped his head and gave her a greedy kiss. The lovely sense of relaxation she had felt seeped away as delicious lightning crept back.

Jeremy began moving faster and then faster, his jaw clenched. Betsy tried to stifle wanton sounds by kissing his shoulders and his neck, but she ended up licking his sweat, and that made her moan. He somehow moved harder and faster until she clung to him with everything she had.

Their bodies moved as one, breaths shuddering, eyes locked on each other.

"Damn it, I love you," Jeremy whispered, his voice strained and harsh.

She would have smiled. She would have answered in kind, or thanked him, or . . . something. Instead, she watched as his eyes closed, head rearing back, his breath hoarse. Something ferocious, delicious slammed through her.

He waited, sweat glistening on his face, cheekbones tight, until Betsy lay beneath him dazed with pleasure.

Then he caught her hips, pulling them up to him.

Letting go with a hoarse shout.

# Chapter Twenty-two

*J*eremy woke from sleep with a tingle of alarm. Dawn was creeping into the chamber, which was nothing unusual: He often watched the sky turn rosy in the morning.

Then his mind cleared and memories flooded back: the way Betsy's hair fell around his face the second time they made love, when he coaxed her into sitting on him, the moment when she decided to play a naughty Cupid and licked him until he shuddered uncontrollably, hoarse groans erupting from his throat because the ache in his loins ruled him. That and the light in Betsy's eyes that said she wanted *him* with no regard to his title, or his shame.

For a few minutes he savored that memory, letting healing grace settle into his bones. He had a wife (almost). And . . . thinking of the night, and his utter disregard for condoms, children. Possibly children. Probably children, given that she had sobbed his name, and then breathlessly told him that she wanted to spend every night like this.

Yes, children.

A girl with Wilde eyebrows and a naughty giggle. A boy . . . a future marquess.

Grégoire had scarcely disguised his disappointment when Jeremy returned from war unscathed. He wouldn't welcome the children. Perhaps Grégoire, in his resentment, had spread rumors about Jeremy's supposed cowardice on the battlefield.

He could imagine the kindling fury in Betsy's eyes if he ever shared that suspicion. She already didn't like his cousin. Grégoire wouldn't be invited to Lindow for Christmas.

But Jeremy would. He had a family now. And he had his father, too.

Perhaps he could talk Betsy into a trip to Gretna Green. Lady Knowe's scowl came into his head and he retracted the idea.

No Gretna Green.

But he'd be damned if more than one night would pass before he saw that blissful surrender on Betsy's face again. That meant children would come sooner rather than later. Too bad he'd walked her back to her room—even if it was only next door.

Except when he turned his head . . . there she was. A rumpled pile of silky hair, a sweet upturned nose, an arm flung over her eyes, just as she did when she was trying to hide, to be the demure lady that she wasn't.

His whole body reacted with a ripple of happiness.

He never intended to love a woman like this, or at all. But there it was. And here she was. He rolled over and slid his hand down her side. She had put on a nightdress before she returned to his bed.

"Betsy," he said, leaning over to kiss her temple. Her closed eyes. Her rosy lips, pillowy and swollen after a night of kissing.

"Mmm."

"Queen Bess, you must return to your chamber," he said, kissing her chin. "Maids will be up and about, if they aren't already."

She turned her head away with a muffled protest and then tried to curl her body away from him. Desire was running through him again, a hungry throb. He only had to look at her to have a cockstand. He was fairly sure it would be like this their entire life.

"Queen of my heart," he whispered, nipping the vulnerable place where her throat met her shoulder.

"Why are you calling me a queen?" Betsy suddenly said, turning toward him.

"You are a queen," Jeremy said. "For one thing, you made your way into my bed against all propriety, so you clearly intend to change the rules in your kingdom."

Betsy giggled. "I washed and went to bed, but it was lonely there. So I came back. You were sleeping."

Jeremy shook his head. "I suppose you take responsibility for that."

She slid one silky leg forward, over his hip. "Shall I prove it?"

He took a deep breath. "I mean to marry you, tomorrow or next week or whenever your family will give you up, but not in the midst of a scandal."

"I don't care if there is one." Betsy rolled onto her side, her face on one arm, eyes peaceful.

He wanted to ask her more, but the day waited. He cupped her cheek with his hand and said, "I shall tell my father and my cousin today that I mean to marry you."

Betsy wrinkled her nose. "I don't like your cousin. I promise to try harder in the future."

"Grégoire is difficult to like," Jeremy said. "But he deserves to hear the news from me."

Betsy scowled. "Why would he assume that he might inherit? Was it so likely you would die on the battlefield?"

"I thought there was a fair chance that I wouldn't survive. I told him myself that even if I wasn't killed, I didn't intend to marry. I meant it . . . then."

Her mouth softened. "Until I came along?"

"Knocked me down as neatly as you pocket a billiard ball," he said, lips ghosting over hers. His emotions felt so naked that he had to phrase them as a jest.

Betsy saw through him. Her eyes were misty and she kissed him sweetly. She'd probably always see through him; his days of sardonic commentary were numbered.

"So you inform Grégoire that he needs to give up his dreams of a title, and I will inform Aunt

Knowe that we must plan for another wedding," Betsy said, sometime later. "I must write to Father and Ophelia as well. I'm not sure how long they planned to stay in Scotland, but it's entirely possible they could get snowed in and stay there for months."

"Our marriage must happen before spring," Jeremy said, smoothing the tumbled hair from her brow. "No condom means babies."

Thankfully, she looked happy at the prospect.

"You'll only have had one Season," he said, a qualm striking him.

"I disliked it," she said flatly. "After I mastered the art of being a damsel, it all became remarkably tedious. If you want to avoid balls, I will never complain."

"In its original definition, a 'damsel' was a virgin," Jeremy said. "A docile mouse of a virgin."

He saw her mouth twitch.

"*You* are a wild woman, a wild queen. You gave me that, Bess, and it's the best gift I was ever given." He let the truth in his words shine in his eyes.

A smile eased her lips, but he wasn't finished.

"We will make love until we know the feeling of each other's skin as well as our own. So that we can arouse the other with little more than a kiss. So that the curves of your body are as well known to me as the angles of mine to you."

He saw her wildness then, proud and true. Sure enough, she reached out and curled her hand tightly around his rigid cock. "You will know the stroke of my fingers as well as your own? Given what you told me about Etonian schoolboys, I will have to practice day and night."

"I'll never be satisfied by a solitary pleasure," he said hoarsely. "Not after this. Not after you."

"And I feel an ache inside myself, where you belong," Betsy whispered, caressing him with a slow, tight movement. Her hips swayed, as if touching him was making her squirm with pleasure.

Jeremy swept a hand under Betsy's nightdress and then around the sweet curve of her hip. Her legs fell apart invitingly. She was satin smooth, plump and wet . . . welcoming.

"I've never made love to a woman in the morning," he whispered.

Her brow darkened. "You will never make love to another woman, morning or night," she said with a touch of Wilde arrogance.

"That's true," he said peacefully. He rolled over and fitted himself to her as readily as an arrow to a bow, poised to fly. "Are you certain you're not sore, Bess?"

She shifted under him, her hips moving in a hungry language he was beginning to learn. "No," she said, and then cleared her throat. "Perhaps a little, but I want you . . . Oh!"

He rubbed the blunt head of his cock against her sleek warmth and listened as the breath caught in her throat.

"We can do other things," he said, registering that his voice had dropped to a hoarse whisper.

"I am aching, and not because I'm sore," Betsy said firmly.

Still he hesitated. "We have time—"

She arched against him, an involuntary gasp coming from her lungs. "You feel so *good*."

"It will be easier like this," Jeremy said, rolling over so she was on top. He hissed with pleasure as she slowly sank down, rippling around him. They kissed, and her tangled silk cloud of hair fell about them like a curtain once again, keeping the world out.

Or reshaping a new world, just the two of them, trembling, kissing, moving lazily, steadily, as if they were climbing a mountain.

Falling off the mountain together in a flurry of sparks. At the end, Betsy collapsed on his chest and he caught his breath, stroking her hair.

Blinking away a watery shimmer in his eyes.

# Chapter Twenty-three

*A*unt Knowe looked up sharply when Betsy put her head around the door, and said, "Well?"

Betsy grinned. "We're getting married—that is, if Father agrees. And even if he doesn't," she added.

Her aunt bounded to her feet and caught Betsy in a tight hug. "Your father will be so pleased, my dear."

"Will he?" Betsy asked. After all, Jeremy had spent most of the autumn in the billiard room, supposedly insensible from liquor, dropping sardonic comments when he bothered to talk at all.

"Yes," Aunt Knowe said. "Your father has great respect for Jeremy. Remember, North fought side by side with Jeremy in several battles."

"I forgot that," Betsy said.

"I can tell you who won't be happy," Aunt Knowe said, with a note of satisfaction in her voice. "That intolerable young man Grégoire. It's rare that I take a dislike to a person—"

"That's not exactly true," Betsy said, giving her aunt a kiss on the cheek. "You have high standards."

"I often disapprove," Aunt Knowe said. "But I rarely dislike. I cannot like Grégoire, for all his manners are ingratiating. His eyes are set close together."

"I know something about him that could be considered immoral," Betsy said. "I haven't mentioned it to Jeremy, but perhaps I shall, once we're married."

Aunt Knowe sat back down and picked up her knitting. "I declare, this piece of yarn gets more tangled every time I look at it."

"I think Grégoire accepts money from a stationer for his sketches," Betsy said. "Remember those prints that showed up virtually overnight, making a fuss about Diana and North's betrothal? That was only a few days after Grégoire visited Jeremy at Lindow for the first time."

"That's hardly evidence," her aunt objected.

"He boasted that everyone can recognize his sketches of the royal family," Betsy said.

"There's nothing illegal about selling sketches to stationers. Believe me, my brother has tried to smother more distasteful prints with no success. Has your maid packed your things yet? I am eager to return to Lindow, and apparently the roads are clear this morning."

"Did the auction house deliver your miniatures?"

"They certainly did." Aunt Knowe beamed.

"May I see the one that looked like a young Wilde?"

"Not just now, darling. They're all packed away. We'll have a light luncheon and then leave for home." She brightened. "If Jeremy informs Grégoire immediately, perhaps the man will take off in a huff and won't accompany us to Lindow."

Betsy shook her head. "It's a sad day when I am more cynical than you, dear Aunt, but if he is feeding images to a stationer, he'll stay close to the Wildes as long as he is able."

"If your father returns from Scotland and suspects, he will *geld* him," Aunt Knowe said, as if she were talking about making a cup of tea.

Betsy choked.

"We know how seriously you take your reputation," her aunt said firmly. "Another child would laugh it off; North didn't even care about being compared to a rapist. A Shakespearean rapist, but still a rapist. You are very different from the rest of your family and we respect that."

Betsy was silent for a moment, watching as her aunt poked at her knitting with a free knitting needle. "I don't care any longer," she said finally.

Her aunt's head jerked up.

"I'm serious." Betsy nodded. "Let him make a scandal out of me. He can sell prints of me across all England, if he wishes."

Aunt Knowe cocked her head. "What if he shows you sneaking into a man's bedchamber?"

"How did you know that?" Betsy asked, only mildly surprised.

"I know my chickens," her aunt said. "What if the prints compare you to your mother, Betsy?"

"I am not my mother," Betsy said stoutly. "In time, everyone will forget, because, as you told me, dear Aunt, I'm a Wilde. There might be an enormous fuss at first, but once we're married? And when we've been married a decade? I think not."

Her aunt's smile widened. "I'm so happy for you, Betsy."

"He says he loves me."

"Everyone has known that for months. The man can't take his eyes off you."

"I thought he didn't really notice me until North's wedding," Betsy said, and then she gasped. "You didn't!"

"Didn't what?" her aunt asked innocently.

"You deliberately sent Thaddeus down to the billiard room to propose to me because you knew Jeremy was there!"

Aunt Knowe dropped her knitting on the table and rose. "Am I not your favorite aunt?"

"You're my only aunt," Betsy replied.

"Well, you are my favorite eldest niece," Aunt Knowe said, swooping down and kissing Betsy on the cheek. "I couldn't bear to see you listlessly turning down yet another proposal. I was becoming somewhat worried that one of those gentlemen would coax you into making a mistake."

"Did you send Jeremy there first?"

"Of course I did," her aunt said with aplomb. "He was desperate to escape from the ballroom.

It was the act of a good host to direct him to retire."

Betsy began to laugh. "You are *evil*, Aunt Knowe. Evil!"

"I try," her aunt said, slinging her arm around Betsy's shoulder. "Now come along, you nearly-married woman. I am starving."

"How did you know that I joined Jeremy last night? He very properly escorted me to my door."

"I couldn't sleep," her aunt said. "I will have you know, my dear, that there's nothing proper about a gentleman escorting a young lady to her bedchamber in the dark of night, especially given a long pause at the door."

"True," Betsy said. But she grinned anyway. "I was the one who decided it was too lonely in bed and returned to his room."

"I found myself very grateful that these walls are so thick. Now that you children aren't children any longer," she clarified.

Betsy was grateful too, given that she seemed unable to stay silent when Jeremy's hands, let alone his mouth, ranged over her body.

They were stowed in the carriage, ready to return to Lindow, before she saw him again. He put his head into the carriage and nodded, his eyes on Betsy's face. "I'll be traveling to the castle with my family."

"That answers the question about whether Bisset-Caron is returning to Lindow," Aunt Knowe said with a sigh, as the Wilde carriage began moving.

"Jeremy means to tell his father and cousin that

we are marrying," Betsy said. "A blow for Grégoire, who apparently had ambitions to inherit Jeremy's title."

"A fool is a fool is a fool," Aunt Knowe said. "I suppose he expected Jeremy would fall in battle, and it grew into a habit of mind. I suspect he knows of Jeremy's reaction to fireworks, given an irritable comment he dropped at some point."

"He made an unpleasant comment about it yesterday. He couldn't use that incident to take away Jeremy's title, could he?"

"Oh, no," Aunt Knowe said comfortably. "That only works in melodramas. For one thing, Jeremy's father is still alive. And for another, Jeremy is patently sane and we could attest to it. A mere word from your father would squash any foolish petition Grégoire might try."

"I expect Grégoire is not dangerous, just disappointed," Betsy said.

"Exactly. Don't forget tiresome."

JEREMY WOULD HAVE echoed Lady Knowe, if he knew her judgment. The journey to Lindow took two hours, given snow and ice on the roads. The entire time was taken up by a monologue on the subject of Jeremy's unfitness for marriage, delivered, naturally, by his cousin. His father rolled his eyes and then fell asleep in a corner.

Jeremy had never given Grégoire much thought. His cousin had been at Eton, but two years behind him. Jeremy had met the younger boy when Grégoire tracked him down on the first day of term and declared himself to be Jeremy's closest relative.

The fact didn't interest him then, and it didn't interest him now.

Grégoire had grown into a man who paid far too much attention to the color of his stockings.

"I don't say this for my own benefit, but due to concern for our ancient name," he said now, a patent falsehood. "A man who's spent time in Bedlam ought not to assume the title."

"How did you know that I spent time in Bedlam?" Jeremy asked.

Grégoire shrugged. "Someone must have told me."

"Not good enough," Jeremy said. He leaned forward slightly and let his expression say the rest.

Grégoire was a pampered only son, not a man who would ever conceive of taking up a place in the artillery or any other branch of the military. He shied away. "Your valet, if you must know. When you disappeared, he sent about to your club and I happened to be there. We were worried that you'd come to harm."

"I see," Jeremy said, controlling his irritation. "It must have been disappointing when I turned up, hearty and well, at Lindow Castle. Did you hope that I had slipped into the Thames?"

"Of course not!" Grégoire said, looking as indignant as was possible for such a slippery fellow. "I have my own fortune and no need for yours." He fondly caressed the large sapphire he wore on his left hand, supposedly in honor of his French mother.

"As I told you, dear cousin, my concern is for the blood we share, and the antiquity of our illustrious name."

"Your mother was French, in case you've forgotten," Jeremy pointed out. "And you changed your name to hers, so we no longer share a name."

Grégoire's eyes hardened. "I am English to the core."

"So my valet told you I was missing, and then later shared my experience in Bedlam as well?" Apparently it was time to pension off his valet; the man was too old to be merely shown the door.

"That is irrelevant," Grégoire retorted. "Prints circulating through London depict you wrapped in a white jacket, raving and wigless." He lowered his voice. "I didn't want to mention them before the marquess; I know the shame would cause him tremendous pain."

Jeremy's jaw tightened.

"Prints are also circulating that depict you hiding behind a tree while the men of your platoon gasp their final breaths," Grégoire said. "As a member of the family, I find those the most objectionable."

"Do you?" Jeremy asked.

"It is axiomatic that the heir to the marquessate should not be reviled for cowardice, nor pitied for madness," Grégoire announced.

Jeremy sat back, crossed his arms over his chest, and said, "Grégoire, I am going to marry the oldest daughter of the Duke of Lindow. It will do you no good to try to have me committed for madness."

His cousin gasped. Overdoing it, to Jeremy's mind.

"What a loathsome suggestion! It is up to you, not I, to ensure the future of the family name, but if you do not care, then you do not."

"I do not," Jeremy confirmed.

"What if you become insane again? You were violent and had to be restrained."

A flare of true anger lit in Jeremy's belly. "You bothered to find out all the details."

"You *are* my only cousin," Grégoire said.

"Perhaps we would both be more comfortable if we eschewed the relationship," Jeremy suggested.

He received another appalled look. "Family cannot be 'eschewed,'" his cousin said flatly. "I will pray to the Blessed Virgin that you have no more violent episodes."

It probably would not lead to harmony if Jeremy pointed out that the Blessed Virgin played quite a small role in English prayers, as opposed to French ones, so he propped himself in the corner and closed his eyes, imitating his father.

Somehow feigned sleep became real sleep, and he woke only when the carriage began rattling over the cobblestones of Lindow Castle.

Opposite him, Grégoire was plucking the curls of his wig to shining ringlets.

Jeremy stretched. An unusual feeling of bodily satisfaction spread through him.

"Why must you wear that wig without powder?" Grégoire said, peevishness leaking into his voice. "It doesn't reflect well on us."

"There is no 'us,'" Jeremy stated.

The carriage drew to a stop. Jeremy pushed open the door and jumped down without waiting for a groom. He needed Betsy, and more Betsy.

Last night her untidy hair, her slumberous eyes, her happy gleam made his chest hurt with an emotion he scarcely knew. He craved her, the way he had once craved whisky.

For him, there was only Bess, or Betsy, or Boadicea.

The private woman, the polite society damsel, the warrior queen.

She wasn't in her bedchamber. Or the billiard room. The damned castle was so large that he searched for her for an hour, enduring sixty minutes of blazing and thwarted desire.

When he found Lady Knowe, she shook her head at him and said, "I sent her to the brewery to judge the October ale."

Jeremy blinked.

"You are stealing a future duchess," Lady Knowe told him. "Betsy is trained to be the Lady of the Castle and oversee every room."

"She will make a magnificent future marchioness," he countered. "Shall I write to her father in Scotland and ask for her hand in marriage? Or request that he return to Lindow?"

"I sent off a messenger this morning. Not that they'll be surprised."

"*I'm* surprised," Jeremy told her.

Her laughter followed him down the corridor. Following Prism's directions, Jeremy walked out the west entrance of the castle. Someone had shoveled a path through the snow covering the archery field, so he followed it. The sun was shining, but a yellow cast to the air suggested that more snow might come.

The archery targets had acquired hats of snow that all tilted to the same side, presumably away from storm wind. He followed footprints through the archery field to a low, ancient building. The lintel was so low that Jeremy had to bend his head to push open the door and enter.

The smell of beer inside the brewery gave the air a thick quality. The odor came to him in a rush of grassy, citrusy hops, with an undernote of malt and a yeasty splash on top.

Betsy was seated at the far side of the room, sitting back from a rough wooden table so that skirts of pale blue brocade could flow out to either side. Her hair was powdered and caught up with butterflies whose wings trembled as she moved. A white fur cloak was thrown over a hogshead to the side.

She was speaking to an old man with an enormous mustache.

"Good afternoon," Jeremy said, walking toward them.

To his sharp delight, she glowed with pleasure to see him. "Lord Jeremy," she cried. "Do come meet our marvelous brewmaster, Herr Horn. We are about to try the October ale."

Jeremy shook hands with Mr. Horn and then sat down opposite Betsy. Mr. Horn went to fetch some ale and a glass for Jeremy.

"I didn't expect to see you here," Betsy said.

Jeremy grinned. "You'll get used to seeing me follow you about. So this is a brewhouse? I don't believe I've ever been in the one on my father's estate."

"We're very lucky to have Herr Horn," she told him. "Someone in the family meets with him to discuss the ales three times a year. The October ale waits for two years, plus there's dark ale, and blond beer. My sisters and I take turns with Aunt Knowe. My older brothers used to do their duty, and the younger children will come along as well."

"The better to shape future duchesses?"

"How will we respect our food and drink if we don't respect the making of it?"

"You just quoted Lady Knowe, did you not?"

Betsy laughed. "She's my mother, for all purposes."

Mr. Horn returned with three glasses and a pitcher. He poured the pale ale slowly, with reverence, into Betsy's glass, allowing for just the right amount of bitter, snowy foam. "The ale is well-hopped, as Her Ladyship prefers," he noted.

"Aunt Knowe thinks that hops have medicinal properties," Betsy added, as Mr. Horn poured more beer.

"That is as may be," the brewmaster said. "Hops make an excellent bitter beer, light-bodied and blond, as we call it."

"Herr Horn, thank you for sharing your creation with us," Betsy said. She picked up her glass and swirled it, holding it so that light from the lamp struck golden notes through the beer.

"It's a fair color," Mr. Horn acknowledged.

Betsy took a delicate sniff from the glass and then a swallow, so Jeremy followed suit. The three of them sat for a moment in silence, letting the bittersweet taste fill their mouths. Betsy licked the foam from her upper lip, and Jeremy had to take a gulp of ale to stop himself from licking it for her.

"You've outdone yourself, Herr Horn," she said, sipping once more.

"We dried the malt with coke," Mr. Horn said, putting down his mug and looking expectantly at Betsy.

"Is that what gives it a fruity taste, something like black cherries?"

The old man grinned at her. "Ach, but you would have made a rare brewmaster, Lady Boadicea! What you're tasting there is the effect of using a peck of peas against half a peck of wheat. What do you think of it, Lord Jeremy?"

"It tastes like summer malt," Jeremy said. He lifted his mug. "You're a magician and an undoubted master, Herr Horn."

The brewmaster's mustache flared up almost to the top of his ruddy cheeks. "I had fine hops to work with."

"Lady Knowe asked if you would be kind enough to share the first taste with her," Betsy said. "She would have joined me, but she's not quite herself today. Perhaps hoppy ale will be healing."

Lady Knowe seemed perfectly hearty when Jeremy saw her a half hour ago, but mischief hung in the air about Betsy, the reckless pleasure with which she donned boy's breeches.

"We're none of us getting any younger," Mr. Horn acknowledged, hustling over to refill his pitcher from a hogshead to the side. "I'll bring it to her myself. Will you accompany me, Lady Boadicea?"

"I'll finish this marvelous brew," she said. And then, with a private twinkle, "Lord Jeremy will escort me to the castle."

As the door shut behind Mr. Horn, they leaned forward at the same moment, as if choreographed. Jeremy groaned as Betsy's tongue met his. She tasted like sweet beer and Bess, a potent combination that made his head swim.

He stood up so fast that his stool fell over. Betsy laughed as he placed their glasses to the side.

"I want you." His voice was raw and deep. He rounded the table and crouched before her, taking in the way her breasts swelled above her bodice, the flush in her cheeks, the bright gleam in her eyes. Her collarbones were as exquisite as the rest of her, edging her breasts like the delicate framework of a cathedral window. "You're so damned beautiful," he breathed.

Her eyes searched his face. "As are you."

Raw lust bit at him, and he grabbed her fur cape, throwing it down on the table. "A bed fit for a lady."

She began giggling, a sound like pure joy turned to song. "We can't do that here."

"Ah, but we can." He picked her up with a kiss, and put her down on the fur, shifting his hands just in time to trap her panniers before they flipped into the air.

"Most men can't manage that," she said, grinning at him.

"I've been watching you maneuver into chairs for months now," he admitted. He pulled up her skirts, but found another under it, and another under that. "How many layers are you wearing?"

Her eyes had darkened from sky blue to something more tempestuous. "At least bar the door," she said.

He pulled up the last layer, a thin chemise, and then turned to cross the room and slam the bar in place. He returned to find her propped on her elbows, her legs dangling over the side of the table, emerging from a froth of pale blue and snowy white petticoats. She wore pale blue stockings, and above the ribbons that held them up, her thighs were plump and creamy.

"Come," she said, holding out a hand.

He was there in a rush, crouching and pushing her legs apart.

She gave a little scream and tried to sit up. "Angelic behavior," he reminded her. Simple hunger roughened his voice. "You taste wonderful."

"You're looking at me in the daylight," Betsy exclaimed, "and we aren't even in a bed."

"You are exquisite." He leaned forward to lick the delicate, fluted petals between her legs. His hands were clasped on her knees so he knew when she began trembling, with small, surprised cries.

He licked with patient intensity, building her pleasure until she was begging. Each word soaked into his soul. He was learning his lady's ways, what made her cry out, writhe, draw up one knee in ecstasy. He knew it to be one of the most important lessons of his lifetime.

All the time, desire mounted ferocious demands in his own body, until he was shaking as much as she was. When he finally let go of one of her knees and pushed two thick fingers inside, she exploded with a scream.

He stayed with her through it, lapping her gently, turning his head to kiss the inside of her knee and, when she quieted but for small gasps, her upper thigh. Then he straightened and drew her forward, just enough to meet his cock.

He paused long enough to catch a smile from languorous eyes before he leaned over to kiss her, taking her mouth at the moment he took her body. Her arms wound around him, clinging to him, holding him to this world. Their hearts beat the same frantic rhythm as he sank into her.

"Does it hurt?" he whispered into her mouth, ready to withdraw.

Her eyes opened and he saw sharp joy there along with hunger. "No," she whispered back. She wriggled and he bit out a groan at the sensation. "It feels uncomfortable but at the same time . . . won't you please move, Jeremy? The way you did last night?"

His mind went blank and he couldn't think of the proper response: "My pleasure" would be absurd.

But it *was* his pleasure: not just the act of it, but the way her soft mouth clung to his, and the way her hands wandered, bolder than they had been the night before. She managed to free his shirt and ran her hands over his nipples, jolting his senses.

He loved every joyful syllable of her laughter, and he loved it when she fell silent but for small sounds that transformed to aching moans.

A fierce male satisfaction grew inside him when she wound her legs around his hips, sobbing out demands with raw erotic fever. His cock deep inside her, he cupped her face in his hands and said, "I love you, and you're mine."

His heart squeezed, meeting her shining eyes.

"I love you too," she whispered.

Afterward, he carried her home, wrapped in her white cloak. "She fell," he told Prism, who looked mildly alarmed.

"I'm fine," Betsy said, raising her head from his chest.

"I'll take her upstairs," Jeremy told the butler. "She may have twisted her ankle. She may have to rest in bed for the day."

She managed to muffle her giggle against his coat.

# Chapter Twenty-four

*W*hen Betsy called Winnie and asked for supper in her room hours later, Jeremy didn't bother to hide behind the curtains or whatever it was that gentlemen did in melodramas.

She was his, and that was the end of it.

She had fallen asleep, her hair a midnight cloud tangled around her shoulders—he'd washed out the powder, but they made love rather than comb out her curls—when a gentle knock on the door brought a note.

It was from Grégoire: *I am in the library. I wish to say goodbye, as I shall return to London early in the morning.*

Jeremy frowned at the note. He hadn't liked the look on Grégoire's face when he talked of Bedlam. Nor that his cousin detailed the print that depicted Jeremy hiding behind a tree with a familiarity that suggested he sketched it. Grégoire's anger seemed to hide a different emotion, a suggestive and disturbing thought.

He pulled the covers up to Betsy's chin and dropped a kiss on her hair.

When he reached the library, Grégoire was seated, reading a book. Jeremy frowned. The scene was staged: but to what end? His cousin had always been a pain in the arse, but Grégoire's instinct for drama was moving past annoying to something else.

"Cousin," Grégoire said, rising, putting his book to the side, and sweeping into a bow. "I have a grave matter that I wish to raise with you before I leave for London."

Jeremy dropped into the chair opposite him without returning his bow. "What is it?"

"I accept that you have formed an understanding with Lady Boadicea."

"You could call it that."

Grégoire's eyes darkened.

"Since you sent that note to her bedchamber, you know that it is far more than an 'understanding,'" Jeremy supplied.

"It would be morally wrong to marry her."

Jeremy didn't roll his eyes, but only because he had decided to limit insults to words. "Your reasoning?"

"You were damaged in the war," Grégoire said, leaning forward. His eyes were so earnest that Jeremy almost missed the calculation in their depths. "You are not the man you used to be."

He paused, presumably to allow Jeremy to absorb this terrible news.

"True," Jeremy said. He leaned back in his chair, examining Grégoire as carefully as he might a colonial soldier. He'd always known that his cousin wanted to inherit the title, but now ambition seemed to have gone further than wistfulness.

It was remarkably annoying. Betsy lay in a bed upstairs, and he could be there, running a hand around her breasts, tasting her again, making her ache until her eyes softened and she began to beg him.

"Go on," he ordered, irritation lacing his voice.

Grégoire arranged his features into an expression of deep concern, but something about his eyes looked feral. Jeremy didn't move a muscle, but he abruptly realized that the room was a battlefield, albeit without cannon fire.

"You were in Bedlam for over a week," Grégoire said, putting his cards on the table. "While there, you were violent and had to be restrained. I spoke to the attendants myself. They brought in three men to subdue you."

"That was surprisingly solicitous of you," Jeremy drawled.

"I *do* care for this family, unlike you," Grégoire retorted. "If you marry Lady Boadicea, you will injure her the next time you fall into a fit. You will damage your wife, and quite possibly your children as well. You might kill them."

Jeremy clenched his teeth together. It wasn't a solution to kill his cousin, though it felt like a necessity. "Just to clarify, you didn't know I was in Bedlam until Parth rescued me?"

"Certainly not. I dislike interfering in matters

of the heart," Grégoire said with a pious smirk, "but I feel that the duke ought to be informed of the particulars of your stay amongst the madmen. Any father would wish to know of it."

"'Amongst the madmen,'" Jeremy echoed. "Nice phrase." He gave Grégoire a flat look, a soldier's warning.

His cousin paled slightly. "I could bring the attendants to Lindow Castle to talk to His Grace," he said shrilly. "No man would allow his daughter to marry a man with a tendency toward violent fits. You don't remember what happened, do you?"

Jeremy didn't. It bothered him, the gap in his memory that stretched from the sound of exploding fireworks to waking in Parth's house.

"You can't risk it," Grégoire said, ladling compassion into his voice, as if he thought Jeremy was agonizing over the experience. "You would be destroyed, cousin, if you injured your wife or children. Yet the damage caused by war is irredeemable." He reached out to the book he had been reading. "This doctor attributes such effects to cardiac damage. Soldiers can be suddenly stricken with visions of warriors attacking them. They do the same to their loved ones, unbeknownst to themselves."

Grégoire decided to demonstrate his ability to read. "*They raise a wild cry as if their throats were being cut even then and there. They fight as bitterly as if they were gnawed by the fangs of panthers or of fierce lions.*"

It was a valid concern so Jeremy thought about it while Grégoire amused himself by reading aloud more depictions of soldiers *in extremis.*

Jeremy had no doubt but that some men did experience illusions and respond to them violently. Yet he had been surprised by the charge that he had been violent to the point of needing a straitjacket. On the other hand, he hadn't bothered to investigate. Likely all patients were restrained, and complaints about violence made things easier for the attendants.

He didn't believe it, in his case: not because he was incapable of violence, but because no one had reported dead attendants.

If his experience at war had taught him anything, it was how to kill in hand-to-hand combat. It was a skill he wished he didn't have, but too late. If he had truly believed he was facing enemy combatants, at least one attendant would have died and most likely three to four.

Grégoire's artful disclosure that attendants had actually described fighting with him suggested that the truth was different from what he'd been told. Jeremy held up his hand, and his cousin stopped reading mid-sentence.

Then he leaned forward and smiled, showing his teeth. Grégoire actually flinched, which showed some sense. "What do you want?"

"I want to preserve the Thurrock line!" Grégoire shrilled. "You—you are not fit. You have never been fit. A future marquess shouldn't go to war, risking everything. You could have died when your colonel deserted—"

He stopped.

"How did you know that?" Jeremy asked, his voice grating. "The general buried the question of desertion. The official story is that conflicting orders left my platoon alone on the battlefield, and I told no one but my father."

Grégoire shrugged. "You really think that secrets remain secrets?"

It was a good answer. Grégoire could have bribed someone, which would have been easy enough.

The issue was irrelevant.

"I did not fight the attendants, and I will never injure my wife," Jeremy said, pacing the words so that Grégoire could not miss the import. "Nor my children. I don't know what happened in Bedlam, but I don't believe I was violent."

"Your confidence in yourself is touching but meaningless, since you have no memory of the episode," Grégoire scoffed. "You are not a reliable witness and I am quite certain the duke will agree with me."

Jeremy was certain that the duke would consider the lack of dead bodies a clue—besides, a bribed attendant could be bribed again to tell the truth.

"What's more," Grégoire said, "it wasn't the only time, was it? You lost consciousness during that episode with Lady Diana's mother. After you were shot, you showed little sign of knowing where you were. The grooms felt you might have attacked the entire party if a well-placed order from Lord Northbridge had not jolted you back to yourself."

Yet he remembered everything of that afternoon, from the shot, to the rushing noise in his ears, to his own violent—*verbal*—reaction.

"They'd never heard such blasphemy," Grégoire said. "Like a beast, they said. In front of ladies too! Your eyes were blank, and you only came to yourself when Lord Northbridge barked an order."

It was true. Luckily he had the strong feeling that no language would startle Betsy, if that part of the episode recurred.

"Men have killed their wives, even strangled their babes in similar fits. They find themselves back in the heat of battle. They smell the smoke of gunpowder, when there is none. They think they are in a field strewn with dead bodies and hostile soldiers. I can show you a book if you wish."

"No, thanks," Jeremy said. "I regret the pain those men experience, but my reactions are not as extreme."

"If you're so certain, you should demonstrate it," Grégoire spat.

They'd reached the crux of the matter, the reason Grégoire asked for this meeting.

"How would I do that?"

"I can prove that you pose a risk to your wife and even your unborn children," Grégoire said. He reached down to a case by his chair and pulled out a pistol. Before he was conscious of moving, Jeremy had the pistol in his right hand and Grégoire's wrist in his left.

"What are you doing?" his cousin cried.

Jeremy moved back a step, dropping Grégoire's

wrist. Grégoire began shaking it as if his bones had been crushed. "I'm looking at a man who wants my title; why would I allow you to wield a weapon in my presence?"

"I'm trying to help!" Grégoire squealed. "I don't need your money. I never have. I speak this truth for the good of the family. You're a menace to those you love, and all I want to do is demonstrate it."

"By shooting me." It wasn't a question.

"Of course not!" Grégoire's eyes bulged with indignation.

Jeremy actually believed him. Grégoire was a monster, but a sneaky one. Probably not a murderer. At least, not face-to-face. Murder left a mark on a man that he recognized, even if the death happened on a battlefield.

He looked down at the pistol. "What the hell are you thinking, keeping a loaded gun in the castle?"

"This book says that men lose their senses when they hear a shot," Grégoire said, pointing. "If I shoot that pistol, you'll fall into a state. I'll *prove* to you that it would be immoral to marry."

Jeremy almost scoffed at him, but there was just enough of a question in his own mind . . . "If I became violent, I could injure you," he pointed out.

Kill him, more likely.

"I'll duck behind the screen," Grégoire said, pointing to a tall screen just by the window, designed to hide a chamber pot. "You won't know I'm here. Remember, you won't be yourself."

"Then how will I know what happened?"

"We could summon a witness."

"We'll have a hundred. You're talking about shooting a pistol in the middle of the night."

"Obviously I would shoot out the window," Grégoire said. "You can shoot the weapon yourself, if you prefer."

"I *do* prefer," Jeremy said. An "accidental" death might be within Grégoire's capabilities.

"If others hear the shot and join us, it will simply prove my point, won't it?" Grégoire moved over to the sideboard. "I need something to steady my nerves. Whisky?"

The man was hoping to befuddle him. Jeremy was growing more curious about this demonstration by the second. Men had committed murder for the title of squire, let alone marquess.

Grégoire handed him a glass of whisky.

Jeremy tossed it back with a silent apology to Lady Knowe. Grégoire obviously didn't know that he was unaffected by whisky, whereas Grégoire had been notorious at Oxford for his inability to hold his liquor.

He poured himself another glass and refilled Grégoire's as well. "Shall we drink to my marriage?" And, meeting Grégoire's stony gaze, "No?"

"To the gods of war," Grégoire said, drinking.

Jeremy didn't join him, as those particular gods were no friends of his. "You surprise me," he observed. "Those gods surely failed you when I returned safe and sound."

"You may be safe, but sound?" Grégoire's smile flickered like a serpent's tongue. "Let's drink to the exquisite Lady Boadicea." The ghost of a

French accent hung around Grégoire's vowels; the whisky was already affecting him.

"Queen Boadicea was a failed warrior, much as you were," Grégoire said, raising his glass. "It must create a bond between you."

Jeremy tossed off the toast and put down his glass.

An icy sensation was building in his chest. Grégoire was right about one thing. The thought of a red welt across Betsy's cheek made his heart stop. He had carried her home from the brewhouse; her bones were as delicate as a bird's in comparison to his.

If he mistook her for a soldier and threw her against a wall . . .

He might kill her indeed. A shard of agony speared through him at the thought, throwing him back onto the field where flies circled the faces of dead men, and every death was his fault. If he . . . if that happened to Betsy or to anyone he loved, it would flay him to the bone.

For months, he had sat in a corner of the billiard room and shook silently, trying to barricade his mind against the memory of war and failing. It had been quiet in the corner, and dark.

No sounds, no smells, nothing to rip him out of his fragile hold on reality and hurl him into the past.

He'd been a coward.

"You think that a gunshot would do it?" he asked hoarsely.

"Look what happened at Vauxhall," Grégoire said. "You can simply shoot my pistol out the window. We'll call it an accidental shot that happened while I was cleaning the weapon before leaving tomorrow."

As if anyone would believe that Grégoire cleaned his own weapons.

Jeremy rubbed his hands over his face, thinking. He had nothing to lose, because he actually was sure of his own mind. It wasn't whole, by any means. But he had spent months staring into the dark, brooding over what happened.

The darkness didn't own him any longer.

"Right," he said. He shoved open the window and pointed Grégoire's pistol into the darkness.

"Aim at the sky," Grégoire cried.

The sound exploded in the small room with the force of a cannon.

# Chapter Twenty-five

$\mathcal{B}$etsy woke at the sound of a gunshot. She sat up, shocked to find she was naked, shocked to find she was alone.

Footsteps pounded down the corridor and paused. "If you have a man in there, send him down," her aunt bellowed. "There's a burglar in the castle!"

Betsy swung her feet out of bed. The moon was shining in the window, but she couldn't see her nightdress. She pulled on her wrapper and knotted it tightly. No slippers, but the boots she had worn to the auction stood against the side of the room. She stamped into them and started out into the corridor.

She followed loud voices to the library and froze in the doorway.

Jeremy was lying on the floor, her aunt kneeling beside him. Her heart skipped a beat. She threw herself across the room and dropped at his side. "Is he shot? Is he—"

"No," Aunt Knowe barked. "There's been a damned fool game and when he wakes up, I plan to kill him myself."

"No blood," Betsy said on a gasp, her hands flying over Jeremy's chest. He felt warm, his heartbeat reassuringly strong.

"Yet he's insensible," her aunt said, frowning. She was holding his wrist, counting his pulse.

"Jeremy doesn't play games," Betsy said. She stood up, trusting him to Aunt Knowe. Prism was there; servants milled about. Jeremy's father burst through the door. A smell of gun smoke lingered in the air.

Grégoire was just where she would have expected, off to the side wearing an expression of elaborate concern. She marched toward him, brushing past the butler.

"What did you do?" she demanded. Unlike the rest of them, he wasn't dressed for bed. His shirt collar was ripped and he wore no wig. His hair was disheveled.

She was startled to see true dislike in Grégoire's eyes, though his troubled expression deepened. "My cousin and I discussed the impairment he had suffered in the war."

Everyone turned to look.

"And?" Betsy demanded.

"My cousin shot the pistol out the window to prove to himself that he suffered no ill effects. Unfortunately there *were* effects. He attacked me." Grégoire waved his hand to indicate his torn collar.

"Nonsense," Aunt Knowe said flatly. "If Jeremy attacked you, you'd be dead."

"I might have been," Grégoire retorted. "Luckily my valet was able to subdue him."

The marquess had been crouching beside his son, but now he rose and came to stand at Betsy's shoulder. She glanced up, surprised to realize that Jeremy had inherited more from his father than she realized. The marquess's amiable countenance had taken on an altogether darker cast.

Grégoire moved sharply and then clarified, "My valet saved my life!"

"It appears your valet struck Lord Jeremy violently on the head," Aunt Knowe said. "He'd better hope that His Lordship recovers quickly."

Betsy whirled. Her aunt was gently holding Jeremy's head. "A knot is rising very quickly. All the same, I am surprised that he isn't awake."

"He's not himself," Grégoire stated. "He suffers from an injury that is not uncommon among soldiers." He turned to Betsy. "If you marry him, he may kill you without knowing it. He may *brutalize* you or your children."

"You pathetic little worm," Betsy spat, taking a step closer to him.

He looked down his nose, an expression of blinding contempt on his face. "You dare say that to me? *You?* I would rue the day that a strumpet became the Marchioness of Thurrock! Like mother, like daughter." He turned and raised his voice. "I had to rout my cousin out of this slut's bedchamber this night."

Before Betsy could answer, a powerful thunk split the air. Grégoire actually came off his feet before he slammed into a wall and slid down it.

"My son is incapacitated," the marquess said grimly, "so I defended the family honor for him."

It had finally happened: Betsy had been called a slut and compared to her mother in public. The sky didn't fall.

"I say," Grégoire bleated, pushing himself up into a sitting position. "Haven't I been attacked enough for one night?"

A heavyset man was sliding toward the door. It had to be Grégoire's valet. "Stop him," she called. Two footmen lunged toward the man.

Aunt Knowe had been waving *sal volatile* under Jeremy's nose. "He moved," she reported, tapping his cheek. "Time to wake up and slaughter your cousin, Jeremy."

"I heard that!" Grégoire said, from where he sat against the wall, dabbing his lip with a handkerchief.

Betsy marched over to him, her boots thumping loudly. "I would demand an apology, except you're right," she said. "Jeremy *was* in my bedchamber because we plan to marry and have many, many children. You will never inherit."

"I believe your father will disagree," Grégoire said with a titter. "You may have given my cousin your maidenhead, but will your father agree to your very life being threatened?"

Behind her, Aunt Knowe growled, "What an imbecile."

"I agree," Betsy said.

She moved even closer to Grégoire. He looked up and sneered. "Are you planning to slap me? It won't change the truth, and the truth *will* out!"

"I expect you're right," Betsy said. It was enormously satisfying to slam her boot between his legs. She enjoyed the gasp and the utter shock in his eyes before he screamed and rolled to the side, curling into a ball and rocking back and forth.

A strong arm wrapped around her shoulder before she could draw back her leg and do it again. "Jeremy will be proud of us, don't you think?" a deep voice asked.

Betsy grinned up at the marquess.

"Jeremy is awake. Someone take that fool valet away and question him," Aunt Knowe ordered, getting to her feet.

Betsy flew back to Jeremy and knelt at his side. He stared at her, squinting, then put a hand on her cheek. "Hello, beautiful," he murmured.

"Do you know who I am?"

"My wife," he said, his eyelids closing on a smile.

"*Wife?*" Grégoire rolled up to his knees. "That's a lie!"

"You're the fool," Aunt Knowe said, staring down at him, arms crossed over her chest. "It's the easiest thing in the world to acquire a license, you imbecile."

Betsy squeezed Jeremy's hand. Perhaps Aunt Knowe was right, but to the best of her knowledge, Jeremy hadn't acquired such a license. Yet.

"Unless you want me to second my niece and

kick any of your future offspring into eternity," Aunt Knowe said grimly, "tell me what you did to her husband."

"I did nothing! My valet cracked him over the head because he was about to murder me. Tell them, Jardin."

The valet was standing near the door, a footman at each arm. "I defended my master."

Betsy kissed Jeremy on the lips and he opened his eyes again. "What happened?" she asked.

He frowned.

"You shot a pistol," she prompted.

He sat up and his hand went straight to the back of his head. "Bloody hell."

"You went mad, just as I predicted," Grégoire shrilled. He was on his feet, glaring around the room. "The shot went off and he began growling like a wild animal and lunged at me. I expect he thought I was another soldier."

"I don't remember that," Jeremy said.

"You wouldn't," Grégoire said, his voice more confident. "You didn't remember Bedlam either, did you?"

"How does *he* know about that?" Aunt Knowe asked.

The marquess moved to Jeremy's side. "Bedlam?" Jeremy's father's voice was anguished.

Jeremy held out his hand and after an infinitesimal pause, his father pulled him to his feet. "Nothing important. Grégoire bribed the attendants for details, the better to circulate a print of it," Jeremy explained.

He looked to Betsy and she flew to him, nestling against his chest.

"I'm fine," he said. "Hell of a headache. Who knocked me out?"

"My valet saved my life," Grégoire repeated. "Did you marry that woman?"

Jeremy's arm tightened around Betsy. "Not yet."

"You ignore evidence at your own peril! I wouldn't be at all surprised if a year from now your wife is found shot dead and your only excuse will be that you can't remember."

"Never!" Betsy said, turning so that her back was to Jeremy's front, as if she could defend him with her body.

"He cannot marry you," Grégoire said flatly. "For all my cousin acts like a beast, he's a gentleman. A surprisingly ethical one too." His voice was bitter. "A hero on the battlefield, by all accounts."

"You would know." Jeremy looked at his father. "He knew the details of what happened in the colonies."

The marquess nodded. "I'll take care of it." Betsy felt suddenly sorry for Grégoire. But not very much.

"We need to talk," Jeremy said to Betsy, turning her gently in his arms.

"He can't marry you, because he genuinely cares for you," Grégoire said. "I know him. The fear that he might hurt you at any moment would be between you your entire life. You—"

"Enough," Jeremy said curtly. Whatever was in his gaze made the words dry up in Grégoire's mouth. Jeremy turned to Aunt Knowe, standing beside the marquess, both of them looking like soldiers waiting for orders. "Thank you."

Betsy took a deep breath.

She didn't like the edge in his voice. She didn't like the feeling that he'd made a decision without her, one that could change the current of her life.

But it wasn't a fight she chose to have in public.

She slipped her hand into his. "I think you should rest."

"We will take care of this situation," Aunt Knowe said. She folded her arms over her chest and gave Jeremy a level stare. "Don't disappoint me and play the fool."

# Chapter Twenty-six

$\mathcal{J}$eremy walked beside Betsy, the splitting pain in his head not helped by the loud sound of her boots. It felt as if Grégoire's valet had slammed him with a brick.

He was beginning to wonder just how far Grégoire had gone to put Jeremy in situations where he *might* die. Wrapped in a straitjacket, drugged, with no one knowing any better? People died all the time in Bedlam.

He pushed the thought away. His father and Lady Knowe would discover the truth. There was a time when he would have demanded to question the valet and his cousin, trusting no one but himself.

But now he had family.

Betsy pushed him down onto the side of the bed and then kicked off her boots and clambered up onto the bed to sit beside him. "How badly does your head hurt?"

"Like the devil. Betsy—"

"I don't care how much of a gentleman you are," she flashed, interrupting. "You're not allowed to push me away. You would never injure me. In fact, there's something very odd about his entire story."

Her eyes were wide and strained. Jeremy reached out, meaning to pull her into his lap, but she shook him off.

"Listen to me," she said fiercely. "You will never injure me. I won't allow it. I'll throw sausages at your head, if that's what's needed to wake you up."

Something resembling laughter rose in his chest.

"You offered for me and I shall hold you to it." She sounded confident, but a tear slid down the curve of her cheek.

"Bess," Jeremy said, his throat tight, but she didn't let him finish. Instead she pounced on him. Clamped her mouth onto his.

He should . . .

The thought slid away. Her tongue slipped into his mouth. She kissed him with heart-aching tenderness.

Betsy put her love, her belief, and her loyalty into that kiss. And her courage, because her heart was hammering a fearful rhythm. "I won't let you go," she gasped, between kisses. "Don't throw me away." Tears stung her eyes. "You won't hurt me." She stopped, unable to find the right words. "You won't," she whispered, her throat raw.

"It would rip me apart if I injured you," Jeremy said. One hand caressed the curve of her cheek. "You understand, don't you?"

"You would never hurt me if you were in your right mind. If you thought I was an enemy soldier, you might try. I would stop you." Her voice broke. "I *promise* that."

He swooped down, kissing her with so much passionate intensity that a tingle of hope went through her. "I told you that the gentleman in me was burned away by the war," he growled.

She hadn't believed him then or now.

He nipped her lip. "For God's sake, Bess, I'm sitting in the bedchamber of a virgin whom I deflowered before marriage."

Sure enough, the man looking at her was burning with primitive, raw desire and possession. "I mean to keep you," he said harshly.

A smile broke out on her face.

"I'll keep drinking Lady Knowe's tisanes, and I'll avoid whisky, and I'll spend my life in the stables, but I won't give you up."

She sighed into his mouth, her breath joining his. "Truly?"

"Not until your life or mine comes to an end."

"Not even then," she whispered. "Promise?"

Jeremy managed to smile at her.

Love flooded through him, changing his very essence, making him new. "I promise," he said huskily. "And beyond."

Betsy pulled back enough to meet his eyes. "We'll have to start going to chapel on Sundays," she said, the love in her voice settling on his skin like a caress.

"We could simply act like the angels we saw," Jeremy murmured, tipping her backward. "Bess,

I don't think I will injure you. I don't believe I ripped Grégoire's shirt."

She nodded. "That was odd, wasn't it? It ripped along the collar."

"As if the stitches had been previously loosened," he agreed. "I don't believe I would become violent even if fireworks went off under my chair. I know myself a hell of a lot better than I did before I went to war." He brushed a kiss across her lips.

"If you had become violent," Betsy said, "Grégoire would have been the one lying on the floor immobile, wouldn't he?"

Jeremy nodded. His eyes were unapologetic. "I was trained as a warrior, and hardened under hellish circumstances, Betsy. If I become violent, it won't be pretty."

"But that means . . ."

"It calls into question the story I was told about Bedlam," he agreed. "I can't say that I really care, though, as long as you don't."

"I *do*," Betsy said fiercely. "Your cousin is . . . I don't have words for what he is!"

"My cousin is being questioned by my father and your aunt," Jeremy said, his eyes laughing. "'In mortal danger' might describe Grégoire."

"He deserves it," she said stoutly.

"He's a fool," Jeremy said, nudging her with his hips.

"Your head?" Betsy asked.

"It hurts," Jeremy admitted. He rolled his hips again. "I can be distracted."

Betsy grinned. "I'll see what I can do."

# Chapter Twenty-seven

$\mathcal{G}$régoire bribed the colonel to flee," the marquess declared, fury nearly choking him. "The man wasn't a coward, as the ministry thought: He was a criminal who took a bribe!"

Jeremy narrowed his eyes. "How was that possible?"

"Grégoire sent a man to the colonies with money and a mandate to put you in danger. The same man followed you after you returned to London," Lady Knowe said. "He took advantage of the fireworks episode to have you whisked off to Bedlam, drugged to the gills, and bound in a straitjacket. Meanwhile, Grégoire stayed far away in case your unfortunate demise was ever questioned."

Jeremy nodded.

"How can you be so calm?" his fierce warrior queen demanded. Betsy's hands were on her hips, as she scowled at him. "That man tried to take your life! He's almost a murderer."

"Grégoire refuses to admit it, but he *is* a murderer," Lady Knowe put in. "Grégoire's wish to ensure that Jeremy died on the battlefield led directly to the death of many men."

"I was furious when you told me that the general had decided to excuse your colonel's cowardly behavior. Now I'll have the colonel court-martialed," the marquess growled. "The man has no honor. None."

Jeremy didn't care.

Oh, he cared for his men; it felt like a physical blow, knowing that their lives were lost owing to one man's greed for a title.

But he didn't care what happened to the colonel. What's done was done.

His father didn't agree. "I'll see your reputation restored if I have to rip the War Office apart brick by brick," the marquess hissed.

"Good!" Betsy said. "What about Grégoire?"

"Attempted murder charges would stick," the marquess said. He hesitated. "If his father were alive, my brother would ask me to allow Grégoire to flee the country, with the promise that he never return to England."

"Yes," Jeremy said flatly. No justice could make up for the lives lost. Grégoire rotting in prison wouldn't do it; the colonel court-martialed wouldn't do it.

"Only if his sapphire and anything else he owns are forfeit, and given to the families of Jeremy's lost men," Betsy ordered, folding her arms over her chest.

His father was obviously impressed. Lady Knowe

wrapped an arm around her. "I trained her well," she said with a chuckle.

"Where is Grégoire?" Jeremy asked.

"Locked in the chapel," Lady Knowe said. "It's cold but not freezing. I told him to contemplate his sins."

"And the valet?"

"He escaped—which means that Prism decided that he wasn't to blame. Prism has strong feelings about servants who are compelled to obey orders," Lady Knowe said. She grimaced. "I expect the man will go straight to a stationery shop, Betsy, and sell a thrilling description of this evening for new etchings. I am sorry about that."

"My reputation is ruined," Betsy said, looking unmoved.

"Society will forget in time," Jeremy said. He took her in his arms. "I thought perhaps you would like to take a wedding trip."

Her eyes lit up. "Where shall we go?"

"Anywhere you like," Jeremy said. He tucked a strand of hair behind her ear. "You could wear breeches when you wished, and be a lady when you didn't."

She hugged him as tightly as she could.

"As long as you're always mine," Jeremy said in a low voice. "My warrior, my queen, and the love of my life."

Betsy looked up, her eyes shining, and Jeremy saw his future in them.

# Chapter Twenty-eight

*Just over a year later*

"The new vicar is coming to tea," Aunt Knowe called, bustling into the drawing room.

"Poor Father Duddleston," Viola said mournfully. She was seated on a sofa unpicking her aunt's tangled knitting. "He only had a few more weeks before he retired."

"He died doing what he loved best," her aunt said. "I'm sure that the new vicar . . . what's his name? Mr. Marlowe. I'm sure he'll be as good."

"Is he married?" Joan asked. Now that she and Viola would be finally debuting in a matter of months, she thought of marriage constantly.

Viola poked at the knitting. *She* had no interest in marriage, and though she'd managed to postpone their debut for a year, it loomed in front of them now.

"He's betrothed to a Miss Pettigrew," Aunt Knowe reported. "Her grandfather is an archbishop, so it's all very appropriate. I've invited her to stay with us for a time." She jumped back to her feet. "I'd better warn Prism; I believe I forgot to mention it."

"I have many ideas for the parish school," Viola said. "Father Duddleston was so resistant to change."

"You'll have no time for that," Joan said. She jumped up and whirled around, following the steps of a country dance. "I can't wait, I can't wait."

Viola willed away the nausea that rose in her stomach. "I wish you would just allow me to wait another year."

"You'd come up with an excuse and never debut at all," Joan said briskly. "You'd spend your life puttering about the parish, teaching children silly rhymes and doing good works."

"No retching in lemon trees from nerves, or spending an evening hiding in the retiring room," Viola said.

"You must fight your shyness," Joan urged, not for the first time. "I worry about you."

Viola's main worries had to do with the horrors of the Season. She could scarcely manage eating with strangers.

"What if you never meet a man to love, because you are immured in the country?" Joan demanded. "Would you be happy living Aunt Knowe's life?"

"Why not? She is beloved by many, and she has all of us," Viola said. "I think she is very lucky."

"There's no *man* in her life," her sister exclaimed, exasperated. "No husband! Remember the way Betsy watches Jeremy under her lashes, or the way North gazes at Diana with adoration? Don't you want to feel the same?"

"No," Viola said decidedly. "It seems most uncomfortable."

"I want a man to look at me desperately."

Viola knew better than to express her opinion because Joan had drama in her bones, and Viola didn't. Viola was also not a Wilde, even though she was raised with them, and the difference was telling. "How many men have come through this castle in the last year?" she asked instead. "Young, unmarried ones, I mean."

"Likely over thirty," Joan said, thinking about it. "There had to be at least that many at Diana's wedding."

"I have never met a single man whom I'd like to spend time with," Viola stated. "Not one."

Joan frowned. "You are being deliberately difficult, Viola. Just think of all the handsome men who pursued Betsy. She said no to all of them, though there were at least four whom I would have considered."

"I wouldn't consider any of them."

Aunt Knowe swept back into the room, looking even more harried. "My dears, isn't this fun? Mr. Marlowe and Miss Pettigrew have arrived a day early; such a lovely surprise!"

Viola and Joan jumped to their feet.

"My nieces, Lady Joan and Miss Viola Astley," Aunt Knowe said. "Miss Pettigrew and Mr. Marlowe."

Viola always looked to women first; having attended a girls' seminary, she was comfortable in female company. Unfortunately, she knew immediately that Miss Pettigrew was not the sort of woman who would put her at her ease—more like the type who would plague her with advice.

She could weather suggestions from those she loved, but she loathed the guidance of strangers, who all seemed to think that they knew the key to overcoming her shyness. Miss Pettigrew definitely knew what was best for everyone in the room. You could see it in her eyes, and the way her head was held high.

At the moment she had inclined it just enough to make it clear that she recognized the secular power of a duke's sister and daughters, but her virtue mattered more than their position in society.

Viola smiled and turned to the new vicar, hoping that he had sweet eyes, like Father Huddleston's.

He hadn't.

# *Epilogue*

*Belmain Manor*
*Country Seat of the Marquess of Thurrock*
*Eight years later*

*T*he billiard room of Belmain Manor was like a sitting room in other houses, or so the oldest daughter of the house, Lady Penny, thought. Her friends' families gathered in sitting rooms or libraries comfortably full of overstuffed chairs, dogs, and books. The Roden family gathered in the billiard room, because it was big enough for two billiard tables—plus overstuffed chairs, dogs, and books.

Just now Penny was sitting on a high stool, her elbows propped on the gleaming sides of her mother's favorite table, watching her parents play.

It was her mama's birthday. Her father, the marquess, didn't care for billiards nearly as much as her mama did, but he always agreed to play on special occasions. This was their third game, and so far they were tied at one each.

They were playing with new rules, which meant that they kept switching back and forth, and both of them got lots of tries to sink balls. It was her father's turn now, so he rounded the table, stopping to kiss her mother on the way. "Last game," he said.

Mama groaned, because she loved to play, almost as much as she loved being a mother to Penny and her brother.

Not quite, though.

"You need to rest," Father said. It was only late afternoon but her mother had grown round with another baby, and Father kept dragging her away to nap. Actually, he did that even when Mama wasn't carrying a child.

"But first we have to give you our present," he added.

The marquess leaned over the table and sighted down the cue. Penny watched carefully as he lined up the billiard cue with the new leather cap that her mother adored so much.

The ball went *thunk* with a pleasing noise, ricocheted from one wall, hit another, and barely missed the pocket.

Penny frowned. Her father had shown Penny that stroke only a week ago, and he'd done it over and over and over, until she could trace the exact path in her mind. He never missed it, not *once*.

She opened her mouth, but before she could say anything, Papa scooped her off the stool. "Shall we give Mama her present?"

"Yes," she said. "But Papa—"

"Our secret," he whispered, putting one finger on her lips.

"Hmm," Penny said.

She knew a losing argument when she saw it, so she skipped off to get the present instead. It was wrapped in silk. Her mother had seated herself in one of the widest chairs, and of course Peter had climbed in her lap and started sucking his thumb.

"Here," Penny said, holding it out. "It's from us. Me too."

Papa sat down on one arm of the chair and wrapped an arm around Mama, so Penny climbed onto the other arm.

"I have such a wonderful family," her mother said mistily.

"Open it!" Peter cried, popping his revoltingly wet thumb out of his mouth.

Inside the bundle was a tiny portrait, smaller than was really useful, to Penny's mind. But she had to admit that it was pretty. It was painted in glowing, shiny paint by a friend of her mother's. He was so old that his brush kept shaking when he painted it, but somehow it had turned out all right.

Her mother held it up.

Hardly bigger than her palm, Penny's beloved grandfather, the late marquess, smiled from the gold frame, Penny nestled on his lap.

"It was finished just before he died," the late marquess's son said, touching his father's cheek. "He loved Penny so much."

"I know I shouldn't cry," her mother said, and then she burst into tears. "It's just that I'm so lucky."

Penny wrapped her arms around her mother's neck, and Peter squirmed around and hugged her too. And her father wrapped his arms around all of them.

"Happy birthday, Queen Bess," he whispered.

# A Note about October Ale, Auction Houses, & PTSD

*A* romance author's historical research clusters around questions of daily life. I need to know what kind of lamp could be carried from room to room in 1790, what kinds of ale a ducal brewhouse might have made and what that beer would have tasted like, as well as who was famous for painting miniatures (Samuel Finney, for one!).

Many of these questions are small, but they can make a large difference to a plot. For example, were women allowed to visit auction houses and bid on items? Many of the people who passed through Christie's doors in the 1790s would have been art dealers or collectors. Christie's Auction House kindly confirmed that women did attend their auctions, although they likely did not bid. Other auction houses may have forbidden women altogether, though I know of none with salacious cupids on the ceiling.

Sometimes, I deliberately go against historical fact, and for that, I apologize. The hymn "Amazing Grace" was published in 1779, and so my hero could not have heard it as a child. But I wanted Jeremy, in the dark and in the profound silence of falling snow, to suddenly hear his father sing, *"I once was lost but now am found. Was blind but now I see."* Jeremy's family was waiting for him, waiting for the moment when he learned to see once again.

Throughout human history, PTSD has been chronicled and described. The description that Grégoire reads aloud was written by Lucretius in 50 B.C. and translated by William Ellery Leonard. I want to add here that one of my readers kindly shared the symptoms that she faced and still faces after engaging in the war in Iraq. I am so grateful to her for revisiting experiences that are so painful.

## By Eloisa James

# Say No to the Duke

They moved toward each other as if they were following the steps of a very slow, very grand country dance. One that was danced by kings and queens and countryfolk alike.

When they were beside each other, she squared her shoulders and met his eyes. "I decided to come to you. I hope that is all right."

"I do believe that you are the bravest woman I've ever met," he replied.

He couldn't have said anything better; Betsy felt herself begin to glow. "I haven't been brave to this point, but I have made up my mind to change. I outlawed being nervous, but now I need to outlaw being afraid." She hesitated. "I have chosen courage, and now I choose happiness."

"I love you as you are," he whispered, and then his mouth came down on hers.

Her breath caught in her throat because their tongues met as if they kissed every day, every night. He tasted *right*, which sent a shiver through her whole body and pushed her against him gently, the way a pebble might roll up a beach when the tide comes in.

One doesn't fight the tide.

**Charles Lutwidge Dodgson (Lewis Carroll)** (1832–98) attended Rugby School for four years and matriculated at Christ Church, Oxford, in May 1850. In 1855, he was appointed mathematical lecturer at Christ Church, a position he held until 1881. Late in the year 1865, he published, under the pseudonym Lewis Carroll, *Alice's Adventures in Wonderland*—the Alice of the title being patterned after a daughter of Dean Liddell of the college. In 1869 came *Phantasmagoria*, in 1871 *Through the Looking-Glass*, in 1876 *The Hunting of the Snark*, and in 1883 *Rhyme and Reason*. During the years in which Lewis Carroll was delighting children of all ages, C. L. Dodgson was publishing mathematical works, the most famous of these being *Euclid and His Modern Rivals* (1879). Though his authorship of the Alice books was well-known, he shied away from publicity, stating, "Mr. Dodgson neither claimed nor acknowledged any connection with the books not published under his name."

**Martin Gardner** (1914–2010) was a science writer who for twenty-five years wrote the "Mathematical Games" column in *Scientific American*. He authored some seventy books about mathematics, science, philosophy, and literature, including two novels and a collection of short stories. His *Annotated Alice* and *More Annotated Alice* were combined into a single *Annotated Alice*. He also wrote *The Annotated Snark* and edited *The Universe in a Handkerchief*, a collection of Carroll's writings about recreational mathematics, puzzles, ciphers, wordplay, and games.

**Jeffrey Meyers**, a fellow of the Royal Society of Literature, is the author of numerous biographies including *Samuel Johnson: The Struggle*; *The Genius and The Goddess: Arthur Miller and Marilyn Monroe*; *George Orwell: Life and Art*—his fifth work on Orwell; and *John Huston: Courage and Art*. Thirty of his books have been translated into fourteen languages and published on six continents.

# Alice's Adventures in Wonderland

# &

# Through the Looking-Glass

*Lewis Carroll*

Illustrations by John Tenniel

With an Introduction by
Martin Gardner
and an Afterword by
Jeffrey Meyers

SIGNET CLASSICS

SIGNET CLASSICS
Published by the Penguin Group
Penguin Group (USA) LLC, 375 Hudson Street,
New York, New York 10014

🐧

USA | Canada | UK | Ireland | Australia | New Zealand | India | South Africa | China
penguin.com
A Penguin Random House Company

Published by Signet Classics, an imprint of New American Library,
a division of Penguin Group (USA) LLC

First Signet Classics Printing, April 1960
First Signet Classics Printing (Meyers Afterword), March 2012

Ⓒ  REGISTERED TRADEMARK—MARCA REGISTRADA

ISBN 978-0-451-53200-8

Printed in the United States of America
10   9

# INTRODUCTION

ALTHOUGH MANY ADULTS dislike fantasy, preferring fiction about the real world, it is surprising how many great literary works are fantasies. One thinks of Homer's *Iliad* and *Odyssey,* Virgil's *Aeneid,* Dante's *Divine Comedy,* Goethe's *Faust,* Shakespeare's *Tempest* and *Midsummer Night's Dream,* and scores of fantasy novels that have outlasted myriads of once admired works of realism.

Among books for children almost all the classics are fantasies: P. L. Travers's *Mary Poppins,* Barrie's *Peter Pan,* French fairy tales by Perrault, German fairy tales by Grimm, Danish tales by Andersen, Italy's *Pinocchio,* Kipling's *Just-So* stories, C. S. Lewis's *Narnia,* the Oz books of L. Frank Baum, and of course Lewis Carroll's two books about Alice. At the moment, J. K. Rowling's incredibly popular books about Harry Potter, boy wizard, are fantasies, but whether they will become classics remains to be seen.

It's hard to understand, but some adults, including a few peculiar psychologists, think fantasy is bad for children. G. K. Chesterton considered this belief close to mortal sin. His marvelous essay "The Dragon's Grandmother" (you'll find it in his book *Tremendous Trifles*) is, in my opinion, the best defense of juvenile fantasy ever written.

"I met a man the other day," Chesterton opens his essay, "who did not believe in fairy tales. I do not mean that he did not believe in the incidents narrated in them. . . . The man I speak of disbelieved in fairy tales in an even more amazing and perverted sense. He actually thought that fairy tales ought not to be told to children."

Chesterton recalls his efforts to wade through some modern novels about the actual world. When this became tiresome he saw a copy of Grimm on the table and gave "a cry of indecent joy. Here at least, here at last, one could find a little common sense. I opened the book and my eyes fell on those splendid and satisfying words, 'The Dragon's Grandmother.'"

At that moment, the monster who hated fairy tales entered the room. Here is what Chesterton said to him:

> It is far easier to believe in a million fairy tales than to believe in one man who does not like fairy tales. I would rather kiss Grimm instead of a Bible and swear to all his stories as if they were thirty-nine articles than say seriously and out of my heart that there can be such a man as you; that you are not some temptation of the devil or some delusion from the void. Look at these plain, homely, practical words. "The Dragon's Grandmother," that is all right; that is rational almost to the verge of rationalism. If there was a dragon, he had a grandmother. But you—you had no grandmother! If you had known one, she would have taught you to love fairy tales.

> It seemed to me that he did not follow me with sufficient delicacy, so I moderated my tone. "Can you not see," I said, "that fairy tales in their essence are quite solid and straightforward; but that this everlasting fiction about modern life is in its nature essentially incredible? Folklore means that the soul is sane, but that the universe is wild and full of marvels. Realism means that the world is dull and full of routine, but that the soul is sick and screaming. The problem of the fairy tale is—what will a healthy man do with a fantastic world? The problem of the modern novel is—what will a madman do with a dull world? In the fairy tales the cosmos goes mad; but the hero does not go mad. In the modern novels the hero is mad before the book begins, and suffers from the harsh steadiness and cruel sanity of the cosmos.

"The cosmos goes mad; but the hero does not go mad." It's an accurate description of Alice as she strolls through the mad world of Wonderland and the equally mad world behind the looking-glass. It is an accurate description of Dorothy as she walks the Yellow Brick Road in the mad world of Oz.

There really are curious persons so down on fantasy that they find no pleasure in Carroll's Alice books. Consider what H. L. Mencken says about them in his autobiographical *Happy Days*:

> I was a grown man, and far gone in sin, before I ever brought myself to tackle "Alice in Wonderland," and even then I made some big skips and wondered sadly how and why such feeble jocosity had got so high a reputation. I am willing to grant that it must be a masterpiece, as my betters allege—but not to *my* taste, not for *me*.

Lewis Carroll, whose real name was Charles Lutwidge Dodgson, was a shy bachelor who taught elementary mathematics at Oxford University's Christ Church, and who had a passion for photography when that art was in its infancy. He loved attractive little girls much more than boys. He was especially fond of the real Alice, Alice Liddell, daughter of the dean of Christ Church. Her last name rhymes with "fiddle." Carroll puns three times on the name's closeness to "little" in his prefatory poem to the first Alice book, and again in Chapter 7 where he writes about the three little girls (Alice had two sisters) who lived at the bottom of a well. There is convincing evidence that Carroll was romantically in love with Alice.

Morton Cohen, in his splendid biography of Carroll, speculates that Carroll may actually have approached Mr. and Mrs. Liddell with a suggestion that he wished to marry Alice someday. At any rate, Mrs. Liddell suddenly decided that Carroll should stop seeing Alice, and she burned all his letters to her. The page in Carroll's diary for the time when this occurred has been torn from the diary and presumably destroyed. It is widely believed that in the second Alice book, Carroll intended the White Knight to be a caricature of himself. When he waves good-bye to Alice, as she moves to the final square of the chessboard to become a queen, the scene represents his final sad parting with the only child friend he truly loved.

Among Carroll's superb photographs of famous persons and young children were hundreds of pictures of unclad little girls. After gossip implied there was something unhealthy in such picture taking, Carroll destroyed all his nude negatives. The four that survived are reproduced in Morton Cohen's beautiful volume, *Reflections in a Looking Glass: A Centennial Celebration of Lewis Carroll, Photographer.*

There is no question that Carroll's fondness for young girls, and photographing them without clothes, was in his mind a completely innocent admiration of their charms. He was a devout Anglican, an ordained deacon who often preached in nearby churches. His religious opinions were strictly orthodox except for an heretical refusal to believe God would eternally punish anyone, including Satan. Entries in his diary constantly repeat a yearning to obey God's will and to be forgiven for sins that are never specified.

Lewis Carroll was born in 1832, in Cheshire, England, the third of eleven children of the Reverend Charles Dodgson, an Anglican priest. Although Carroll's major hobby was photography, he was also fond of showing magic tricks to child friends and taking them to see conjuring shows. He liked to form a handkerchief into a mouse, then make it jump from his hand when he stroked it. He would fold from paper what he called "paper pistols" that made a loud bang when swung through the air. He was an avid patron of the theater, though frequently offended by stage profanity and scenes he considered sacrilegious or licentious. The famous actress Ellen Terry was a lifelong friend.

The first Alice book had its origin in a story Carroll told Alice and her two sisters when they were on a rowing trip up the Isis, a branch of the Thames. Alice begged him to write it down for her. This he did, calling it *Alice's Adventures Underground.* Carroll himself illustrated the tale, though his artistic ability, as he recognized, was poor. He presented a hand-lettered copy to Alice, and it was later published as a small book. The story differs in many interesting ways from the final printed version, and it lacks such episodes as the Pig and Pepper chapter and the Mad Tea-Party. If you are curious to read it, Dover has a paperback reprint.

Both Alice books reflect Carroll's interest in games. Among his dozens of privately printed pamphlets, many describe games he himself invented. They include variations of croquet, games played with pieces on a checkerboard, and a game he called "doublets" in which one tried in the fewest possible steps to change one word to another by altering one letter at a time, at each step forming a common word. In the first Alice book, playing cards provide the roles of courtiers, queens, kings, and laborers. In the sequel, cards are replaced by the kings, queens, and knights of chess. Each book is rich in wordplay, nonsense verse, mathematical whimsy, and logical paradoxes.

The Alice books swarm with sly implications that Victorian readers would grasp at once, but today have to be explained by footnotes such as you will find in the 1999 edition of my *Annotated Alice*. I will give only one amusing instance. When Humpty Dumpty shakes hands with Alice he extends only one finger. In Victorian days, when someone shook hands with a person of inferior social status, it was customary to extend only two fingers. Humpty, in the great pride that went before his fall, carries this ugly custom to its extreme.

Tenniel's illustrations also have subtle features that are easily missed. Look carefully at the picture of Humpty seated on the wall. A cross section of the wall on the right reveals that the wall has a narrow ridge, like an inverted V. This of course renders the egg's seat extremely precarious. In the picture of the Queen of Hearts asking Alice "What's your name, child?" see if you can find the White Rabbit. After Alice has gone through the looking-glass, note the grin on the back of the clock and the gargoyle face below the mantel. Tenniel slyly shaded the nose of the Jack of Hearts to suggest that he was a heavy drinker. For much more about Tenniel and his art see *The Tenniel Illustrations to the "Alice" Books,* a delightful study by Michael Hancher (1985).

*Alice's Adventures in Wonderland* was first published by London's Macmillan in 1865. The covers are red cloth, with gold lettering on the spine. On the front cover is a picture of Alice holding a pig; on the back a picture of the Cheshire Cat. The print run was two thousand. Because Tenniel strongly objected to the quality of the printing of his pictures, Carroll was forced at considerable expense to make a new printing. Copies of the first run were sold to an American publisher. The book was such a success that by 1899 there had been twenty-six new printings. Carroll continued to correct printer's errors and make small changes in the text until the eighty-nine thousandth was issued in 1897, a year before his death.

Macmillan published *Through the Looking-Glass* in 1872. It, too, was bound in red cloth, with the Red Queen on the front cover and the White Queen on the back. It sold even faster than the first Alice book. Fifteen thousand copies were bought in the first seven weeks.

After Carroll's death, at age sixty-five, new editions of his Alice books began to appear with illustrations by other artists. In 1901, Harper and Brothers published in America an edition of the first Alice book with pictures by the American artist Peter Newell. The following year it issued Newell's illustrated edition of the second Alice book. His eighty full-page plates are reproduced in my *More Annotated Alice* (1990). Since then scores of artists, including the famous illustrator Arthur Rackham, have tried their hand on the Alice books. *The Illustrators of Alice* (1972), edited by Graham Overden, is devoted to the history of illustrated editions of Alice, with many handsome reproductions of their art. Some recent artists take extreme liberties. For example, Barry Moser's art for the second Alice book gives Humpty the face of Richard Nixon!

So many translations of Alice into other languages have been made that mathematician and Carroll collector Warren Weaver wrote an entire book about them, *Alice in Many Tongues* (1964). So many plays and musicals were based on Alice that Charles C. Lovett covers their history in *Alice on Stage* (1990). A checklist of motion pictures about Alice, by David Schaefer, will be found at the back of the 1999 Norton edition of my *Annotated Alice*.

Many biographies of Carroll have been written, and several book collections made of his correspondence. A two-volume expurgated edition of Carroll's diary, edited by Roger Lancelyn Green, appeared in 1954. An uncut edition of the diary, edited by Edward Wakeling, is now being issued in many volumes. Alice Liddell has her own biography, *The Real Alice* (1981), by Anne Clarke.

Aside from his books about mathematics and logic, and collections of his poetry, Carroll wrote two other fantasies. A long novel about two fairy children was published in two volumes: *Sylvie and Bruno* (1889) and *Sylvie and Bruno Concluded* (1893). His great nonsense ballad *The Hunting of the Snark,* illustrated by Henry Holiday, appeared in 1876. You'll find its history, along with numerous footnotes, in my *Annotated Snark* (1962). The ballad tells of a crew of bizarre adventurers who set sail to find an elusive monster called the Snark. It also was illustrated by Peter Newell, as well as by many other artists since.

Carroll's long comic poem *Phantasmagoria,* about a friendly ghost, was recently published by Prometheus Books. Several books deal with Carroll's writings about puzzles and recreational mathematics, including my *Universe in a Handkerchief* (1996). For a detailed and annotated bibliography of all of Carroll's writings, the classic reference is *The Lewis Carroll Handbook,* by Sidney Herbert Williams and Falconer Madan, revised and updated by Roger Green in 1962. Other bibliographies, essay collections, and critical studies of Carroll's work are far too numerous to mention.

The Lewis Carroll Society of North America publishes a news bulletin entitled *The Knight Letter,* and sponsors two annual conventions. In England, an older Lewis Carroll Society, founded in 1969, issues a scholarly periodical, *The Carrollian* (formerly *Jabberwocky*), edited by Anne Clarke Amor, and a newsletter called *Bandersnatch.* A Canadian Carroll Society publishes *White Rabbit Tales,* its newsletter, and there is a recently organized Carroll Society of Japan. Carroll has an extensive following in Japan, where some sixty editions of the Alice books are currently in print!

You won't find the Alice books reprinted in Mortimer Adler's set of *The Great Books of the Western World,* but I venture to state the following: It is permissible today to consider a person educated even if he or she has not read, say,

*Das Kapital,* or books by Hegel and Freud, or indeed more than half the volumes in Adler's series. On the other hand, I would not consider a person educated who has never read Carroll's Alice books. Among the great characters of imaginative literature, Alice has become as immortal as Don Quixote, Huckleberry Finn, Captain Ahab, Sherlock Holmes, and Dorothy Gale of Kansas. If you are not yet acquainted with Alice's adventures in Wonderland and behind the mirror, read on and enjoy!

—Martin Gardner

# Alice's Adventures
# in Wonderland
# &
# Through the
# Looking-Glass

All in the golden afternoon
    Full leisurely we glide;
For both our oars, with little skill,
    By little arms are plied,
While little hands make vain pretence
    Our wanderings to guide.

Ah, cruel Three! In such an hour,
    Beneath such dreamy weather,
To beg a tale of breath too weak
    To stir the tiniest feather!
Yet what can one poor voice avail
    Against three tongues together?

Imperious Prima flashes forth
    Her edict "to begin it"—
In gentler tones Secunda hopes
    "There will be nonsense in it"—
While Tertia interrupts the tale
    Not more than once a minute.

Anon, to sudden silence won,
    In fancy they pursue
The dream-child moving through a land
    Of wonders wild and new,
In friendly chat with bird or beast—
    And half believe it true.

And ever, as the story drained
    The wells of fancy dry,
And faintly strove that weary one
    To put the subject by,
"The rest next time—" "It is next time!"
    The happy voices cry.

*Thus grew the tale of Wonderland:*
 *Thus slowly, one by one,*
*Its quaint events were hammered out—*
 *And now the tale is done,*
*And home we steer, a merry crew,*
 *Beneath the setting sun.*

*Alice! A childish story take,*
 *And with a gentle hand*
*Lay it where Childhood's dreams are twined*
 *In Memory's mystic band,*
*Like pilgrim's withered wreath of flowers*
 *Plucked in a far-off land.*

# CONTENTS

# ALICE'S ADVENTURES IN WONDERLAND

# I

## *Down the Rabbit-Hole*

ALICE WAS BEGINNING to get very tired of sitting by her sister on the bank, and of having nothing to do: once or twice she had peeped into the book her sister was reading, but it had no pictures or conversations in it, "and what is the use of a book," thought Alice, "without pictures or conversations?"

So she was considering in her own mind (as well as she could, for the hot day made her feel very sleepy and stupid), whether the pleasure of making a daisy-chain would be worth the trouble of getting up and picking the daisies, when suddenly a White Rabbit with pink eyes ran close by her.

There was nothing so *very* remarkable in that; nor did Alice think it so *very* much out of the way to hear the Rabbit say to itself "Oh dear! Oh dear! I shall be too late!" (when she thought it over afterwards, it occurred to her that she ought to have wondered at this, but at the time it all seemed quite natural); but when the Rabbit actually *took a watch out of its waistcoat-pocket,* and looked at it, and then hurried on, Alice started to her feet, for it flashed across her mind that she had never before seen a rabbit with either a waistcoat-pocket, or a watch to take out of it, and, burning with curiosity, she ran across the field after it, and was just in time to see it pop down a large rabbit-hole under the hedge.

In another moment down went Alice after it, never once considering how in the world she was to get out again.

The rabbit-hole went straight on like a tunnel for some way, and then dipped suddenly down, so suddenly that Alice had not a moment to think about stopping herself before she found herself falling down what seemed to be a very deep well.

Either the well was very deep, or she fell very slowly, for she had plenty of time as she went down to look about her, and to wonder what was going to happen next. First, she tried to look down and make out what she was coming to, but it was too dark to see anything: then she looked at the sides of the well, and noticed that they were filled with cupboards and book-shelves: here and there she saw maps and pictures hung upon pegs. She took down a jar from one of the shelves as she passed: it was labeled "ORANGE MARMALADE," but to her great disappointment it was empty: she did not like to drop the jar, for fear of killing somebody underneath, so managed to put it into one of the cupboards as she fell past it.

"Well!" thought Alice to herself. "After such a fall as this, I shall think nothing of tumbling down-stairs! How brave they'll all think me at home! Why, I wouldn't say anything about it, even if I fell off the top of the house!" (Which was very likely true.)

Down, down, down. Would the fall *never* come to an end? "I wonder how many miles I've fallen by this time?" she said aloud. "I must be getting somewhere near the centre of the earth. Let me see: that would be four thousand miles down, I think—" (for, you see, Alice had learnt several things of this sort in her lessons in the school-room, and though this was not a *very* good opportunity for showing off her knowledge, as there was no one to listen to her, still it was good practice to say it over) "—yes, that's about the right distance—but then I wonder what Latitude or Longitude I've got to?" (Alice had not the slightest idea what Latitude was, or Longitude either, but she thought they were nice grand words to say.)

Presently she began again. "I wonder if I shall fall right

*through* the earth! How funny it'll seem to come out among the people that walk with their heads downwards! The antipathies, I think—" (she was rather glad there *was* no one listening, this time, as it didn't sound at all the right word) "—but I shall have to ask them what the name of the country is, you know. Please, Ma'am, is this New Zealand? Or Australia?" (and she tried to curtsey as she spoke—fancy *curtseying* as you're falling through the air! Do you think you could manage it?) "And what an ignorant little girl she'll think me for asking! No, it'll never do to ask: perhaps I shall see it written up somewhere."

Down, down, down. There was nothing else to do, so Alice soon began talking again. "Dinah'll miss me very much to-night, I should think!" (Dinah was the cat.) "I hope they'll remember her saucer of milk at tea-time. Dinah, my dear! I wish you were down here with me! There are no mice in the air, I'm afraid, but you might catch a bat, and that's very like a mouse, you know. But do cats eat bats, I wonder?" And here Alice began to get rather sleepy, and went on saying to herself, in a dreamy sort of way, "Do cats eat bats? Do cats eat bats?" and sometimes "Do bats eat cats?" for, you see, as she couldn't answer either question, it didn't much matter which way she put it. She felt that she was dozing off, and had just begun to dream that she was walking hand in hand with Dinah, and was saying to her very earnestly, "Now, Dinah, tell me the truth: did you ever eat a bat?," when suddenly, thump! thump! down she came upon a heap of sticks and dry leaves, and the fall was over.

Alice was not a bit hurt, and she jumped up on to her feet in a moment: she looked up, but it was all dark overhead; before her was another long passage, and the White Rabbit was still in sight, hurrying down it. There was not a moment to be lost: away went Alice like the wind, and was just in time to hear it say, as it turned a corner, "Oh my ears and whiskers, how late it's getting!" She was close behind it when she turned the corner, but the Rabbit was no longer to be seen: she found herself in a long, low hall, which was lit up by a row of lamps hanging from the roof.

There were doors all round the hall, but they were all locked; and when Alice had been all the way down one side and up the other, trying every door, she walked sadly down the middle, wondering how she was ever to get out again.

Suddenly she came upon a little three-legged table, all made of solid glass; there was nothing on it but a tiny golden key, and Alice's first idea was that this might belong to one of the doors of the hall; but alas! either the locks were too large, or the key was too small, but at any rate it would not open any of them. However, on the second time round, she came upon a low curtain she had not noticed before, and behind it was a little door about fifteen inches high: she tried the little golden key in the lock, and to her great delight it fitted!

Alice opened the door and found that it led into a small passage, not much larger than a rat-hole: she knelt down and looked along the passage into the loveliest garden you ever saw. How she longed to get out of that dark hall, and wander about among those beds of bright flowers and those cool fountains, but she could not even get her head through the doorway; "and even if my head *would* go through," thought poor Alice, "it would be of very little use without my shoulders. Oh, how I wish I could shut up like a telescope! I think I could, if I only knew how to begin." For, you see, so many out-of-the-way things had happened lately that Alice had begun to think that very few things indeed were really impossible.

There seemed to be no use in waiting by the little door, so she went back to the table, half hoping she might find another key on it, or at any rate a book of rules for shutting people up like telescopes: this time she found a little bottle on it ("which certainly was not here before," said Alice), and tied round the neck of the bottle was a paper label, with the words "DRINK ME" beautifully printed on it in large letters.

It was all very well to say "Drink me," but the wise little Alice was not going to do *that* in a hurry. "No, I'll look first," she said, "and see whether it's marked '*poison*' or not"; for she had read several nice little stories about children who had got burnt, and eaten up by wild beasts, and other unpleasant things, all because they *would* not remember the simple rules their friends had taught them: such as, that a red-hot poker will burn you if you hold it too long; and that, if you cut your finger *very* deeply with a knife, it usually bleeds; and she had never forgotten that, if you drink much from a bottle marked "poison," it is almost certain to disagree with you, sooner or later.

However, this bottle was *not* marked "poison," so Alice ventured to taste it, and finding it very nice (it had, in fact, a sort of mixed flavour of cherry-tart, custard, pine-apple, roast turkey, toffy, and hot buttered toast), she very soon finished it off.

"What a curious feeling!" said Alice. "I must be shutting up like a telescope."

And so it was indeed: she was now only ten inches high, and her face brightened up at the thought that she was now the right size for going through the little door into that lovely garden. First, however, she waited for a few minutes to see if she was going to shrink any further: she felt a little nervous about this; "for it might end, you know," said Alice to herself, "in my going out altogether, like a candle. I wonder what I should be like then?" And she tried to fancy what the flame of a candle looks like after the candle is blown out, for she could not remember ever having seen such a thing.

After a while, finding that nothing more happened, she decided on going into the garden at once; but, alas for poor Alice! when she got to the door, she found she had forgotten the little golden key, and when she went back to the table for it, she found she could not possibly reach it: she could see it quite plainly through the glass, and she tried her best to climb up one of the legs of the table, but it was too slippery; and when she had tired herself out with trying, the poor little thing sat down and cried.

"Come, there's no use in crying like that!" said Alice to herself, rather sharply, "I advise you to leave off this minute!" She generally gave herself very good advice (though she very seldom followed it), and sometimes she scolded herself so severely as to bring tears into her eyes; and once she remembered trying to box her own ears for having cheated herself in a game of croquet she was playing against herself, for this curious child was very fond of pretending to be two people. "But it's no use now," thought poor Alice, "to pretend to be two people! Why, there's hardly enough of me left to make *one* respectable person!"

Soon her eye fell on a little glass box that was lying under the table: she opened it, and found in it a very small cake, on which the words "EAT ME" were beautifully marked in currants. "Well, I'll eat it," said Alice, "and if it makes me grow larger, I can reach the key; and if it makes me grow smaller, I can creep under the door; so either way I'll get into the garden, and I don't care which happens!"

She ate a little bit, and said anxiously to herself "Which way? Which way?" holding her hand on the top of her head to feel which way it was growing, and she was quite surprised to find that she remained the same size: to be sure, this is what generally happens when one eats cake; but Alice had got so much into the way of expecting nothing but out-of-the-way things to happen, that it seemed quite dull and stupid for life to go on in the common way.

So she set to work, and very soon finished off the cake.

     \*     \*     \*     \*     \*     \*     \*

       \*     \*     \*     \*     \*     \*

     \*     \*     \*     \*     \*     \*     \*

# II

## *The Pool of Tears*

"CURIOUSER AND CURIOUSER!" cried Alice (she was so much surprised, that for the moment she quite forgot how to speak good English). "Now I'm opening out like the largest telescope that ever was! Good-bye, feet!" (for when she looked down at her feet, they seemed to be almost out of sight, they were getting so far off). "Oh, my poor little feet, I wonder who will put on your shoes and stockings for you now, dears? I'm sure *I* shan't be able! I shall be a great deal too far off to trouble myself about you: you must manage the best way you can—but I must be kind to them," thought Alice, "or perhaps they won't walk the way I want to go! Let me see. I'll give them a new pair of boots for Christmas."

And she went on planning to herself how she would manage it. "They must go by the carrier," she thought; "and how funny it'll seem, sending presents to one's own feet! And how odd the directions will look!

> *Alice's Right Foot, Esq.,*
> *Hearthrug,*
> *near the Fender.*
> *(with Alice's love).*

Oh dear, what nonsense I'm talking!"

Just at this moment her head struck against the roof of the hall: in fact she was now rather more than nine feet high, and she at once took up the little golden key and hurried off to the garden door.

Poor Alice! It was as much as she could do, lying down on one side, to look through into the garden with one eye; but to get through was more hopeless than ever: she sat down and began to cry again.

"You ought to be ashamed of yourself," said Alice, "a great girl like you" (she might well say this), "to go on crying in this way! Stop this moment, I tell you!" But she went on all the same, shedding gallons of tears, until there was a large pool all round her, about four inches deep and reaching half down the hall.

After a time she heard a little pattering of feet in the distance, and she hastily dried her eyes to see what was coming. It was the White Rabbit returning, splendidly dressed, with a pair of white kid-gloves in one hand and a large fan in the other: he came trotting along in a great hurry, muttering to himself as he came, "Oh! the Duchess, the Duchess! Oh! *Won't* she be savage if I've kept her waiting?" Alice felt so desperate that she was ready to ask help of any one: so, when the Rabbit came near her, she began, in a low, timid voice, "If you please, Sir——" The Rabbit started violently, dropped the white kid-gloves and the fan, and skurried away into the darkness as hard as he could go.

Alice took up the fan and gloves, and, as the hall was very hot, she kept fanning herself all the time she went on talking. "Dear, dear! How queer everything is to-day! And yesterday things went on just as usual. I wonder if I've been changed in the night? Let me think: *was* I the same when I got up this morning? I almost think I can remember feeling a little different. But if I'm not the same, the next question is 'Who in the world am I?' Ah, *that's* the great puzzle!" And she began thinking over all the children she knew, that were of the same age as herself, to see if she could have been changed for any of them.

"I'm sure I'm not Ada," she said, "for her hair goes in such long ringlets, and mine doesn't go in ringlets at all; and I'm sure I can't be Mabel, for I know all sorts of things, and she, oh, she knows such a very little! Besides, *she's* she, and *I'm* I, and—oh dear, how puzzling it all is! I'll try if I know all the things I used to know. Let me see: four times five is twelve, and four times six is thirteen, and four times seven is—oh dear! I shall never get to twenty at that rate! However, the Multiplication-Table doesn't signify: let's try Geography. London is the capital of Paris, and Paris is the capital of Rome, and Rome—no, *that's* all wrong, I'm certain! I must have been changed for Mabel! I'll try and say *'How doth the little—'* " and she crossed her hands on her lap, as if she were saying lessons, and began to repeat it, but her voice sounded hoarse and strange, and the words did not come the same as they used to do:—

> *"How doth the little crocodile*
> *Improve his shining tail,*
> *And pour the waters of the Nile*
> *On every golden scale!*
>
> *"How cheerfully he seems to grin,*
> *How neatly spreads his claws,*
> *And welcomes little fishes in,*
> *With gently smiling jaws!"*

"I'm sure those are not the right words," and her eyes filled with tears again as she we[nt on,] Mabel after all, and I shall have to go and li[ve in that] little house, and have next to no toys to play with, [and oh,] so many lessons to learn! No, I've made up my m[ind;] if I'm Mabel, I'll stay down here! It'll be no use th[eir putting] their heads down and saying, 'Come up again, dear[!' I] shall only look up and say 'Who am I, then? Tell me that first, and then, if I like being that person, I'll come up: if not, I'll stay down here till I'm somebody else'—but, oh dear!" cried Alice, with a sudden burst of tears, "I do wish they *would* put their heads down! I am so *very* tired of being all alone here!"

As she said this she looked down at her hands, and was surprised to see that she had put on one of the Rabbit's little white kid-gloves while she was talking. "How *can* I have done that?" she thought. "I must be growing small again." She got up and went to the table to measure herself by it, and found that, as nearly as she could guess, she was now about two feet high, and was going on shrinking rapidly: she soon found out that the cause of this was the fan she was holding, and she dropped it hastily, just in time to save herself from shrinking away altogether.

"That *was* a narrow escape!" said Alice, a good deal frightened at the sudden change, but very glad to find herself still in existence. "And now for the garden!" And she ran with all speed back to the little door; but alas! the little door was shut again, and the little golden key was lying on the glass table as before, "and things are worse than ever," thought the poor child, "for I never was so small as this before, never! And I declare it's too bad, that it is!"

As she said these words her foot slipped, and in another moment, splash! she was up to her chin in salt water. Her first idea was that she had somehow fallen into the sea, "and in that case I can go back by railway," she said to herself.

had been to the seaside once in her life, and had come the general conclusion that, wherever you go to on the English coast, you find a number of bathing-machines in the sea, some children digging in the sand with wooden spades, then a row of lodging-houses, and behind them a railway-station.) However, she soon made out that she was in the pool of tears which she had wept when she was nine feet high.

"I wish I hadn't cried so much!" said Alice, as she swam about, trying to find her way out. "I shall be punished for it now, I suppose, by being drowned in my own tears! That *will* be a queer thing, to be sure! However, everything is queer to-day."

Just then she heard something splashing about in the pool a little way off, and she swam nearer to make out what it was: at first she thought it must be a walrus or hippopotamus, but then she remembered how small she was now, and she soon made out that it was only a mouse, that had slipped in like herself.

"Would it be of any use, now," thought Alice, "to speak to this mouse? Everything is so out-of-the-way down here, that I should think very likely it can talk: at any rate there's no harm in trying." So she began: "O Mouse, do you know the way out of this pool? I am very tired of swimming about here, O Mouse!" (Alice thought this must be the right way of speaking to a mouse: she had never done such a thing before, but she remembered having seen in her brother's Latin Grammar, "A mouse—of a mouse—to a mouse—a mouse—O mouse!") The mouse looked at her rather inquisitively, and seemed to her to wink with one of its little eyes, but it said nothing.

"Perhaps it doesn't understand English," thought Alice. "I daresay it's a French mouse, come over with William the Conqueror." (For, with all her knowledge of history, Alice had no very clear notion how long ago anything had happened.) So she began again: "Où est ma chatte?," which was the first sentence in her French lesson-book. The Mouse gave a sudden leap out of the water, and seemed to quiver all over with fright. "Oh, I beg your pardon!" cried Alice hastily, afraid that she had hurt the poor animal's feelings. "I quite forgot you didn't like cats."

"Not like cats!" cried the Mouse in a shrill, passionate voice. "Would *you* like cats, if you were me?"

"Well, perhaps not," said Alice in a soothing tone: "don't be angry about it. And yet I wish I could show you our cat Dinah. I think you'd take a fancy to cats, if you could only see her. She is such a dear quiet thing," Alice went on, half to herself, as she swam lazily about in the pool, "and she sits purring so nicely by the fire, licking her paws and washing her face—and she is such a nice soft thing to nurse—and

she's such a capital one for catching mice——oh, I beg your pardon!" cried Alice again, for this time the Mouse was bristling all over, and she felt certain it must be really offended. "We won't talk about her any more, if you'd rather not."

"We, indeed!" cried the Mouse, who was trembling down to the end of its tail. "As if *I* would talk on such a subject! Our family always *hated* cats: nasty, low, vulgar things! Don't let me hear the name again!"

"I won't indeed!" said Alice, in a great hurry to change the subject of conversation. "Are you—are you fond—of—of dogs?" The Mouse did not answer, so Alice went on eagerly: "There is such a nice little dog near our house, I should like to show you! A little bright-eyed terrier, you know, with oh, such long curly brown hair! And it'll fetch things when you throw them, and it'll sit up and beg for its dinner, and all sorts of things—I can't remember half of them—and it belongs to a farmer, you know, and he says it's so useful, it's worth a hundred pounds! He says it kills all the rats and—oh dear!" cried Alice in a sorrowful tone. "I'm afraid I've offended it again!" For the Mouse was swimming away from her as hard as it could go, and making quite a commotion in the pool as it went.

So she called softly after it, "Mouse dear! Do come back again, and we won't talk about cats or dogs either, if you don't like them!" When the Mouse heard this, it turned round and swam slowly back to her: its face was quite pale (with passion, Alice thought), and it said, in a low, trembling voice, "Let us get to the shore, and then I'll tell you my history, and you'll understand why it is I hate cats and dogs."

It was high time to go, for the pool was getting quite crowded with the birds and animals that had fallen into it: there was a Duck and a Dodo, a Lory and an Eaglet, and several other curious creatures. Alice led the way, and the whole party swam to the shore.

# III

## A Caucus-Race and a Long Tale

THEY WERE INDEED a queer-looking party that assembled on the bank—the birds with draggled feathers, the animals with their fur clinging close to them, and all dripping wet, cross, and uncomfortable.

The first question of course was how to get dry again: they had a consultation about this, and after a few minutes it seemed quite natural to Alice to find herself talking familiarly with them, as if she had known them all her life. Indeed, she had quite a long argument with the Lory, who at last turned sulky, and would only say "I'm older than you, and must know better." And this Alice would not allow, without knowing how old it was, and as the Lory positively refused to tell its age, there was no more to be said.

At last the Mouse, who seemed to be a person of some

authority among them, called out "Sit down, all of you, and listen to me! *I'll* soon make you dry enough!" They all sat down at once, in a large ring, with the Mouse in the middle. Alice kept her eyes anxiously fixed on it, for she felt sure she would catch a bad cold if she did not get dry very soon.

"Ahem!" said the Mouse with an important air. "Are you all ready? This is the driest thing I know. Silence all round, if you please! 'William the Conqueror, whose cause was favoured by the pope, was soon submitted to by the English, who wanted leaders, and had been of late much accustomed to usurpation and conquest. Edwin and Morcar, the earls of Mercia and Northumbria——' "

"Ugh!" said the Lory, with a shiver.

"I beg your pardon?" said the Mouse, frowning, but very politely: "Did you speak?"

"Not I!" said the Lory, hastily.

"I thought you did," said the Mouse. "I proceed. 'Edwin and Morcar, the earls of Mercia and Northumbria, declared for him; and even Stigand, the patriotic archbishop of Canterbury, found it advisable——' "

"Found *what?*" said the Duck.

"Found *it*," the Mouse replied rather crossly: "of course you know what 'it' means."

"I know what 'it' means well enough, when *I* find a thing," said the Duck: "it's generally a frog, or a worm. The question is, what did the archbishop find?"

The Mouse did not notice this question, but hurriedly went on, " '——found it advisable to go with Edgar Atheling to meet William and offer him the crown. William's conduct at first was moderate. But the insolence of his Normans——' How are you getting on now, my dear?" it continued, turning to Alice as it spoke.

"As wet as ever," said Alice in a melancholy tone: "it doesn't seem to dry me at all."

"In that case," said the Dodo solemnly, rising to its feet, "I move that the meeting adjourn, for the immediate adoption of more energetic remedies——"

"Speak English!" said the Eaglet. "I don't know the meaning of half those long words, and what's more, I don't believe you do either!" And the Eaglet bent down its head to hide a smile: some of the other birds tittered audibly.

"What I was going to say," said the Dodo in an offended tone, "was, that the best thing to get us dry would be a Caucus-race."

"What *is* a Caucus-race?" said Alice; not that she much wanted to know, but the Dodo had paused as if it thought that *somebody* ought to speak, and no one else seemed inclined to say anything.

"Why," said the Dodo, "the best way to explain it is to do it." (And, as you might like to try the thing yourself, some winter-day, I will tell you how the Dodo managed it.)

First it marked out a race-course, in a sort of circle ("the exact shape doesn't matter," it said), and then all the party were placed along the course, here and there. There was no "One, two, three, and away!," but they began running when they liked, and left off when they liked, so that it was not easy to know when the race was over. However, when they had been running half an hour or so, and were quite dry again, the Dodo suddenly called out "The race is over!," and they all crowded round it, panting, and asking "But who has won?"

This question the Dodo could not answer without a great deal of thought, and it sat for a long time with one finger pressed upon its forehead (the position in which you usually see Shakespeare, in the pictures of him), while the rest waited in silence. At last the Dodo said "*Everybody* has won, and *all* must have prizes."

"But who is to give the prizes?" quite a chorus of voices asked.

"Why, *she,* of course," said the Dodo, pointing to Alice with one finger; and the whole party at once crowded round her, calling out, in a confused way, "Prizes! Prizes!"

Alice had no idea what to do, and in despair she put her hand in her pocket, and pulled out a box of comfits (luckily the salt water had not got into it), and handed them round as prizes. There was exactly one a-piece, all round.

"But she must have a prize herself, you know," said the Mouse.

"Of course," the Dodo replied very gravely. "What else have you got in your pocket?" it went on, turning to Alice.

"Only a thimble," said Alice sadly.

"Hand it over here," said the Dodo.

Then they all crowded round her once more while the Dodo solemnly presented the thimble, saying, "We beg your acceptance of this elegant thimble"; and, when it had finished this short speech, they all cheered.

Alice thought the whole thing very absurd, but they all looked so grave that she did not dare to laugh; and, as she could not think of anything to say, she simply bowed, and took the thimble, looking as solemn as she could.

The next thing was to eat the comfits: this caused some noise and confusion, as the large birds complained that they could not taste theirs, and the small ones choked and had to be patted on the back. However, it was over at last, and they sat down again in a ring, and begged the Mouse to tell them something more.

"You promised to tell me your history, you know," said Alice, "and why it is you hate—C and D," she added in a whisper, half afraid that it would be offended again.

"Mine is a long and a sad tale," said the Mouse, turning to Alice, and sighing.

"It *is* a long tail, certainly," said Alice, looking down with wonder at the Mouse's tail; "but why do you call it sad?" And she kept on puzzling about it while the Mouse was speaking, so that her idea of the tale was something like this:——"Fury said to
                        a mouse, That
                          he met in the
                            house, 'Let
                              us both go
                                to law: *I*
                                  will prose-
                                    cute *you*.—
                                  Come, I'll
                                  take no de-
                                  nial: We
                                  must have
                                the trial;
                              For really
                              this morn-
                            ing I've
                          nothing
                        to do.'
                      Said the
                          mouse to
                            the cur,
                              'Such a
                                trial, dear
                                sir, With
                                  no jury
                                    or judge,
                                      would
                                        be wast-
                                      ing our
                                    breath.'
                                  'I'll be
                                  judge,
                              I'll be
                            jury,'
                        said
                      cun-
                      ning
                        old
                          Fury;
                            'I'll
                              try
                                the
                                  whole
                                    cause,
                                    and
                                  con-
                                demn
                          you to
                  death.'"

"You are not attending!" said the Mouse to Alice, severely. "What are you thinking of?"

"I beg your pardon," said Alice very humbly: "you had got to the fifth bend, I think?"

"I had *not!*" cried the Mouse, sharply and very angrily.

"A knot!" said Alice, always ready to make herself useful, and looking anxiously about her. "Oh, do let me help to undo it!"

"I shall do nothing of the sort," said the Mouse, getting up and walking away. "You insult me by talking such nonsense!"

"I didn't mean it!" pleaded poor Alice. "But you're so easily offended, you know!"

The Mouse only growled in reply.

"Please come back, and finish your story!" Alice called after it. And the others all joined in chorus "Yes, please do!" But the Mouse only shook its head impatiently, and walked a little quicker.

"What a pity it wouldn't stay!" sighed the Lory, as soon as it was quite out of sight. And an old Crab took the opportunity of saying to her daughter "Ah, my dear! Let this be a lesson to you never to lose *your* temper!" "Hold your tongue, Ma!" said the young Crab, a little snappishly. "You're enough to try the patience of an oyster!"

"I wish I had our Dinah here, I know I do!" said Alice aloud, addressing nobody in particular. "She'd soon fetch it back!"

"And who is Dinah, if I might venture to ask the question?" said the Lory.

Alice replied eagerly, for she was always ready to talk about her pet: "Dinah's our cat. And she's such a capital one for catching mice, you can't think! And oh, I wish you could see her after the birds! Why, she'll eat a little bird as soon as look at it!"

This speech caused a remarkable sensation among the party. Some of the birds hurried off at once: one old Magpie began wrapping itself up very carefully, remarking, "I really must be getting home: the night-air doesn't suit my throat!" And a Canary called out in a trembling voice, to its children, "Come away, my dears! It's high time you were all in bed!"

On various pretexts they all moved off, and Alice was soon left alone.

"I wish I hadn't mentioned Dinah!" she said to herself in a melancholy tone. "Nobody seems to like her, down here, and I'm sure she's the best cat in the world! Oh, my dear Dinah! I wonder if I shall ever see you any more!" And here poor Alice began to cry again, for she felt very lonely and low-spirited. In a little while, however, she again heard a little pattering of footsteps in the distance, and she looked up eagerly, half hoping that the Mouse had changed its mind, and was coming back to finish its story.

# IV

## The Rabbit
## Sends in a Little Bill

IT WAS THE White Rabbit, trotting slowly back again, and looking anxiously about as it went, as if it had lost something; and she heard it muttering to itself, "The Duchess! The Duchess! Oh my dear paws! Oh my fur and whiskers! She'll get me executed, as sure as ferrets are ferrets! Where *can* I have dropped them, I wonder!" Alice guessed in a moment that it was looking for the fan and the pair of white kid-gloves, and she very good-naturedly began hunting about for them, but they were nowhere to be seen—everything seemed to have changed since her swim in the pool, and the great hall, with the glass table and the little door, had vanished completely.

Very soon the Rabbit noticed Alice, as she went hunting about, and called out to her in an angry tone, "Why, Mary Ann, what *are* you doing out here? Run home this moment, and fetch me a pair of gloves and a fan! Quick, now!" And Alice was so much frightened that she ran off at once in the direction it pointed to, without trying to explain the mistake that it had made.

"He took me for his housemaid," she said to herself as she ran. "How surprised he'll be when he finds out who I am! But I'd better take him his fan and gloves—that is, if I can find them." As she said this, she came upon a neat little house, on the door of which was a bright brass plate with the name "W. RABBIT" engraved upon it. She went in without knocking, and hurried upstairs, in great fear lest she should meet the real Mary Ann, and be turned out of the house before she had found the fan and gloves.

"How queer it seems," Alice said to herself, "to be going messages for a rabbit! I suppose Dinah'll be sending me on messages next!" And she began fancying the sort of thing that would happen: "'Miss Alice! Come here directly, and get ready for your walk!' 'Coming in a minute, nurse! But I've got to watch this mousehole till Dinah comes back, and see that the mouse doesn't get out.' Only I don't think," Alice went on, "that they'd let Dinah stop in the house if it began ordering people about like that!"

By this time she had found her way into a tidy little room with a table in the window, and on it (as she had hoped) a fan and two or three pairs of tiny white kid-gloves: she took up the fan and a pair of the gloves, and was just going to leave the room, when her eye fell upon a little bottle that stood near the looking-glass. There was no label this time with the words "DRINK ME," but nevertheless she uncorked it and put it to her lips. "I know *something* interesting is sure to happen," she said to herself, "whenever I eat or drink anything: so I'll just see what this bottle does. I do hope it'll make me grow large again, for really I'm quite tired of being such a tiny little thing!"

It did so indeed, and much sooner than she had expected: before she had drunk half the bottle, she found her head pressing against the ceiling, and had to stoop to save her neck from being broken. She hastily put down the bottle, saying to herself "That's quite enough—I hope I shan't grow any more—As it is, I can't get out at the door—I do wish I hadn't drunk quite so much!"

Alas! It was too late to wish that! She went on growing, and growing, and very soon had to kneel down on the floor: in another minute there was not even room for this, and she tried the effect of lying down, with one elbow against the door, and the other arm curled round her head. Still she went on growing, and, as a last resource, she put one arm out of the window, and one foot up the chimney, and said to herself, "Now I can do no more, whatever happens. What *will* become of me?"

Luckily for Alice, the little magic bottle had now had its

full effect, and she grew no larger: still it was very uncomfortable, and, as there seemed to be no sort of chance of her ever getting out of the room again, no wonder she felt unhappy.

"It was much pleasanter at home," thought poor Alice, "when one wasn't always growing larger and smaller, and being ordered about by mice and rabbits. I almost wish I hadn't gone down that rabbit-hole—and yet—and yet—it's rather curious, you know, this sort of life! I do wonder what *can* have happened to me! When I used to read fairy-tales, I fancied that kind of thing never happened, and now here I am in the middle of one! There ought to be a book written about me, that there ought! And when I grow up, I'll write one— but I'm grown up now," she added in a sorrowful tone: "at least there's no room to grow up any more *here*.

"But then," thought Alice, "shall I *never* get any older than I am now? That'll be a comfort, one way—never to be an old woman—but then—always to have lessons to learn! Oh, I shouldn't like *that!*

"Oh, you foolish Alice!" she answered herself. "How can you learn lessons in here? Why, there's hardly room for *you*, and no room at all for any lesson-books!"

And so she went on, taking first one side and then the other, and making quite a conversation of it altogether, but after a few minutes she heard a voice outside, and stopped to listen.

"Mary Ann! Mary Ann!" said the voice. "Fetch me my

gloves this moment!" Then came a little pattering of feet on
the stairs. Alice knew it was the Rabbit coming to look for
her, and she trembled till she shook the house, quite forgetting that she was now about a thousand times as large as the
Rabbit, and had no reason to be afraid of it.

Presently the Rabbit came up to the door, and tried to
open it; but, as the door opened inwards, and Alice's elbow
was pressed hard against it, that attempt proved a failure.
Alice heard it say to itself "Then I'll go round and get in at
the window."

"*That* you won't!" thought Alice, and, after waiting till
she fancied she heard the Rabbit just under the window, she
suddenly spread out her hand, and made a snatch in the air.

She did not get hold of anything, but she heard a little
shriek and a fall, and a crash
of broken glass, from which
she concluded that it was just
possible it had fallen into a
cucumber-frame, or some-
thing of the sort.

Next came an angry
voice—the Rabbit's—"Pat!
Pat! Where are you?" And
then a voice she had never
heard before, "Sure then
I'm here! Digging for ap-
ples, yer honour!"

"Digging for apples, in-
deed!" said the Rabbit an-
grily. "Here! Come and help me out of *this!*" (Sounds of
more broken glass.) "Now tell me, Pat, what's that in the
window?"

"Sure, it's an arm, yer honour!" (He pronounced it "ar-
rum.")

"An arm, you goose! Who ever saw one that size? Why, it
fills the whole window!"

"Sure, it does, yer honour: but it's an arm for all that."

"Well, it's got no business there, at any rate: go and take
it away!"

There was a long silence after this, and Alice could only hear whispers now and then; such as "Sure, I don't like it, yer honour, at all, at all!" "Do as I tell you, you coward!", and at last she spread out her hand again, and made another snatch in the air. This time there were *two* little shrieks, and more sounds of broken glass. "What a number of cucumber-frames there must be!" thought Alice. "I wonder what they'll do next! As for pulling me out of the window, I only wish they *could!* I'm sure *I* don't want to stay in here any longer!"

She waited for some time without hearing anything more: at last came a rumbling of little cart-wheels, and the sound of a good many voices all talking together: she made out the words, "Where's the other ladder?—Why, I hadn't to bring but one. Bill's got the other—Bill! Fetch it here, lad!—Here, put 'em up at this corner—No, tie 'em together first—they don't reach half high enough yet—Oh, they'll do well enough. Don't be particular—Here, Bill! Catch hold of this rope—Will the roof bear?—Mind that loose slate—Oh, it's coming down! Heads below!" (a loud crash)—"Now, who did that?—It was Bill, I fancy—Who's to go down the chimney?—Nay, *I* shan't! *You* do it!—*That* I won't, then!—Bill's got to go down—Here, Bill! The master says you've got to go down the chimney!"

"Oh, so Bill's got to come down the chimney, has he?" said Alice to herself. "Why, they seem to put everything upon Bill! I wouldn't be in Bill's place for a good deal: this fire-place is narrow, to be sure; but I *think* I can kick a little!"

She drew her foot as far down the chimney as she could, and waited till she heard a little animal (she couldn't guess of what sort it was) scratching and scrambling about in the chimney close above her: then, saying to herself "This is Bill," she gave one sharp kick, and waited to see what would happen next.

The first thing she heard was a general chorus of "There goes Bill!" then the Rabbit's voice alone—"Catch him, you by the hedge!" then silence, and then another confusion of voices—"Hold up his head—Brandy now—Don't choke him—How was it, old fellow? What happened to you? Tell us all about it!"

Last came a little feeble, squeaking voice ("That's Bill,"

thought Alice), "Well, I hardly know—No more, thank ye; I'm better now—but I'm a deal too flustered to tell you— all I know is, something comes at me like a Jack-in-the-box, and up I goes like a sky-rocket!"

"So you did, old fellow!" said the others.

"We must burn the house down!" said the Rabbit's voice, and Alice called out, as loud as she could, "If you do, I'll set Dinah at you!"

There was a dead silence instantly, and Alice thought to herself "I wonder what they *will* do next! If they had any sense, they'd take the roof off." After a minute or two, they began moving about again, and Alice heard the Rabbit say "A barrowful will do, to begin with."

"A barrowful of *what?*" thought Alice. But she had not long to doubt, for the next mo-

ment a shower of little pebbles came rattling in at the window, and some of them hit her in the face. "I'll put a stop to this," she said to herself, and shouted out "You'd better not do that again!," which produced another dead silence.

Alice noticed, with some surprise, that the pebbles were all turning into little cakes as they lay on the floor, and a bright idea came into her head. "If I eat one of these cakes," she thought, "it's sure to make *some* change in my size; and, as it can't possibly make me larger, it must make me smaller, I suppose."

So she swallowed one of the cakes, and was delighted to find that she began shrinking directly. As soon as she was small enough to get through the door, she ran out of the house, and found quite a crowd of little animals and birds waiting outside. The poor little Lizard, Bill, was in the middle, being held up by two guinea-pigs, who were giving it something out of a bottle. They all made a rush at Alice the moment she appeared; but she ran off as hard as she could, and soon found herself safe in a thick wood.

"The first thing I've got to do," said Alice to herself, as she wandered about in the wood, "is to grow to my right size again; and the second thing is to find my way into that lovely garden. I think that will be the best plan."

It sounded an excellent plan, no doubt, and very neatly and simply arranged; the only difficulty was, that she had not the smallest idea how to set about it; and, while she was peering about anxiously among the trees, a little sharp bark just over her head made her look up in a great hurry.

An enormous puppy was looking down at her with large round eyes, and feebly stretching out one paw, trying to touch her. "Poor little thing!" said Alice, in a coaxing tone, and she tried hard to whistle to it; but she was terribly frightened all the time at the thought that it might be hungry, in which case it would be very likely to eat her up in spite of all her coaxing.

Hardly knowing what she did, she picked up a little bit of stick, and held it out to the puppy: whereupon the puppy jumped into the air off all its feet at once, with a yelp of delight, and rushed at the stick, and made believe to worry it: then Alice dodged behind a great thistle, to keep herself from being run over; and, the moment she appeared on the other side, the puppy made another rush at the stick, and tumbled head over heels in its hurry to get hold of it: then Alice, thinking it was very like having a game of play with a cart-horse, and expecting every moment to be trampled under its feet, ran round the thistle again: then the puppy began a series of short charges at the stick, running a very little way forwards each time and a long way back, and barking hoarsely all the while, till at last it sat down a good way off, panting, with its tongue hanging out of its mouth, and its great eyes half shut.

This seemed to Alice a good opportunity for making her

escape: so she set off at once, and ran till she was quite tired and out of breath, and till the puppy's bark sounded quite faint in the distance.

"And yet what a dear little puppy it was!" said Alice, as she leant against a buttercup to rest herself, and fanned herself with one of the leaves. "I should have liked teaching it tricks very much, if—if I'd only been the right size to do it! Oh dear! I'd nearly forgotten that I've got to grow up again! Let me see—how *is* it to be managed? I suppose I ought to eat or drink something or other; but the great question is, 'What?'"

The great question certainly was "What?" Alice looked all round her at the flowers and the blades of grass, but she could not see anything that looked like the right thing to eat or drink under the circumstances. There was a large mushroom growing near her, about the same height as herself; and, when she had looked under it, and on both sides of it, and behind it, it occurred to her that she might as well look and see what was on the top of it.

She stretched herself up on tiptoe, and peeped over the

edge of the mushroom, and her eyes immediately met those of a large blue caterpillar, that was sitting on the top, with its arms folded, quietly smoking a long hookah, and taking not the smallest notice of her or of anything else.

# V

---

## *Advice from a Caterpillar*

THE CATERPILLAR and Alice looked at each other for some time in silence: at last the Caterpillar took the hookah out of its mouth, and addressed her in a languid, sleepy voice.

"Who are *you?*" said the Caterpillar.

This was not an encouraging opening for a conversation. Alice replied, rather shyly, "I—I hardly know, Sir, just at present—at least I know who I *was* when I got up this morning, but I think I must have been changed several times since then."

"What do you mean by that?" said the Caterpillar, sternly. "Explain yourself!"

"I can't explain *myself,* I'm afraid, Sir," said Alice, "because I'm not myself, you see."

"I don't see," said the Caterpillar.

"I'm afraid I can't put it more clearly," Alice replied, very politely, "for I can't understand it myself, to begin with; and being so many different sizes in a day is very confusing."

"It isn't," said the Caterpillar.

"Well, perhaps you haven't found it so yet," said Alice; "but when you have to turn into a chrysalis—you will some day, you know—and then after that into a butterfly, I should think you'll feel it a little queer, won't you?"

"Not a bit," said the Caterpillar.

"Well, perhaps *your* feelings may be different," said Alice: "all I know is, it would feel very queer to *me.*"

"You!" said the Caterpillar contemptuously. "Who are *you?*"

Which brought them back again to the beginning of the conversation. Alice felt a little irritated at the Caterpillar's making such *very* short remarks, and she drew herself up and said, very gravely, "I think you ought to tell me who *you* are, first."

"Why?" said the Caterpillar.

Here was another puzzling question; and, as Alice could not think of any good reason, and the Caterpillar seemed to be in a *very* unpleasant state of mind, she turned away.

"Come back!" the Caterpillar called after her. "I've something important to say!"

This sounded promising, certainly. Alice turned and came back again.

"Keep your temper," said the Caterpillar.

"Is that all?" said Alice, swallowing down her anger as well as she could.

"No," said the Caterpillar.

Alice thought she might as well wait, as she had nothing else to do, and perhaps after all it might tell her something worth hearing. For some minutes it puffed away without speaking; but at last it unfolded its arms, took the hookah out of its mouth again, and said, "So you think you're changed, do you?"

"I'm afraid I am, Sir," said Alice. "I can't remember things as I used—and I don't keep the same size for ten minutes together!"

"Can't remember *what* things?" said the Caterpillar.

"Well, I've tried to say *'How doth the little busy bee,'* but it all came different!" Alice replied in a very melancholy voice.

"Repeat *'You are old, Father William,'*" said the Caterpillar.

Alice folded her hands, and began:—

> " *'You are old, Father William,' the young man said,*
>     *'And your hair has become very white;*
>  *And yet you incessantly stand on your head—*
>     *Do you think, at your age, it is right?'*

" 'In my youth,' Father William replied to his son,
  'I feared it might injure the brain;
But, now that I'm perfectly sure I have none,
  Why, I do it again and again.'

" 'You are old,' said the youth, 'as I mentioned before,
  And have grown most uncommonly fat;
Yet you turned a back-somersault in at the door—
  Pray, what is the reason of that?'

" 'In my youth,' said the sage, as he shook his grey locks,
   'I kept all my limbs very supple
By the use of this ointment—one shilling the box—
   Allow me to sell you a couple?'

" 'You are old,' said the youth, 'and your jaws are too weak
   For anything tougher than suet;
Yet you finished the goose, with the bones and the beak—
   Pray, how did you manage to do it?'

" 'In my youth,' said his father, 'I took to the law,
   And argued each case with my wife;
And the muscular strength, which it gave to my jaw,
   Has lasted the rest of my life.'

" 'You are old,' said the youth, 'one would hardly suppose
   That your eye was as steady as ever;
Yet you balanced an eel on the end of your nose—
   What made you so awfully clever?'

" '*I have answered three questions, and that is enough,'*
  *Said his father. 'Don't give yourself airs!*
*Do you think I can listen all day to such stuff?*
  *Be off, or I'll kick you down-stairs!'* "

"That is not said right," said the Caterpillar.

"Not *quite* right, I'm afraid," said Alice timidly: "some of the words have got altered."

"It is wrong from beginning to end," said the Caterpillar, decidedly, and there was silence for some minutes.

The Caterpillar was the first to speak.

"What size do you want to be?" it asked.

"Oh, I'm not particular as to size," Alice hastily replied; "only one doesn't like changing so often, you know."

"I *don't* know," said the Caterpillar.

Alice said nothing: she had never been so much contradicted in all her life before, and she felt that she was losing her temper.

"Are you content now?" said the Caterpillar.

"Well, I should like to be a *little* larger, Sir, if you wouldn't mind," said Alice: "three inches is such a wretched height to be."

"It is a very good height indeed!" said the Caterpillar angrily, rearing itself upright as it spoke (it was exactly three inches high).

"But I'm not used to it!" pleaded poor Alice in a piteous tone. And she thought to herself "I wish the creatures wouldn't be so easily offended!"

"You'll get used to it in time," said the Caterpillar; and it put the hookah into its mouth, and began smoking again.

This time Alice waited patiently until it chose to speak again. In a minute or two the Caterpillar took the hookah out of its mouth, and yawned once or twice, and shook itself. Then it got down off the mushroom, and crawled away into the grass, merely remarking, as it went, "One side will make you grow taller, and the other side will make you grow shorter."

"One side of *what?* The other side of *what?*" thought Alice to herself.

"Of the mushroom," said the Caterpillar, just as if she had asked it aloud; and in another moment it was out of sight.

Alice remained looking thoughtfully at the mushroom for a minute, trying to make out which were the two sides of it; and, as it was perfectly round, she found this a very difficult question. However, at last she stretched her arms round it as far as they would go, and broke off a bit of the edge with each hand.

"And now which is which?" she said to herself, and nibbled a little of the right-hand bit to try the effect. The next moment she felt a violent blow underneath her chin: it had struck her foot!

She was a good deal frightened by this very sudden change, but she felt that there was no time to be lost, as she was shrinking rapidly: so she set to work at once to eat some of the other bit. Her chin was pressed so closely against her foot, that there was hardly room to open her mouth; but she did it at last, and managed to swallow a morsel of the left-hand bit.

        *        *        *        *        *

"Come, my head's free at last!" said Alice in a tone of delight, which changed into alarm in another moment, when she found that her shoulders were nowhere to be found: all she could see, when she looked down, was an immense length of neck, which seemed to rise like a stalk out of a sea of green leaves that lay far below her.

"What *can* all that green stuff be?" said Alice. "And where *have* my shoulders got to? And oh, my poor hands, how is it I can't see you?" She was moving them about as she spoke, but no result seemed to follow, except a little shaking among the distant green leaves.

As there seemed to be no chance of getting her hands up to her head, she tried to get her head down to *them,* and was delighted to find that her neck would bend about easily in any direction, like a serpent. She had just succeeded in curving it down into a graceful zigzag, and was going to dive in among the leaves, which she found to be nothing but the tops of the trees under which she had been wandering, when a sharp hiss made her draw back in a hurry: a large pigeon had flown into her face, and was beating her violently with its wings.

"Serpent!" screamed the Pigeon.

"I'm *not* a serpent!" said Alice indignantly. "Let me alone!"

"Serpent, I say again!" repeated the Pigeon, but in a more subdued tone, and added, with a kind of sob, "I've tried every way, but nothing seems to suit them!"

"I haven't the least idea what you're talking about," said Alice.

"I've tried the roots of trees, and I've tried banks, and I've tried hedges," the Pigeon went on, without attending to her; "but those serpents! There's no pleasing them!"

Alice was more and more puzzled, but she thought there was no use in saying anything more till the Pigeon had finished.

"As if it wasn't trouble enough hatching the eggs," said the Pigeon; "but I must be on the look-out for serpents, night and day! Why, I haven't had a wink of sleep these three weeks!"

"I'm very sorry you've been annoyed," said Alice, who was beginning to see its meaning.

"And just as I'd taken the highest tree in the wood," continued the Pigeon, raising its voice to a shriek, "and just as I was thinking I should be free of them at last, they must needs come wriggling down from the sky! Ugh, Serpent!"

"But I'm *not* a serpent, I tell you!" said Alice. "I'm a——— I'm a———"

"Well! *What* are you?" said the Pigeon. "I can see you're trying to invent something!"

"I—I'm a little glrl," said Alice, rather doubtfully, as she remembered the number of changes she had gone through that day.

"A likely story indeed!" said the Pigeon, in a tone of the deepest contempt. "I've seen a good many little girls in my time, but never *one* with such a neck as that! No, no! You're a serpent; and there's no use denying it. I suppose you'll be telling me next that you never tasted an egg!"

"I *have* tasted eggs, certainly," said Alice, who was a very truthful child; "but little girls eat eggs quite as much as serpents do, you know."

"I don't believe it," said the Pigeon; "but if they do, why, then they're a kind of serpent: that's all I can say."

This was such a new idea to Alice, that she was quite silent for a minute or two, which gave the Pigeon the opportunity of adding "You're looking for eggs, I know *that* well enough; and what does it matter to me whether you're a little girl or a serpent?"

"It matters a good deal to *me*," said Alice hastily; "but I'm not looking for eggs, as it happens; and, if I was, I shouldn't want *yours:* I don't like them raw."

"Well, be off, then!" said the Pigeon in a sulky tone, as it settled down again into its nest. Alice crouched down among the trees as well as she could, for her neck kept getting entangled among the branches, and every now and then she had to stop and untwist it. After a while she remembered that she still held the pieces of mushroom in her hands, and she set to work very carefully, nibbling first at one and then at the other, and growing sometimes taller, and sometimes shorter, until she had succeeded in bringing herself down to her usual height.

It was so long since she had been anything near the right size, that it felt quite strange at first; but she got used to it in a few minutes, and began talking to herself, as usual, "Come, there's half my plan done now! How puzzling all these changes are! I'm never sure what I'm going to be, from one minute to another! However, I've got back to my right size: the next thing is, to get into that beautiful garden—how *is* that to be done, I wonder?" As she said this, she came suddenly upon an open place, with a little house in it about four feet high. "Whoever lives there," thought Alice, "it'll never do to come upon them *this* size: why, I should frighten them out of their wits!" So she began nibbling at the right-hand bit again, and did not venture to go near the house till she had brought herself down to nine inches high.

# VI

---

## *Pig and Pepper*

FOR A MINUTE or two she stood looking at the house, and wondering what to do next, when suddenly a footman in livery came running out of the wood—(she considered him to

be a footman because he was in livery: otherwise, judging by his face only, she would have called him a fish)—and rapped loudly at the door with his knuckles. It was opened by another footman in livery, with a round face, and large eyes like a frog; and both footmen, Alice noticed, had powdered hair that curled all over their heads. She felt very curious to know what it was all about, and crept a little way out of the wood to listen.

The Fish-Footman began by producing from under his arm a great letter, nearly as large as himself, and this he handed over to the other, saying, in a solemn tone, "For the Duchess. An invitation from the Queen to play croquet." The Frog-Footman repeated, in the same solemn tone, only changing the order of the words a little, "From the Queen. An invitation for the Duchess to play croquet."

Then they both bowed low, and their curls got entangled together.

Alice laughed so much at this, that she had to run back into the wood for fear of their hearing her; and, when she next peeped out, the Fish-Footman was gone, and the other was sitting on the ground near the door, staring stupidly up into the sky.

Alice went timidly up to the door, and knocked.

"There's no sort of use in knocking," said the Footman, "and that for two reasons. First, because I'm on the same side of the door as you are: secondly, because they're making such a noise inside, no one could possibly hear you." And certainly there *was* a most extraordinary noise going on within—a constant howling and sneezing, and every now and then a great crash, as if a dish or kettle had been broken to pieces.

"Please, then," said Alice, "how am I to get in?"

"There might be some sense in your knocking," the Footman went on, without attending to her, "if we had the door between us. For instance, if you were *inside,* you might knock, and I could let you out, you know." He was looking up into the sky all the time he was speaking, and this Alice thought decidedly uncivil. "But perhaps he can't help it," she said to herself; "his eyes are so *very* nearly at the top of his head. But at any rate he might answer questions.—How am I to get in?" she repeated, aloud.

"I shall sit here," the Footman remarked, "till tomorrow——"

At this moment the door of the house opened, and a large plate came skimming out, straight at the Footman's head: it just grazed his nose, and broke to pieces against one of the trees behind him.

"——or next day, maybe," the Footman continued in the same tone, exactly as if nothing had happened.

"How am I to get in?" asked Alice again, in a louder tone.

"*Are* you to get in at all?" said the Footman. "That's the first question, you know."

It was, no doubt: only Alice did not like to be told so. "It's really dreadful," she muttered to herself, "the way all the creatures argue. It's enough to drive one crazy!"

The Footman seemed to think this a good opportunity for repeating his remark, with variations. "I shall sit here," he said, "on and off, for days and days."

"But what am *I* to do?" said Alice.

"Anything you like," said the Footman, and began whistling.

"Oh, there's no use in talking to him," said Alice desperately: "he's perfectly idiotic!" And she opened the door and went in.

The door led right into a large kitchen, which was full of smoke from one end to the other: the Duchess was sitting on a three-legged stool in the middle, nursing a baby; the cook was leaning over the fire, stirring a large cauldron which seemed to be full of soup.

"There's certainly too much pepper in that soup!" Alice said to herself, as well as she could for sneezing.

There was certainly too much of it in the *air*. Even the Duchess sneezed occasionally; and as for the baby, it was sneezing and howling alternately without a moment's pause. The only two creatures in the kitchen that did *not* sneeze, were the cook, and a large cat, which was sitting on the hearth and grinning from ear to ear.

"Please, would you tell me," said Alice, a little timidly, for she was not quite sure whether it was good manners for her to speak first, "why your cat grins like that?"

"It's a Cheshire-Cat," said the Duchess, "and that's why. Pig!"

She said the last word with such sudden violence that Alice quite jumped; but she saw in another moment that it was addressed to the baby, and not to her, so she took courage, and went on again:—

"I didn't know that Cheshire-Cats always grinned; in fact, I didn't know that cats *could* grin."

"They all can," said the Duchess; "and most of 'em do."

"I don't know of any that do," Alice said very politely, feeling quite pleased to have got into a conversation.

"You don't know much," said the Duchess; "and that's a fact."

Alice did not at all like the tone of this remark, and thought it would be as well to introduce some other subject of conversation. While she was trying to fix on one, the cook took the cauldron of soup off the fire, and at once set to work throwing everything within her reach at the Duchess and the baby—the fire-irons came first; then followed a shower of saucepans, plates, and dishes. The Duchess took no notice of them even when they hit her; and the baby was howling so much already, that it was quite impossible to say whether the blows hurt it or not.

"Oh, *please* mind what you're doing!" cried Alice, jumping up and down in an agony of terror. "Oh, there goes his *precious* nose!," as an unusually large saucepan flew close by it, and very nearly carried it off.

"If everybody minded their own business," the Duchess said, in a hoarse growl, "the world would go round a deal faster than it does."

"Which would *not* be an advantage," said Alice, who felt very glad to get an opportunity of showing off a little of her knowledge. "Just think what work it would make with the day and night! You see the earth takes twenty-four hours to turn round on its axis——"

"Talking of axes," said the Duchess, "chop off her head!"

Alice glanced rather anxiously at the cook, to see if she meant to take the hint; but the cook was busily stirring the soup, and seemed not to be listening, so she went on again: "Twenty-four hours, I *think;* or is it twelve? I——"

"Oh, don't bother *me,*" said the Duchess. "I never could abide figures." And with that she began nursing her child again, singing a sort of lullaby to it as she did so, and giving it a violent shake at the end of every line:—

> *"Speak roughly to your little boy,*
> *And beat him when he sneezes:*
> *He only does it to annoy,*
> *Because he knows it teases."*

CHORUS

(in which the cook and the baby joined):—

> *"Wow! wow! wow!"*

While the Duchess sang the second verse of the song, she kept tossing the baby violently up and down, and the poor little thing howled so, that Alice could hardly hear the words:—

> *"I speak severely to my boy,*
> *I beat him when he sneezes;*
> *For he can thoroughly enjoy*
> *The pepper when he pleases!"*

CHORUS

> *"Wow! wow! wow!"*

"Here! You may nurse it a bit, if you like!" said the Duchess to Alice, flinging the baby at her as she spoke. "I must go and get ready to play croquet with the Queen," and she hurried out of the room. The cook threw a frying-pan after her as she went, but it just missed her.

Alice caught the baby with some difficulty, as it was a queer-shaped little creature, and held out its arms and legs in all directions, "just like a star-fish," thought Alice. The poor little thing was snorting like a steam-engine when she caught it, and kept doubling itself up and straightening itself out again, so that altogether, for the first minute or two, it was as much as she could do to hold it.

As soon as she had made out the proper way of nursing it (which was to twist it up into a sort of knot, and then keep tight hold of its right ear and left foot, so as to prevent its undoing itself), she carried it out into the open air. "If I don't take this child away with me," thought Alice, "they're sure to kill it in a day or two. Wouldn't it be murder to leave it behind?" She said the last words out loud, and the little thing grunted in reply (it had left off sneezing by this time). "Don't grunt," said Alice: "that's not at all a proper way of expressing yourself."

The baby grunted again, and Alice looked very anxiously into its face to see what was the matter with it. There could be no doubt that it had a *very* turn-up nose, much more like a snout than a real nose: also its eyes were getting extremely small for a baby: altogether Alice did not like the look of the thing at all. "But perhaps it was only sobbing," she thought, and looked into its eyes again, to see if there were any tears.

No, there were no tears. "If you're going to turn into a pig, my dear," said Alice, seriously, "I'll have nothing more to do with you. Mind now!" The poor little thing sobbed again (or grunted, it was impossible to say which), and they went on for some while in silence.

Alice was just beginning to think to herself, "Now, what am I to do with this creature when I get it home?" when it grunted again, so violently, that she looked down into its face in some alarm. This time there could be *no* mistake about it: it was neither more nor less than a pig, and she felt that it would be quite absurd for her to carry it any further.

So she set the little creature down, and felt quite relieved to see it trot away quietly into the wood. "If it had grown up," she said to herself, "it would have been a dreadfully ugly child: but it makes rather a handsome pig, I think." And she began thinking over other children she knew, who might do very well as pigs, and was just saying to herself "if one only knew the right way to change them——" when she was a little startled by seeing the Cheshire-Cat sitting on a bough of a tree a few yards off.

The Cat only grinned when it saw Alice. It looked good-natured, she thought: still it had *very* long claws and a great many teeth, so she felt it ought to be treated with respect.

"Cheshire-Puss," she began, rather timidly, as she did not at all know whether it would like the name: however, it only grinned a little wider. "Come, it's pleased so far," thought Alice, and she went on. "Would you tell me, please, which way I ought to go from here?"

"That depends a good deal on where you want to get to," said the Cat.

"I don't much care where——" said Alice.

"Then it doesn't matter which way you go," said the Cat.

"——so long as I get *somewhere,*" Alice added as an explanation.

"Oh, you're sure to do that," said the Cat, "if you only walk long enough."

Alice felt that this could not be denied, so she tried another question. "What sort of people live about here?"

"In *that* direction," the Cat said, waving its right paw round, "lives a Hatter: and in *that* direction," waving the other paw, "lives a March Hare. Visit either you like: they're both mad."

"But I don't want to go among mad people," Alice remarked.

"Oh, you can't help that," said the Cat: "we're all mad here. I'm mad. You're mad."

"How do you know I'm mad?" said Alice.

"You must be," said the Cat, "or you wouldn't have come here."

Alice didn't think that proved it at all: however, she went on: "And how do you know that you're mad?"

"To begin with," said the Cat, "a dog's not mad. You grant that?"

"I suppose so," said Alice.

"Well, then," the Cat went on, "you see a dog growls when it's angry, and wags its tail when it's pleased. Now *I* growl when I'm pleased, and wag my tail when I'm angry. Therefore I'm mad."

"*I* call it purring, not growling," said Alice.

"Call it what you like," said the Cat. "Do you play croquet with the Queen to-day?"

"I should like it very much," said Alice, "but I haven't been invited yet."

"You'll see me there," said the Cat, and vanished.

Alice was not much surprised at this, she was getting so well used to queer things happening. While she was still looking at the place where it had been, it suddenly appeared again.

"By-the-bye, what became of the baby?" said the Cat. "I'd nearly forgotten to ask."

"It turned into a pig," Alice answered very quietly, just as if the Cat had come back in a natural way.

"I thought it would," said the Cat, and vanished again.

Alice waited a little, half expecting to see it again, but it did not appear, and after a minute or two she walked on in the direction in which the March Hare was said to live. "I've seen hatters before," she said to herself: "the March Hare will be much the most interesting, and perhaps, as this is May it won't be raving mad—at least not so mad as it was in March." As she said this, she looked up, and there was the Cat again, sitting on a branch of a tree.

"Did you say 'pig,' or 'fig'?" said the Cat.

"I said 'pig,'" replied Alice; "and I wish you wouldn't keep appearing and vanishing so suddenly: you make one quite giddy."

"All right," said the Cat; and this time it vanished quite slowly, beginning with the end of the tail, and ending with the grin, which remained some time after the rest of it had gone.

"Well! I've often seen a cat without a grin," thought Alice; "but a grin without a cat! It's the most curious thing I ever saw in all my life!"

She had not gone much farther before she came in sight of the house of the March Hare: she thought it must be the right house, because the chimneys were shaped like ears and the roof was thatched with fur. It was so large a house, that she did not like to go nearer till she had nibbled some more of the left-hand bit of mushroom, and raised herself to about two feet high: even then she walked up towards it rather timidly, saying to herself, "Suppose it should be raving mad after all! I almost wish I'd gone to see the Hatter instead!"

# VII

## A Mad Tea-Party

THERE WAS A table set out under a tree in front of the house, and the March Hare and the Hatter were having tea at it: a Dormouse was sitting between them, fast asleep, and the other two were using it as a cushion, resting their elbows on it, and talking over its head. "Very uncomfortable for the Dormouse," thought Alice; "only, as it's asleep, I suppose it doesn't mind."

The table was a large one, but the three were all crowded together at one corner of it. "No room! No room!" they cried out when they saw Alice coming. "There's *plenty* of room!" said Alice indignantly, and she sat down in a large arm-chair at one end of the table.

"Have some wine," the March Hare said in an encouraging tone.

Alice looked all round the table, but there was nothing on it but tea. "I don't see any wine," she remarked.

"There isn't any," said the March Hare.

"Then it wasn't very civil of you to offer it," said Alice angrily.

"It wasn't very civil of you to sit down without being invited," said the March Hare.

"I didn't know it was *your* table," said Alice: "it's laid for a great many more than three."

"Your hair wants cutting," said the Hatter. He had been looking at Alice for some time with great curiosity, and this was his first speech.

"You should learn not to make personal remarks," Alice said with some severity: "it's very rude."

The Hatter opened his eyes very wide on hearing this; but all he *said* was "Why is a raven like a writing-desk?"

"Come, we shall have some fun now!" thought Alice. "I'm glad they've begun asking riddles—I believe I can guess that," she added aloud.

"Do you mean that you think you can find out the answer to it?" said the March Hare.

"Exactly so," said Alice.

"Then you should say what you mean," the March Hare went on.

"I do," Alice hastily replied; "at least—at least I mean what I say—that's the same thing, you know."

"Not the same thing a bit!" said the Hatter. "Why, you might just as well say that 'I see what I eat' is the same thing as 'I eat what I see'!"

"You might just as well say," added the March Hare, "that 'I like what I get' is the same thing as 'I get what I like'!"

"You might just as well say," added the Dormouse, which seemed to be talking in its sleep, "that 'I breathe when I sleep' is the same thing as 'I sleep when I breathe'!"

"It *is* the same thing with you," said the Hatter, and here the conversation dropped, and the party sat silent for a minute, while Alice thought over all she could remember about ravens and writing-desks, which wasn't much.

The Hatter was the first to break the silence. "What day of the month is it?" he said, turning to Alice: he had taken his watch out of his pocket, and was looking at it uneasily, shaking it every now and then, and holding it to his ear.

Alice considered a little, and then said, "The fourth."

"Two days wrong!" sighed the Hatter. "I told you butter wouldn't suit the works!" he added, looking angrily at the March Hare.

"It was the *best* butter," the March Hare meekly replied.

"Yes, but some crumbs must have got in as well," the Hatter grumbled: "you shouldn't have put it in with the bread-knife."

The March Hare took the watch and looked at it gloomily: then he dipped it into his cup of tea, and looked at it again: but he could think of nothing better to say than his first remark, "It was the *best* butter, you know."

Alice had been looking over his shoulder with some curiosity. "What a funny watch!" she remarked. "It tells the day of the month, and doesn't tell what o'clock it is!"

"Why should it?" muttered the Hatter. "Does *your* watch tell you what year it is?"

"Of course not," Alice replied very readily: "but that's because it stays the same year for such a long time together."

"Which is just the case with *mine*," said the Hatter.

Alice felt dreadfully puzzled. The Hatter's remark seemed to her to have no sort of meaning in it, and yet it was certainly English. "I don't quite understand you," she said, as politely as she could.

"The Dormouse is asleep again," said the Hatter, and he poured a little hot tea upon its nose.

The Dormouse shook its head impatiently, and said, without opening its eyes, "Of course, of course: just what I was going to remark myself."

"Have you guessed the riddle yet?" the Hatter said, turning to Alice again.

"No, I give it up," Alice replied. "What's the answer?"

"I haven't the slightest idea," said the Hatter.

"Nor I," said the March Hare.

Alice sighed wearily. "I think you might do something better with the time," she said, "than wasting it in asking riddles that have no answers."

"If you knew Time as well as I do," said the Hatter, "you wouldn't talk about wasting *it*. It's *him*."

"I don't know what you mean," said Alice.

"Of course you don't!" the Hatter said, tossing his head contemptuously. "I dare say you never even spoke to Time!"

"Perhaps not," Alice cautiously replied; "but I know I have to beat time when I learn music."

"Ah! That accounts for it," said the Hatter. "He won't stand beating. Now, if you only kept on good terms with him, he'd do almost anything you liked with the clock.

"For instance, suppose it were nine o'clock in the morning, just time to begin lessons: you'd only have to whisper a hint to Time, and round goes the clock in a twinkling! Half-past one, time for dinner!"

("I only wish it was," the March Hare said to itself in a whisper.)

"That would be grand, certainly," said Alice thoughtfully: "but then—I shouldn't be hungry for it, you know."

"Not at first, perhaps," said the Hatter: "but you could keep it to half-past one as long as you liked."

"Is that the way *you* manage?" Alice asked.

The Hatter shook his head mournfully. "Not I!" he replied. "We quarrelled last March——just before *he* went mad, you know——" (pointing with his teaspoon at the March Hare), "——it was at the great concert given by the Queen of Hearts, and I had to sing

> *'Twinkle, twinkle, little bat!*
> *How I wonder what you're at!'*

You know the song, perhaps?"

"I've heard something like it," said Alice.

"It goes on, you know," the Hatter continued, "in this way:—

> *'Up above the world you fly,*
> *Like a tea-tray in the sky.*
> *Twinkle, twinkle——'*

Here the Dormouse shook itself, and began singing in its sleep *"Twinkle, twinkle, twinkle, twinkle——"* and went on so long that they had to pinch it to make it stop.

"Well, I'd hardly finished the first verse," said the Hatter, "when the Queen bawled out 'He's murdering the time! Off with his head!'"

"How dreadfully savage!" exclaimed Alice.

"And ever since that," the Hatter went on in a mournful tone, "he won't do a thing I ask! It's always six o'clock now."

A bright idea came into Alice's head. "Is that the reason so many tea-things are put out here?" she asked.

"Yes, that's it," said the Hatter with a sigh: "it's always tea-time, and we've no time to wash the things between whiles."

"Then you keep moving round, I suppose?" said Alice.

"Exactly so," said the Hatter: "as the things get used up."

"But what happens when you come to the beginning again?" Alice ventured to ask.

"Suppose we change the subject," the March Hare interrupted, yawning. "I'm getting tired of this. I vote the young lady tells us a story."

"I'm afraid I don't know one," said Alice, rather alarmed at the proposal.

"Then the Dormouse shall!" they both cried. "Wake up, Dormouse!" And they pinched it on both sides at once.

The Dormouse slowly opened its eyes. "I wasn't asleep,"

it said in a hoarse, feeble voice, "I heard every word you fellows were saying."

"Tell us a story!" said the March Hare.

"Yes, please do!" pleaded Alice.

"And be quick about it," added the Hatter, "or you'll be asleep again before it's done."

"Once upon a time there were three little sisters," the Dormouse began in a great hurry; "and their names were Elsie, Lacie, and Tillie; and they lived at the bottom of a well——"

"What did they live on?" said Alice, who always took a great interest in questions of eating and drinking.

"They lived on treacle," said the Dormouse, after thinking a minute or two.

"They couldn't have done that, you know," Alice gently remarked. "They'd have been ill."

"So they were," said the Dormouse; "*very* ill."

Alice tried a little to fancy to herself what such an extraordinary way of living would be like, but it puzzled her too much: so she went on: "But why did they live at the bottom of a well?"

"Take some more tea," the March Hare said to Alice, very earnestly.

"I've had nothing yet," Alice replied in an offended tone: "so I can't take more."

"You mean you can't take *less*," said the Hatter: "it's very easy to take *more* than nothing."

"Nobody asked *your* opinion," said Alice.

"Who's making personal remarks now?" the Hatter asked triumphantly.

Alice did not quite know what to say to this: so she helped herself to some tea and bread-and-butter, and then turned to the Dormouse, and repeated her question. "Why did they live at the bottom of a well?"

The Dormouse again took a minute or two to think about it, and then said, "It was a treacle-well."

"There's no such thing!" Alice was beginning very angrily, but the Hatter and the March Hare went "Sh! sh!" and the Dormouse sulkily remarked "If you can't be civil, you'd better finish the story for yourself."

"No, please go on!" Alice said very humbly. "I won't interrupt you again. I dare say there may be *one.*"

"One, indeed!" said the Dormouse indignantly. However, he consented to go on. "And so these three little sisters—they were learning to draw, you know——"

"What did they draw?" said Alice, quite forgetting her promise.

"Treacle," said the Dormouse, without considering at all, this time.

"I want a clean cup," interrupted the Hatter: "let's all move one place on."

He moved on as he spoke, and the Dormouse followed him: the March Hare moved into the Dormouse's place, and Alice rather unwillingly took the place of the March Hare. The Hatter was the only one who got any advantage from the change; and Alice was a good deal worse off than before, as the March Hare had just upset the milk-jug into his plate.

Alice did not wish to offend the Dormouse again, so she began very cautiously: "But I don't understand. Where did they draw the treacle from?"

"You can draw water out of a water-well," said the Hatter; "so I should think you could draw treacle out of a treacle-well—eh, stupid?"

"But they were *in* the well," Alice said to the Dormouse, not choosing to notice this last remark.

"Of course they were," said the Dormouse: "well in."

This answer so confused poor Alice, that she let the Dormouse go on for some time without interrupting it.

"They were learning to draw," the Dormouse went on, yawning and rubbing its eyes, for it was getting very sleepy; "and they drew all manner of things—everything that begins with an M——"

"Why with an M?" said Alice.

"Why not?" said the March Hare.

Alice was silent.

The Dormouse had closed its eyes by this time, and was going off into a doze; but, on being pinched by the Hatter, it woke up again with a little shriek, and went on: "——that begins with an M, such as mouse-traps, and the moon, and memory, and muchness—you know you say things are 'much of a muchness'—did you ever see such a thing as a drawing of a muchness?"

"Really, now you ask me," said Alice, very much confused, "I don't think——"

"Then you shouldn't talk," said the Hatter.

This piece of rudeness was more than Alice could bear: she got up in great disgust, and walked off: the Dormouse fell asleep instantly, and neither of the others took the least notice of her going, though she looked back once or twice, half hop-

ing that they would call after her: the last time she saw them, they were trying to put the Dormouse into the teapot.

"At any rate I'll never go *there* again!" said Alice as she picked her way through the wood. "It's the stupidest tea-party I ever was at in all my life!"

Just as she said this, she noticed that one of the trees had a door leading right into it. "That's very curious!" she thought. "But everything's curious to-day. I think I may as well go in at once." And in she went.

Once more she found herself in the long hall, and close to the little glass table. "Now, I'll manage better this time," she said to herself, and began by taking the little golden key, and unlocking the door that led into the garden. Then she set to work nibbling at the mushroom (she had kept a piece of it in her pocket) till she was about a foot high: then she walked down the little passage: and *then*—she found herself at last in the beautiful garden, among the bright flower-beds and the cool fountains.

# VIII

## The Queen's Croquet-Ground

A LARGE ROSE-TREE stood near the entrance of the garden: the roses growing on it were white, but there were three gardeners at it, busily painting them red. Alice thought this a very curious thing, and she went nearer to watch them, and, just as she came up to them, she heard one of them say "Look out now, Five! Don't go splashing paint over me like that!"

"I couldn't help it," said Five, in a sulky tone. "Seven jogged my elbow."

On which Seven looked up and said "That's right, Five! Always lay the blame on others!"

"*You'd* better not talk!" said Five. "I heard the Queen say only yesterday you deserved to be beheaded."

"What for?" said the one who had spoken first.

"That's none of *your* business, Two!" said Seven.

"Yes, it *is* his business!" said Five. "And I'll tell him— it was for bringing the cook tulip-roots instead of onions."

Seven flung down his brush, and had just begun "Well, of all the unjust things—" when his eye chanced to fall upon Alice, as she stood watching them, and he checked himself suddenly: the others looked round also, and all of them bowed low.

"Would you tell me, please," said Alice, a little timidly, "why you are painting those roses?"

Five and Seven said nothing, but looked at Two. Two began, in a low voice, "Why, the fact is, you see, Miss, this here ought to have been a *red* rose-tree, and we put a white one in by mistake; and, if the Queen was to find it out, we should all have our heads cut off, you know. So you see, Miss, we're doing our best, afore she comes, to—" At this moment, Five, who had been anxiously looking across the garden, called out "The Queen! The Queen!," and the three gardeners instantly threw themselves flat upon their faces. There was a sound of many footsteps, and Alice looked round, eager to see the Queen.

First came ten soldiers carrying clubs; these were all shaped like the three gardeners, oblong and flat, with their hands and feet at the corners: next the ten courtiers: these were ornamented all over with diamonds, and walked two and two, as the soldiers did. After these came the royal children; there were ten of them, and the little dears came jumping merrily along hand in hand, in couples: they were all ornamented with hearts. Next came the guests, mostly Kings and Queens, and among them Alice recognised the White Rabbit: it was talking in a hurried nervous manner, smiling at everything that was said, and went by without noticing her. Then followed the Knave of Hearts, carrying the King's crown on a crimson velvet cushion; and, last of all this grand procession, came THE KING AND QUEEN OF HEARTS.

Alice was rather doubtful whether she ought not to lie down on her face like the three gardeners, but she could not remember ever having heard of such a rule at processions; "and besides, what would be the use of a procession," thought she, "if people had all to lie down on their faces, so that they couldn't see it?" So she stood where she was, and waited.

When the procession came opposite to Alice, they all stopped and looked at her, and the Queen said, severely, "Who is this?" She said it to the Knave of Hearts, who only bowed and smiled in reply.

"Idiot!" said the Queen, tossing her head impatiently; and, turning to Alice, she went on, "What's your name, child?"

"My name is Alice, so please your Majesty," said Alice very politely; but she added, to herself, "Why, they're only a pack of cards, after all. I needn't be afraid of them!"

"And who are *these?*" said the Queen, pointing to the three gardeners who were lying round the rose-tree; for, you see, as they were lying on their faces, and the pattern on their backs was the same as the rest of the pack, she could not tell whether they were gardeners, or soldiers, or courtiers, or three of her own children.

"How should *I* know?" said Alice, surprised at her own courage. "It's no business of *mine.*"

The Queen turned crimson with fury, and, after glaring at her for a moment like a wild beast, began screaming "Off with her head! Off with——"

"Nonsense!" said Alice, very loudly and decidedly, and the Queen was silent.

The King laid his hand upon her arm, and timidly said "Consider, my dear: she is only a child!"

The Queen turned angrily away from him, and said to the Knave "Turn them over!"

The Knave did so, very carefully, with one foot.

"Get up!" said the Queen in a shrill, loud voice, and the three gardeners instantly jumped up, and began bowing to the King, the Queen, the royal children, and everybody else.

"Leave off that!" screamed the Queen. "You make me giddy." And then, turning to the rose-tree, she went on, "What *have* you been doing here?"

"May it please your Majesty," said Two, in a very humble tone, going down on one knee as he spoke, "we were trying——"

"*I* see!" said the Queen, who had meanwhile been examining the roses. "Off with their heads!" and the procession moved on, three of the soldiers remaining behind to execute the unfortunate gardeners, who ran to Alice for protection.

"You shan't be beheaded!" said Alice, and she put them into a large flower-pot that stood near. The three soldiers wandered about for a minute or two, looking for them, and then quietly marched off after the others.

"Are their heads off?" shouted the Queen.

"Their heads are gone, if it please your Majesty!" the soldiers shouted in reply.

"That's right!" shouted the Queen. "Can you play croquet?"

The soldiers were silent, and looked at Alice, as the question was evidently meant for her.

"Yes!" shouted Alice.

"Come on, then!" roared the Queen, and Alice joined the procession, wondering very much what would happen next.

"It's—it's a very fine day!" said a timid voice at her side. She was walking by the White Rabbit, who was peeping anxiously into her face.

"Very," said Alice. "Where's the Duchess?"

"Hush! Hush!" said the Rabbit in a low, hurried tone. He looked anxiously over his shoulder as he spoke, and then raised himself upon tiptoe, put his mouth close to her ear, and whispered "She's under sentence of execution."

"What for?" said Alice.

"Did you say 'What a pity!'?" the Rabbit asked.

"No, I didn't," said Alice. "I don't think it's at all a pity. I said 'What for?'"

"She boxed the Queen's ears——" the Rabbit began. Alice gave a little scream of laughter. "Oh, hush!" the Rabbit whispered in a frightened tone. "The Queen will hear you! You see she came rather late, and the Queen said——"

"Get to your places!" shouted the Queen in a voice of thunder, and people began running about in all directions, tumbling up against each other: however, they got settled down in a minute or two, and the game began.

Alice thought she had never seen such a curious croquet-ground in her life: it was all ridges and furrows; the croquet balls were live hedgehogs, and the mallets live flamingoes, and the soldiers had to double themselves up and stand on their hands and feet, to make the arches.

The chief difficulty Alice found at first was in managing her flamingo: she succeeded in getting its body tucked away, comfortably enough, under her arm, with its legs hanging down, but generally, just as she had got its neck nicely straightened out, and was going to give the hedgehog a blow with its head, it *would* twist itself round and look up into her face, with such a puzzled expression that she could not help bursting out laughing; and, when she had got its head down, and was going to begin again, it was very provoking to find that the hedgehog had unrolled itself, and was in the act of crawling away: besides all this, there was generally a ridge or a furrow in the way wherever she wanted to send the hedgehog to, and, as the doubled-up soldiers were always getting up and walking off to other parts of the ground, Alice soon came to the conclusion that it was a very difficult game indeed.

The players all played at once without waiting for turns, quarrelling all the while, and fighting for the hedgehogs; and in a very short time the Queen was in a furious passion, and went stamping about, and shouting "Off with his head!" or "Off with her head!" about once in a minute.

Alice began to feel very uneasy: to be sure, she had not as yet had any dispute with the Queen, but she knew that it might happen any minute, "and then," thought she, "what would become of me? They're dreadfully fond of beheading people here: the great wonder is, that there's any one left alive!"

She was looking about for some way of escape, and wondering whether she could get away without being seen, when she noticed a curious appearance in the air: it puzzled her very much at first, but after watching it a minute or two she made it out to be a grin, and she said to herself "It's the Cheshire-Cat: now I shall have somebody to talk to."

"How are you getting on?" said the Cat, as soon as there was mouth enough for it to speak with.

Alice waited till the eyes appeared, and then nodded. "It's no use speaking to it," she thought, "till its ears have come, or at least one of them." In another minute the whole head appeared, and then Alice put down her flamingo, and began an account of the game, feeling very glad she had some one to listen to her. The Cat seemed to think that there was enough of it now in sight, and no more of it appeared.

"I don't think they play at all fairly," Alice began, in rather a complaining tone, "and they all quarrel so dreadfully one can't hear oneself speak—and they don't seem to have any rules in particular; at least, if there are, nobody attends to them—and you've no idea how confusing it is all the things being alive: for instance, there's the arch I've got to go through next walking about at the other end of the ground— and I should have croqueted the Queen's hedgehog just now, only it ran away when it saw mine coming!"

"How do you like the Queen?" said the Cat in a low voice.

"Not at all," said Alice: "she's so extremely—" Just then she noticed that the Queen was close behind her, listening: so she went on "—likely to win, that it's hardly worth while finishing the game."

The Queen smiled and passed on.

"Who *are* you talking to?" said the King, coming up to Alice, and looking at the Cat's head with great curiosity.

"It's a friend of mine—a Cheshire-Cat," said Alice: "allow me to introduce it."

"I don't like the look of it at all," said the King: "however, it may kiss my hand, if it likes."

"I'd rather not," the Cat remarked.

"Don't be impertinent," said the King, "and don't look at me like that!" He got behind Alice as he spoke.

"A cat may look at a king," said Alice. "I've read that in some book, but I don't remember where."

"Well, it must be removed," said the King very decidedly; and he called to the Queen, who was passing at the moment, "My dear! I wish you would have this cat removed!"

The Queen had only one way of settling all difficulties, great or small. "Off with his head!" she said without even looking round.

"I'll fetch the executioner myself," said the King eagerly, and he hurried off.

Alice thought she might as well go back and see how the game was going on, as she heard the Queen's voice in the distance, screaming with passion. She had already heard her sentence three of the players to be executed for having missed their turns, and she did not like the look of things at all, as the game was in such confusion that she never knew whether it was her turn or not. So she went off in search of her hedgehog.

The hedgehog was engaged in a fight with another hedge-

hog, which seemed to Alice an excellent opportunity for cro-
queting one of them with the other: the only difficulty was,
that her flamingo was gone across to the other side of the
garden, where Alice could see it trying in a helpless sort of
way to fly up into a tree.

By the time she had caught the flamingo and brought it
back, the fight was over, and both the hedgehogs were out of
sight: "but it doesn't matter much," thought Alice, "as all the
arches are gone from this side of the ground." So she tucked
it away under her arm, that it might not escape again, and
went back to have a little more conversation with her friend.

When she got back to the Cheshire-Cat, she was surprised
to find quite a large crowd collected round it: there was a
dispute going on between the executioner, the King, and the
Queen, who were all talking at once, while all the rest were
quite silent, and looked very uncomfortable.

The moment Alice appeared, she was appealed to by all three to settle the question, and they repeated their arguments to her, though, as they all spoke at once, she found it very hard to make out exactly what they said.

The executioner's argument was, that you couldn't cut off a head unless there was a body to cut it off from: that he had never had to do such a thing before, and he wasn't going to begin at *his* time of life.

The King's argument was that anything that had a head could be beheaded, and that you weren't to talk nonsense.

The Queen's argument was that, if something wasn't done about it in less than no time, she'd have everybody executed, all round. (It was this last remark that had made the whole party look so grave and anxious.)

Alice could think of nothing else to say but "It belongs to the Duchess: you'd better ask *her* about it."

"She's in prison," the Queen said to the executioner: "fetch her here." And the executioner went off like an arrow.

The Cat's head began fading away the moment he was gone, and, by the time he had come back with the Duchess, it had entirely disappeared: so the King and the executioner ran wildly up and down looking for it, while the rest of the party went back to the game.

# IX

## The Mock Turtle's Story

"You can't think how glad I am to see you again, you dear old thing!" said the Duchess, as she tucked her arm affectionately into Alice's, and they walked off together.

Alice was very glad to find her in such a pleasant temper, and thought to herself that perhaps it was only the pepper that had made her so savage when they met in the kitchen.

"When *I'm* a Duchess," she said to herself (not in a very hopeful tone, though), "I won't have any pepper in my kitchen *at all*. Soup does very well without—Maybe it's always pepper that makes people hot-tempered," she went on, very much pleased at having found out a new kind of rule, "and vinegar that makes them sour—and camomile that makes them bitter—and—and barley-sugar and such things that make children sweet-tempered. I only wish people knew *that:* then they wouldn't be so stingy about it, you know——"

She had quite forgotten the Duchess by this time, and was a little startled when she heard her voice close to her ear. "You're thinking about something, my dear, and that makes you forget to talk. I can't tell you just now what the moral of that is, but I shall remember it in a bit."

"Perhaps it hasn't one," Alice ventured to remark.

"Tut, tut, child!" said the Duchess. "Everything's got a moral, if only you can find it." And she squeezed herself up closer to Alice's side as she spoke.

Alice did not much like her keeping so close to her: first, because the Duchess was *very* ugly, and secondly, because she was exactly the right height to rest her chin on Alice's shoulder, and it was an uncomfortably sharp chin. However, she did not like to be rude: so she bore it as well as she could.

"The game's going on rather better now," she said, by way of keeping up the conversation a little.

"'Tis so," said the Duchess: "and the moral of that is—'Oh, 'tis love, 'tis love, that makes the world go round!'"

"Somebody said," Alice whispered, "that it's done by everybody minding their own business!"

"Ah well! It means much the same thing," said the Duchess, digging her sharp little chin into Alice's shoulder as she added, "and the moral of *that* is—'Take care of the sense, and the sounds will take care of themselves.'"

"How fond she is of finding morals in things!" Alice thought to herself.

"I dare say you're wondering why I don't put my arm round your waist," the Duchess said, after a pause: "the reason is, that I'm doubtful about the temper of your flamingo. Shall I try the experiment?"

"He might bite," Alice cautiously replied, not feeling at all anxious to have the experiment tried.

"Very true," said the Duchess: "flamingoes and mustard both bite. And the moral of that is—'Birds of a feather flock together.'"

"Only mustard isn't a bird," Alice remarked.

"Right, as usual," said the Duchess: "what a clear way you have of putting things!"

"It's a mineral, I *think*," said Alice.

"Of course it is," said the Duchess, who seemed ready to agree to everything that Alice said: "there's a large mustard-mine near here. And the moral of that is—'The more there is of mine, the less there is of yours.'"

"Oh, I know," exclaimed Alice, who had not attended to this last remark. "It's a vegetable. It doesn't look like one, but it is."

"I quite agree with you," said the Duchess; "and the moral of that is—'Be what you would seem to be'—or, if you'd like it put more simply—'Never imagine yourself not to be otherwise than what it might appear to others that what you were or might have been was not otherwise than what you had been would have appeared to them to be otherwise.'"

"I think I should understand that better," Alice said very politely, "if I had it written down: but I can't quite follow it as you say it."

"That's nothing to what I could say if I chose," the Duchess replied, in a pleased tone.

"Pray don't trouble yourself to say it any longer than that," said Alice.

"Oh, don't talk about trouble!" said the Duchess. "I make you a present of everything I've said as yet."

"A cheap sort of present!" thought Alice. "I'm glad they don't give birthday-presents like that!" But she did not venture to say it out loud.

"Thinking again?" the Duchess asked, with another dig of her sharp little chin.

"I've a right to think," said Alice sharply, for she was beginning to feel a little worried.

"Just about as much right," said the Duchess, "as pigs have to fly; and the m——"

But here, to Alice's great surprise, the Duchess's voice died away, even in the middle of her favourite word "moral," and the arm that was linked into hers began to tremble. Alice looked up, and there stood the Queen in front of them, with her arms folded, frowning like a thunderstorm.

"A fine day, your Majesty!" the Duchess began in a low, weak voice.

"Now, I give you fair warning," shouted the Queen, stamping on the ground as she spoke; "either you or your head must be off, and that in about half no time! Take your choice!"

The Duchess took her choice, and was gone in a moment.

"Let's go on with the game," the Queen said to Alice; and Alice was too much frightened to say a word, but slowly followed her back to the croquet-ground.

The other guests had taken advantage of the Queen's absence, and were resting in the shade: however, the moment they saw her, they hurried back to the game, the Queen merely remarking that a moment's delay would cost them their lives.

All the time they were playing the Queen never left off quarrelling with the other players, and shouting "Off with his head!" or "Off with her head!" Those whom she sentenced were taken into custody by the soldiers, who of course had to leave off being arches to do this, so that, by the end of half an hour or so, there were no arches left, and all the players, except the King, the Queen, and Alice, were in custody and under sentence of execution.

Then the Queen left off, quite out of breath, and said to Alice, "Have you seen the Mock Turtle yet?"

"No," said Alice. "I don't even know what a Mock Turtle is."

"It's the thing Mock Turtle Soup is made from," said the Queen.

"I never saw one, or heard of one," said Alice.

"Come on, then," said the Queen, "and he shall tell you his history."

As they walked off together, Alice heard the King say in a low voice, to the company generally, "You are all pardoned." "Come, *that's* a good thing!" she said to herself, for she had felt quite unhappy at the number of executions the Queen had ordered.

They very soon came upon a Gryphon, lying fast asleep in the sun. (If you don't know what a Gryphon is, look at the picture.) "Up, lazy thing!" said the Queen, "and take this young lady to see the Mock Turtle, and to hear his history. I must go back and see after some executions I have ordered"; and she walked off, leaving Alice alone with the Gryphon. Alice did not quite like the look of the creature, but on the whole she thought it would be quite as safe to stay with it as to go after that savage Queen: so she waited.

The Gryphon sat up and rubbed its eyes: then it watched the Queen till she was out of sight: then it chuckled. "What fun!" said the Gryphon, half to itself, half to Alice.

"What *is* the fun?" said Alice.

"Why, *she*," said the Gryphon. "It's all her fancy, that: they never executes nobody, you know. Come on!"

"Everybody says 'come on!' here," thought Alice, as she went slowly after it: "I never was so ordered about before in all my life, never!"

They had not gone far before they saw the Mock Turtle in the distance, sitting sad and lonely on a little ledge of rock, and, as they came nearer, Alice could hear him sighing as if his heart would break. She pitied him deeply. "What is his sorrow?" she asked the Gryphon. And the Gryphon answered, very nearly in the same words as before, "It's all his fancy, that: he hasn't got no sorrow, you know. Come on!"

So they went up to the Mock Turtle, who looked at them with large eyes full of tears, but said nothing.

"This here young lady," said the Gryphon, "she wants for to know your history, she do."

"I'll tell it her," said the Mock Turtle in a deep, hollow tone: "sit down, both of you, and don't speak a word till I've finished."

So they sat down, and nobody spoke for some minutes. Alice thought to herself, "I don't see how he can *ever* finish, if he doesn't begin." But she waited patiently.

"Once," said the Mock Turtle at last, with a deep sigh, "I was a real Turtle."

These words were followed by a very long silence, broken only by an occasional exclamation of "Hjckrrh!" from the Gryphon, and the constant heavy sobbing of the Mock Turtle. Alice was very nearly getting up and saying, "Thank you, Sir, for your interesting story," but she could not help thinking there *must* be more to come, so she sat still and said nothing.

"When we were little," the Mock Turtle went on at last, more calmly, though still sobbing a little now and then, "we went to school in the sea. The master was an old Turtle—we used to call him Tortoise——"

"Why did you call him Tortoise, if he wasn't one?" Alice asked.

"We called him Tortoise because he taught us," said the Mock Turtle angrily. "Really you are very dull!"

"You ought to be ashamed of yourself for asking such a simple question," added the Gryphon; and then they both sat silent and looked at poor Alice, who felt ready to sink into the earth. At last the Gryphon said to the Mock Turtle, "Drive on, old fellow! Don't be all day about it!," and he went on in these words:—

"Yes, we went to school in the sea, though you mayn't believe it——"

"I never said I didn't!" interrupted Alice.

"You did," said the Mock Turtle.

"Hold your tongue!" added the Gryphon, before Alice could speak again. The Mock Turtle went on.

"We had the best of educations—in fact, we went to school every day——"

"*I've* been to a day-school, too," said Alice. "You needn't be so proud as all that."

"With extras?" asked the Mock Turtle, a little anxiously.

"Yes," said Alice: "we learned French and music."

"And washing?" said the Mock Turtle.

"Certainly not!" said Alice indignantly.

"Ah! Then yours wasn't a really good school," said the Mock Turtle, in a tone of great relief. "Now, at *ours,* they had, at the end of the bill, 'French, music, *and washing*—extra.'"

"You couldn't have wanted it much," said Alice; "living at the bottom of the sea."

"I couldn't afford to learn it," said the Mock Turtle with a sigh. "I only took the regular course."

"What was that?" enquired Alice.

"Reeling and Writhing, of course, to begin with," the Mock Turtle replied; "and then the different branches of Arithmetic—Ambition, Distraction, Uglification, and Derision."

"I never heard of 'Uglification,'" Alice ventured to say. "What is it?"

The Gryphon lifted up both its paws in surprise. "Never heard of uglifying!" it exclaimed. "You know what to beautify is, I suppose?"

"Yes," said Alice doubtfully: "it means—to—make—anything—prettier."

"Well, then," the Gryphon went on, "if you don't know what to uglify is, you *are* a simpleton."

Alice did not feel encouraged to ask any more questions about it: so she turned to the Mock Turtle, and said "What else had you to learn?"

"Well, there was Mystery," the Mock Turtle replied, counting off the subjects on his flappers,—"Mystery, ancient and modern, with Seaography: then Drawling—the Drawling-master was an old conger-eel, that used to come once a week: *he* taught us Drawling, Stretching, and Fainting in Coils."

"What was *that* like?" said Alice.

"Well, I can't show it you, myself," the Mock Turtle said: "I'm too stiff. And the Gryphon never learnt it."

"Hadn't time," said the Gryphon: "I went to the Classical master, though. He was an old crab, *he* was."

"I never went to him," the Mock Turtle said with a sigh. "He taught Laughing and Grief, they used to say."

"So he did, so he did," said the Gryphon, sighing in his turn; and both creatures hid their faces in their paws.

"And how many hours a day did you do lessons?" said Alice, in a hurry to change the subject.

"Ten hours the first day," said the Mock Turtle: "nine the next, and so on."

"What a curious plan!" exclaimed Alice.

"That's the reason they're called lessons," the Gryphon remarked: "because they lessen from day to day."

This was quite a new idea to Alice, and she thought it over a little before she made her next remark. "Then the eleventh day must have been a holiday?"

"Of course it was," said the Mock Turtle.

"And how did you manage on the twelfth?" Alice went on eagerly.

"That's enough about lessons," the Gryphon interrupted in a very decided tone. "Tell her something about the games now."

# X

## The Lobster-Quadrille

THE MOCK TURTLE sighed deeply, and drew the back of one flapper across his eyes. He looked at Alice and tried to speak, but, for a minute or two, sobs choked his voice. "Same as if he had a bone in his throat," said the Gryphon; and it set to work shaking him and punching him in the back. At last the Mock Turtle recovered his voice, and, with tears running down his cheeks, he went on again:—

"You may not have lived much under the sea——" ("I haven't," said Alice)——"and perhaps you were never even introduced to a lobster——" (Alice began to say "I once tasted——" but checked herself hastily, and said, "No, never")——"so you can have no idea what a delightful thing a Lobster-Quadrille is!"

"No, indeed," said Alice. "What sort of a dance is it?"

"Why," said the Gryphon, "you first form into a line along the seashore——"

"Two lines!" cried the Mock Turtle. "Seals, turtles, salmon, and so on: then, when you've cleared all the jelly-fish out of the way——"

"*That* generally takes some time," interrupted the Gryphon.

"—you advance twice——"

"Each with a lobster as a partner!" cried the Gryphon.

"Of course," the Mock Turtle said: "advance twice, set to partners——"

"—change lobsters, and retire in same order," continued the Gryphon.

"Then, you know," the Mock Turtle went on, "you throw the——"

"The lobsters!" shouted the Gryphon, with a bound into the air.

"—as far out to sea as you can——"

"Swim after them!" screamed the Gryphon.

"Turn a somersault in the sea!" cried the Mock Turtle, capering wildly about.

"Change lobsters again!" yelled the Gryphon at the top of its voice.

"Back to land again, and—that's all the first figure," said the Mock Turtle, suddenly dropping his voice; and the the two creatures, who had been jumping about like mad things all this time, sat down again very sadly and quietly, and looked at Alice.

"It must be a very pretty dance," said Alice timidly.

"Would you like to see a little of it?" said the Mock Turtle.

"Very much indeed," said Alice.

"Come, let's try the first figure!" said the Mock Turtle to the Gryphon. "We can do it without lobsters, you know. Which shall sing?"

"Oh, *you* sing," said the Gryphon. "I've forgotten the words."

So they began solemnly dancing round and round Alice, every now and then treading on her toes when they passed too close, and waving their fore-paws to mark the time, while the Mock Turtle sang this, very slowly and sadly:—

" 'Will you walk a little faster?' said a whiting to a snail,
'There's a porpoise close behind us, and he's treading on my tail.
See how eagerly the lobsters and the turtles all advance!
They are waiting on the shingle—will you come and join the dance?
  Will you, won't you, will you, won't you, will you join the dance?
  Will you, won't you, will you, won't you, won't you join the dance?'

" 'You can really have no notion how delightful it will be
When they take us up and throw us, with the lobsters, out to sea!'
But the snail replied 'Too far, too far!' and gave a look askance—
Said he thanked the whiting kindly, but he would not join the dance.
  Would not, could not, would not, could not, would not join the dance.
  Would not, could not, would not, could not, could not join the dance.

" 'What matters it how far we go?" his scaly friend replied,
'There is another shore, you know, upon the other side.
The further off from England the nearer is to France—
Then turn not pale, beloved snail, but come and join the dance.
  Will you, won't you, will you, won't you, will you join the dance?
  Will you, won't you, will you, won't you, won't you join the dance?'"

"Thank you, it's a very interesting dance to watch," said Alice, feeling very glad that it was over at last: "and I do so like that curious song about the whiting!"

"Oh, as to the whiting," said the Mock Turtle, "they—you've seen them, of course?"

"Yes," said Alice, "I've often seen them at dinn——" she checked herself hastily.

"I don't know where Dinn may be," said the Mock Turtle; "but if you've seen them so often, of course you know what they're like?"

"I believe so," Alice replied thoughtfully. "They have their tails in their mouths—and they're all over crumbs."

"You're wrong about the crumbs," said the Mock Turtle: "crumbs would all wash off in the sea. But they *have* their tails in their mouths; and the reason is—" here the Mock Turtle yawned and shut his eyes. "Tell her about the reason and all that," he said to the Gryphon.

"The reason is," said the Gryphon, "that they *would* go with the lobsters to the dance. So they got thrown out to sea. So they had to fall a long way. So they got their tails fast in their mouths. So they couldn't get them out again. That's all."

"Thank you," said Alice, "it's very interesting. I never knew so much about a whiting before."

"I can tell you more than that, if you like," said the Gryphon. "Do you know why it's called a whiting?"

"I never thought about it," said Alice. "Why?"

*"It does the boots and shoes,"* the Gryphon replied very solemnly.

Alice was thoroughly puzzled. "Does the boots and shoes!" she repeated in a wondering tone.

"Why, what are *your* shoes done with?" said the Gryphon. "I mean, what makes them so shiny?"

Alice looked down at them, and considered a little before she gave her answer. "They're done with blacking, I believe."

"Boots and shoes under the sea," the Gryphon went on in a deep voice, "are done with whiting. Now you know."

"And what are they made of?" Alice asked in a tone of great curiosity.

"Soles and eels, of course," the Gryphon replied, rather impatiently: "any shrimp could have told you that."

"If I'd been the whiting," said Alice, whose thoughts were still running on the song, "I'd have said to the porpoise 'Keep back, please! We don't want *you* with us!'"

"They were obliged to have him with them," the Mock Turtle said. "No wise fish would go anywhere without a porpoise."

"Wouldn't it, really?" said Alice, in a tone of great surprise.

"Of course not," said the Mock Turtle. "Why, if a fish came to *me,* and told me he was going a journey, I should say 'With what porpoise?' "

"Don't you mean 'purpose'?" said Alice.

"I mean what I say," the Mock Turtle replied, in an offended tone. And the Gryphon added "Come, let's hear some of *your* adventures."

"I could tell you my adventures—beginning from this morning," said Alice a little timidly; "but it's no use going back to yesterday, because I was a different person then."

"Explain all that," said the Mock Turtle.

"No, no! The adventures first," said the Gryphon in an impatient tone: "explanations take such a dreadful time."

So Alice began telling them her adventures from the time when she first saw the White Rabbit. She was a little nervous about it, just at first, the two creatures got so close to her, one on each side, and opened their eyes and mouths so *very* wide; but she gained courage as she went on. Her listeners were perfectly quiet till she got to the part about her repeating *"You are old, Father William,"* to the Caterpillar, and the words all coming different, and then the Mock Turtle drew a long breath, and said, "That's very curious!"

"It's all about as curious as it can be," said the Gryphon.

"It all came different!" the Mock Turtle repeated thoughtfully. "I should like to hear her try and repeat something now. Tell her to begin." He looked at the Gryphon as if he thought it had some kind of authority over Alice.

"Stand up and repeat ' *'Tis the voice of the sluggard,'* " said the Gryphon.

"How the creatures order one about, and make one repeat lessons!" thought Alice. "I might just as well be at school at once." However, she got up, and began to repeat it, but her head was so full of the Lobster-Quadrille, that she hardly knew what she was saying; and the words came very queer indeed:—

" 'Tis the voice of the lobster: I heard him declare,
'You have baked me too brown, I must sugar my hair.'
As a duck with its eyelids, so he with his nose
Trims his belt and his buttons, and turns out his toes.
When the sands are all dry, he is gay as a lark,
And will talk in contemptuous tones of the Shark:
But, when the tide rises and sharks are around,
His voice has a timid and tremulous sound."

"That's different from what *I* used to say when I was a child," said the Gryphon.

"Well, I never heard it before," said the Mock Turtle; "but it sounds uncommon nonsense."

Alice said nothing: she had sat down again with her face in her hands, wondering if anything would *ever* happen in a natural way again.

"I should like to have it explained," said the Mock Turtle.

"She can't explain it," said the Gryphon hastily. "Go on with the next verse."

"But about his toes?" the Mock Turtle persisted. "How *could* he turn them out with his nose, you know?"

"It's the first position in dancing," Alice said; but she was dreadfully puzzled by the whole thing, and longed to change the subject.

"Go on with the next verse," the Gryphon repeated impatiently: "it begins '*I passed by his garden.*'" Alice did not dare to disobey, though she felt sure it would all come wrong, and she went on in a trembling voice:—

> *"I passed by his garden, and marked, with one eye,*
> *How the Owl and the Panther were sharing a pie:*
> *The Panther took pie-crust, and gravy, and meat,*
> *While the Owl had the dish as its share of the treat.*
> *When the pie was all finished, the Owl, as a boon,*
> *Was kindly permitted to pocket the spoon:*
> *While the Panther received knife and fork with a growl,*
> *And concluded the banquet by——"*

"What *is* the use of repeating all that stuff," the Mock Turtle interrupted, "if you don't explain it as you go on? It's by far the most confusing thing *I* ever heard!"

"Yes, I think you'd better leave off," said the Gryphon, and Alice was only too glad to do so.

"Shall we try another figure of the Lobster-Quadrille?" the Gryphon went on. "Or would you like the Mock Turtle to sing you another song?"

"Oh, a song, please, if the Mock Turtle would be so kind," Alice replied, so eagerly that the Gryphon said, in a rather offended tone, "Hm! No accounting for tastes! Sing her '*Turtle Soup*,' will you, old fellow?"

The Mock Turtle sighed deeply, and began, in a voice sometimes choked with sobs, to sing this:—

> *"Beautiful Soup, so rich and green,*
> *Waiting in a hot tureen!*
> *Who for such dainties would not stoop?*
> *Soup of the evening, beautiful Soup!*
> *Soup of the evening, beautiful Soup!*
> *Beau—ootiful Soo—oop!*
> *Beau—ootiful Soo—oop!*
> *Soo—oop of the e—e—evening,*
> *Beautiful, beautiful Soup!*

*"Beautiful Soup! Who cares for fish,*
*Game, or any other dish?*
*Who would not give all else for two*
*Pennyworth only of beautiful Soup?*
*Pennyworth only of beautiful Soup?*
*Beau—ootiful Soo—oop!*
*Beau—ootiful Soo—oop!*
*Soo—oop of the e—e—evening,*
*Beautiful, beauti—FUL SOUP!"*

"Chorus again!" cried the Gryphon, and the Mock Turtle had just begun to repeat it, when a cry of "The trial's beginning!" was heard in the distance.

"Come on!" cried the Gryphon, and, taking Alice by the hand, it hurried off, without waiting for the end of the song.

"What trial is it?" Alice panted as she ran; but the Gryphon only answered "Come on!" and ran the faster, while more and more faintly came, carried on the breeze that followed them, the melancholy words:—

*"Soo—oop of the e—e—evening,*
*Beautiful, beautiful Soup!"*

# XI

## *Who Stole the Tarts?*

THE KING AND QUEEN of Hearts were seated on their throne when they arrived, with a great crowd assembled about them—all sorts of little birds and beasts, as well as the whole pack of cards: the Knave was standing before them, in chains, with a soldier on each side to guard him; and near the King was the White Rabbit, with a trumpet in one hand, and a scroll of parchment in the other. In the very middle of the court was a table, with a large dish of tarts upon it: they looked so good, that it made Alice quite hungry to look at them—"I wish they'd get the trial done," she thought, "and hand round the refreshments!" But there seemed to be no chance of this; so she began looking at everything about her to pass away the time.

Alice had never been in a court of justice before, but she had read about them in books, and she was quite pleased to find that she knew the name of nearly everything there. "That's the judge," she said to herself, "because of his great wig."

The judge, by the way, was the King; and, as he wore his crown over the wig (look at the frontispiece if you want to see how he did it), he did not look at all comfortable, and it was certainly not becoming.

"And that's the jury-box," thought Alice; "and those twelve creatures" (she was obliged to say "creatures," you see, because some of them were animals, and some were birds), "I suppose they are the jurors." She said this last word two or three times over to herself, being rather proud of it: for she thought, and rightly too, that very few little girls of her age knew the meaning of it at all. However, "jurymen," would have done just as well.

The twelve jurors were all writing very busily on slates. "What are they doing?" Alice whispered to the Gryphon. "They can't have anything to put down yet, before the trial's begun."

"They're putting down their names," the Gryphon whispered in reply, "for fear they should forget them before the end of the trial."

"Stupid things!" Alice began in a loud indignant voice, but she stopped herself hastily, for the White Rabbit cried out "Silence in the court!," and the King put on his spectacles and looked anxiously round, to make out who was talking.

Alice could see, as well as if she were looking over their shoulders, that all the jurors were writing down "Stupid things!" on their slates, and she could even make out that one of them didn't know how to spell "stupid," and that he had to ask his neighbour to tell him. "A nice muddle their slates'll be in before the trial's over!" thought Alice.

One of the jurors had a pencil that squeaked. This, of course, Alice could *not* stand, and she went round the court and got behind him, and very soon found an opportunity of taking it away. She did it so quickly that the poor little juror (it was Bill, the Lizard) could not make out at all what had become of it; so, after hunting all about for it, he was obliged to write with one finger for the rest of the day; and this was of very little use, as it left no mark on the slate.

"Herald, read the accusation!" said the King.

On this the White Rabbit blew three blasts on the trumpet, and then unrolled the parchment scroll, and read as follows:—

> *"The Queen of Hearts, she made some tarts,*
> *All on a summer day:*
> *The Knave of Hearts, he stole those tarts*
> *And took them quite away!"*

"Consider your verdict," the King said to the jury.

"Not yet, not yet!" the Rabbit hastily interrupted. "There's a great deal to come before that!"

"Call the first witness," said the King; and the White Rabbit blew three blasts on the trumpet, and called out "First witness!"

The first witness was the Hatter. He came in with a teacup in one hand and a piece of bread-and-butter in the other. "I beg pardon, your Majesty," he began, "for bringing these in; but I hadn't quite finished my tea when I was sent for."

"You ought to have finished," said the King. "When did you begin?"

The Hatter looked at the March Hare, who had followed him into the court, arm-in-arm with the Dormouse. "Fourteenth of March, I *think* it was," he said.

"Fifteenth," said the March Hare.

"Sixteenth," added the Dormouse.

"Write that down," the King said to the jury; and the jury eagerly wrote down all three dates on their slates, and then added them up, and reduced the answer to shillings and pence.

"Take off your hat," the King said to the Hatter.

"It isn't mine," said the Hatter.

"*Stolen!*" the King exclaimed, turning to the jury, who instantly made a memorandum of the fact.

"I keep them to sell," the Hatter added as an explanation. "I've none of my own. I'm a hatter."

Here the Queen put on her spectacles, and began staring hard at the Hatter, who turned pale and fidgeted.

"Give your evidence," said the King; "and don't be nervous, or I'll have you executed on the spot."

This did not seem to encourage the witness at all: he kept shifting from one foot to the other, looking uneasily at the Queen, and in his confusion he bit a large piece out of his teacup instead of the bread-and-butter.

Just at this moment Alice felt a very curious sensation, which puzzled her a good deal until she made out what it was: she was beginning to grow larger again, and she thought at first she would get up and leave the court; but on second thoughts she decided to remain where she was as long as there was room for her.

"I wish you wouldn't squeeze so," said the Dormouse, who was sitting next to her. "I can hardly breathe."

"I can't help it," said Alice very meekly: "I'm growing."

"You've no right to grow *here*," said the Dormouse.

"Don't talk nonsense," said Alice more boldly: "you know you're growing too."

"Yes, but *I* grow at a reasonable pace," said the Dormouse: "not in that ridiculous fashion." And he got up very sulkily and crossed over to the other side of the court.

All this time the Queen had never left off staring at the Hatter, and, just as the Dormouse crossed the court, she said to one of the officers of the court, "Bring me the list of the singers in the last concert!" on which the wretched Hatter trembled so, that he shook off both his shoes.

"Give your evidence," the King repeated angrily, "or I'll have you executed, whether you're nervous or not."

"I'm a poor man, your Majesty," the Hatter began, in a trembling voice, "and I hadn't begun my tea—not above a week or so—and what with the bread-and-butter getting so thin—and the twinkling of the tea——"

"The twinkling of *what?*" said the King.

"It *began* with the tea," the Hatter replied.

"Of course twinkling *begins* with a T!" said the King sharply. "Do you take me for a dunce? Go on!"

"I'm a poor man," the Hatter went on, "and most things twinkled after that—only the March Hare said——"

"I didn't!" the March Hare interrupted in a great hurry.

"You did!" said the Hatter.

"I deny it!" said the March Hare.

"He denies it," said the King: "leave out that part."

"Well, at any rate, the Dormouse said——" the Hatter went on, looking anxiously round to see if he would deny it too: but the Dormouse denied nothing, being fast asleep.

"After that," continued the Hatter, "I cut some more bread-and-butter——"

"But what did the Dormouse say?" one of the jury asked.

"That I can't remember," said the Hatter.

"You *must* remember," remarked the King, "or I'll have you executed."

The miserable Hatter dropped his teacup and bread-and-butter, and went down on one knee. "I'm a poor man, your Majesty," he began.

"You're a *very* poor *speaker*," said the King.

Here one of the guinea-pigs cheered, and was immediately suppressed by the officers of the court. (As that is rather a hard word, I will just explain to you how it was done. They had a large canvas bag, which tied up at the mouth with strings: into this they slipped the guinea-pig, head first, and then sat upon it.)

"I'm glad I've seen that done," thought Alice. "I've so often read in the newspapers, at the end of trials, 'There was some attempt at applause, which was immediately suppressed by the officers of the court,' and I never understood what it meant till now."

"If that's all you know about it, you may stand down," continued the King.

"I can't go no lower," said the Hatter: "I'm on the floor, as it is."

"Then you may *sit* down," the King replied.

Here the other guinea-pig cheered, and was suppressed.

"Come, that finishes the guinea-pigs!" thought Alice. "Now we shall get on better."

"I'd rather finish my tea," said the Hatter, with an anxious look at the Queen, who was reading the list of singers.

"You may go," said the King, and the Hatter hurriedly left the court, without even waiting to put his shoes on.

"——and just take his head off outside," the Queen added to one of the officers; but the Hatter was out of sight before the officer could get to the door.

"Call the next witness!" said the King.

The next witness was the Duchess's cook. She carried the pepper-box in her hand, and Alice guessed who it was, even before she got into the court, by the way the people near the door began sneezing all at once.

"Give your evidence," said the King.

"Shan't," said the cook.

The King looked anxiously at the White Rabbit, who said, in a low voice, "Your Majesty must cross-examine *this* witness."

"Well, if I must, I must," the King said with a melancholy air, and, after folding his arms and frowning at the cook till his eyes were nearly out of sight, he said in a deep voice, "What are tarts made of?"

"Pepper, mostly," said the cook.

"Treacle," said a sleepy voice behind her.

"Collar that Dormouse!" the Queen shrieked out. "Behead that Dormouse! Turn that Dormouse out of court! Suppress him! Pinch him! Off with his whiskers!"

For some minutes the whole court was in confusion, getting the Dormouse turned out, and, by the time they had settled down again, the cook had disappeared.

"Never mind!" said the King, with an air of great relief.

"Call the next witness." And, he added, in an undertone to the Queen, "Really, my dear, *you* must cross-examine the next witness. It quite makes my forehead ache!"

Alice watched the White Rabbit as he fumbled over the list, feeling very curious to see what the next witness would be like, "—for they haven't got much evidence *yet*," she said to herself. Imagine her surprise, when the White Rabbit read out, at the top of his shrill little voice, the name "Alice!"

# XII

## *Alice's Evidence*

"HERE!" CRIED ALICE, quite forgetting in the flurry of the moment how large she had grown in the last few minutes, and she jumped up in such a hurry that she tipped over the jury-box with the edge of her skirt, upsetting all the jurymen on to the heads of the crowd below, and there they lay sprawling about, reminding her very much of a globe of gold-fish she had accidentally upset the week before.

"Oh, I *beg* your pardon!" she exclaimed in a tone of great dismay, and began picking them up again as quickly as she could, for the accident of the gold-fish kept running in her head, and she had a vague sort of idea that they must be collected at once and put back into the jury-box, or they would die.

"The trial cannot proceed," said the King, in a very grave voice, "until all the jurymen are back in their proper places—*all*," he repeated with great emphasis, looking hard at Alice as he said so.

Alice looked at the jury-box, and saw that, in her haste, she had put the Lizard in head downwards, and the poor little thing was waving its tail about in a melancholy way, being quite unable to move. She soon got it out again, and put it right; "not that it signifies much," she said to herself; "I should think it would be *quite* as much use in the trial one way up as the other."

As soon as the jury had a little recovered from the shock of being upset, and their slates and pencils had been found and handed back to them, they set to work very diligently to write out a history of the accident, all except the Lizard, who seemed too much overcome to do anything but sit with its mouth open, gazing up into the roof of the court.

"What do you know about this business?" the King said to Alice.

"Nothing," said Alice.

"Nothing *whatever?*" persisted the King.

"Nothing *whatever,*" said Alice.

"That's very important," the King said, turning to the jury. They were just beginning to write this down on their slates, when the White Rabbit interrupted: "*Un*important, your Majesty means, of course," he said, in a very respectful tone, but frowning and making faces at him as he spoke.

"*Un*important, of course, I meant," the King hastily said, and went on to himself in an undertone, "important—unimportant—unimportant—important——" as if he were trying which word sounded best.

Some of the jury wrote it down "important," and some "unimportant." Alice could see this, as she was near enough to look over their slates; "but it doesn't matter a bit," she thought to herself.

At this moment the King, who had been for some time busily writing in his notebook, called out "Silence!" and read out from his book, "Rule Forty-two. *All persons more than a mile high to leave the court."*

Everybody looked at Alice.

*"I'm* not a mile high," said Alice.

"You are," said the King.

"Nearly two miles high," added the Queen.

"Well, I shan't go, at any rate," said Alice: "besides, that's not a regular rule: you invented it just now."

"It's the oldest rule in the book," said the King.

"Then it ought to be Number One," said Alice.

The King turned pale, and shut his notebook hastily. "Consider your verdict," he said to the jury, in a low trembling voice.

"There's more evidence to come yet, please your Majesty," said the White Rabbit, jumping up in a great hurry; "this paper has just been picked up."

"What's in it?" said the Queen.

"I haven't opened it yet," said the White Rabbit; "but it seems to be a letter, written by the prisoner to—to somebody."

"It must have been that," said the King, "unless it was written to nobody, which isn't usual, you know."

"Who is it directed to?" said one of the jurymen.

"It isn't directed at all," said the White Rabbit: "in fact, there's nothing written on the *outside*." He unfolded the paper as he spoke, and added "It isn't a letter, after all: it's a set of verses."

"Are they in the prisoner's handwriting?" asked another of the jurymen.

"No, they're not," said the White Rabbit, "and that's the queerest thing about it." (The jury all looked puzzled.)

"He must have imitated somebody else's hand," said the King. (The jury all brightened up again.)

"Please, your Majesty," said the Knave, "I didn't write it, and they can't prove I did: there's no name signed at the end."

"If you didn't sign it," said the King, "that only makes the matter worse. You *must* have meant some mischief, or else you'd have signed your name like an honest man."

There was a general clapping of hands at this: it was the first really clever thing the King had said that day.

"That *proves* his guilt, of course," said the Queen: "so, off with——"

"It doesn't prove anything of the sort!" said Alice. "Why, you don't even know what they're about!"

"Read them," said the King.

The White Rabbit put on his spectacles. "Where shall I begin, please your Majesty?" he asked.

"Begin at the beginning," the King said, very gravely, "and go on till you come to the end: then stop."

There was dead silence in the court, whilst the White Rabbit read out these verses:——

> *"They told me you had been to her,*
> *And mentioned me to him:*
> *She gave me a good character,*
> *But said I could not swim.*
>
> *He sent them word I had not gone*
> *(We know it to be true):*
> *If she should push the matter on,*
> *What would become of you?*
>
> *I gave her one, they gave him two,*
> *You gave us three or more;*
> *They all returned from him to you,*
> *Though they were mine before.*
>
> *If I or she should chance to be*
> *Involved in this affair,*
> *He trusts to you to set them free,*
> *Exactly as we were.*
>
> *My notion was that you had been*
> *(Before she had this fit)*
> *An obstacle that came between*
> *Him, and ourselves, and it.*

*Don't let him know she liked them best,*
   *For this must ever be*
*A secret, kept from all the rest,*
   *Between yourself and me."*

"That's the most important piece of evidence we've heard yet," said the King, rubbing his hands; "so now let the jury——"

"If any one of them can explain it," said Alice (she had grown so large in the last few minutes that she wasn't a bit afraid of interrupting him), "I'll give him sixpence. *I* don't

believe there's an atom of meaning in it."

The jury all wrote down on their slates, *"She* doesn't believe there's an atom of meaning in it," but none of them atten,.ed to explain the paper.

"If there's no meaning in it," said the King, "that saves a world of trouble, you know, as we needn't try to find any. And yet I don't know," he went on, spreading out the verses on his knee, and looking at them with one eye; "I seem to see some meaning in them, after all. '—*said I could not swim—'* you can't swim, can you?" he added, turning to the Knave.

The Knave shook his head sadly. "Do I look like it?" he said. (Which he certainly did *not,* being made entirely of cardboard.)

"All right, so far," said the King; and he went on muttering over the verses to himself: "*'We know it to be true—'* that's the jury, of course—*'If she should push the matter on'*—that must be the Queen—*'What would become of you?'*—What, indeed!—*'I gave her one, they gave him two'*—why, that must be what he did with the tarts, you know—"

"But it goes on *'they all returned from him to you,'*" said Alice.

"Why, there they are!" said the King triumphantly, pointing to the tarts on the table. "Nothing can be clearer than *that.* Then again—*'before she had this fit'*—you never had *fits,* my dear, I think?" he said to the Queen.

"Never!" said the Queen, furiously, throwing an inkstand at the Lizard as she spoke. (The unfortunate little Bill had left off writing on his slate with one finger, as he found it made no mark; but he now hastily began again, using the ink, that was trickling down his face, as long as it lasted.)

"Then the words don't *fit* you," said the King, looking round the court with a smile. There was a dead silence.

"It's a pun!" the King added in an angry tone, and everybody laughed. "Let the jury consider their verdict," the King said, for about the twentieth time that day.

"No, no!" said the Queen. "Sentence first—verdict afterwards."

"Stuff and nonsense!" said Alice loudly. "The idea of having the sentence first!"

"Hold your tongue!" said the Queen, turning purple.

"I won't!" said Alice.

"Off with her head!" the Queen shouted at the top of her voice. Nobody moved.

"Who cares for you?" said Alice (she had grown to her full size by this time). "You're nothing but a pack of cards!"

At this the whole pack rose up into the air, and came flying down upon her; she gave a little scream, half of fright and half of anger, and tried to beat them off, and found herself lying on the bank, with her head in the lap of her sister, who was gently brushing away some dead leaves that had fluttered down from the trees upon her face.

"Wake up, Alice dear!" said her sister. "Why, what a long sleep you've had!"

"Oh, I've had such a curious dream!" said Alice, and she told her sister, as well as she could remember them, all these strange Adventures of hers that you have just been reading about; and when she had finished, her sister kissed her, and said, "It *was* a curious dream, dear, certainly: but now run in to your tea; it's getting late." So Alice got up and ran off, thinking while she ran, as well she might, what a wonderful dream it had been.

\*  \*  \*

But her sister sat still just as she left her, leaning her head on her hand, watching the setting sun, and thinking of little Alice and all her wonderful Adventures, till she too began dreaming after a fashion, and this was her dream:—

First, she dreamed of little Alice herself: once again the tiny hands were clasped upon her knee, and the bright eager eyes were looking up into hers—she could hear the very tones of her voice, and see that queer little toss of her head to keep back the wandering hair that *would* always get into her eyes—and still as she listened, or seemed to listen, the whole place around her became alive with the strange creatures of her little sister's dream.

The long grass rustled at her feet as the White Rabbit hurried by—the frightened Mouse splashed his way through the neighbouring pool—she could hear the rattle of the teacups as the March Hare and his friends shared their never-ending meal, and the shrill voice of the Queen ordering off her unfortunate guests to execution—once more the pig-baby was sneezing on the Duchess's knee, while plates and dishes crashed around it—once more the shriek of the Gryphon, the squeaking of the Lizard's slate-pencil, and the choking of the suppressed guinea-pigs, filled the air, mixed up with the distant sob of the miserable Mock Turtle.

So she sat on, with closed eyes, and half believed herself in Wonderland, though she knew she had but to open them again, and all would change to dull reality—the grass would be only rustling in the wind, and the pool rippling to the waving of the reeds—the rattling teacups would change to tinkling sheep-bells, and the Queen's shrill cries to the voice of the shepherd-boy—and the sneeze of the baby, the shriek of the Gryphon, and all the other queer noises, would change (she knew) to the confused clamour of the busy farm-yard—while the lowing of the cattle in the distance would take the place of the Mock Turtle's heavy sobs.

Lastly, she pictured to herself how this same little sister of hers would, in the after-time, be herself a grown woman; and how she would keep, through all her riper years, the simple and loving heart of her childhood; and how she would gather about her other little children, and make *their* eyes bright and eager with many a strange tale, perhaps even with the dream of Wonderland of long ago; and how she would feel with all their simple sorrows, and find a pleasure in all their simple joys, remembering her own child-life, and the happy summer days.

# THROUGH THE
# LOOKING-GLASS
## AND WHAT ALICE FOUND THERE

# AUTHOR'S PREFACE

AS THE CHESS-PROBLEM, given on page 112, has puzzled some of my readers, it may be well to explain that it is correctly worked out, so far as the *moves* are concerned. The *alternation* of Red and White is perhaps not so strictly observed as it might be, and the "castling" of the three Queens is merely a way of saying that they entered the palace: but the "check" of the White King at move 6, the capture of the Red Knight at move 7, and the final "checkmate" of the Red King, will be found, by any one who will take the trouble to set the pieces and play the moves as directed, to be strictly in accordance with the laws of the game.

The new words, in the poem "Jabberwocky" (see pages 124–126), have given rise to some differences of opinion as to their pronunciation: so it may be well to give instructions on *that* point also. Pronounce "slithy" as if it were the two words "sly, the"; make the "g" *hard* in "gyre" and "gimble": and pronounce "rath" to rhyme with "bath."

*Christmas, 1896.*

*Child of the pure unclouded brow*
    *And dreaming eyes of wonder!*
*Though time be fleet, and I and thou*
    *Are half a life asunder,*
*Thy loving smile will surely hail*
*The love-gift of a fairy-tale.*

*I have not seen thy sunny face,*
    *Nor heard thy silver laughter:*
*No thought of me shall find a place*
    *In thy young life's hereafter—*
*Enough that now thou wilt not fail*
*To listen to my fairy-tale.*

*A tale begun in other days,*
    *When summer suns were glowing—*
*A simple chime, that served to time*
    *The rhythm of our rowing—*
*Whose echoes live in memory yet,*
*Though envious years would say "forget."*

*Come, hearken then, ere voice of dread,*
    *With bitter tidings laden,*
*Shall summon to unwelcome bed*
    *A melancholy maiden!*
*We are but older children, dear,*
*Who fret to find our bedtime near.*

Without, the frost, the blinding snow,
  The storm-wind's moody madness—
Within, the firelight's ruddy glow,
  And childhood's nest of gladness.
The magic words shall hold thee fast:
Thou shalt not heed the raving blast.

And, though the shadow of a sigh
  May tremble through the story,
For "happy summer days" gone by,
  And vanish'd summer glory—
It shall not touch, with breath of bale,
  The pleasance of our fairy-tale.

# CONTENTS

**RED**

**WHITE**

*White Pawn (Alice) to play, and win in eleven moves.*

# CHRISTMAS-GREETINGS

## [FROM A FAIRY TO A CHILD]

*Lady dear, if Fairies may*
  *For a moment lay aside*
*Cunning tricks and elfish play,*
  *'Tis at happy Christmas-tide.*

*We have heard the children say—*
  *Gentle children, whom we love—*
*Long ago, on Christmas Day,*
  *Came a message from above.*

*Still, as Christmas-tide comes round,*
  *They remember it again—*
*Echo still the joyful sound*
  *"Peace on earth, good-will to men!"*

*Yet the hearts must childlike be*
  *Where such heavenly guests abide;*
*Unto children, in their glee,*
  *All the year is Christmas-tide!*

*Thus, forgetting tricks and play*
  *For a moment, Lady dear,*
*We would wish you, if we may,*
  *Merry Christmas, glad New Year!*

*Christmas, 1867.*

# I

## *Looking-Glass House*

ONE THING was certain, that the *white* kitten had had nothing to do with it—it was the black kitten's fault entirely. For the white kitten had been having its face washed by the old cat for the last quarter of an hour (and bearing it pretty well, considering): so you see that it *couldn't* have had any hand in the mischief.

The way Dinah washed her children's faces was this: first she held the poor thing down by its ear with one paw, and then with the other paw she rubbed its face all over, the wrong way, beginning at the nose: and just now, as I said, she was hard at work on the white kitten, which was lying quite still and trying to purr—no doubt feeling that it was all meant for its good.

But the black kitten had been finished with earlier in the afternoon, and so, while Alice was sitting curled up in a corner of the great arm-chair, half talking to herself and half asleep, the kitten had been having a grand game of romps with the ball of worsted Alice had been trying to wind up, and had been rolling it up and down till it had all come un-done again; and there it was, spread over the hearth-rug, all knots and tangles, with the kitten running after its own tail in the middle.

"Oh, you wicked wicked little thing!" cried Alice, catch-ing up the kitten, and giving it a little kiss to make it under-stand that it was in disgrace. "Really, Dinah ought to have taught you better manners! You *ought,* Dinah, you know you ought!" she added, looking reproachfully at the old cat, and speaking in as cross a voice as she could manage—and then she scrambled back into the arm-chair, taking the kitten and the worsted with her, and began winding up the ball again. But she didn't get on very fast, as she was talking all the time, sometimes to the kitten, and sometimes to herself. Kitty sat very demurely on her knee, pretending to watch the prog-ress of the winding, and now and then putting out one paw and gently touching the ball, as if it would be glad to help if it might.

"Do you know what to-morrow is, Kitty?" Alice began. "You'd have guessed if you'd been up in the window with me—only Dinah was making you tidy, so you couldn't. I was watching the boys getting in sticks for the bonfire—and it wants plenty of sticks, Kitty! Only it got so cold, and it snowed so, they had to leave off. Never mind, Kitty, we'll go and see the bonfire to-morrow." Here Alice wound two or three turns of the worsted round the kitten's neck, just to see how it would look: this led to a scramble, in which the ball rolled down upon the floor, and yards and yards of it got unwound again.

"Do you know, I was so angry, Kitty," Alice went on, as soon as they were comfortably settled again, "when I saw all the mischief you had been doing, I was very nearly opening the window, and putting you out into the snow! And you'd have deserved it, you little mischievous darling! What have you got to say for yourself? Now don't interrupt me!" she went on, holding up one finger. "I'm going to tell you all your faults. Number one: you squeaked twice while Dinah was washing your face this morning. Now you can't deny it, Kitty: I heard you! What's that you say?" (pretending that the kitten was speaking). "Her paw went into your eye? Well, that's *your* fault, for keeping your eyes open—if you'd shut them tight up, it wouldn't have happened. Now don't make any more excuses, but listen! Number two: you pulled Snowdrop away by the tail just as I had put down the saucer of

milk before her! What, you were thirsty, were you? How do you know she wasn't thirsty too? Now for number three: you unwound every bit of the worsted while I wasn't looking!

"That's three faults, Kitty, and you've not been punished for any of them yet. You know I'm saving up all your punishments for Wednesday week—Suppose they had saved up all *my* punishments?" she went on, talking more to herself than the kitten. "What *would* they do at the end of a year? I should be sent to prison, I suppose, when the day came. Or—let me see—suppose each punishment was to be going without a dinner: then, when the miserable day came, I should have to go without fifty dinners at once! Well, I shouldn't mind *that* much! I'd far rather go without them than eat them!

"Do you hear the snow against the window-panes, Kitty? How nice and soft it sounds! Just as if some one was kissing the window all over outside. I wonder if the snow *loves* the trees and fields, that it kisses them so gently? And then it covers them up snug, you know, with a white quilt; and perhaps it says 'Go to sleep, darlings, till the summer comes again.' And when they wake up in the summer, Kitty, they dress themselves all in green, and dance about—whenever the wind blows—oh, that's very pretty!" cried Alice, dropping the ball of worsted to clap her hands. "And I do so *wish* it was true! I'm sure the woods look sleepy in the autumn, when the leaves are getting brown.

"Kitty, can you play chess? Now, don't smile, my dear, I'm asking it seriously. Because, when we were playing just now, you watched just as if you understood it: and when I said 'Check!' you purred! Well, it *was* a nice check, Kitty, and really I might have won, if it hadn't been for that nasty Knight, that came wriggling down among my pieces. Kitty, dear, let's pretend——" And here I wish I could tell you half the things Alice used to say, beginning with her favourite phrase "Let's pretend." She had had quite a long argument with her sister only the day before—all because Alice had begun with "Let's pretend we're kings and queens"; and her sister, who liked being very exact, had argued that they couldn't, because there were only two of them, and Alice had been reduced at last to say "Well, *you* can be one of them, then, and *I'll* be all the rest." And once she had really frightened her old nurse by shouting suddenly in her ear, "Nurse! Do let's pretend that I'm a hungry hyaena, and you're a bone!"

But this is taking us away from Alice's speech to the kitten. "Let's pretend that you're the Red Queen, Kitty! Do you know, I think if you sat up and folded your arms, you'd look exactly like her. Now do try, there's a dear!" And Alice got the Red Queen off the table, and set it up before the kitten as a model for it to imitate: however, the thing didn't succeed, principally, Alice said, because the kitten wouldn't fold its arms properly. So, to punish it, she held it up to the Looking-Glass, that it might see how sulky it was, "—and if you're not good directly," she added, "I'll put you through into Looking-Glass House. How would you like *that?*

"Now, if you'll only attend, Kitty, and not talk so much,

I'll tell you all my ideas about Looking-Glass House. First, there's the room you can see through the glass—that's just the same as our drawing-room, only the things go the other way. I can see all of it when I get upon a chair—all but the bit just behind the fireplace. Oh! I do so wish I could see *that* bit! I want so much to know whether they've a fire in the winter: you never *can* tell, you know, unless our fire smokes, and then smoke comes up in that room too—but that may be only pretence, just to make it look as if they had a fire. Well then, the books are something like our books, only the words go the wrong way: I know *that,* because I've held up one of our books to the glass, and then they hold up one in the other room.

"How would you like to live in Looking-Glass House, Kitty? I wonder if they'd give you milk in there? Perhaps Looking-Glass milk isn't good to drink—but oh, Kitty! now we come to the passage. You can just see a little *peep* of the passage in Looking-Glass House, if you leave the door of our drawing-room wide open: and it's very like our passage as far as you can see, only you know it may be quite different on beyond. Oh, Kitty, how nice it would be if we could only get through into Looking-Glass House! I'm sure it's got, oh! such beautiful things in it! Let's pretend there's a way of getting through into it, somehow, Kitty. Let's pretend the glass has got all soft like gauze, so that we can get through. Why, it's turning into a sort of mist now, I declare! It'll be easy enough to get through——" She was up on the chimney-piece while she said this, though she hardly knew how she had got there. And certainly the glass *was* beginning to melt away, just like a bright silvery mist.

In another moment Alice was through the glass, and had jumped lightly down into the Looking-Glass room. The very first thing she did was to look whether there was a fire in the fireplace, and she was quite pleased to find that there was a real one, blazing away as brightly as the one she had left behind. "So I shall be as warm here as I was in the old room," thought Alice: "warmer, in fact, because there'll be no one here to scold me away from the fire. Oh, what fun it'll be, when they see me through the glass in here, and can't get at me!"

Then she began looking about, and noticed that what could be seen from the old room was quite common and un-interesting, but that all the rest was as different as possible. For instance, the pictures on the wall next the fire seemed to be all alive, and the very clock on the chimney-piece (you know you can only see the back of it in the Looking-Glass) had got the face of a little old man, and grinned at her.

"They don't keep this room so tidy as the other," Alice thought to herself, as she noticed several of the chessmen down in the hearth among the cinders; but in another moment, with a little "Oh!" of surprise, she was down on her hands and knees watching them. The chessmen were walking about, two and two!

"Here are the Red King and the Red Queen," Alice said (in a whisper, for fear of frightening them), "and there are the White King and the White Queen sitting on the edge of the shovel—and here are two Castles walking arm in arm—I don't think they can hear me," she went on, as she put her

head closer down, "and I'm nearly sure they can't see me. I feel somehow as if I was getting invisible——"

Here something began squeaking on the table behind Alice, and made her turn her head just in time to see one of the White Pawns roll over and begin kicking: she watched it with great curiosity to see what would happen next.

"It is the voice of my child!" the White Queen cried out, as she rushed past the King, so violently that she knocked him over among the cinders. "My precious Lily! My imperial kitten!" and she began scrambling wildly up the side of the fender.

"Imperial fiddlestick!" said the King, rubbing his nose,

which had been hurt by the fall. He had a right to be a *little* annoyed with the Queen, for he was covered with ashes from head to foot.

Alice was very anxious to be of use, and, as the poor little Lily was nearly screaming herself into a fit, she hastily picked up the Queen and set her on the table by the side of her noisy little daughter.

The Queen gasped, and sat down: the rapid journey through the air had quite taken away her breath, and for a minute or two she could do nothing but hug the little Lily in silence. As soon as she had recovered her breath a little, she called out to the White King, who was sitting sulkily among the ashes, "Mind the volcano!"

"What volcano?" said the King, looking up anxiously into the fire, as if he thought that was the most likely place to find one.

"Blew—me—up," panted the Queen, who was still a little out of breath. "Mind you come up—the regular way—don't get blown up!"

Alice watched the White King as he slowly struggled up from bar to bar, till at last she said "Why, you'll be hours and hours getting to the table, at that rate. I'd far better help you, hadn't I?" But the King took no notice of the question: it was quite clear that he could neither hear her nor see her.

So Alice picked him up very gently, and lifted him across more slowly than she had lifted the Queen, that she mightn't take his breath away; but, before she put him on the table, she thought she might as well dust him a little, he was so covered with ashes.

She said afterwards that she had never seen in all her life such a face as the King made, when he found himself held in the air by an invisible hand, and being dusted: he was far too much astonished to cry out, but his eyes and his mouth went on getting larger and larger, and rounder and rounder, till her hand shook so with laughing that she nearly let him drop upon the floor.

"Oh! *please* don't make such faces, my dear!" she cried out, quite forgetting that the King couldn't hear her. "You make me laugh so that I can hardly hold you! And don't keep your mouth so wide open! All the ashes will get into it— there, now I think you're tidy enough!" she added, as she smoothed his hair, and set him upon the table near the Queen.

The King immediately fell flat on his back, and lay perfectly still; and Alice was a little alarmed at what she had done, and went round the room to see if she could find any water to throw over him. However, she could find nothing but a bottle of ink, and when she got back with it she found he had recovered, and he and the Queen were talking together in a frightened whisper—so low, that Alice could hardly hear what they said.

The King was saying "I assure you, my dear, I turned cold to the very ends of my whiskers!"

To which the Queen replied "You haven't got any whiskers."

"The horror of that moment," the King went on, "I shall never, *never* forget!"

"You will, though," the Queen said, "if you don't make a memorandum of it."

Alice looked on with great interest as the King took an enormous memorandum-book out of his pocket, and began writing. A sudden thought struck her, and she took hold of the end of the pencil, which came some way over his shoulder, and began writing for him.

The poor King looked puzzled and unhappy, and struggled with the pencil for some time without saying anything; but Alice was too strong for him, and at last he panted out "My dear! I really *must* get a thinner pencil. I can't manage this one a bit: it writes all manner of things that I don't intend——"

"What manner of things?" said the Queen, looking over the book (in which Alice had put *"The White Knight is sliding down the poker. He balances very badly"*). "That's not a memorandum of *your* feelings!"

There was a book lying near Alice on the table, and while she sat watching the White King (for she was still a little anxious about him, and had the ink all ready to throw over him, in case he fainted again), she turned over the leaves, to find some part that she could read, "—for it's all in some language I don't know," she said to herself.

It was like this.

**.YXↃOWЯƎᙠᙠAႱ**

*'Twas brillig, and the slithy toves
   Did gyre and gimble in the wabe:
All mimsy were the borogoves,
   And the mome raths outgrabe.*

She puzzled over this for some time, but at last a bright thought struck her. "Why, it's a Looking-Glass book, of course! And, if I hold it up to a glass, the words will all go the right way again."

This was the poem that Alice read.

### JABBERWOCKY.

>*'Twas brillig, and the slithy toves
>   Did gyre and gimble in the wabe:
>All mimsy were the borogoves,
>   And the mome raths outgrabe.*

>*"Beware the Jabberwock, my son!
>   The jaws that bite, the claws that catch!
>Beware the Jubjub bird, and shun
>   The frumious Bandersnatch!"*

He took his vorpal sword in hand:
  Long time the manxome foe he sought—
So rested he by the Tumtum tree,
  And stood awhile in thought.

And, as in uffish thought he stood,
  The Jabberwock, with eyes of flame,
Came whiffling through the tulgey wood,
  And burbled as it came!

*One, two! One, two! And through and through*
    *The vorpal blade went snicker-snack!*
*He left it dead, and with its head*
    *He went galumphing back.*

*"And hast thou slain the Jabberwock?*
    *Come to my arms, my beamish boy!*
*O frabjous day! Callooh! Callay!"*
    *He chortled in his joy.*

*'Twas brillig, and the slithy toves*
    *Did gyre and gimble in the wabe:*
*All mimsy were the borogoves,*
    *And the mome raths outgrabe.*

"It seems very pretty," she said when she had finished it, "but it's *rather* hard to understand!" (You see she didn't like to confess, even to herself, that she couldn't make it out at all.) "Somehow it seems to fill my head with ideas—only I don't exactly know what they are! However, *somebody* killed *something:* that's clear, at any rate—

"But oh!" thought Alice, suddenly jumping up, "if I don't make haste, I shall have to go back through the Looking-Glass, before I've seen what the rest of the house is like! Let's have a look at the garden first!" She was out of the room in a moment, and ran down stairs—or, at least, it wasn't exactly running, but a new invention for getting down stairs quickly and easily, as Alice said to herself. She just kept the tips of her fingers on the hand-rail, and floated gently down without even touching the stairs with her feet: then she floated on through the hall, and would have gone straight out at the door in the same way, if she hadn't caught hold of the door-post. She was getting a little giddy with so much float-ing in the air, and was rather glad to find herself walking again in the natural way.

# II

## The Garden of Live Flowers

"I SHOULD SEE the garden far better," said Alice to herself, "if I could get to the top of that hill: and here's a path that leads straight to it—at least, no, it doesn't do *that*——" (after going a few yards along the path, and turning several sharp corners), "but I suppose it will at last. But how curiously it twists! It's more like a corkscrew than a path! Well, *this* turn goes to the hill, I suppose—no, it doesn't! This goes straight back to the house! Well then, I'll try it the other way."

And so she did: wandering up and down, and trying turn after turn, but always coming back to the house, do what she would. Indeed, once, when she turned a corner rather more quickly than usual, she ran against it before she could stop herself.

"It's no use talking about it," Alice said, looking up at the house and pretending it was arguing with her. "I'm *not* going in again yet. I know I should have to get through the Looking-Glass again——back into the old room——and there'd be an end of all my adventures!"

So, resolutely turning her back upon the house, she set out once more down the path, determined to keep straight on till she got to the hill. For a few minutes all went on well, and she was just saying "I really *shall* do it this time——" when the path gave a sudden twist and shook itself (as she described it afterwards), and the next moment she found herself actually walking in at the door.

"Oh, it's too bad!" she cried. "I never saw such a house for getting in the way! Never!"

However, there was the hill full in sight, so there was

nothing to be done but start again. This time she came upon a large flower-bed, with a border of daisies, and a willow-tree growing in the middle.

"O Tiger-Lily!" said Alice, addressing herself to one that was waving gracefully about in the wind, "I *wish* you could talk!"

"We *can* talk!" said the Tiger-Lily, "when there's anybody worth talking to."

Alice was so astonished that she couldn't speak for a minute: it quite seemed to take her breath away. At length, as the Tiger-Lily only went on waving about, she spoke again, in a timid voice—almost in a whisper. "And can *all* the flowers talk?"

"As well as *you* can," said the Tiger-Lily. "And a great deal louder."

"It isn't manners for us to begin, you know," said the Rose, "and I really was wondering when you'd speak! Said I to myself, 'Her face has got *some* sense in it, though it's not a clever one!' Still, you're the right colour, and that goes a long way."

"I don't care about the colour," the Tiger-Lily remarked. "If only her petals curled up a little more, she'd be all right."

Alice didn't like being criticized, so she began asking questions. "Aren't you sometimes frightened at being planted out here, with nobody to take care of you?"

"There's the tree in the middle," said the Rose. "What else is it good for?"

"But what could it do, if any danger came?" Alice asked.

"It could bark," said the Rose.

"It says 'Bough-wough!'" cried a Daisy. "That's why its branches are called boughs!"

"Didn't you know *that?*" cried another Daisy. And here they all began shouting together, till the air seemed quite full of little shrill voices. "Silence, every one of you!" cried the Tiger-Lily, waving itself passionately from side to side, and trembling with excitement. "They know I can't get at them!" it panted, bending its quivering head towards Alice, "or they wouldn't dare to do it!"

"Never mind!" Alice said in a soothing tone, and, stooping down to the daisies, who were just beginning again, she whispered "If you don't hold your tongues, I'll pick you!"

There was silence in a moment, and several of the pink daisies turned white.

"That's right!" said the Tiger-Lily. "The daisies are worst of all. When one speaks, they all begin together, and it's enough to make one wither to hear the way they go on!"

"How is it you can all talk so nicely?" Alice said, hoping to get it into a better temper by a compliment. "I've been in many gardens before, but none of the flowers could talk."

"Put your hand down, and feel the ground," said the Tiger-Lily. "Then you'll know why."

Alice did so. "It's very hard," she said; "but I don't see what that has to do with it."

"In most gardens," the Tiger-Lily said, "they make the beds too soft—so that the flowers are always asleep."

This sounded a very good reason, and Alice was quite pleased to know it. "I never thought of that before!" she said.

"It's *my* opinion that you never think *at all*," the Rose said, in a rather severe tone.

"I never saw anybody that looked stupider," a Violet said, so suddenly, that Alice quite jumped; for it hadn't spoken before.

"Hold *your* tongue!" cried the Tiger-Lily. "As if *you* ever saw anybody! You keep your head under the leaves, and snore away there, till you know no more what's going on in the world, than if you were a bud!"

"Are there any more people in the garden besides me?" Alice said, not choosing to notice the Rose's last remark.

"There's one other flower in the garden that can move about like you," said the Rose. "I wonder how you do it——" ("You're always wondering," said the Tiger-Lily), "but she's more bushy than you are."

"Is she like me?" Alice asked eagerly, for the thought crossed her mind, "There's another little girl in the garden, somewhere!"

"Well, she has the same awkward shape as you," the Rose said: "but she's redder—and her petals are shorter, I think."

"They're done up close, like a dahlia," said the Tiger-Lily: "not tumbled about, like yours."

"But that's not *your* fault," the Rose added kindly. "You're beginning to fade, you know—and then one can't help one's petals getting a little untidy."

Alice didn't like this idea at all: so, to change the subject, she asked "Does she ever come out here?"

"I daresay you'll see her soon," said the Rose. "She's one of the kind that has nine spikes, you know."

"Where does she wear them?" Alice asked with some curiosity.

"Why, all round her head, of course," the Rose replied. "I was wondering *you* hadn't got some too. I thought it was the regular rule."

"She's coming!" cried the Larkspur. "I hear her footstep, thump, thump, along the gravel-walk!"

Alice looked round eagerly and found that it was the Red Queen. "She's grown a good deal!" was her first remark. She had indeed: when Alice first found her in the ashes, she had been only three inches high—and here she was, half a head taller than Alice herself!

"It's the fresh air that does it," said the Rose: "wonderfully fine air it is, out here."

"I think I'll go and meet her," said Alice, for, though the flowers were interesting enough, she felt that it would be far grander to have a talk with a real Queen.

"You can't possibly do that," said the Rose: "*I* should advise you to walk the other way."

This sounded nonsense to Alice, so she said nothing, but set off at once towards the Red Queen. To her surprise she lost sight of her in a moment, and found herself walking in at the front-door again.

A little provoked, she drew back, and, after looking everywhere for the Queen (whom she spied out at last, a long way off), she thought she would try the plan, this time, of walking in the opposite direction.

It succeeded beautifully. She had not been walking a minute before she found herself face to face with the Red Queen, and full in sight of the hill she had been so long aiming at.

"Where do you come from?" said the Red Queen. "And where are you going? Look up, speak nicely, and don't twiddle your fingers all the time."

Alice attended to all these directions, and explained, as well as she could, that she had lost her way.

"I don't know what you mean by *your* way," said the Queen: "all the ways about here belong to *me*—but why did you come out here at all?" she added in a kinder tone. "Curtsey while you're thinking what to say. It saves time."

Alice wondered a little at this, but she was too much in awe of the Queen to disbelieve it. "I'll try it when I go home," she thought to herself, "the next time I'm a little late for dinner."

"It's time for you to answer now," the Queen said, looking at her watch: "open your mouth a *little* wider when you speak, and always say 'your Majesty.'"

"I only wanted to see what the garden was like, your Majesty——"

"That's right," said the Queen, patting her on the head, which Alice didn't like at all: "though, when you say 'garden'—*I've* seen gardens, compared with which this would be a wilderness."

Alice didn't dare to argue the point, but went on: "—and I thought I'd try and find my way to the top of that hill——"

"When you say 'hill,'" the Queen interrupted, "*I* could show you hills, in comparison with which you'd call that a valley."

"No, I shouldn't," said Alice, surprised into contradicting her at last: "a hill *can't* be a valley, you know. That would be nonsense——"

The Red Queen shook her head. "You may call it 'nonsense' if you like," she said, "but *I've* heard nonsense, compared with which that would be as sensible as a dictionary!"

Alice curtseyed again, as she was afraid from the Queen's tone that she was a *little* offended: and they walked on in silence till they got to the top of the little hill.

For some minutes Alice stood without speaking, looking out in all directions over the country—and a most curious country it was. There were a number of tiny little brooks running straight across it from side to side, and the ground between was divided up into squares by a number of little green hedges, that reached from brook to brook.

"I declare it's marked out just like a large chessboard!"

Alice said at last. "There ought to be some men moving about somewhere—and so there are!" she added in a tone of delight, and her heart began to beat quick with excitement as she went on. "It's a great huge game of chess that's being played—all over the world—if this *is* the world at all, you know. Oh, what fun it is! How I wish I was one of them! I wouldn't mind being a Pawn, if only I might join—though of course I should *like* to be a Queen, best."

She glanced rather shyly at the real Queen as she said this, but her companion only smiled pleasantly, and said "That's easily managed. You can be the White Queen's Pawn, if you like, as Lily's too young to play; and you're in the Second Square to begin with: when you get to the Eighth Square you'll be a Queen——" Just at this moment, somehow or other, they began to run.

Alice never could quite make out, in thinking it over afterwards, how it was that they began: all she remembers is, that they were running hand in hand, and the Queen went so fast that it was all she could do to keep up with her: and still the Queen kept crying "Faster! Faster!," but Alice felt she *could not* go faster, though she had no breath left to say so.

The most curious part of the thing was, that the trees and the other things round them never changed their places at all: however fast they went, they never seemed to pass anything. "I wonder if all the things move along with us?" thought poor puzzled Alice. And the Queen seemed to guess her thoughts, for she cried "Faster! Don't try to talk!"

Not that Alice had any idea of doing *that*. She felt as if she would never be able to talk again, she was getting so much out of breath: and still the Queen cried "Faster! Faster!," and dragged her along. "Are we nearly there?" Alice managed to pant out at last.

"Nearly there!" the Queen repeated. "Why, we passed it ten minutes ago! Faster!" And they ran on for a time in silence, with the wind whistling in Alice's ears, and almost blowing her hair off her head, she fancied.

"Now! Now!" cried the Queen. "Faster! Faster!" And they went so fast that at last they seemed to skim through the air, hardly touching the ground with their feet, till suddenly, just as Alice was getting quite exhausted, they stopped, and she found herself sitting on the ground, breathless and giddy.

The Queen propped her up against a tree, and said kindly, "You may rest a little, now."

Alice looked round her in great surprise. "Why, I do believe we've been under this tree the whole time! Everything's just as it was!"

"Of course it is," said the Queen. "What would you have it?"

"Well, in *our* country," said Alice, still panting a little, "you'd generally get to somewhere else—if you ran very fast for a long time as we've been doing."

"A slow sort of country!" said the Queen. "Now, *here,* you see, it takes all the running *you* can do, to keep in the same place. If you want to get somewhere else, you must run at least twice as fast as that!"

"I'd rather not try, please!" said Alice. "I'm quite content to stay here—only I *am* so hot and thirsty!"

"I know what *you'd* like!" the Queen said good-naturedly, taking a little box out of her pocket. "Have a biscuit?"

Alice thought it would not be civil to say "No," though it wasn't at all what she wanted. So she took it, and ate it as well as she could: and it was *very* dry: and she thought she had never been so nearly choked in all her life.

"While you're refreshing yourself," said the Queen, "I'll just take the measurements." And she took a ribbon out of her pocket, marked in inches, and began measuring the ground, and sticking little pegs in here and there.

"At the end of two yards," she said, putting in a peg to mark the distance, "I shall give you your directions—have another biscuit?"

"No, thank you," said Alice: "one's *quite* enough!"

"Thirst quenched, I hope?" said the Queen.

Alice did not know what to say to this, but luckily the Queen did not wait for an answer, but went on. "At the end of *three* yards I shall repeat them—for fear of your forgetting them. At the end of *four,* I shall say good-bye. And at the end of *five,* I shall go!"

She had got all the pegs put in by this time, and Alice looked on with great interest as she returned to the tree, and then began slowly walking down the row.

At the two-yard peg she faced round, and said "A pawn goes two squares in its first move, you know. So you'll go *very* quickly through the Third Square—by railway, I should think—and you'll find yourself in the Fourth Square in no time. Well, *that* square belongs to Tweedledum and Tweedledee—the Fifth is mostly water—the Sixth belongs to Humpty Dumpty——But you make no remark?"

"I—I didn't know I had to make one—just then," Alice faltered out.

"You *should* have said," the Queen went on in a tone of grave reproof, " 'It's extremely kind of you to tell me all this'—however, we'll suppose it said—the Seventh Square is all forest—however, one of the Knights will show you the way—and in the Eighth Square we shall be Queens together, and it's all feasting and fun!" Alice got up and curtseyed, and sat down again.

At the next peg the Queen turned again, and this time she said "Speak in French when you can't think of the English for a thing—turn out your toes as you walk—and remember who you are!" She did not wait for Alice to curtsey, this time, but walked on quickly to the next peg, where she turned for a moment to say "Good-bye," and then hurried on to the last.

How it happened, Alice never knew, but exactly as she came to the last peg, she was gone. Whether she vanished into the air, or whether she ran quickly into the wood ("and she *can* run very fast!" thought Alice), there was no way of guessing, but she was gone, and Alice began to remember that she was a Pawn, and that it would soon be time for her to move.

# III

## Looking-Glass Insects

OF COURSE THE first thing to do was to make a grand survey of the country she was going to travel through. "It's something very like learning geography," thought Alice, as she stood on tiptoe in hopes of being able to see a little further. "Principal rivers—there *are* none. Principal mountains—I'm on the only one, but I don't think it's got any name. Principal towns—why, what *are* those creatures, making honey down there? They can't be bees—nobody ever saw bees a mile off, you know——" and for some time she stood silent, watching one of them that was bustling about among the flowers, poking its proboscis into them, "just as if it was a regular bee," thought Alice.

However, this was anything but a regular bee: in fact, it was an elephant—as Alice soon found out, though the idea quite took her breath away at first. "And what enormous flowers they must be!" was her next idea. "Something like cottages with the roofs taken off, and stalks put to them—and what quantities of honey they must make! I think I'll go down and—no, I won't go *just* yet," she went on, checking herself just as she was beginning to run down the hill, and trying to find some excuse for turning shy so suddenly. "It'll never do to go down among them without a good long branch to brush them away—and what fun it'll be when they ask me how I liked my walk. I shall say 'Oh, I liked it well enough—' (here came the favourite little toss of the head), 'only it *was* so dusty and hot, and the elephants *did* tease so!'

"I think I'll go down the other way," she said after a pause;

"and perhaps I may visit the elephants later on. Besides, I *do* so want to get into the Third Square!"

So, with this excuse, she ran down the hill, and jumped over the first of the six little brooks.

"Tickets, please!" said the Guard, putting his head in at the window. In a moment everybody was holding out a ticket: they were about the same size as the people, and quite seemed to fill the carriage.

"Now then! Show your ticket, child!" the Guard went on, looking angrily at Alice. And a great many voices all said together ("like the chorus of a song," thought Alice) "Don't keep him waiting, child! Why, his time is worth a thousand pounds a minute!"

"I'm afraid I haven't got one," Alice said in a frightened tone: "there wasn't a ticket-office where I came from." And again the chorus of voices went on. "There wasn't room for one where she came from. The land there is worth a thousand pounds an inch!"

"Don't make excuses," said the Guard: "you should have bought one from the engine-driver." And once more the chorus of voices went on with "The man that drives the engine. Why, the smoke alone is worth a thousand pounds a puff!"

Alice thought to herself "Then there's no use in speaking." The voices didn't join in, *this* time, as she hadn't spoken, but, to her great surprise, they all *thought* in chorus (I hope you understand what *thinking in chorus* means—for I must confess that *I* don't), "Better say nothing at all. Language is worth a thousand pounds a word!"

"I shall dream about a thousand pounds tonight, I know I shall!" thought Alice.

All this time the Guard was looking at her, first through a

telescope, then through a microscope, and then through an opera-glass. At last he said "You're traveling the wrong way," and shut up the window, and went away.

"So young a child," said the gentleman sitting opposite to her (he was dressed in white paper), "ought to know which way she's going, even if she doesn't know her own name!"

A Goat, that was sitting next to the gentleman in white, shut his eyes and said in a loud voice, "She ought to know her way to the ticket-office, even if she doesn't know her alphabet!"

There was a Beetle sitting next the Goat (it was a very queer carriage-full of passengers altogether), and, as the rule seemed to be that they should all speak in turn, *he* went on with "She'll have to go back from here as luggage!"

Alice couldn't see who was sitting beyond the Beetle, but a hoarse voice spoke next. "Change engines——" it said, and there it choked and was obliged to leave off.

"It sounds like a horse," Alice thought to herself. And an extremely small voice, close to her ear, said "You might make a joke on that—something about 'horse' and 'hoarse,' you know."

Then a very gentle voice in the distance said, "She must be labeled 'Lass, with care,' you know——"

And after that other voices went on ("What a number of

people there are in the carriage!" thought Alice), saying "She must go by post, as she's got a head on her——" "She must be sent as a message by the telegraph——" "She must draw the train herself the rest of the way——" and so on.

But the gentleman dressed in white paper leaned forwards and whispered in her ear, "Never mind what they all say, my dear, but take a return-ticket every time the train stops."

"Indeed I shan't!" Alice said rather impatiently. "I don't belong to this railway journey at all—I was in a wood just now—and I wish I could get back there!"

"You might make a joke on *that*," said the little voice close to her ear: "something about 'you *would* if you could,' you know."

"Don't tease so," said Alice, looking about in vain to see where the voice came from. "If you're so anxious to have a joke made, why don't you make one yourself?"

The little voice sighed deeply. It was *very* unhappy, evidently, and Alice would have said something pitying to comfort it, "if it would only sigh like other people!" she thought. But this was such a wonderfully small sigh, that she wouldn't have heard it at all, if it hadn't come *quite* close to her ear. The consequence of this was that it tickled her ear very much, and quite took off her thoughts from the unhappiness of the poor little creature.

"I know you are a friend," the little voice went on: "a dear friend, and an old friend. And you won't hurt me, though I *am* an insect."

"What kind of insect?" Alice inquired, a little anxiously. What she really wanted to know was, whether it could sting or not, but she thought this wouldn't be quite a civil question to ask.

"What, then you don't——" the little voice began, when it was drowned by a shrill scream from the engine, and everybody jumped up in alarm, Alice among the rest.

The Horse, who had put his head out of the window, quietly drew it in and said "It's only a brook we have to jump over." Everybody seemed satisfied with this, though Alice felt a little nervous at the idea of trains jumping at all. "However, it'll take us into the Fourth Square, that's some comfort!" she said to herself. In another moment she felt the carriage rise straight up into the air, and in her fright she caught at the thing nearest to her hand, which happened to be the Goat's beard.

But the beard seemed to melt away as she touched it, and she found herself sitting quietly under a tree—while the Gnat (for that was the insect she had been talking to) was balancing itself on a twig just over her head, and fanning her with its wings.

It certainly was a *very* large Gnat: "about the size of a chicken," Alice thought. Still, she couldn't feel nervous with it, after they had been talking together so long.

"—then you don't like *all* insects?" the Gnat went on, as quietly as if nothing had happened.

"I like them when they can talk," Alice said. "None of them ever talk, where *I* come from."

"What sort of insects do you rejoice in, where *you* come from?" the Gnat inquired.

"I don't *rejoice* in insects at all," Alice explained, "because I'm rather afraid of them—at least the large kinds. But I can tell you the names of some of them."

"Of course they answer to their names?" the Gnat remarked carelessly.

"I never knew them do it."

"What's the use of their having names," the Gnat said, "if they won't answer to them?"

"No use to *them*," said Alice; "but it's useful to the people that name them, I suppose. If not, why do things have names at all?"

"I can't say," the Gnat replied. "Further on, in the wood down there, they've got no names—however, go on with your list of insects: you're wasting time."

"Well, there's the Horse-fly," Alice began, counting off the names on her fingers.

"All right," said the Gnat. "Half way up that bush, you'll see a Rocking-horse-fly, if you look. It's made entirely of wood, and gets about by swinging itself from branch to branch."

"What does it live on?" Alice asked, with great curiosity.

"Sap and sawdust," said the Gnat. "Go on with the list."

Alice looked at the Rocking-horse-fly with great interest, and made up her mind that it must have been just repainted, it looked so bright and sticky; and then she went on.

"And there's the Dragon-fly."

"Look on the branch above your head," said the Gnat, "and there you'll find a Snap-dragon-fly. Its body is made of plum-pudding, its wings of holly-leaves, and its head is a raisin burning in brandy."

"And what does it live on?" Alice asked, as before.

"Frumenty and mince-pie," the Gnat replied; "and it makes its nest in a Christmas-box."

"And then there's the Butterfly," Alice went on, after she had taken a good look at the insect with its head on fire, and had thought to herself, "I wonder if that's the reason insects are so fond of flying into candles—because they want to turn into Snap-dragon-flies!"

"Crawling at your feet," said the Gnat (Alice drew her feet back in some alarm), "you may observe a Bread-and-butter-fly. Its wings are thin slices of bread-and-butter, its body is a crust, and its head is a lump of sugar."

"And what does *it* live on?"

"Weak tea with cream in it."

A new difficulty came into Alice's head. "Supposing it couldn't find any?" she suggested.

"Then it would die, of course."

"But that must happen very often," Alice remarked thoughtfully.

"It always happens," said the Gnat.

After this, Alice was silent for a minute or two, pondering. The Gnat amused itself meanwhile by humming round and round her head: at last it settled again and remarked "I suppose you don't want to lose your name?"

"No, indeed," Alice said, a little anxiously.

"And yet I don't know," the Gnat went on in a careless tone: "only think how convenient it would be if you could manage to go home without it! For instance, if the governess wanted to call you to your lessons, she would call out 'Come here——,' and there she would have to leave off, because there wouldn't be any name for her to call, and of course you wouldn't have to go, you know."

"That would never do, I'm sure," said Alice: "the governess would never think of excusing me lessons for that. If she couldn't remember my name, she'd call me 'Miss,' as the servants do."

"Well, if she said 'Miss,' and didn't say anything more,"

the Gnat remarked, "of course you'd miss your lessons. That's a joke. I wish *you* had made it."

"Why do you wish *I* had made it?" Alice asked. "It's a very bad one."

But the Gnat only sighed deeply, while two large tears came rolling down its cheeks.

"You shouldn't make jokes," Alice said, "if it makes you so unhappy."

Then came another of those melancholy little sighs, and this time the poor Gnat really seemed to have sighed itself away, for, when Alice looked up, there was nothing whatever to be seen on the twig, and, as she was getting quite chilly with sitting still so long, she got up and walked on.

She very soon came to an open field, with a wood on the other side of it: it looked much darker than the last wood, and Alice felt a *little* timid about going into it. However, on second thoughts, she made up her mind to go on: "for I certainly won't go *back*," she thought to herself, and this was the only way to the Eighth Square.

"This must be the wood," she said thoughtfully to herself, "where things have no names. I wonder what'll become of *my* name when I go in? I shouldn't like to lose it at all—because they'd have to give me another, and it would be almost certain to be an ugly one. But then the fun would be, trying to find the creature that had got my old name! That's just like the advertisements, you know, when people lose dogs—'*answers to the name of "Dash": had on a brass collar*'—just fancy calling everything you met 'Alice,' till one of them answered! Only they wouldn't answer at all, if they were wise."

She was rambling on in this way when she reached the wood: it looked very cool and shady. "Well, at any rate it's a great comfort," she said as she stepped under the trees, "after being so hot, to get into the—into the—into *what?*" she went on, rather surprised at not being able to think of the word. "I mean to get under the—under the—under *this,* you know!" putting her hand on the trunk of the tree. "What *does* it call itself, I wonder? I do believe it's got no name—why, to be sure it hasn't!"

She stood silent for a minute, thinking: then she suddenly

began again. "Then it really *has* happened, after all! And now, who am I? I *will* remember, if I can! I'm determined to do it!" But being determined didn't help her much, and all she could say, after a great deal of puzzling, was "L, I *know* it begins with L!"

Just then a Fawn came wandering by: it looked at Alice with its large gentle eyes, but didn't seem at all frightened. "Here then! Here then!" Alice said, as she held out her hand and tried to stroke it; but it only started back a little, and then stood looking at her again.

"What do you call yourself?" the Fawn said at last. Such a soft sweet voice it had!

"I wish I knew!" thought poor Alice. She answered, rather sadly, "Nothing, just now."

"Think again," it said: "that won't do."

Alice thought, but nothing came of it. "Please, would you tell me what *you* call yourself?" she said timidly. "I think that might help a little."

"I'll tell you, if you'll come a little further on," the Fawn said. "I can't remember *here.*"

So they walked on together through the wood, Alice with her arms clasped lovingly round the soft neck of the Fawn, till they came out into another open field, and here the Fawn gave a sudden bound into the air, and shook itself free from Alice's arm. "I'm a Fawn!" it cried out in a voice of delight. "And, dear me! you're a human child!" A sudden look of alarm came into its beautiful brown eyes, and in another moment it had darted away at full speed.

Alice stood looking after it, almost ready to cry with vexation at having lost her dear little fellow-traveler so suddenly. "However, I know my name now," she said: "that's *some* comfort. Alice—Alice—I won't forget it again. And now, which of these finger-posts ought I to follow, I wonder?"

It was not a very difficult question to answer, as there was only one road through the wood, and the two finger-posts both pointed along it. "I'll settle it," Alice said to herself, "when the road divides and they point different ways."

But this did not seem likely to happen. She went on and on, a long way, but, wherever the road divided, there were sure to be two finger-posts pointing the same way, one marked "TO TWEEDLEDUM'S HOUSE," and the other "TO THE HOUSE OF TWEEDLEDEE."

"I do believe," said Alice at last, "that they live in the *same* house! I wonder I never thought of that before—But I can't stay there long. I'll just call and say 'How d'ye do?' and ask them the way out of the wood. If I could only get to the Eighth Square before it gets dark!" So she wandered on, talking to herself as she went, till, on turning a sharp corner, she came upon two fat little men, so suddenly that she could not help starting back, but in another moment she recovered herself, feeling sure that they must be . . .

# IV

## *Tweedledum and Tweedledee*

THEY WERE STANDING under a tree, each with an arm round the other's neck, and Alice knew which was which in a moment, because one of them had "DUM" embroidered on his collar, and the other "DEE." "I suppose they've each got 'TWEEDLE' round at the back of the collar," she said to herself.

They stood so still that she quite forgot they were alive, and she was just going round to see if the word "TWEEDLE" was written at the back of each collar when she was startled by a voice coming from the one marked "DUM."

"If you think we're wax-works," he said, "you ought to pay, you know. Wax-works weren't made to be looked at for nothing. Nohow!"

"Contrariwise," added the one marked "DEE," "if you think we're alive, you ought to speak."

"I'm sure I'm very sorry," was all Alice could say; for the words of the old song kept ringing through her head like the ticking of a clock, and she could hardly help saying them out loud:—

> *"Tweedledum and Tweedledee*
> *Agreed to have a battle;*
> *For Tweedledum said Tweedledee*
> *Had spoiled his nice new rattle.*
>
> *Just then flew down a monstrous crow,*
> *As black as a tar-barrel;*
> *Which frightened both the heroes so,*
> *They quite forgot their quarrel!"*

"I know what you're thinking about," said Tweedledum; "but it isn't so, nohow."

"Contrariwise," continued Tweedledee, "if it was so, it might be; and if it were so, it would be; but as it isn't, it ain't. That's logic."

"I was thinking," Alice said very politely, "which is the best way out of this wood: it's getting so dark. Would you tell me, please?"

But the fat little men only looked at each other and grinned.

They looked so exactly like a couple of great schoolboys, that Alice couldn't help pointing her finger at Tweedledum, and saying "First Boy!"

"Nohow!" Tweedledum cried out briskly, and shut his mouth up again with a snap.

"Next Boy!" said Alice, passing on to Tweedledee, though she felt quite certain he would only shout "Contrariwise!" and so he did.

"You've begun wrong!" cried Tweedledum. "The first thing in a visit is to say 'How d'ye do?' and shake hands!" And here the two brothers gave each other a hug, and then they held out the two hands that were free, to shake hands with her.

Alice did not like shaking hands with either of them first, for fear of hurting the other one's feelings; so, as the best way out of the difficulty, she took hold of both hands at once: the next moment they were dancing round in a ring. This seemed quite natural (she remembered afterwards), and she was not even surprised to hear music playing: it seemed to come from the tree under which they were dancing and it was done (as well as she could make it out) by the branches rubbing one across the other, like fiddles and fiddle-sticks.

"But it certainly *was* funny" (Alice said afterwards, when she was telling her sister the history of all this), "to find myself singing *'Here we go round the mulberry bush.'* I don't know when I began it, but somehow I felt as if I'd been singing it a long long time!"

The other two dancers were fat, and very soon out of breath. "Four times round is enough for one dance," Tweedledum panted out, and they left off dancing as suddenly as they had begun: the music stopped at the same moment.

Then they let go of Alice's hands, and stood looking at her for a minute: there was a rather awkward pause, as Alice didn't know how to begin a conversation with people she had just been dancing with. "It would never do to say 'How d'ye do?' *now*," she said to herself: "we seem to have got beyond that, somehow!"

"I hope you're not much tired?" she said at last.

"Nohow. And thank you *very* much for asking," said Tweedledum.

"So *much* obliged!" added Tweedledee. "You like poetry?"

"Ye-es, pretty well—*some* poetry," Alice said doubtfully. "Would you tell me which road leads out of the wood?"

"What shall I repeat to her?" said Tweedledee, looking round at Tweedledum with great solemn eyes, and not noticing Alice's question.

"*'The Walrus and the Carpenter'* is the longest," Tweedledum replied, giving his brother an affectionate hug.

Tweedledee began instantly:

*"The sun was shining——"*

Here Alice ventured to interrupt him. "If it's *very* long," she said, as politely as she could, "would you please tell me first which road——"

Tweedledee smiled gently, and began again:

> *"The sun was shining on the sea,*
>   *Shining with all his might:*
> *He did his very best to make*
>   *The billows smooth and bright—*
> *And this was odd, because it was*
>   *The middle of the night.*
>
> *"The moon was shining sulkily,*
>   *Because she thought the sun*
> *Had got no business to be there*
>   *After the day was done—*
> *'It's very rude of him,' she said,*
>   *'To come and spoil the fun!'*
>
> *"The sea was wet as wet could be,*
>   *The sands were dry as dry.*
> *You could not see a cloud because*
>   *No cloud was in the sky:*
> *No birds were flying overhead—*
>   *There were no birds to fly.*
>
> *"The Walrus and the Carpenter*
>   *Were walking close at hand:*
> *They wept like anything to see*
>   *Such quantities of sand:*
> *'If this were only cleared away,'*
>   *They said, 'it would be grand!'*
>
> *" 'If seven maids with seven mops*
>   *Swept it for half a year,*
> *Do you suppose,' the Walrus said,*
>   *'That they could get it clear?'*
> *'I doubt it,' said the Carpenter,*
>   *And shed a bitter tear.*

" 'O Oysters, come and walk with us!'
    The Walrus did beseech.
'A pleasant walk, a pleasant talk,
    Along the briny beach:
We cannot do with more than four,
    To give a hand to each.'

"The eldest Oyster looked at him,
    But never a word he said:
The eldest Oyster winked his eye,
    And shook his heavy head—
Meaning to say he did not choose
    To leave the oyster-bed.

"But four young Oysters hurried up,
    All eager for the treat:
Their coats were brushed, their faces washed,
    Their shoes were clean and neat—
And this was odd, because, you know,
    They hadn't any feet.

"Four other Oysters followed them,
    And yet another four;

*And thick and fast they came at last,*
*And more, and more, and more—*
*All hopping through the frothy waves,*
*And scrambling to the shore.*

*"The Walrus and the Carpenter*
*Walked on a mile or so,*
*And then they rested on a rock*
*Conveniently low:*
*And all the little Oysters stood*
*And waited in a row.*

*" 'The time has come,' the Walrus said,*
*'To talk of many things:*
*Of shoes—and ships—and sealing-wax—*
*Of cabbages—and kings—*
*And why the sea is boiling hot—*
*And whether pigs have wings.'*

*" 'But wait a bit,' the Oysters cried,*
*'Before we have our chat;*
*For some of us are out of breath,*
*And all of us are fat!'*
*'No hurry!' said the Carpenter.*
*They thanked him much for that.*

" 'A loaf of bread,' the Walrus said,
 'Is what we chiefly need:
Pepper and vinegar besides
 Are very good indeed—
Now, if you're ready, Oysters dear,
 We can begin to feed.'

" 'But not on us!' the Oysters cried,
 Turning a little blue.
'After such kindness, that would be
 A dismal thing to do!'
'The night is fine,' the Walrus said.
 'Do you admire the view?

" 'It was so kind of you to come!
 And you are very nice!'
The Carpenter said nothing but
 'Cut us another slice.
I wish you were not quite so deaf—
 I've had to ask you twice!'

" 'It seems a shame,' the Walrus said,
 'To play them such a trick,
After we've brought them out so far,
 And made them trot so quick!'

> The Carpenter said nothing but
>    'The butter's spread too thick!'

> " 'I weep for you,' the Walrus said:
>    'I deeply sympathize.'
> With sobs and tears he sorted out
>    Those of the largest size,
> Holding his pocket-handkerchief
>    Before his streaming eyes.

> " 'O Oysters,' said the Carpenter,
>    'You've had a pleasant run!
> Shall we be trotting home again?'
>    But answer came there none—
> And this was scarcely odd, because
>    They'd eaten every one."

"I like the Walrus best," said Alice: "because he was a *little* sorry for the poor oysters."

"He ate more than the Carpenter, though," said Tweedledee. "You see he held his handkerchief in front, so that the Carpenter couldn't count how many he took: contrariwise."

"That was mean!" Alice said indignantly. "Then I like the Carpenter best—if he didn't eat so many as the Walrus."

"But he ate as many as he could get," said Tweedledum.

This was a puzzler. After a pause, Alice began, "Well! They were *both* very unpleasant characters——" Here she checked herself in some alarm, at hearing something that sounded to her like the puffing of a large steam-engine in the wood near them, though she feared it was more likely to be a wild beast. "Are there any lions or tigers about here?" she asked timidly.

"It's only the Red King snoring," said Tweedledee.

"Come and look at him!" the brothers cried, and they each took one of Alice's hands, and led her up to where the King was sleeping.

"Isn't he a *lovely* sight?" said Tweedledum.

Alice couldn't say honestly that he was. He had a tall red night-cap on, with a tassel, and he was lying crumpled up into a sort of untidy heap, and snoring loud—"fit to snore his head off!" as Tweedledum remarked.

"I'm afraid he'll catch cold with lying on the damp grass," said Alice, who was a very thoughtful little girl.

"He's dreaming now," said Tweedledee: "and what do you think he's dreaming about?"

Alice said "Nobody can guess that."

"Why, about *you!*" Tweedledee exclaimed, clapping his hands triumphantly. "And if he left off dreaming about you, where do you suppose you'd be?"

"Where I am now, of course," said Alice.

"Not you!" Tweedledee retorted contemptuously. "You'd be nowhere. Why, you're only a sort of thing in his dream!"

"If that there King was to wake," added Tweedledum, "you'd go out—bang!—just like a candle!"

"I shouldn't!" Alice exclaimed indignantly. "Besides, if *I'm* only a sort of thing in his dream, what are *you,* I should like to know?"

"Ditto," said Tweedledum.

"Ditto, ditto!" cried Tweedledee.

He shouted this so loud that Alice couldn't help saying "Hush! You'll be waking him, I'm afraid, if you make so much noise."

"Well, it's no use *your* talking about waking him," said Tweedledum, "when you're only one of the things in his dream. You know very well you're not real."

"I *am* real!" said Alice, and began to cry.

"You won't make yourself a bit realler by crying," Tweedledee remarked: "there's nothing to cry about."

"If I wasn't real," Alice said—half-laughing through her

tears, it all seemed so ridiculous—"I shouldn't be able to cry."

"I hope you don't suppose those are *real* tears?" Tweedledum interrupted in a tone of great contempt.

"I know they're talking nonsense," Alice thought to herself: "and it's foolish to cry about it." So she brushed away her tears, and went on, as cheerfully as she could, "At any rate I'd better be getting out of the wood, for really it's coming on very dark. Do you think it's going to rain?"

Tweedledum spread a large umbrella over himself and his brother, and looked up into it. "No, I don't think it is," he said: "at least—not under *here*. Nohow."

"But it may rain *outside?*"

"It may—if it chooses," said Tweedledee: "we've no objection. Contrariwise."

"Selfish things!" thought Alice, and she was just going to say "Good-night" and leave them, when Tweedledum sprang out from under the umbrella, and seized her by the wrist.

"Do you see *that?*" he said, in a voice choking with passion, and his eyes grew large and yellow all in a moment, as he pointed with a trembling finger at a small white thing lying under the tree.

"It's only a rattle," Alice said, after a careful examination of the little white thing. "Not a rattle-*snake,* you know," she added hastily, thinking that he was frightened: "only an old rattle—quite old and broken."

"I knew it was!" cried Tweedledum, beginning to stamp about wildly and tear his hair. "It's spoilt, of course!" Here he looked at Tweedledee, who immediately sat down on the ground, and tried to hide himself under the umbrella.

Alice laid her hand upon his arm, and said, in a soothing tone, "You needn't be so angry about an old rattle."

"But it *isn't* old!" Tweedledum cried, in a greater fury than ever. "It's *new,* I tell you—I bought it yesterday—my nice NEW RATTLE!" and his voice rose to a perfect scream.

All this time Tweedledee was trying his best to fold up the umbrella, with himself in it: which was such an extraordinary thing to do, that it quite took off Alice's attention from the angry brother. But he couldn't quite succeed, and it ended in his rolling over, bundled up in the umbrella, with only his head out: and there he lay, opening and shutting his mouth and his large eyes—"looking more like a fish than anything else," Alice thought.

"Of course you agree to have a battle?" Tweedledum said in a calmer tone.

"I suppose so," the other sulkily replied, as he crawled out of the umbrella: "only *she* must help us to dress up, you know."

So the two brothers went off hand in hand into the wood, and returned in a minute with their arms full of things—such as bolsters, blankets, hearth-rugs, table-cloths, dish-covers, and coal-scuttles. "I hope you're a good hand at pinning and tying strings?" Tweedledum remarked. "Every one of these things has got to go on, somehow or other."

Alice said afterwards she had never seen such a fuss made about anything in all her life—the way those two bustled about—and the quantity of things they put on—and the trouble they gave her in tying strings and fastening buttons—"Really they'll be more like bundles of old clothes than anything else, by the time they're ready!" she said to herself, as she arranged a bolster round the neck of Tweedledee, "to keep his head from being cut off," as he said.

"You know," he added very gravely, "it's one of the most

serious things that can possibly happen to one in a battle—to get one's head cut off."

Alice laughed loud: but she managed to turn it into a cough, for fear of hurting his feelings.

"Do I look very pale?" said Tweedledum, coming up to have his helmet tied on. (He *called* it a helmet, though it certainly looked much more like a saucepan.)

"Well—yes—a *little,*" Alice replied gently.

"I'm very brave, generally," he went on in a low voice: "only to-day I happen to have a headache."

"And *I've* got a toothache!" said Tweedledee, who had overheard the remark. "I'm far worse than you!"

"Then you'd better not fight to-day," said Alice, thinking it a good opportunity to make peace.

"We *must* have a bit of a fight, but I don't care about going on long," said Tweedledum. "What's the time now?"

Tweedledee looked at his watch, and said "Half-past four."

"Let's fight till six, and then have dinner," said Tweedledum.

"Very well," the other said, rather sadly: "and *she* can watch us—only you'd better not come *very* close," he added: "I generally hit every thing I can see—when I get really excited."

"And *I* hit every thing within reach," cried Tweedledum, "whether I can see it or not!"

Alice laughed. "You must hit the *trees* pretty often, I should think," she said.

Tweedledum looked round him with a satisfied smile. "I don't suppose," he said, "there'll be a tree left standing, for ever so far round, by the time we've finished!"

"And all about a rattle!" said Alice, still hoping to make them a *little* ashamed of fighting for such a trifle.

"I shouldn't have minded it so much," said Tweedledum, "if it hadn't been a new one."

"I wish the monstrous crow would come!" thought Alice.

"There's only one sword, you know," Tweedledum said to his brother: "but *you* can have the umbrella—it's quite as sharp. Only we must begin quick. It's getting as dark as it can."

"And darker," said Tweedledee.

It was getting dark so suddenly that Alice thought there must be a thunderstorm coming on. "What a thick black cloud that is!" she said. "And how fast it comes! Why, I do believe it's got wings!"

"It's the crow!" Tweedledum cried out in a shrill voice of alarm; and the two brothers took to their heels and were out of sight in a moment.

Alice ran a little way into the wood, and stopped under a large tree. "It can never get at me *here*," she thought: "it's far too large to squeeze itself in among the trees. But I wish it wouldn't flap its wings so—it makes quite a hurricane in the wood—here's somebody's shawl being blown away!"

# V

## Wool and Water

SHE CAUGHT THE shawl as she spoke, and looked about for the owner: in another moment the White Queen came running wildly through the wood, with both arms stretched out wide, as if she were flying, and Alice very civilly went to meet her with the shawl.

"I'm very glad I happened to be in the way," Alice said, as she helped her to put on her shawl again.

The White Queen only looked at her in a helpless frightened sort of way, and kept repeating something in a whisper to herself that sounded like "Bread-and-butter, bread-and-butter," and Alice felt that if there was to be any conversation at all, she must manage it herself. So she began rather timidly: "Am I addressing the White Queen?"

"Well, yes, if you call that a-dressing," the Queen said. "It isn't *my* notion of the thing, at all."

Alice thought it would never do to have an argument at the very beginning of their conversation, so she smiled and said "If your Majesty will only tell me the right way to begin, I'll do it as well as I can."

"But I don't want it done at all!" groaned the poor Queen. "I've been a-dressing myself for the last two hours."

It would have been all the better, as it seemed to Alice, if she had got some one else to dress her, she was so dreadfully untidy. "Every single thing's crooked," Alice thought to herself, "and she's all over pins!——May I put your shawl straight for you?" she added aloud.

"I don't know what's the matter with it!" the Queen said, in a melancholy voice. "It's out of temper, I think. I've pinned it here, and I've pinned it there, but there's no pleasing it!"

"It *can't* go straight, you know, if you pin it all on one side," Alice said, as she gently put it right for her; "and, dear me, what a state your hair is in!"

"The brush has got entangled in it!" the Queen said with a sigh. "And I lost the comb yesterday."

Alice carefully released the brush, and did her best to get the hair into order. "Come, you look rather better now!" she said, after altering most of the pins. "But really you should have a lady's-maid!"

"I'm sure I'll take *you* with pleasure!" the Queen said. "Twopence a week, and jam every other day."

Alice couldn't help laughing, as she said "I don't want you to hire *me*—and I don't care for jam."

"It's very good jam," said the Queen.

"Well, I don't want any *to-day,* at any rate."

"You couldn't have it if you *did* want it," the Queen said. "The rule is, jam to-morrow and jam yesterday—but never jam *to-day.*"

"It *must* come sometimes to 'jam to-day,'" Alice objected.

"No, it can't," said the Queen. "It's jam every *other* day: to-day isn't any *other* day, you know."

"I don't understand you," said Alice. "It's dreadfully confusing!"

"That's the effect of living backwards," the Queen said kindly: "it always makes one a little giddy at first——"

"Living backwards!" Alice repeated in great astonishment. "I never heard of such a thing!"

"——but there's one great advantage in it, that one's memory works both ways."

"I'm sure *mine* only works one way," Alice remarked. "I can't remember things before they happen."

"It's a poor sort of memory that only works backwards," the Queen remarked.

"What sort of things do *you* remember best?" Alice ventured to ask.

"Oh, things that happened the week after next," the Queen replied in a careless tone. "For instance, now," she went on, sticking a large piece of plaster on her finger as she spoke, "there's the King's Messenger. He's in prison now, being punished: and the trial doesn't even begin till next Wednesday: and of course the crime comes last of all."

"Suppose he never commits the crime?" said Alice.

"That would be all the better, wouldn't it?" the Queen said, as she bound the plaster round her finger with a bit of ribbon.

Alice felt there was no denying *that.* "Of course it would be all the better," she said: "but it wouldn't be all the better his being punished."

"You're wrong *there,* at any rate," said the Queen. "Were *you* ever punished?"

"Only for faults," said Alice.

"And you were all the better for it, I know!" the Queen said triumphantly.

"Yes, but then I *had* done the things I was punished for," said Alice: "that makes all the difference."

"But if you *hadn't* done them," the Queen said, "that would have been better still; better, and better, and better!" Her voice went higher with each "better," till it got quite to a squeak at last.

Alice was just beginning to say "There's a mistake somewhere——," when the Queen began screaming, so loud that she had to leave the sentence unfinished. "Oh, oh, oh!" shouted the Queen, shaking her hand about as if she wanted to shake it off. "My finger's bleeding! Oh, oh, oh, oh!"

Her screams were so exactly like the whistle of a steam-engine, that Alice had to hold both her hands over her ears.

"What *is* the matter?" she said, as soon as there was a chance of making herself heard. "Have you pricked your finger?"

"I haven't pricked it *yet*," the Queen said, "but I soon shall—oh, oh, oh!"

"When do you expect to do it?" Alice asked, feeling very much inclined to laugh.

"When I fasten my shawl again," the poor Queen groaned out: "the brooch will come undone directly. Oh, oh!" As she said the words the brooch flew open, and the Queen clutched wildly at it, and tried to clasp it again.

"Take care!" cried Alice. "You're holding it all crooked!" And she caught at the brooch; but it was too late: the pin had slipped, and the Queen had pricked her finger.

"That accounts for the bleeding, you see," she said to Alice with a smile. "Now you understand the way things happen here."

"But why don't you scream *now?*" Alice asked, holding her hands ready to put over her ears again.

"Why, I've done all the screaming already," said the Queen. "What would be the good of having it all over again?"

By this time it was getting light. "The crow must have flown away, I think," said Alice: "I'm so glad it's gone. I thought it was the night coming on."

"I wish *I* could manage to be glad!" the Queen said. "Only

I never can remember the rule. You must be very happy, living in this wood, and being glad whenever you like!"

"Only it is so *very* lonely here!" Alice said in a melancholy voice; and, at the thought of her loneliness, two large tears came rolling down her cheeks.

"Oh, don't go on like that!" cried the poor Queen, wringing her hands in despair. "Consider what a great girl you are. Consider what a long way you've come to-day. Consider what o'clock it is. Consider anything, only don't cry!"

Alice could not help laughing at this, even in the midst of her tears. "Can *you* keep from crying by considering things?" she asked.

"That's the way it's done," the Queen said with great decision: "nobody can do two things at once, you know. Let's consider your age to begin with—how old are you?"

"I'm seven and a half, exactly."

"You needn't say 'exactly,'" the Queen remarked. "I can believe it without that. Now I'll give *you* something to believe. I'm just one hundred and one, five months and a day."

"I can't believe *that!*" said Alice.

"Can't you?" the Queen said in a pitying tone. "Try again: draw a long breath, and shut your eyes."

Alice laughed. "There's no use trying," she said: "one *can't* believe impossible things."

"I daresay you haven't had much practice," said the Queen. "When I was your age, I always did it for half-an-hour a day. Why, sometimes I've believed as many as six impossible things before breakfast. There goes the shawl again!"

The brooch had come undone as she spoke, and a sudden gust of wind blew the Queen's shawl across a little brook. The Queen spread out her arms again, and went flying after it, and this time she succeeded in catching it for herself. "I've got it!" she cried in a triumphant tone. "Now you shall see me pin it on again, all by myself!"

"Then I hope your finger is better now?" Alice said very politely, as she crossed the little brook after the Queen.

    *       *       *       *       *

      *       *       *       *

  *       *       *       *       *

"Oh, much better!" cried the Queen, her voice rising into a squeak as she went on. "Much be-etter! Be-etter! Be-e-e-etter! Be-e-ehh!" The last word ended in a long bleat, so like a sheep that Alice quite started.

She looked at the Queen, who seemed to have suddenly wrapped herself up in wool. Alice rubbed her eyes, and looked again. She couldn't make out what had happened at all. Was she in a shop? And was that really—was it really a *sheep* that was sitting on the other side of the counter? Rub as she would, she could make nothing more of it: she was in a little dark shop, leaning with her elbows on the counter, and opposite to her was an old Sheep, sitting in an arm-chair, knitting, and every now and then leaving off to look at her through a great pair of spectacles.

"What is it you want to buy?" the Sheep said at last, looking up for a moment from her knitting.

"I don't *quite* know yet," Alice said very gently. "I should like to look all round me first, if I might."

"You may look in front of you, and on both sides, if you like," said the Sheep; "but you can't look *all* round you—unless you've got eyes at the back of your head."

But these, as it happened, Alice had *not* got: so she contented herself with turning round, looking at the shelves as she came to them.

The shop seemed to be full of all manner of curious things—but the oddest part of it all was that, whenever she looked hard at any shelf, to make out exactly what it had on it, that particular shelf was always quite empty, though the others round it were crowded as full as they could hold.

"Things flow about so here!" she said at last in a plaintive tone, after she had spent a minute or so in vainly pursuing a large bright thing, that looked sometimes like a doll and sometimes like a work-box, and was always in the shelf next above the one she was looking at. "And this one is the most provoking of all—but I'll tell you what—" she added, as a sudden thought struck her. "I'll follow it up to the very top shelf of all. It'll puzzle it to go through the ceiling, I expect!"

But even this plan failed: the "thing" went through the ceiling as quietly as possible, as if it were quite used to it.

"Are you a child or a teetotum?" the Sheep said, as she took up another pair of needles. "You'll make me giddy soon, if you go on turning round like that." She was now working with fourteen pairs at once, and Alice couldn't help looking at her in great astonishment.

"How *can* she knit with so many?" the puzzled child thought to herself. "She gets more and more like a porcupine every minute!"

"Can you row?" the Sheep asked, handing her a pair of knitting-needles as she spoke.

"Yes, a little—but not on land—and not with needles——" Alice was beginning to say, when suddenly the needles turned into oars in her hands, and she found they were in a little boat, gliding along between banks: so there was nothing for it but to do her best.

"Feather!" cried the Sheep, as she took up another pair of needles.

This didn't sound like a remark that needed any answer: so Alice said nothing, but pulled away. There was something very queer about the water, she thought, as every now and then the oars got fast in it, and would hardly come out again.

"Feather! Feather!" the Sheep cried again, taking more needles. "You'll be catching a crab directly."

"A dear little crab!" thought Alice. "I should like that."

"Didn't you hear me say 'Feather'?" the Sheep cried angrily, taking up quite a bunch of needles.

"Indeed I did," said Alice: "you've said it very often—and very loud. Please, where *are* the crabs?"

"In the water, of course!" said the Sheep, sticking some of the needles into her hair, as her hands were full. "Feather, I say!"

"*Why* do you say 'Feather' so often?" Alice asked at last, rather vexed. "I'm not a bird!"

"You are," said the Sheep: "you're a little goose."

This offended Alice a little, so there was no more conversation for a minute or two, while the boat glided gently on, sometimes among beds of weeds (which made the oars stick fast in the water, worse than ever), and sometimes under trees, but always with the same tall river-banks frowning over their heads.

"Oh, please! There are some scented rushes!" Alice cried in a sudden transport of delight. "There really are—and *such* beauties!"

"You needn't say 'please' to *me* about 'em," the Sheep said, without looking up from her knitting: "I didn't put 'em there, and I'm not going to take 'em away."

"No, but I meant—please, may we wait and pick some?" Alice pleaded. "If you don't mind stopping the boat for a minute."

"How am *I* to stop it?" said the Sheep. "If you leave off rowing, it'll stop of itself."

So the boat was left to drift down the stream as it would, till it glided gently in among the waving rushes. And then the little sleeves were carefully rolled up, and the little arms were plunged in elbow-deep, to get hold of the rushes a good long way down before breaking them off—and for a while Alice forgot all about the Sheep and the knitting, as she bent over the side of the boat, with just the ends of her tangled hair dipping into the water—while with bright eager eyes she caught at one bunch after another of the darling scented rushes.

"I only hope the boat won't tipple over!" she said to herself. "Oh, *what* a lovely one! Only I couldn't quite reach it."

And it certainly *did* seem a little provoking ("almost as if it happened on purpose," she thought) that, though she managed to pick plenty of beautiful rushes as the boat glided by, there was always a more lovely one that she couldn't reach.

"The prettiest are always further!" she said at last, with a sigh at the obstinacy of the rushes in growing so far off, as, with flushed cheeks and dripping hair and hands, she scrambled back into her place, and began to arrange her new-found treasures.

What mattered it to her just then that the rushes had begun to fade, and to lose all their scent and beauty, from the very moment that she picked them? Even real scented rushes, you know, last only a very little while—and these, being dream-rushes, melted away almost like snow, as they lay in heaps at her feet—but Alice hardly noticed this, there were so many other curious things to think about.

They hadn't gone much farther before the blade of one of the oars got fast in the water and *wouldn't* come out again (so Alice explained it afterwards), and the consequence was that the handle of it caught her under the chin, and, in spite of a series of little shrieks of "Oh, oh, oh!" from poor Alice, it swept her straight off the seat, and down among the heap of rushes.

However, she wasn't a bit hurt, and was soon up again: the Sheep went on with her knitting all the while, just as if nothing had happened. "That was a nice crab you caught!" she remarked, as Alice got back into her place, very much relieved to find herself still in the boat.

"Was it? I didn't see it," said Alice, peeping cautiously over the side of the boat into the dark water. "I wish it hadn't let go—I should so like a little crab to take home with me!" But the Sheep only laughed scornfully, and went on with her knitting.

"Are there many crabs here?" said Alice.

"Crabs, and all sorts of things," said the Sheep: "plenty of choice, only make up your mind. Now, what *do* you want to buy?"

"To buy!" Alice echoed in a tone that was half astonished and half frightened—for the oars, and the boat, and the river, had vanished all in a moment, and she was back again in the little dark shop.

"I should like to buy an egg, please," she said timidly. "How do you sell them?"

"Fivepence farthing for one—twopence for two," the Sheep replied.

"Then two are cheaper than one?" Alice said in a surprised tone, taking out her purse.

"Only you *must* eat them both, if you buy two," said the Sheep.

"Then I'll have *one,* please," said Alice, as she put the money down on the counter. For she thought to herself, "They mightn't be at all nice, you know."

The Sheep took the money, and put it away in a box: then she said "I never put things into people's hands—that would never do—you must get it for yourself." And so saying, she went off to the other end of the shop, and set the egg upright on a shelf.

"I wonder *why* it wouldn't do?" thought Alice, as she groped her way among the tables and chairs, for the shop was very dark towards the end. "The egg seems to get further away the more I walk towards it. Let me see, is this a chair? Why, it's got branches, I declare! How very odd to find trees growing here! And actually here's a little brook! Well, this is the very queerest shop I ever saw!"

So she went on, wondering more and more at every step, as everything turned into a tree the moment she came up to it, and she quite expected the egg to do the same.

# VI

## *Humpty Dumpty*

HOWEVER, THE EGG only got larger and larger, and more and more human: when she had come within a few yards of it, she saw that it had eyes and a nose and mouth; and, when she had come close to it, she saw clearly that it was HUMPTY DUMPTY himself. "It can't be anybody else!" she said to herself. "I'm as certain of it, as if his name were written all over his face!"

It might have been written a hundred times, easily, on that enormous face. Humpty Dumpty was sitting, with his legs crossed like a Turk, on the top of a high wall—such a narrow one that Alice quite wondered how he could keep his balance—and, as his eyes were steadily fixed in the opposite direction, and he didn't take the least notice of her, she thought he must be a stuffed figure, after all.

"And how exactly like an egg he is!" she said aloud, standing with her hands ready to catch him, for she was every moment expecting him to fall.

"It's *very* provoking," Humpty Dumpty said after a long silence, looking away from Alice as he spoke, "to be called an egg—*very!*"

"I said you *looked* like an egg, Sir," Alice gently explained. "And some eggs are very pretty, you know," she added, hoping to turn her remark into a sort of compliment.

"Some people," said Humpty Dumpty, looking away from her as usual, "have no more sense than a baby!"

Alice didn't know what to say to this: it wasn't at all like conversation, she thought, as he never said anything to *her;* in fact, his last remark was evidently addressed to a tree—so she stood and softly repeated to herself:—

> *"Humpty Dumpty sat on a wall:*
> *Humpty Dumpty had a great fall.*
> *All the King's horses and all the King's men*
> *Couldn't put Humpty Dumpty in his place again."*

"That last line is much too long for the poetry," she added, almost out loud, forgetting that Humpty Dumpty would hear her.

"Don't stand chattering to yourself like that," Humpty Dumpty said, looking at her for the first time, "but tell me your name and your business."

"My *name* is Alice, but——"

"It's a stupid name enough!" Humpty Dumpty interrupted impatiently. "What does it mean?"

*"Must* a name mean something?" Alice asked doubtfully.

"Of course it must," Humpty Dumpty said with a short laugh: *"my* name means the shape I am—and a good handsome shape it is, too. With a name like yours, you might be any shape, almost."

"Why do you sit out here all alone?" said Alice, not wishing to begin an argument.

"Why, because there's nobody with me!" cried Humpty Dumpty. "Did you think I didn't know the answer to *that?* Ask another."

"Don't you think you'd be safer down on the ground?" Alice went on, not with any idea of making another riddle, but simply in her good-natured anxiety for the queer creature. "That wall is so *very* narrow!"

"What tremendously easy riddles you ask!" Humpty Dumpty growled out. "Of course I don't think so! Why, if ever I *did* fall off—which there's no chance of—but *if* I did——" Here he pursed up his lips, and looked so solemn and grand that Alice could hardly help laughing. *"If* I *did* fall," he went on, *"the King has promised me*—ah, you may turn pale, if you like! You didn't think I was going to say that, did you? *The King has promised me—with his very own mouth*—to—to——"

"To send all his horses and all his men," Alice interrupted, rather unwisely.

"Now I declare that's too bad!" Humpty Dumpty cried,

breaking into a sudden passion. "You've been listening at doors— and behind trees—and down chimneys—or you couldn't have known it!"

"I haven't, indeed!" Alice said very gently. "It's in a book."

"Ah, well! They may write such things in a *book*," Humpty Dumpty said in a calmer tone. "That's what you call a History of England, that is. Now, take a good look at me! I'm one that has spoken to a King, *I* am: mayhap you'll never see such another: and, to show you I'm not proud, you may shake hands with me!" And he grinned almost from ear to ear, as he leant forwards (and as nearly as possible fell off the wall in doing so) and offered Alice his hand. She watched him a little anxiously as she took it. "If he smiled much more the ends of his mouth might meet behind," she thought: "and then I don't know *what* would happen to his head! I'm afraid it would come off!"

"Yes, all his horses and all his men," Humpty Dumpty went on. "They'd pick me up again in a minute, *they* would! However, this conversation is going on a little too fast: let's go back to the last remark but one."

"I'm afraid I can't quite remember it," Alice said, very politely.

"In that case we start afresh," said Humpty Dumpty, "and it's my turn to choose a subject——" ("He talks about it just as if it was a game!" thought Alice.) "So here's a question for you. How old did you say you were?"

Alice made a short calculation, and said "Seven years and six months."

"Wrong!" Humpty Dumpty exclaimed triumphantly. "You never said a word like it!"

"I thought you meant 'How old *are* you?'" Alice explained.

"If I'd meant that, I'd have said it," said Humpty Dumpty.

Alice didn't want to begin another argument, so she said nothing.

"Seven years and six months!" Humpty Dumpty repeated thoughtfully. "An uncomfortable sort of age. Now if you'd asked *my* advice, I'd have said 'Leave off at seven'—but it's too late now."

"I never ask advice about growing," Alice said indignantly.

"Too proud?" the other enquired.

Alice felt even more indignant at this suggestion. "I mean," she said, "that one can't help growing older."

"*One* can't, perhaps," said Humpty Dumpty; "but *two* can. With proper assistance, you might have left off at seven."

"What a beautiful belt you've got on!" Alice suddenly remarked. (They had had quite enough of the subject of age, she thought: and, if they really were to take turns in choosing subjects, it was *her* turn now.) "At least," she corrected herself on second thoughts, "a beautiful cravat, I should have said—no, a belt, I mean—I beg your pardon!" she added in dismay, for Humpty Dumpty looked thoroughly offended, and she began to wish she hadn't chosen that subject. "If only I knew," she thought to herself, "which was neck and which was waist!"

Evidently Humpty Dumpty was very angry, though he said nothing for a minute or two. When he *did* speak again, it was in a deep growl.

"It is a—*most*—*provoking*—thing," he said at last, "when a person doesn't know a cravat from a belt!"

"I know it's very ignorant of me," Alice said, in so humble a tone that Humpty Dumpty relented.

"It's a cravat, child, and a beautiful one, as you say. It's a present from the White King and Queen. There now!"

"Is it really?" said Alice, quite pleased to find that she *had* chosen a good subject, after all.

"They gave it me," Humpty Dumpty continued thoughtfully, as he crossed one knee over the other and clasped his hands round it, "they gave it me—for an un-birthday present."

"I beg your pardon?" Alice said with a puzzled air.

"I'm not offended," said Humpty Dumpty.

"I mean, what *is* an un-birthday present?"

"A present given when it isn't your birthday, of course."

Alice considered a little. "I like birthday presents best," she said at last.

"You don't know what you're talking about!" cried Humpty Dumpty. "How many days are there in a year?"

"Three hundred and sixty-five," said Alice.

"And how many birthdays have you?"

"One."

"And if you take one from three hundred and sixty-five, what remains?"

"Three hundred and sixty-four, of course."

Humpty Dumpty looked doubtful. "I'd rather see that done on paper," he said.

Alice couldn't help smiling as she took out her memorandum-book, and worked the sum for him:

$$\begin{array}{r} 365 \\ \underline{1} \\ 364 \end{array}$$

Humpty Dumpty took the book, and looked at it carefully. "That seems to be done right——" he began.

"You're holding it upside down!" Alice interrupted.

"To be sure I was!" Humpty Dumpty said gaily, as she turned it round for him. "I thought it looked a little queer. As I was saying, that *seems* to be done right—though I haven't time to look it over thoroughly just now—and that shows that there are three hundred and sixty-four days when you might get un-birthday presents——"

"Certainly," said Alice.

"And only *one* for birthday presents, you know. There's glory for you!"

"I don't know what you mean by 'glory,'" Alice said.

Humpty Dumpty smiled contemptuously. "Of course you don't—till I tell you. I meant 'there's a nice knock-down argument for you!'"

"But 'glory' doesn't mean a 'nice knock-down argument,'" Alice objected.

"When *I* use a word," Humpty Dumpty said, in rather a scornful tone, "it means just what I choose it to mean—neither more nor less."

"The question is," said Alice, "whether you *can* make words mean so many different things."

"The question is," said Humpty Dumpty, "which is to be master—that's all."

Alice was too much puzzled to say anything; so after a minute Humpty Dumpty began again. "They've a temper, some of them—particularly verbs: they're the proudest—adjectives you can do anything with, but not verbs—however, *I* can manage the whole lot of them! Impenetrability! That's what *I* say!"

"Would you tell me, please," said Alice, "what that means?"

"Now you talk like a reasonable child," said Humpty Dumpty, looking very much pleased. "I meant by 'impenetrability' that we've had enough of that subject, and it would be just as well if you'd mention what you mean to do next, as I suppose you don't mean to stop here all the rest of your life."

"That's a great deal to make one word mean," Alice said in a thoughtful tone.

"When I make a word do a lot of work like that," said Humpty Dumpty, "I always pay it extra."

"Oh!" said Alice. She was too much puzzled to make any other remark.

"Ah, you should see 'em come round me of a Saturday night," Humpty Dumpty went on, wagging his head gravely from side to side, "for to get their wages, you know."

(Alice didn't venture to ask what he paid them with; and so you see I can't tell *you*.)

"You seem very clever at explaining words, Sir," said Alice. "Would you kindly tell me the meaning of the poem called 'Jabberwocky'?"

"Let's hear it," said Humpty Dumpty. "I can explain all the poems that ever were invented—and a good many that haven't been invented just yet."

This sounded very hopeful, so Alice repeated the first verse:—

> " 'Twas brillig, and the slithy toves
>     Did gyre and gimble in the wabe:
> All mimsy were the borogoves,
>     And the mome raths outgrabe."

"That's enough to begin with," Humpty Dumpty interrupted: "there are plenty of hard words there. *'Brillig'* means four o'clock in the afternoon—the time when you begin *broiling* things for dinner."

"That'll do very well," said Alice: "and *'slithy'*?"

"Well, *'slithy'* means 'lithe and slimy.' 'Lithe' is the same as 'active.' You see it's like a portmanteau—there are two meanings packed up into one word."

"I see it now," Alice remarked thoughtfully: "and what are *'toves'*?"

"Well, *'toves'* are something like badgers—they're something like lizards—and they're something like corkscrews."

"They must be very curious-looking creatures."

"They are that," said Humpty Dumpty: "also they make their nests under sun-dials—also they live on cheese."

"And what's to *'gyre'* and to *'gimble'*?"

"To *'gyre'* is to go round and round like a gyroscope. To *'gimble'* is to make holes like a gimblet."

"And *'the wabe'* is the grass-plot round a sun-dial, I suppose?" said Alice, surprised at her own ingenuity.

"Of course it is. It's called *'wabe,'* you know, because it goes a long way before it, and a long way behind it——"

"And a long way beyond it on each side," Alice added.

"Exactly so. Well then, *'mimsy'* is 'flimsy and miserable'

(there's another portmanteau for you). And a *'borogove'* is a thin shabby-looking bird with its feathers sticking out all round—something like a live mop."

"And then *'mome raths'?"* said Alice. "I'm afraid I'm giving you a great deal of trouble."

"Well, a *'rath'* is a sort of green pig: but *'mome'* I'm not certain about. I think it's short for 'from home'—meaning that they'd lost their way, you know."

"And what does *'outgrabe'* mean?"

"Well, *'outgribing'* is something between bellowing and whistling, with a kind of sneeze in the middle: however, you'll hear it done, maybe—down in the wood yonder—and, when you've once heard it, you'll be *quite* content. Who's been repeating all that hard stuff to you?"

"I read it in a book," said Alice. "But I *had* some poetry repeated to me much easier than that, by—Tweedledee, I think it was."

"As to poetry, you know," said Humpty Dumpty, stretching out one of his great hands, *"I* can repeat poetry as well as other folk, if it comes to that——"

"Oh, it needn't come to that!" Alice hastily said, hoping to keep him from beginning.

"The piece I'm going to repeat," he went on without noticing her remark, "was written entirely for your amusement."

Alice felt that in that case she really *ought* to listen to it; so she sat down, and said "Thank you" rather sadly.

> *"In winter, when the fields are white,*
> *I sing this song for your delight——*

only I don't sing it," he added, as an explanation.

"I see you don't," said Alice.

"If you can *see* whether I'm singing or not, you've sharper eyes than most," Humpty Dumpty remarked severely. Alice was silent.

> *"In spring, when woods are getting green,*
> *I'll try and tell you what I mean."*

"Thank you very much," said Alice.

> *"In summer, when the days are long,*
> *Perhaps you'll understand the song:*

> *"In autumn, when the leaves are brown,*
> *Take pen and ink, and write it down."*

"I will, if I can remember it so long," said Alice.

"You needn't go on making remarks like that," Humpty Dumpty said: "they're not sensible, and they put me out.

> *"I sent a message to the fish:*
> *I told them 'This is what I wish.'*

> *"The little fishes of the sea,*
> *They sent an answer back to me.*

> *"The little fishes' answer was*
> *'We cannot do it, Sir, because——'"*

"I'm afraid I don't quite understand," said Alice.
"It gets easier further on," Humpty Dumpty replied.

> *"I sent to them again to say*
> *'It will be better to obey.'*

> *"The fishes answered, with a grin,*
> *'Why, what a temper you are in!'*

> *"I told them once, I told them twice:*
> *They would not listen to advice.*

> *"I took a kettle large and new,*
> *Fit for the deed I had to do.*

> *"My heart went hop, my heart went thump:*
> *I filled the kettle at the pump.*

> *"Then some one came to me and said*
> *'The little fishes are in bed.'*

> *"I said to him, I said it plain,*
> *'Then you must wake them up again.'*

> *"I said it very loud and clear:*
> *I went and shouted in his ear."*

Humpty Dumpty raised his voice almost to a scream as he repeated this verse, and Alice thought, with a shudder, "I wouldn't have been the messenger for *anything!*"

> *"But he was very stiff and proud:*
> *He said 'You needn't shout so loud!'*

> *"And he was very proud and stiff:*
> *He said 'I'd go and wake them, if——'*

*"I took a corkscrew from the shelf:
I went to wake them up myself.*

*"And when I found the door was locked,
I pulled and pushed and kicked and knocked.*

*"And when I found the door was shut,
I tried to turn the handle, but——"*

There was a long pause.

"Is that all?" Alice timidly asked.

"That's all," said Humpty Dumpty. "Good-bye."

This was rather sudden, Alice thought: but, after such a *very* strong hint that she ought to be going, she felt that it would hardly be civil to stay. So she got up, and held out her hand. "Good-bye, till we meet again!" she said as cheerfully as she could.

"I shouldn't know you again if we *did* meet," Humpty Dumpty replied in a discontented tone, giving her one of his fingers to shake: "you're so exactly like other people."

"The face is what one goes by, generally," Alice remarked in a thoughtful tone.

"That's just what I complain of," said Humpty Dumpty. "Your face is the same as everybody has—the two eyes, so——" (marking their places in the air with his thumb) "nose in the middle, mouth under. It's always the same. Now if you had the two eyes on the same side of the nose, for instance—or the mouth at the top—that would be *some* help."

"It wouldn't look nice," Alice objected. But Humpty Dumpty only shut his eyes, and said "Wait till you've tried."

Alice waited a minute to see if he would speak again, but, as he never opened his eyes or took any further notice of her, she said "Good-bye!" once more, and, getting no answer to this, she quietly walked away: but she couldn't help saying to herself, as she went, "of all the unsatisfactory—" (she repeated this aloud, as it was a great comfort to have such a long word to say) "of all the unsatisfactory people I *ever* met——" She never finished the sentence, for at this moment a heavy crash shook the forest from end to end.

# VII

## *The Lion and the Unicorn*

THE NEXT MOMENT soldiers came running through the wood, at first in twos and threes, then ten or twenty together, and at last in such crowds that they seemed to fill the whole forest. Alice got behind a tree, for fear of being run over, and watched them go by.

She thought that in all her life she had never seen soldiers so uncertain on their feet: they were always tripping over something or other, and whenever one went down, several more always fell over him, so that the ground was soon covered with little heaps of men.

Then came the horses. Having four feet, these managed rather better than the foot-soldiers; but even *they* stumbled now and then; and it seemed to be a regular rule that, whenever a horse stumbled, the rider fell off instantly. The confusion got worse every moment, and Alice was very glad to get out of the wood into an open place, where she found the White King seated on the ground, busily writing in his memorandum-book.

"I've sent them all!" the King cried in a tone of delight, on seeing Alice. "Did you happen to meet any soldiers, my dear, as you came through the wood?"

"Yes, I did," said Alice: "several thousand, I should think."

"Four thousand two hundred and seven, that's the exact number," the King said, referring to his book. "I couldn't send all the horses, you know, because two of them are wanted in the game. And I haven't sent the two Messengers, either. They're both gone to the town. Just look along the road, and tell me if you can see either of them."

"I see nobody on the road," said Alice.

"I only wish *I* had such eyes," the King remarked in a fretful tone. "To be able to see Nobody! And at that distance too! Why, it's as much as *I* can do to see real people, by this light!"

All this was lost on Alice, who was still looking intently along the road, shading her eyes with one hand. "I see somebody now!" she exclaimed at last. "But he's coming very slowly—and what curious attitudes he goes into!" (For the Messenger kept skipping up and down, and wriggling like an eel, as he came along, with his great hands spread out like fans on each side.)

"Not at all," said the King. "He's an Anglo-Saxon Messenger—and those are Anglo-Saxon attitudes. He only does them when he's happy. His name is Haigha." (He pronounced it so as to rhyme with "mayor.")

"I love my love with an H," Alice couldn't help beginning, "because he is Happy. I hate him with an H, because he is Hideous. I fed him with—with—with Ham-sandwiches and Hay. His name is Haigha, and he lives——"

"He lives on the Hill," the King remarked simply, without the least idea that he was joining in the game, while Alice was still hesitating for the name of a town beginning with H.

"The other Messenger's called Hatta. I must have *two,* you know—to come and go. One to come, and one to go."

"I beg your pardon?" said Alice.

"It isn't respectable to beg," said the King.

"I only meant that I didn't understand," said Alice. "Why one to come and one to go?"

"Don't I tell you?" the King repeated impatiently. "I must have *two*—to fetch and carry. One to fetch, and one to carry."

At this moment the Messenger arrived: he was far too much out of breath to say a word, and could only wave his hands about, and make the most fearful faces at the poor King.

"This young lady loves you with an H," the King said, introducing Alice in the hope of turning off the Messenger's attention from himself—but it was of no use—the Anglo-Saxon attitudes only got more extraordinary every moment, while the great eyes rolled wildly from side to side.

"You alarm me!" said the King. "I feel faint——Give me a ham sandwich!"

On which the Messenger, to Alice's great amusement, opened a bag that hung round his neck, and handed a sandwich to the King, who devoured it greedily.

"Another sandwich!" said the King.

"There's nothing but hay left now," the Messenger said, peeping into the bag.

"Hay, then," the King murmured in a faint whisper.

Alice was glad to see that it revived him a good deal. "There's nothing like eating hay when you're faint," he remarked to her, as he munched away.

"I should think throwing cold water over you would be better," Alice suggested: "—or some sal-volatile."

"I didn't say there was nothing *better*," the King replied. "I said there was nothing *like* it." Which Alice did not venture to deny.

"Who did you pass on the road?" the King went on, holding out his hand to the Messenger for some more hay.

"Nobody," said the Messenger.

"Quite right," said the King: "this young lady saw him too. So of course Nobody walks slower than you."

"I do my best," the Messenger said in a sullen tone. "I'm sure nobody walks much faster than I do!"

"He can't do that," said the King, "or else he'd have been here first. However, now you've got your breath, you may tell us what's happened in the town."

"I'll whisper it," said the Messenger, putting his hands to his mouth in the shape of a trumpet and stooping so as to get close to the King's ear. Alice was sorry for this, as she wanted to hear the news too. However, instead of whispering, he simply shouted, at the top of his voice, "They're at it again!"

"Do you call *that* a whisper?" cried the poor King, jumping up and shaking himself. "If you do such a thing again, I'll have you buttered! It went through and through my head like an earthquake!"

"It would have to be a very tiny earthquake!" thought Alice. "Who are at it again?" she ventured to ask.

"Why, the Lion and the Unicorn, of course," said the King.

"Fighting for the crown?"

"Yes, to be sure," said the King: "and the best of the joke is, that it's *my* crown all the while! Let's run and see them." And they trotted off, Alice repeating to herself, as she ran, the words of the old song:—

*"The Lion and the Unicorn were fighting for the crown:*
*The Lion beat the Unicorn all round the town.*
*Some gave them white bread, some gave them brown:*
*Some gave them plum-cake and drummed them out of*
*     town.*

"Does——the one——that wins——get the crown?" she
asked, as well as she could, for the run was putting her quite
out of breath.

"Dear me, no!" said the King. "What an idea!"

"Would you—be good enough——" Alice panted out,
after running a little further, "to stop a minute—just to get—
one's breath again?"

"I'm *good* enough," the King said, "only I'm not *strong*
enough. You see, a minute goes by so fearfully quick. You
might as well try to stop a Bandersnatch!"

Alice had no more breath for talking; so they trotted on in
silence, till they came into sight of a great crowd, in the middle of which the Lion and Unicorn were fighting. They were
in such a cloud of dust, that at first Alice could not make out
which was which; but she soon managed to distinguish the
Unicorn by his horn.

They placed themselves close to where Hatta, the other
Messenger, was standing watching the fight, with a cup of tea
in one hand and a piece of bread-and-butter in the other.

"He's only just out of prison, and he hadn't finished his
tea when he was sent in," Haigha whispered to Alice: "and
they only give them oyster-shells in there—so you see he's
very hungry and thirsty. How are you, dear child?" he went
on, putting his arm affectionately round Hatta's neck.

Hatta looked round and nodded, and went on with his
bread-and-butter.

"Were you happy in prison, dear child?" said Haigha.

Hatta looked round once more, and this time a tear or two
trickled down his cheek; but not a word would he say.

"Speak, can't you!" Haigha cried impatiently. But Hatta
only munched away, and drank some more tea.

"Speak, won't you!" cried the King. "How are they getting on with the fight?"

Hatta made a desperate effort, and swallowed a large

piece of bread-and-butter. "They're getting on very well," he said in a choking voice: "each of them has been down about eighty-seven times."

"Then I suppose they'll soon bring the white bread and the brown?" Alice ventured to remark.

"It's waiting for 'em now," said Hatta; "this is a bit of it as I'm eating."

There was a pause in the fight just then, and the Lion and the Unicorn sat down, panting, while the King called out "Ten minutes allowed for refreshments!" Haigha and Hatta set to work at once, carrying round trays of white and brown bread. Alice took a piece to taste, but it was *very* dry.

"I don't think they'll fight any more to-day," the King said to Hatta: "go and order the drums to begin." And Hatta went bounding away like a grasshopper.

For a minute or two Alice stood silent, watching him. Suddenly she brightened up. "Look, look!" she cried, point-ing eagerly. "There's the White Queen running across the country! She came flying out of the wood over yonder—— How fast those Queens *can* run!"

"There's some enemy after her, no doubt," the King said, without even looking round. "That wood's full of them."

"But aren't you going to run and help her?" Alice asked, very much surprised at his taking it so quietly.

"No use, no use!" said the King. "She runs so fearfully quick. You might as well try to catch a Bandersnatch! But I'll make a memorandum about her, if you like——She's a dear good creature," he repeated softly to himself, as he opened his memorandum-book. "Do you spell 'creature' with a double 'e'?"

At this moment the Unicorn sauntered by them, with his hands in his pockets. "I had the best of it this time?" he said to the King, just glancing at him as he passed.

"A little—a little," the King replied, rather nervously. "You shouldn't have run him through with your horn, you know."

"It didn't hurt him," the Unicorn said carelessly, and he was going on, when his eye happened to fall upon Alice: he turned round instantly, and stood for some time looking at her with an air of the deepest disgust.

"What—is—this?" he said at last.

"This is a child!" Haigha replied eagerly, coming in front of Alice to introduce her, and spreading out both his hands towards her in an Anglo-Saxon attitude. "We only found it to-day. It's as large as life, and twice as natural!"

"I always thought they were fabulous monsters!" said the Unicorn. "Is it alive?"

"It can talk," said Haigha solemnly.

The Unicorn looked dreamily at Alice, and said "Talk, child."

Alice could not help her lips curling up into a smile as she began: "Do you know, I always thought Unicorns were fabulous monsters, too? I never saw one alive before!"

"Well, now that we *have* seen each other," said the Unicorn, "if you'll believe in me, I'll believe in you. Is that a bargain?"

"Yes, if you like," said Alice.

"Come, fetch out the plum-cake, old man!" the Unicorn went on, turning from her to the King. "None of your brown bread for me!"

"Certainly—certainly!" the King muttered, and beckoned

to Haigha. "Open the bag!" he whispered. "Quick! Not that one—that's full of hay!"

Haigha took a large cake out of the bag, and gave it to Alice to hold, while he got out a dish and carving-knife. How they all came out of it Alice couldn't guess. It was just like a conjuring-trick, she thought.

The Lion had joined them while this was going on: he looked very tired and sleepy, and his eyes were half shut. "What's this!" he said, blinking lazily at Alice, and speaking in a deep hollow tone that sounded like the tolling of a great bell.

"Ah, what *is* it, now?" the Unicorn cried eagerly. "You'll never guess! *I* couldn't."

The Lion looked at Alice wearily. "Are you animal—or vegetable—or mineral?" he said, yawning at every other word.

"It's a fabulous monster!" the Unicorn cried out, before Alice could reply.

"Then hand round the plum-cake, Monster," the Lion said, lying down and putting his chin on his paws. "And sit down, both of you" (to the King and the Unicorn): "fair play with the cake, you know!"

The King was evidently very uncomfortable at having to

sit down between the two great creatures; but there was no other place for him.

"What a fight we might have for the crown, *now!*" the Unicorn said, looking slyly up at the crown, which the poor King was nearly shaking off his head, he trembled so much.

"I should win easy," said the Lion.

"I'm not so sure of that," said the Unicorn.

"Why, I beat you all round the town, you chicken!" the Lion replied angrily, half getting up as he spoke.

Here the King interrupted, to prevent the quarrel going on: he was very nervous, and his voice quite quivered. "All round the town?" he said. "That's a good long way. Did you go by the old bridge, or the market-place? You get the best view by the old bridge."

"I'm sure I don't know," the Lion growled out as he lay down again. "There was too much dust to see anything. What a time the Monster is, cutting up that cake!"

Alice had seated herself on the bank of a little brook, with the great dish on her knees, and was sawing away diligently with the knife. "It's very provoking!" she said, in reply to the Lion (she was getting quite used to being called "the Monster"). "I've cut several slices already, but they always join on again!"

"You don't know how to manage Looking-Glass cakes," the Unicorn remarked. "Hand it round first, and cut it afterwards."

This sounded nonsense, but Alice very obediently got up, and carried the dish round, and the cake divided itself into three pieces as she did so. *"Now* cut it up," said the Lion, as she returned to her place with the empty dish.

"I say, this isn't fair!" cried the Unicorn, as Alice sat with the knife in her hand, very much puzzled how to begin. "The Monster has given the Lion twice as much as me!"

"She's kept none for herself, anyhow," said the Lion. "Do you like plum-cake, Monster?"

But before Alice could answer him, the drums began.

Where the noise came from, she couldn't make out: the air seemed full of it, and it rang through and through her head till she felt quite deafened. She started to her feet and sprang across the little brook in her terror, and had just time to see the Lion and the Unicorn rise to their feet, with angry looks at being interrupted in their feast, before she dropped to her knees, and put her hands over her ears, vainly trying to shut out the dreadful uproar.

"If *that* doesn't drum them out of town," she thought to herself, "nothing ever will!"

# VIII

## *"It's My Own Invention"*

AFTER A WHILE the noise seemed gradually to die away, till all was dead silence, and Alice lifted up her head in some alarm. There was no one to be seen, and her first thought was that she must have been dreaming about the Lion and the Unicorn and those queer Anglo-Saxon Messengers. However, there was the great dish still lying at her feet, on which she had tried to cut the plum-cake, "So I wasn't dreaming, after all," she said to herself, "unless—unless we're all part of the same dream. Only I do hope it's *my* dream, and not the Red King's! I don't like belonging to another person's dream," she went on in a rather complaining tone: "I've a great mind to go and wake him, and see what happens!"

At this moment her thoughts were interrupted by a loud shouting of "Ahoy! Ahoy! Check!" and a Knight, dressed in crimson armour, came galloping down upon her, brandishing a great club. Just as he reached her, the horse stopped suddenly: "You're my prisoner!" the Knight cried, as he tumbled off his horse.

Startled as she was, Alice was more frightened for him than for herself at the moment, and watched him with some anxiety as he mounted again. As soon as he was comfortably in the saddle, he began once more "You're my——" but here another voice broke in "Ahoy! Ahoy! Check!" and Alice looked round in some surprise for the new enemy.

This time it was a White Knight. He drew up at Alice's side, and tumbled off his horse just as the Red Knight had done; then he got on again, and the two Knights sat and

looked at each other for some time without speaking. Alice
looked from one to the other in some bewilderment.

"She's *my* prisoner, you know!" the Red Knight said at
last.

"Yes, but then *I* came and rescued her!" the White Knight
replied.

"Well, we must fight for her, then," said the Red Knight,
as he took up his helmet (which hung from the saddle, and
was something the shape of a horse's head) and put it on.

"You will observe the Rules of Battle, of course?" the
White Knight remarked, putting on his helmet too.

"I always do," said the Red Knight, and they began bang-
ing away at each other with such fury that Alice got behind a
tree to be out of the way of the blows.

"I wonder, now, what the Rules of Battle are," she said to
herself, as she watched the fight, timidly peeping out from her
hiding-place. "One Rule seems to be, that if one Knight hits
the other, he knocks him off his horse; and, if he misses, he
tumbles off himself—and another Rule seems to be that they

hold their clubs with their arms, as if they were Punch and Judy——What a noise they make when they tumble! Just like a whole set of fire-irons falling into the fender! And how quiet the horses are! They let them get on and off them just as if they were tables!"

Another Rule of Battle, that Alice had not noticed, seemed to be that they always fell on their heads; and the battle ended with their both falling off in this way, side by side. When they got up again, they shook hands, and then the Red Knight mounted and galloped off.

"It was a glorious victory, wasn't it?" said the White Knight, as he came up panting.

"I don't know," Alice said doubtfully. "I don't want to be anybody's prisoner. I want to be a Queen."

"So you will, when you've crossed the next brook," said the White Knight. "I'll see you safe to the end of the wood— and then I must go back, you know. That's the end of my move."

"Thank you very much," said Alice. "May I help you off with your helmet?" It was evidently more than he could manage by himself: however she managed to shake him out of it at last.

"Now one can breathe more easily," said the Knight, putting back his shaggy hair with both hands, and turning his gentle face and large mild eyes to Alice. She thought she had never seen such a strange-looking soldier in all her life.

He was dressed in tin armour, which seemed to fit him very badly, and he had a queer-shaped little deal box fastened across his shoulders, upside-down, and with the lid hanging open. Alice looked at it with great curiosity.

"I see you're admiring my little box," the Knight said in a friendly tone. "It's my own invention—to keep clothes and sandwiches in. You see I carry it upside-down, so that the rain can't get in."

"But the things can get *out*," Alice gently remarked. "Do you know the lid's open?"

"I didn't know it," the Knight said, a shade of vexation passing over his face. "Then all the things must have fallen out! And the box is no use without them." He unfastened it as he spoke, and was just going to throw it into the bushes, when a sudden thought seemed to strike him, and he hung it carefully on a tree. "Can you guess why I did that?" he said to Alice.

Alice shook her head.

"In hopes some bees may make a nest in it—then I should get the honey."

"But you've got a bee-hive—or something like one—fastened to the saddle," said Alice.

"Yes, it's a very good bee-hive," the Knight said in a discontented tone, "one of the best kind. But not a single bee has come near it yet. And the other thing is a mousetrap. I suppose the mice keep the bees out—or the bees keep the mice out, I don't know which."

"I was wondering what the mouse-trap was for," said Alice. "It isn't very likely there would be any mice on the horse's back."

"Not very likely, perhaps," said the Knight; "but, if they *do* come, I don't choose to have them running all about.

"You see," he went on after a pause, "it's as well to be provided for *everything*. That's the reason the horse has all those anklets round his feet."

"But what are they for?" Alice asked in a tone of great curiosity.

"To guard against the bites of sharks," the Knight replied. "It's an invention of my own. And now help me on. I'll go with you to the end of the wood——What's that dish for?"

"It's meant for plum-cake," said Alice.

"We'd better take it with us," the Knight said. "It'll come in handy if we find any plum-cake. Help me to get it into this bag."

This took a long time to manage, though Alice held the bag open very carefully, because the Knight was so *very* awkward in putting in the dish: the first two or three times that he tried he fell in himself instead. "It's rather a tight fit, you see," he said, as they got it in at last; "there are so many candlesticks in the bag." And he hung it to the saddle, which was already loaded with bunches of carrots, and fire-irons, and many other things.

"I hope you've got your hair well fastened on?" he continued as they set off.

"Only in the usual way," Alice said, smiling.

"That's hardly enough," he said, anxiously. "You see the wind is so *very* strong here. It's as strong as soup."

"Have you invented a plan for keeping the hair from being blown off?" Alice enquired.

"Not yet," said the Knight. "But I've got a plan for keeping it from *falling* off."

"I should like to hear it, very much."

"First you take an upright stick," said the Knight. "Then you make your hair creep up it, like a fruit-tree. Now the reason hair falls off is because it hangs *down*—things never fall *upwards*, you know. It's a plan of my own invention. You may try it if you like."

It didn't sound a comfortable plan, Alice thought, and for a few minutes she walked on in silence, puzzling over the

idea, and every now and then stopping to help the poor Knight, who certainly was *not* a good rider.

Whenever the horse stopped (which it did very often), he fell off in front; and, whenever it went on again (which it generally did rather suddenly), he fell off behind. Otherwise he kept on pretty well, except that he had a habit of now and then falling off sideways; and, as he generally did this on the side on which Alice was walking, she soon found that it was the best plan not to walk *quite* close to the horse.

"I'm afraid you've not had much practice in riding," she ventured to say, as she was helping him up from his fifth tumble.

The Knight looked very much surprised, and a little offended at the remark. "What makes you say that?" he asked, as he scrambled back into the saddle, keeping hold of Alice's hair with one hand, to save himself from falling over on the other side.

"Because people don't fall off quite so often, when they've had much practice."

"I've had plenty of practice," the Knight said very gravely: "plenty of practice!"

Alice could think of nothing better to say than "Indeed?" but she said it as heartily as she could. They went on a little way in silence after this, the Knight with his eyes shut, muttering to himself, and Alice watching anxiously for the next tumble.

"The great art of riding," the Knight suddenly began in a loud voice, waving his right arm as he spoke, "is to keep——" Here the sentence ended as suddenly as it had begun, as the Knight fell heavily on the top of his head exactly in the path where Alice was walking. She was quite frightened this time, and said in an anxious tone, as she picked him up, "I hope no bones are broken?"

"None to speak of," the Knight said, as if he didn't mind breaking two or three of them. "The great art of riding, as I was saying, is—to keep your balance properly. Like this, you know——"

He let go the bridle, and stretched out both his arms to show Alice what he meant, and this time he fell flat on his back, right under the horse's feet.

"Plenty of practice!" he went on repeating, all the time that Alice was getting him on his feet again. "Plenty of practice!"

"It's too ridiculous!" cried Alice, losing all her patience this time. "You ought to have a wooden horse on wheels, that you ought!"

"Does that kind go smoothly?" the Knight asked in a tone of great interest, clasping his arms round the horse's neck as he spoke, just in time to save himself from tumbling off again.

"Much more smoothly than a live horse," Alice said, with a little scream of laughter, in spite of all she could do to prevent it.

"I'll get one," the Knight said thoughtfully to himself. "One or two—several."

There was a short silence after this, and then the Knight went on again. "I'm a great hand at inventing things. Now, I daresay you noticed, the last time you picked me up, that I was looking rather thoughtful?"

"You *were* a little grave," said Alice.

"Well, just then I was inventing a new way of getting over a gate——would you like to hear it?"

"Very much indeed," Alice said politely.

"I'll tell you how I came to think of it," said the Knight. "You see, I said to myself 'The only difficulty is with the feet: the *head* is high enough already.' Now, first I put my head on the top of the gate—then the head's high enough—then I stand on my head—then the feet are high enough, you see—then I'm over, you see."

"Yes, I suppose you'd be over when that was done," Alice said thoughtfully: "but don't you think it would be rather hard?"

"I haven't tried it yet," the Knight said, gravely; "so I can't tell for certain—but I'm afraid it *would* be a little hard."

He looked so vexed at the idea, that Alice changed the subject hastily. "What a curious helmet you've got!" she said cheerfully. "Is that your invention too?"

The Knight looked down proudly at his helmet, which hung from the saddle. "Yes," he said; "but I've invented a better one than that—like a sugar-loaf. When I used to wear it, if I fell off the horse, it always touched the ground directly. So I had a *very* little way to fall, you see—But there *was* the danger of falling *into* it, to be sure. That happened to me once—and the worst of it was, before I could get out again, the other White Knight came and put it on. He thought it was his own helmet."

The Knight looked so solemn about it that Alice did not

dare to laugh. "I'm afraid you must have hurt him," she said in a trembling voice, "being on the top of his head."

"I had to kick him, of course," the Knight said, very seriously. "And then he took the helmet off again—but it took hours and hours to get me out. I was as fast as—as lightning, you know."

"But that's a different kind of fastness," Alice objected.

The Knight shook his head. "It was all kinds of fastness with me, I can assure you!" he said. He raised his hands in some excitement as he said this, and instantly rolled out of the saddle, and fell headlong into a deep ditch.

Alice ran to the side of the ditch to look for him. She was rather startled by the fall, as for some time he had kept on very well, and she was afraid that he really *was* hurt this time. However, though she could see nothing but the soles of his feet, she was much relieved to hear that he was talking on in his usual tone. "All kinds of fastness," he repeated: "but it was careless of him to put another man's helmet on—with the man in it, too."

"How *can* you go on talking so quietly, head downwards?" Alice asked, as she dragged him out by the feet, and laid him in a heap on the bank.

The Knight looked surprised at the question. "What does it matter where my body happens to be?" he said. "My mind goes on working all the same. In fact, the more head-downwards I am, the more I keep inventing new things.

"Now the cleverest thing of the sort that I ever did," he

went on after a pause, "was inventing a new pudding during the meat-course."

"In time to have it cooked for the next course?" said Alice. "Well, that *was* quick work, certainly!"

"Well, not the *next* course," the Knight said in a slow thoughtful tone: "no, certainly not the next *course.*"

"Then it would have to be the next day. I suppose you wouldn't have two pudding-courses in one dinner?"

"Well, not the *next* day," the Knight repeated as before: "not the next *day.* In fact," he went on, holding his head down, and his voice getting lower and lower, "I don't believe that pudding ever *was* cooked! In fact, I don't believe that pudding ever *will* be cooked! And yet it was a very clever pudding to invent."

"What did you mean it to be made of?" Alice asked, hoping to cheer him up, for the poor Knight seemed quite low-spirited about it.

"It began with blotting-paper," the Knight answered with a groan.

"That wouldn't be very nice, I'm afraid——"

"Not very nice *alone,*" he interrupted, quite eagerly: "but you've no idea what a difference it makes, mixing it with other things—such as gunpowder and sealing-wax. And here I must leave you." They had just come to the end of the wood.

Alice could only look puzzled: she was thinking of the pudding.

"You are sad," the Knight said in an anxious tone: "let me sing you a song to comfort you."

"Is it very long?" Alice asked, for she had heard a good deal of poetry that day.

"It's long," said the Knight, "but it's very, *very* beautiful. Everybody that hears me sing it—either it brings the *tears* into their eyes, or else——"

"Or else what?" said Alice, for the Knight had made a sudden pause.

"Or else it doesn't, you know. The name of the song is called *'Haddocks' Eyes.'*"

"Oh, that's the name of the song, is it?" Alice said, trying to feel interested.

"No, you don't understand," the Knight said, looking a

little vexed. "That's what the name is *called*. The name really is '*The Aged Aged Man*.'"

"Then I ought to have said 'That's what the *song* is called'?" Alice corrected herself.

"No, you oughtn't: that's quite another thing! The *song* is called '*Ways And Means*': but that's only what it's *called,* you know!"

"Well, what *is* the song, then?" said Alice, who was by this time completely bewildered.

"I was coming to that," the Knight said. "The song really is '*A-sitting On A Gate*': and the tune's my own invention."

So saying, he stopped his horse and let the reins fall on its neck: then, slowly beating time with one hand, and with a faint smile lighting up his gentle foolish face, as if he enjoyed the music of his song, he began.

Of all the strange things that Alice saw in her journey Through the Looking-Glass, this was the one that she always remembered most clearly. Years afterwards she could bring the whole scene back again, as if it had been only yesterday— the mild blue eyes and kindly smile of the Knight—the setting sun gleaming through his hair, and shining on his armour in a blaze of light that quite dazzled her—the horse quietly moving about, with the reins hanging loose on his neck, cropping the grass at her feet—and the black shadows of the forest behind—all this she took in like a picture, as, with one hand shading her eyes, she leant against a tree, watching the strange pair, and listening, in a half-dream, to the melancholy music of the song.

"But the tune *isn't* his own invention," she said to herself: "it's '*I give thee all, I can no more*.'" She stood and listened very attentively, but no tears came into her eyes.

> "I'll tell thee everything I can:
>     There's little to relate.
> I saw an aged aged man,
>     A-sitting on a gate.
> 'Who are you, aged man?' I said.
>     'And how is it you live?'
> And his answer trickled through my head,
>     Like water through a sieve.

*"He said 'I look for butterflies*
   *That sleep among the wheat:*
*I make them into mutton-pies,*
   *And sell them in the street.*
*I sell them unto men,' he said,*
   *'Who sail on stormy seas;*
*And that's the way I get my bread——*
   *A trifle, if you please.'*

*"But I was thinking of a plan*
   *To dye one's whiskers green,*
*And always use so large a fan*
   *That they could not be seen.*
*So, having no reply to give*
   *To what the old man said,*
*I cried 'Come, tell me how you live!'*
   *And thumped him on the head.*

*"His accents mild took up the tale:*
   *He said 'I go my ways,*
*And when I find a mountain-rill,*
   *I set it in a blaze;*
*And thence they make a stuff they call*
   *Rowland's Macassar-Oil—*
*Yet twopence-halfpenny is all*
   *They give me for my toil.'*

*"But I was thinking of a way*
   *To feed oneself on batter,*
*And so go on from day to day*
   *Getting a little fatter.*
*I shook him well from side to side,*
   *Until his face was blue:*
*'Come, tell me how you live,' I cried,*
   *'And what it is you do!'*

*"He said 'I hunt for haddocks' eyes*
   *Among the heather bright,*
*And work them into waistcoat-buttons*
   *In the silent night.*

*And these I do not sell for gold*
  *Or coin of silvery shine,*
*But for a copper halfpenny,*
  *And that will purchase nine.*

*" 'I sometimes dig for buttered rolls,*
  *Or set limed twigs for crabs:*
*I sometimes search the grassy knolls*
  *For wheels of Hansom-cabs.*
*And that's the way' (he gave a wink)*
  *'By which I get my wealth——*
*And very gladly will I drink*
  *Your Honour's noble health.'*

*"I heard him then, for I had just*
  *Completed my design*
*To keep the Menai bridge from rust*
  *By boiling it in wine.*
*I thanked him much for telling me*
  *The way he got his wealth,*
*But chiefly for his wish that he*
  *Might drink my noble health.*

*"And now, if e'er by chance I put*
  *My fingers into glue,*

*Or madly squeeze a right-hand foot*
  *Into a left-hand shoe,*
*Or if I drop upon my toe*
  *A very heavy weight,*
*I weep, for it reminds me so*
*Of that old man I used to know—*
*Whose look was mild, whose speech was slow,*
*Whose hair was whiter than the snow,*
*Whose face was very like a crow,*
*With eyes, like cinders, all aglow,*
*Who seemed distracted with his woe,*
*Who rocked his body to and fro,*
*And muttered mumblingly and low,*
*As if his mouth were full of dough,*
*Who snorted like a buffalo——*
*That summer evening long ago,*
  *A-sitting on a gate."*

As the Knight sang the last words of the ballad, he gathered up the reins, and turned his horse's head along the road by which they had come. "You've only a few yards to go," he said, "down the hill and over that little brook, and then you'll be a Queen——But you'll stay and see me off first?" he added as Alice turned with an eager look in the direction to which he pointed. "I shan't be long. You'll wait and wave your handkerchief when I get to that turn in the road? I think it'll encourage me, you see."

"Of course I'll wait," said Alice: "and thank you very much for coming so far—and for the song—I liked it very much."

"I hope so," the Knight said doubtfully: "but you didn't cry so much as I thought you would."

So they shook hands, and then the Knight rode slowly away into the forest. "It won't take long to see him *off*, I expect," Alice said to herself, as she stood watching him. "There he goes! Right on his head as usual! However, he gets on again pretty easily—that comes of having so many things hung round the horse——" So she went on talking to herself, as she watched the horse walking leisurely along the road, and the Knight tumbling off, first on one side and then on the other. After the fourth or fifth tumble he reached the turn, and then she waved her handkerchief to him, and waited till he was out of sight.

"I hope it encouraged him," she said, as she turned to run down the hill: "and now for the last brook, and to be a Queen! How grand it sounds!" A very few steps brought her to the edge of the brook. "The Eighth Square at last!" she cried as she bounded across, and threw herself down to rest on a lawn

as soft as moss, with little flower-beds dotted about it here and there. "Oh, how glad I am to get here! And what *is* this on my head?" she exclaimed in a tone of dismay, as she put her hands up to something very heavy, that fitted tight all round her head.

"But how *can* it have got there without my knowing it?" she said to herself, as she lifted it off, and set it on her lap to make out what it could possibly be.

It was a golden crown.

# IX

## Queen Alice

"WELL, THIS *IS* GRAND!" said Alice. "I never expected I should be a Queen so soon—and I'll tell you what it is, your Majesty," she went on, in a severe tone (she was always rather fond of scolding herself), "it'll never do for you to be lolling about on the grass like that! Queens have to be dignified, you know!"

So she got up and walked about—rather stiffly just at first, as she was afraid that the crown might come off: but she comforted herself with the thought that there was nobody to see her, "and if I really am a Queen," she said as she sat down again, "I shall be able to manage it quite well in time."

Everything was happening so oddly that she didn't feel a bit surprised at finding the Red Queen and the White Queen sitting close to her, one on each side: she would have liked very much to ask them how they came there, but she feared it would not be quite civil. However, there would be no harm, she thought, in asking if the game was over. "Please, would you tell me——" she began, looking timidly at the Red Queen.

"Speak when you're spoken to!" the Queen sharply interrupted her.

"But if everybody obeyed that rule," said Alice, who was always ready for a little argument, "and if you only spoke when you were spoken to, and the other person always waited for *you* to begin, you see nobody would ever say anything, so that——"

"Ridiculous!" cried the Queen. "Why, don't you see, child——" here she broke off with a frown, and, after thinking for a minute, suddenly changed the subject of the conver-sation. "What do you mean by 'If you really are a Queen'? What right have you to call yourself so? You can't be a Queen, you know, till you've passed the proper examination. And the sooner we begin it, the better."

"I only said 'if'!" poor Alice pleaded in a piteous tone.

The two Queens looked at each other, and the Red Queen remarked, with a little shudder, "She *says* she only said 'if'——"

"But she said a great deal more than that!" the White Queen moaned, wringing her hands, "Oh, ever so much more than that!"

"So you did, you know," the Red Queen said to Alice. "Always speak the truth—think before you speak—and write it down afterwards."

"I'm sure I didn't mean——" Alice was beginning, but the Red Queen interrupted her impatiently.

"That's just what I complain of! You *should* have meant! What do you suppose is the use of a child without any mean-ing? Even a joke should have some meaning—and a child's more important than a joke, I hope. You couldn't deny that, even if you tried with both hands."

"I don't deny things with my *hands*," Alice objected.

"Nobody said you did," said the Red Queen. "I said you couldn't if you tried."

"She's in that state of mind," said the White Queen, "that she wants to deny *something*—only she doesn't know what to deny!"

"A nasty, vicious temper," the Red Queen remarked; and then there was an uncomfortable silence for a minute or two.

The Red Queen broke the silence by saying, to the White Queen, "I invite you to Alice's dinner-party this afternoon."

The White Queen smiled feebly, and said "And I invite *you*."

"I didn't know I was to have a party at all," said Alice; "but, if there *is* to be one, I think *I* ought to invite the guests."

"We gave you the opportunity of doing it," the Red Queen remarked: "but I daresay you've not had many lessons in manners yet?"

"Manners are not taught in lessons," said Alice. "Lessons teach you to do sums, and things of that sort."

"Can you do Addition?" the White Queen asked. "What's one and one and one and one and one and one and one and one and one and one?"

"I don't know," said Alice. "I lost count."

"She can't do Addition," the Red Queen interrupted. "Can you do Subtraction? Take nine from eight."

"Nine from eight I can't, you know," Alice replied very readily: "but——"

"She can't do Subtraction," said the White Queen. "Can you do Division? Divide a loaf by a knife—what's the answer to *that?*"

"I suppose——" Alice was beginning, but the Red Queen answered for her. "Bread-and-butter, of course. Try another Subtraction sum. Take a bone from a dog: what remains?"

Alice considered. "The bone wouldn't remain, of course, if I took it—and the dog wouldn't remain: it would come to bite me—and I'm sure I shouldn't remain!"

"Then you think nothing would remain?" said the Red Queen.

"I think that's the answer."

"Wrong, as usual," said the Red Queen: "the dog's temper would remain."

"But I don't see how——"

"Why, look here!" the Red Queen cried. "The dog would lose its temper, wouldn't it?"

"Perhaps it would," Alice replied cautiously.

"Then if the dog went away, its temper would remain!" the Queen exclaimed triumphantly.

Alice said, as gravely as she could, "They might go different ways." But she couldn't help thinking to herself "What dreadful nonsense we *are* talking!"

"She can't do sums a *bit!*" the Queens said together, with great emphasis.

"Can *you* do sums?" Alice said, turning suddenly on the White Queen, for she didn't like being found fault with so much.

The Queen gasped and shut her eyes. "I can do Addition," she said, "if you give me time—but I can't do Subtraction under *any* circumstances!"

"Of course you know your A B C?" said the Red Queen.

"To be sure I do," said Alice.

"So do I," the White Queen whispered: "we'll often say it over together, dear. And I'll tell you a secret—I can read words of one letter! Isn't *that* grand? However, don't be discouraged. You'll come to it in time."

Here the Red Queen began again. "Can you answer useful questions?" she said. "How is bread made?"

"I know *that!*" Alice cried eagerly. "You take some flour——"

"Where do you pick the flower?" the White Queen asked. "In a garden or in the hedges?"

"Well, it isn't *picked* at all," Alice explained: "it's *ground*——"

"How many acres of ground?" said the White Queen. "You mustn't leave out so many things."

"Fan her head!" the Red Queen anxiously interrupted. "She'll be feverish after so much thinking." So they set to work and fanned her with bunches of leaves, till she had to beg them to leave off, it blew her hair about so.

"She's all right again now," said the Red Queen. "Do you know Languages? What's the French for fiddle-de-dee?"

"Fiddle-de-dee's not English," Alice replied gravely.

"Who ever said it was?" said the Red Queen.

Alice thought she saw a way out of the difficulty, this time. "If you'll tell me what language 'fiddle-de-dee' is, I'll tell you the French for it!" she exclaimed triumphantly.

But the Red Queen drew herself up rather stiffly, and said "Queens never make bargains."

"I wish Queens never asked questions," Alice thought to herself.

"Don't let us quarrel," the White Queen said in an anxious tone. "What is the cause of lightning?"

"The cause of lightning," Alice said very decidedly, for she felt quite certain about this, "is the thunder—no, no!" she hastily corrected herself. "I meant the other way."

"It's too late to correct it," said the Red Queen: "when you've once said a thing, that fixes it, and you must take the consequences."

"Which reminds me——" the White Queen said, looking down and nervously clasping and unclasping her hands, "we had *such* a thunderstorm last Tuesday—I mean one of the last set of Tuesdays, you know."

Alice was puzzled. "In *our* country," she remarked, "there's only one day at a time."

The Red Queen said "That's a poor thin way of doing things. Now *here,* we mostly have days and nights two or three at a time, and sometimes in the winter we take as many as five nights together—for warmth, you know."

"Are five nights warmer than one night, then?" Alice ventured to ask.

"Five times as warm, of course."

"But they should be five times as *cold,* by the same rule——"

"Just so!" cried the Red Queen. "Five times as warm, *and* five times as cold—just as I'm five times as rich as you are, *and* five times as clever!"

Alice sighed and gave it up. "It's exactly like a riddle with no answer!" she thought.

"Humpty Dumpty saw it too," the White Queen went on in a low voice, more as if she were talking to herself. "He came to the door with a corkscrew in his hand——"

"What did he want?" said the Red Queen.

"He said he *would* come in," the White Queen went on,

"because he was looking for a hippopotamus. Now, as it happened, there wasn't such a thing in the house, that morning."

"Is there generally?" Alice asked in an astonished tone.

"Well, only on Thursdays," said the Queen.

"I know what he came for," said Alice: "he wanted to punish the fish, because——"

Here the White Queen began again. "It was *such* a thunderstorm, you can't think!" ("She *never* could, you know," said the Red Queen.) "And part of the roof came off, and ever so much thunder got in—and it went rolling round the room in great lumps—and knocking over the tables and things—till I was so frightened, I couldn't remember my own name!"

Alice thought to herself "I never should *try* to remember my name in the middle of an accident! Where would be the use of it?" but she did not say this aloud, for fear of hurting the poor Queen's feelings.

"Your Majesty must excuse her," the Red Queen said to Alice, taking one of the White Queen's hands in her own, and gently stroking it: "she means well, but she can't help saying foolish things, as a general rule."

The White Queen looked timidly at Alice, who felt she *ought* to say something kind, but really couldn't think of anything at the moment.

"She never was really well brought up," the Red Queen went on: "but it's amazing how good-tempered she is! Pat her on the head, and see how pleased she'll be!" But this was more than Alice had courage to do.

"A little kindness—and putting her hair in papers—would do wonders with her——"

The White Queen gave a deep sigh, and laid her head on Alice's shoulder. "I *am* so sleepy!" she moaned.

"She's tired, poor thing!" said the Red Queen. "Smooth her hair—lend her your nightcap—and sing her a soothing lullaby."

"I haven't got a nightcap with me," said Alice, as she tried to obey the first direction: "and I don't know any soothing lullabies."

"I must do it myself, then," said the Red Queen, and she began:—

> *"Hush-a-by lady, in Alice's lap!*
> *Till the feast's ready, we've time for a nap.*
> *When the feast's over, we'll go to the ball—*
> *Red Queen, and White Queen, and Alice, and all!"*

"And now you know the words," she added, as she put her head down on Alice's other shoulder, "just sing it through to me. I'm getting sleepy, too." In another moment both Queens were fast asleep, and snoring loud.

"What *am* I to do?" exclaimed Alice, looking about in great perplexity, as first one round head, and then the other, rolled down from her shoulder and lay like a heavy lump in her lap. "I don't think it *ever* happened before, that any one had to take care of two Queens asleep at once! No, not in all the History of England—it couldn't, you know, because there never was more than one Queen at a time. Do wake up, you heavy things!" she went on in an impatient tone; but there was no answer but a gentle snoring.

The snoring got more distinct every minute, and sounded more like a tune: at last she could even make out words, and she listened so eagerly that, when the two great heads suddenly vanished from her lap, she hardly missed them.

She was standing before an arched doorway, over which were the words "QUEEN ALICE" in large letters, and on each side of the arch there was a bell-handle; one was marked "Visitors' Bell," and the other "Servants' Bell."

"I'll wait till the song's over," thought Alice, "and then I'll ring the—the—*which* bell must I ring?" she went on, very much puzzled by the names. "I'm not a visitor, and I'm not a servant. There *ought* to be one marked 'Queen,' you know———"

Just then the door opened a little way, and a creature with a long beak put its head out for a moment and said "No admittance till the week after next!" and shut the door again with a bang.

Alice knocked and rang in vain for a long time; but at last a very old Frog, who was sitting under a tree, got up and hobbled slowly towards her: he was dressed in bright yellow, and had enormous boots on.

"What is it, now?" the Frog said in a deep hoarse whisper.

Alice turned round, ready to find fault with anybody. "Where's the servant whose business it is to answer the door?" she began angrily.

"Which door?" said the Frog.

Alice almost stamped with irritation at the slow drawl in which he spoke. *"This* door, of course!"

The Frog looked at the door with his large dull eyes for a minute: then he went nearer and rubbed it with his thumb, as if he were trying whether the paint would come off: then he looked at Alice.

"To answer the door?" he said. "What's it been asking of?" He was so hoarse that Alice could scarcely hear him.

"I don't know what you mean," she said.

"I speaks English, doesn't I?" the Frog went on. "Or are you deaf? What did it ask you?"

"Nothing!" Alice said impatiently. "I've been knocking at it!"

"Shouldn't do that—shouldn't do that——" the Frog muttered. "Wexes it, you know." Then he went up and gave the door a kick with one of his great feet. "You let *it* alone," he panted out, as he hobbled back to his tree, "and it'll let *you* alone, you know."

At this moment the door was flung open, and a shrill voice was heard singing:—

*"To the Looking-Glass world it was Alice that said*
  *'I've a sceptre in hand, I've a crown on my head.*
  *Let the Looking-Glass creatures, whatever they be,*
  *Come and dine with the Red Queen, the White*
    *Queen, and me.'"*

And hundreds of voices joined in the chorus:—

*"Then fill up the glasses as quick as you can,*
  *And sprinkle the table with buttons and bran;*
  *Put cats in the coffee, and mice in the tea—*
  *And welcome Queen Alice with thirty-times-three!"*

Then followed a confused noise of cheering, and Alice thought to herself "Thirty times three makes ninety. I wonder if any one's counting?" In a minute there was silence again, and the same shrill voice sang another verse:—

*" 'O Looking-Glass creatures,' quoth Alice, 'draw near!*
  *'Tis an honour to see me, a favour to hear:*
  *'Tis a privilege high to have dinner and tea*
  *Along with the Red Queen, the White Queen, and me!'"*

Then came the chorus again:—

*"Then fill up the glasses with treacle and ink,*
  *Or anything else that is pleasant to drink:*
  *Mix sand with the cider, and wool with the wine—*
  *And welcome Queen Alice with ninety-times-nine!"*

"Ninety times nine!" Alice repeated in despair. "Oh, that'll never be done! I'd better go in at once——" and in she went, and there was a dead silence the moment she appeared.

Alice glanced nervously along the table, as she walked up the large hall, and noticed that there were about fifty guests, of all kinds: some were animals, some birds, and there were even a few flowers among them. "I'm glad they've come without waiting to be asked," she thought: "I should never have known who were the right people to invite!"

There were three chairs at the head of the table: the Red and White Queens had already taken two of them, but the middle one was empty. Alice sat down in it, rather uncomfortable at the silence, and longing for some one to speak.

At last the Red Queen began. "You've missed the soup and fish," she said. "Put on the joint!" And the waiters set a leg of mutton before Alice, who looked at it rather anxiously, as she had never had to carve a joint before.

"You look a little shy: let me introduce you to that leg of

mutton," said the Red Queen. "Alice——Mutton: Mutton——
Alice." The leg of mutton got up in the dish and made a little
bow to Alice; and Alice returned the bow, not knowing whether
to be frightened or amused.

"May I give you a slice?" she said, taking up the knife and
fork, and looking from one Queen to the other.

"Certainly not," the Red Queen said, very decidedly: "it
isn't etiquette to cut any one you've been introduced to. Remove the joint!" And the waiters carried it off, and brought a
large plum-pudding in its place.

"I won't be introduced to the pudding, please," Alice said
rather hastily, "or we shall get no dinner at all. May I give
you some?"

But the Red Queen looked sulky, and growled
"Pudding——Alice: Alice——Pudding. Remove the pudding!" and the waiters took it away so quickly that Alice
couldn't return its bow.

However, she didn't see why the Red Queen should be the
only one to give orders; so, as an experiment, she called out
"Waiter! Bring back the pudding!," and there it was again in
a moment, like a conjuring-trick. It was so large that she
couldn't help feeling a *little* shy with it, as she had been with
the mutton; however, she conquered her shyness by a great
effort, and cut a slice and handed it to the Red Queen.

"What impertinence!" said the Pudding. "I wonder how
you'd like it, if I were to cut a slice out of *you,* you creature!"

It spoke in a thick, suety sort of voice, and Alice hadn't a
word to say in reply: she could only sit and look at it and
gasp.

"Make a remark," said the Red Queen: "it's ridiculous to
leave all the conversation to the pudding!"

"Do you know, I've had such a quantity of poetry repeated
to me to-day," Alice began, a little frightened at finding that,
the moment she opened her lips, there was dead silence, and
all eyes were fixed upon her; "and it's a very curious thing, I
think—every poem was about fishes in some way. Do you
know why they're so fond of fishes, all about here?"

She spoke to the Red Queen, whose answer was a little
wide of the mark. "As to fishes," she said, very slowly and
solemnly, putting her mouth close to Alice's ear, "her White

Majesty knows a lovely riddle—all in poetry—all about fishes. Shall she repeat it?"

"Her Red Majesty's very kind to mention it," the White Queen murmured into Alice's other ear, in a voice like the cooing of a pigeon. "It would be *such* a treat! May I?"

"Please do," Alice said very politely.

The White Queen laughed with delight, and stroked Alice's cheek. Then she began:

> " *'First, the fish must be caught.'*
> *That is easy: a baby, I think, could have caught it.*
> *'Next, the fish must be bought.'*
> *That is easy: a penny, I think, would have bought it.*
>
> " *'Now cook me the fish!'*
> *That is easy, and will not take more than a minute.*
> *'Let it lie in a dish!'*
> *That is easy, because it already is in it.*
>
> " *'Bring it here! Let me sup!'*
> *It is easy to set such a dish on the table.*
> *'Take the dish-cover up!'*
> *Ah, that is so hard that I fear I'm unable!*
>
> *"For it holds it like glue—*
> *Holds the lid to the dish, while it lies in the middle:*
> *Which is easiest to do,*
> *Un-dish-cover the fish, or dishcover the riddle?"*

"Take a minute to think about it, and then guess," said the Red Queen. "Meanwhile, we'll drink your health—Queen Alice's health!" she screamed at the top of her voice, and all the guests began drinking it directly, and very queerly they managed it: some of them put their glasses upon their heads like extinguishers, and drank all that trickled down their faces—others upset the decanters, and drank the wine as it ran off the edges of the table —and three of them (who looked like kangaroos) scrambled into the dish of roast mutton, and began eagerly lapping up the gravy, "just like pigs in a trough!" thought Alice.

"You ought to return thanks in a neat speech," the Red Queen said, frowning at Alice as she spoke.

"We must support you, you know," the White Queen whispered, as Alice got up to do it, very obediently, but a little frightened.

"Thank you very much," she whispered in reply, "but I can do quite well without."

"That wouldn't be at all the thing," the Red Queen said very decidedly: so Alice tried to submit to it with a good grace.

("And they *did* push so!" she said afterwards, when she was telling her sister the history of the feast. "You would have thought they wanted to squeeze me flat!")

In fact it was rather difficult for her to keep in her place while she made her speech: the two Queens pushed her so, one on each side, that they nearly lifted her up into the air. "I rise to return thanks——" Alice began: and she really *did* rise as she spoke, several inches; but she got hold of the edge of the table, and managed to pull herself down again.

"Take care of yourself!" screamed the White Queen, seizing Alice's hair with both her hands. "Something's going to happen!"

And then (as Alice afterwards described it) all sorts of things happened in a moment. The candles all grew up to the ceiling, looking something like a bed of rushes with fireworks at the top. As to the bottles, they each took a pair of plates, which they hastily fitted on as wings, and so, with forks for legs, went fluttering about in all directions: "and very like birds they look," Alice thought to herself, as well as she could in the dreadful confusion that was beginning.

At this moment she heard a hoarse laugh at her side, and turned to see what was the matter with the White Queen; but, instead of the Queen, there was the leg of mutton sitting in the chair. "Here I am!" cried a voice from the soup-tureen, and Alice turned again, just in time to see the Queen's broad good-natured face grinning at her for a moment over the edge of the tureen, before she disappeared into the soup.

There was not a moment to be lost. Already several of the guests were lying down in the dishes, and the soup-ladle was walking up the table towards Alice's chair, and beckoning to her impatiently to get out of its way.

"I can't stand this any longer!" she cried, as she jumped up and seized the table-cloth with both hands: one good pull, and plates, dishes, guests, and candles came crashing down together in a heap on the floor.

"And as for *you*," she went on, turning fiercely upon the Red Queen, whom she considered as the cause of all the mischief—but the Queen was

no longer at her side—she had suddenly dwindled down to the size of a little doll, and was now on the table, merrily running round and round after her own shawl, which was trailing behind her.

At any other time, Alice would have felt surprised at this, but she was far too much excited to be surprised at anything *now*. "As for *you*," she repeated, catching hold of the little creature in the very act of jumping over a bottle which had just lighted upon the table, "I'll shake you into a kitten, that I will!"

# X

---

## *Shaking*

SHE TOOK HER off the table as she spoke, and shook her backwards and forwards with all her might.

The Red Queen made no resistance whatever: only her face grew very small, and her eyes got large and green: and still, as Alice went on shaking her, she kept on growing shorter—and fatter—and softer—and rounder—and—

# XI

---

## *Waking*

——and it really *was* a kitten, after all.

# XII

## Which Dreamed It?

"Your Red Majesty shouldn't purr so loud," Alice said, rubbing her eyes, and addressing the kitten, respectfully, yet with some severity. "You woke me out of oh! such a nice dream! And you've been along with me, Kitty—all through the Looking-Glass world. Did you know it, dear?"

It is a very inconvenient habit of kittens (Alice had once made the remark) that, whatever you say to them, they *always* purr. "If they would only purr for 'yes,' and mew for 'no,' or any rule of that sort," she had said, "so that one could keep up a conversation! But how *can* you talk with a person if they *always* say the same thing?"

On this occasion the kitten only purred: and it was impossible to guess whether it meant "yes" or "no."

So Alice hunted among the chessmen on the table till she had found the Red Queen: then she went down on her knees on the hearth-rug, and put the kitten and the Queen to look at each other. "Now, Kitty!" she cried, clapping her hands triumphantly. "Confess that was what you turned into!"

("But it wouldn't look at it," she said, when she was explaining the thing afterwards to her sister: "it turned away its head, and pretended not to see it: but it looked a *little* ashamed of itself, so I think it *must* have been the Red Queen.")

"Sit up a little more stiffly, dear!" Alice cried with a merry laugh. "And curtsey while you're thinking what to—what to purr. It saves time, remember!" And she caught it up and gave it one little kiss, "just in honour of its having been a Red Queen."

"Snowdrop, my pet!" she went on, looking over her shoulder at the White Kitten, which was still patiently undergoing its toilet, "when *will* Dinah have finished with your White Majesty, I wonder? That must be the reason you were so untidy in my dream.——Dinah! Do you know that you're scrubbing a White Queen? Really, it's most disrespectful of you!

"And what did *Dinah* turn to, I wonder?" she prattled on, as she settled comfortably down, with one elbow on the rug, and her chin in her hand, to watch the kittens. "Tell me, Dinah, did you turn to Humpty Dumpty? I *think* you did—however, you'd better not mention it to your friends just yet, for I'm not sure.

"By the way, Kitty, if only you'd been really with me in my dream, there was one thing you *would* have enjoyed——I had such a quantity of poetry said to me, all about fishes! To-morrow morning you shall have a real treat. All the time you're eating your breakfast, I'll repeat 'The Walrus and the Carpenter' to you; and then you can make believe it's oysters, dear!

"Now, Kitty, let's consider who it was that dreamed it all. This is a serious question, my dear, and you should *not* go on licking your paw like that—as if Dinah hadn't washed you this morning! You see, Kitty, it *must* have been either me or the Red King. He was part of my dream, of course—but then I was part of his dream, too! *Was* it the Red King, Kitty? You were his wife, my dear, so you ought to know—Oh, Kitty, *do* help to settle it! I'm sure your paw can wait!" But the provoking kitten only began on the other paw, and pretended it hadn't heard the question.

Which do *you* think it was?

*A boat, beneath a sunny sky*
*Lingering onward dreamily*
*In an evening of July—*

*Children three that nestle near,*
*Eager eye and willing ear,*
*Pleased a simple tale to hear—*

*Long has paled that sunny sky:*
*Echoes fade and memories die:*
*Autumn frosts have slain July.*

*Still she haunts me, phantomwise,*
*Alice moving under skies*
*Never seen by waking eyes.*

*Children yet, the tale to hear,*
*Eager eye and willing ear,*
*Lovingly shall nestle near.*

*In a Wonderland they lie,*
*Dreaming as the days go by,*
*Dreaming as the summers die:*

*Ever drifting down the stream—*
*Lingering in the golden gleam—*
*Life, what is it but a dream?*

# AFTERWORD

Lewis Carroll was perhaps the strangest of all the sexually troubled Victorian writers. Thomas Carlyle, John Ruskin and James Barrie were impotent; Edward FitzGerald, Edward Lear, Walter Pater, Gerard Manley Hopkins and A. E. Housman were forced, in that repressive era, to be secret homosexuals. Carroll spent his entire adult life within the male confines of Christ Church, Oxford, first as a student, then as a mathematics tutor, from 1851, when he was nineteen, until his death in 1898. The expansive and voluble Mark Twain, who met him in 1879, called him "the stillest and shyest fullgrown man I have ever met."

Carroll's stammer kept him shy and silent among adults, and he was socially most at ease with children. He liked to befriend and photograph naked preadolescent girls and abhorred brutish little boys. As he earnestly told a friend, "I confess I do *not* admire naked *boys* in pictures. They always seem to need *clothes*: whereas one hardly sees why the lovely forms of girls should *ever* be covered up!" He captured the girls' images with his camera, but lost interest in them as soon as they reached puberty. He was particularly fond of Alice Liddell (pronounced like "middle") and her sisters, the daughters of the dean of his college, and took more discreet though still suggestive photographs of them.

Carroll's biographer Morton Cohen noted how the *Alice* books throb with sexual imagery: "the rabbit hole at the start; the emphasis on eating and drinking; Alice's changing size; Alice outgrowing the size of the Rabbit's house, almost causing it to burst at the seams; the explosive ejection of Bill the Lizard through the chimney of the house; the Pigeon referring to Alice as a kind of serpent; physical beatings, shakings and sneezings; the numerous threats of decapitation."

Carroll poured his passionate and repressed feelings for Alice into the works she inspired, and his admiration and love for his child heroine give the books their enduring power. His fantastic imagination, characters, style, humor, puns, and parodies of nursery rhymes and moralistic poetry appeal to children and adults alike. The *Alice* books are phenomenally popular, even in non-Western cultures that know very little about the polite behavior, social nuances and idiosyncratic wit of academic life in Victorian Oxford.

The books have been translated into more than seventy languages, including a Russian version by Vladimir Nabokov, and have inspired five feature films between 1915 and 2010 as well as plays, operas, operettas, ballets, classical music, musicals and songs. They influenced Beatrix Potter's *Peter Rabbit* books and Kenneth Grahame's *The Wind in the Willows*, in which animals speak and (half or fully dressed) wear clothes. The King of Hearts' cook, like Mr. Toad in *Willows*, stubbornly says, "Shan't." The title of Angus Wilson's novel *Anglo-Saxon Attitudes* comes from Carroll. The *Alice* books were admired by André Breton and the Surrealists, left their mark on Gertrude Stein, Virginia Woolf and T. S. Eliot, and influenced James Joyce's *Finnegans Wake*. Hugh Kenner wrote that "the playing cards, the farcical trial, the animated banquet, the talking flowers, the endless argumentations at cross-purposes, the reversals of time and space, those and other Carrollean motifs recur and recur throughout Joyce's text."

Though Carroll imposed a fanatical, obsessive order on every detail of his life, absolute chaos reigned in his work. The strict logician invented illogical worlds in which all rational forms of behavior disappear. Alice goes down the rabbit hole impulsively headfirst and upside down like the world she enters. Though she's subterranean, there's plenty of light. People and even things behave contrary to normal expectations and are ruled by the Uncertainty Principle. As in Einstein's theories, all motion is relative; time is no longer uniform and absolute. After Alice has sliced the pieces of cake, they join together; the March Hare dips a pocket watch into his tea; during the caucus race everyone "began running when they liked, and left off when they liked, so that it was not easy to know when the race was over" (p. 23).

At the start of the story, after rejecting a dull book with no pictures or dialogue, Alice becomes the heroine—the Underground Girl—of a lively book about herself, enhanced by the amusing drawings of John Tenniel. The charming and complex Alice is a precocious and sophisticated English child, far wiser than her tender years and very clever for a seven-year-old. She is tidy and kindhearted, and loves her pet cat Dinah. She's well brought up and well mannered, offended by rudeness, conscious of her class and sure of her social position. Bookish, thoughtful and talkative, she talks to herself because she meets no other children and is always ready for a little argument. She's commonsensical, curious and eager to learn; grown-up, self-possessed and independent. Though life in Wonderland is a sharp contrast to the secure routine of her Victorian nursery, she's adventurous, adaptable, cool in the face of adversity, brave in danger. Though completely on her own, she never calls out for her mother. She's polite and diplomatic when dealing with a series of extremely touchy and eccentric characters, who appear in swiftly changing scenes, like in a modern movie. She knows a bit of Latin and French, how to play croquet and chess, to swim, row and dance, to scan poetry and to flatter the disagreeable Queen of Hearts. Most important, perhaps, is that she exposes the duplicitous façade of the grown-up world and rejects adult authority. When she finally loses her patience and temper, she tears off the tablecloth and sends "plates, dishes, guests, and candles . . . crashing down together in a heap on the floor" (p. 220), she not only echoes the cook who throws a barrage of pots and pans at the duchess, but also releases a satisfying destructive impulse, like Stanley Kowalski's violent table-clearing scene in Tennessee Williams' *A Streetcar Named Desire*.

The theme of change is dominant in the *Alice* stories. All

children are eager to grow up, but Alice, taking magic food and drink, is shocked by her sudden expansion and contraction. The Cheshire-Cat vanishes, leaving only a lingering grin; the White Queen is transformed into a sheep; the hookah-puffing caterpillar (high on a mushroom) will someday become a fluttering butterfly.

In Homer's *Odyssey*, Circe changed men into swine; in Wonderland, Carroll changed a squalling baby into a squealing piglet. "If it had grown up," Alice says, "it would have been a dreadfully ugly child: but it makes rather a handsome pig" (p. 52). The greatest literary work in Latin literature, on the theme of eternal change, is Ovid's *Metamorphosis*. His translator Horace Gregory wrote that Ovid—as if foreshadowing Carroll—described "the violent and rapid transformations, distortions of normal law and action . . . the miraculous events, the quick changes, the shifts from images of beauty to the grotesque . . . the migration of human souls to trees and stones, even to pools and springs, to birds, to wolves . . . the charm of frightened Daphne into a quivering laurel tree, or a shrewd, quick-witted girl servant into a red-haired weasel."

Like Carroll's, Gregory writes that Ovid's "stories were written to entertain, to charm, to shock their readers." Similarly, there's quite a lot of violence and cruelty in the *Alice* stories. The engaging but pathetic White Knight keeps falling off his horse. Humpty Dumpty is about to be shattered into fragments. The Walrus and the Carpenter devour all the innocent oysters. Tweedledum has a raging tantrum over his broken rattle. The Queen of Hearts, the embodiment of ungovernable fury, constantly threatens capital punishment—"off with his head"—for even the most minor infractions, in striking contrast to the benign image of Queen Victoria. Peter Coveney remarked that in the sequel, *Through the Looking-Glass*, "the tone is perceptibly sharper. The humour is more sardonic. There is more merciless, embittered ridicule. The dream takes on a quality of horror. . . . Alice is subjected to a type of subtle cruelty in a way quite alien to the earlier book. The episode in the railway carriage has all the horror of a sadistic nightmare." Though the changes are as radical, though not as horrific, as in Franz Kafka's man-into-bug

"Metamorphosis," young readers were no doubt more frightened than the cool and gallant Alice.

The word "curious" and its variants—meaning that Alice is inquisitive and Wonderland peculiar—are crucial in the novels. Just before Alice follows the White Rabbit down the rabbit hole, she's "burning with curiosity" (p. 7) about his unusual waistcoat and pocket watch. As her neck telescopes alarmingly to increase her height to nine feet, she exclaims (in a rather restrained phrase) "Curiouser and curiouser!" (p. 14). Indeed, while searching for a stable reality and trying to make sense of all the irrational behavior, she describes her adventures as very absurd, completely unnatural and dreadfully confusing.

Alice's eager curiosity about the weird new world leads inevitably to curiosity about herself and to a quest for her own identity. Alice is deprived of food throughout the novels and at the tea party complains, "I've had nothing yet . . . so I can't take more" (p. 61). But something interesting always happens whenever she manages to eat or drink a magical potion on her own. Right after her first elongation, she asks herself, "Who in the world am I?" (p. 16), and both she and the caterpillar repeat the question. It's difficult to answer because Alice both is and is not her real self.

The most tender and poignant scene in the books illuminates this recurrent question. Wandering in a cool and shady wood—like Eden before the Fall, when Adam first named all the birds and beasts—she meets a gentle, brown-eyed fawn, who's not at all alarmed by her appearance. The two soul mates ask each other's name, but cannot define their own identities. "So they walked on together through the wood, Alice with her arms clasped lovingly round the soft neck of the Fawn, till they came out into another open field, and here the Fawn gave a sudden bound into the air, and shook itself free from Alice's arm" (p. 145). As soon as their identities are defined—as a fawn and a human child—the fawn becomes frightened and darts away at full speed. Alice's identity, the revelation of her real self, inspires fear rather than friendship. In this quietly mysterious episode in *Looking-Glass*, the author and his subject exchange roles: Carroll becomes Alice and Alice the Fawn. It seems to be a parable of Carroll's unhappy estrangement from the real Alice. In 1863, after an obscure argument with the family, Carroll was banished from the Liddell household.

Many other delightfully amusing scenes contain sparkling verse and witty dialogue. When the fancy frog and fish foot-men, wearing eighteenth-century powdered wigs, both bow at the same time, their curls get "entangled together" (p. 47). Alice plays a jolly game of croquet with live hedgehogs as balls and flamingos (held upside down, of course) as mal-leable mallets. The old, fat and white-haired Father William behaves in an unconstrained and unseemly manner by crunching the bones and beaks of fowl, balancing an eel on his nose, turning surprising somersaults and constantly standing (yogalike) on his head. But he has a nutty, metrical explanation for his behavior:

> *"In my youth," Father William replied to his son,*
>    *"I feared it might injure the brain;*
> *But, now that I'm perfectly sure I have none,*
>    *Why, I do it again and again."*     (p. 39)

When Alice asks precise directions from the Cheshire-Cat, she's answered with the kind of perverse logic that trav-elers often get in foreign countries:

> "Would you tell me, please, which way I ought to go from here?"
>
> "That depends a good deal on where you want to get to," said the Cat.
>
> "I don't much care where——" said Alice.
>
> "Then it doesn't matter which way you go," said the Cat.
>
> "——so long as I get *somewhere*," Alice added as an explanation.
>
> "Oh, you're sure to do that," said the Cat, "if you only walk long enough."     (p. 52)

In a witty parody of social gaffes, Carroll has Alice get her own back by inadvertently frightening a series of more ami-able but timorous animals. She tells the Mouse that Dinah is "such a capital one for catching mice—oh, I beg your pardon!" (p. 19) and that the farmer has a "bright-eyed terrier" that " 'kills all the rats and—oh dear!' cried Alice, in a sorrowful tone. 'I'm afraid I've offended it again!' " (p. 20). Still unable to restrain her enthusiasm about killer pets, she boasts to the Magpie and Canary that Dinah will "eat a little bird as soon as look at it" (p. 26). On various polite pretexts—the cold, the lateness of the evening—the traumatized birds hurry off as soon as is decently possible, leaving Alice longing for her predatory Dinah.

The English language lends itself to puns (always difficult to translate) and a lively tradition of comic literary wordplay runs from Jonathan Swift and his friend Thomas Sheridan in the eighteenth century to Joyce and Nabokov in the modern age. In the Mock Turtle chapters, Carroll gives free rein to his manic paronomasia. Many of his puns make fun of school lessons: "We used to call him Tortoise . . . because he taught us" (p. 79); "No wise fish would go anywhere without a porpoise" (p. 87); "Boots and shoes under the sea . . . are done with whiting" and made of "soles and eels" (p. 86); the branches of arithmetic, all with negative connotations, are "Ambition, Distraction, Uglification, and Derision" (p. 81); the art instructor teaches "Drawling, Stretching, and Fainting in Coils" (p. 81); the Classical master instructs in "Laughing and Grief" (p. 81)—Latin and Greek as well as Comedy and Tragedy. Best of all is "Reeling and Writhing" (p. 81), in which the creation of literature, in a fishing metaphor, is a mixture of vertiginous inspiration and acute agony. The series of puns at first throw readers off-balance, then provide pleasure. The puns are complemented by notable proverbial phrases, which Carroll did not invent, but popularized: "grinning like a Cheshire-Cat" (p. 49), "a cat may look at a king" (p. 71) and "mad as a March hare" (p. 54) who goes wild in the mating season.

In *Through the Looking-Glass,* Alice, who has no adventures in her ordinary life, penetrates a drawing room mirror instead of descending into a rabbit hole. This book is structured by a chess game rather than a card game. At the end of *Wonderland*, Alice wakes from her dream; just as at the end of *Looking-Glass*, Alice shakes the Red Queen, "whom she considered as the cause of all the mischief" (p. 220), and wakes to find she's been shaken back to reality and is actually shaking Dinah's black kitten. Both books, like Shakespeare's *The Tempest*, are composed of "such stuff as dreams are made on." The novels are at once a fantasy of improbable events, an imaginary world with a real Liddell girl in it and a playful but serious love poem. We don't know how these tremendous adventures have changed Alice. She wakes from her dream, pets her cat, talks to her sister and resumes—apparently *unchanged*, despite her anarchic wisdom—her familiar, secure and normal life. A new, transformed Alice would require another book.

Carroll wanted Alice Liddell, his ideal reader, to find simple pleasure in "remembering her own child-life, and the happy summer days" (p. 106) when the story was invented. Yet, despite the fantastic and comic elements, the *Alice* books also express surprisingly realistic as well as serious themes. The chorus—"Wow! wow! wow!" (p. 50)—sounds just like a modern college cheer. Humpty Dumpty (whose broad smile meets behind his egg-shaped head) complains that Alice's face is essentially the same as all others. Then, uncannily anticipating Picasso's distorted portraits, he says, "if you had the two eyes on the same side of the nose, for instance—or the mouth at the top—that would be *some* help" (p. 182). The rather static race, which "takes all the running *you* can do, to keep in the same place" (p. 134), suggests the intensely competitive human rat race in the modern world. The White Queen's sardonic slogan—"The rule is, jam to-morrow and jam yesterday—but never jam *to-day*" (p. 161)—foreshadows the deceptive promises to the starving masses made by Communist governments after engineering famines and rewriting the past. Most striking of all is the Queen of Hearts' cruel assertion during the trial of the Knave who stole her tarts: "Sentence first—verdict afterwards" (p. 103). If the accused turns out to be innocent, the sentence presumably stands. This assertion anticipates not only Kafka's *The Trial*, in which Joseph K. is guilty but does not know what crime he's committed, but also judicial procedures—like the Soviet Purge Trials in the late 1930s—in which real-life totalitarian regimes decree the verdict before the trial begins. Like George Orwell's political fable, *Animal Farm*, Carroll's *Alice* books attract readers of all cultures and ages, on various levels of sophistication and understanding.

—Jeffrey Meyers

# SELECTED BIBLIOGRAPHY

**Annotated Editions**

Gardner, Martin. *The Annotated Alice*. New York: Norton, 1999.

Gray, Donald. *Alice in Wonderland*. New York: Norton, 1971.

Haughton, Hugh. *Alice in Wonderland*. London: Penguin, 1998.

**Biographies**

Cohen, Morton. *Lewis Carroll: A Biography*. New York: Knopf, 1995.

Collingwood, Stuart Dodgson. *The Life and Letters of Lewis Carroll*. London: Unwin, 1898.

**Criticism**

Auden, W. H. "Lewis Carroll" (1962). In *Forewords and Afterwords*, 283–93. New York: Vintage, 1974.

Coveney, Peter. *The Image of Childhood*. Revised edition. Baltimore: Penguin, 1967.

Empson, William. "*Alice in Wonderland*: The Child as Swain" (1935). In *Some Versions of Pastoral*, 241–83. New York: New Directions, 1938.

Gernsheim, Helmut. *Lewis Carroll, Photographer*. New York: Dover, 1960.

Kenner, Hugh. "Alice in Chapelizod" (1956). In *Dublin's Joyce*, 276–300. Boston: Beacon, 1967.

Levin, Harry. "Wonderland Revisited." *Kenyon Review* 27 (1965): 591–616.

Phillips, Robert, ed. *Aspects of Alice*. New York: Vintage, 1971.

Rackin, Donald. "Alice's Journey to the End of the Night." *Publications of the Modern Language Association* 81 (1966): 313–26.

Rackin, Donald, ed. *Alice's Adventures in Wonderland: A Critical Handbook*. Belmont, CA: Wadsworth, 1969.

Sale, Roger. "Lewis Carroll." In *Fairy Tales and After: From Snow White to E. B. White,* 101–25. Cambridge, MA.: Harvard University Press, 1978.

Strong, T. B. "Lewis Carroll." *Cornhill Magazine* 4 (March 1898): 303–10.

Wilson, A. N. *The Victorians,* 324–29. New York: Norton, 2003.

Wilson, Edmund. "C. L. Dodgson: The Poet Logician." In *The Shores of Light,* 540–50. New York: Farrar, Straus, 1952.

Woolf, Virginia. "Lewis Carroll" (1939). In *The Moment and Other Essays,* 81–83. New York: Harcourt, 1948.

### About Alice Liddell

Björk, Christina. *The Other Alice: The Story of Alice Liddell and Alice in Wonderland*. Stockholm and New York: R & S Books, 1993.

Clarke, Anne. *The Real Alice: Lewis Carroll's Dream Child*. New York: Stein and Day, 1981.

Cohen, Morton N. *Lewis Carroll and Alice: 1832–1982*. New York: Pierpont Morgan Library, 1982.

Gordon, Colin. *Beyond the Looking Glass: Reflections of Alice and Her Family*. London: Hodder and Stoughton, 1982.

### About John Tenniel

Engen, Rodney. *Sir John Tenniel: Alice's White Knight*. Aldershot, Hants, England: Scolar Press, 1991.

Hancher, Michael. *The Tenniel Illustrations to the "Alice" Books*. Columbus: Ohio State University Press, 1985.

Sarzano, Frances. *Sir John Tenniel*. New York: Pellegrini & Cudahy, 1948.

Simpson, Roger. *Sir John Tenniel: Aspects of His Work*. Rutherford, NJ: Fairleigh Dickinson University Press, 1994.

# Classic Fairy Tales
# for All Ages

**Aesop's Fables** edited by Jack Zipes
This exclusive Signet Classics edition contains over 200 of
Aesop's most enduring and popular fables, translated into
readable, modern English, and beautifully illustrated with classic
19th-century woodcuts.

**Andersen's Fairy Tales** by Hans Christian Andersen
For over one hundred years, these Fairy Tales have charmed and
entertained audiences around the world. The forty-seven tales in this
collection transport the reader into a magical world of the Little
Mermaid, the Red Shoes, and all manner of kings and princesses,
giants and mermaids, witches, and fabulous beasts.

**Just So Stories** by Rudyard Kipling
Here are Kipling's famous stories written to delight children with their
fanciful explanations of how things in the world came to be. Based on
the stories told to him as a child by his Indian nurses, they create a
realm of magical enchantment.

**Complete Fairy Tales** by Oscar Wilde
As Wilde explained, these tales were written "partly for children, and
partly for those who have kept the childlike faculties of wonder and
joy." This volume brings together all of Wilde's lovely, gemlike tales
filled with princes, mermaids, giants, and kings. It also retains the
wonderful and evocative illustrations done for the original editions.

S474

# READ THE TOP 20
# SIGNET CLASSICS

1984 by George Orwell

Animal Farm by George Orwell

Narrative of the Life of Frederick Douglass
by Frederick Douglass

The Inferno by Dante

Romeo and Juliet by William Shakespeare

Why We Can't Wait by Dr. Martin Luther King, Jr.

Nectar in a Sieve by Kamala Markandaya

Frankenstein by Mary Shelley

Beowulf translated by Burton Raffel

Hamlet by William Shakespeare

The Federalist Papers by Alexander Hamilton

The Odyssey by Homer

Macbeth by William Shakespeare

Crime and Punishment by Fyodor Dostoyevsky

The Hound of the Baskervilles
by Sir Arthur Conan Doyle

The Scarlet Letter by Nathaniel Hawthorne

Dr. Jekyll and Mr. Hyde by Robert L. Stevenson

A Midsummer Night's Dream by William Shakespeare

The Classic Slave Narratives by Henry L. Gates

A Tale of Two Cities by Charles Dickens

PENGUIN.COM
FACEBOOK.COM/SIGNETCLASSIC